With a grin, Geoffrey obligingly pecked Rose on the lips

When she wrinkled her nose at the inadequate response, he laughed and drew her to his lap. "Now, my dear, do not become a scolding wife at the very beginning of our marriage, or we shall have nowhere to progress to," he teased, pecking her again, lightly. Then again, not so lightly.

Rose melted into him, tilting her head and offering her lips for a more thorough plunder. The feel of his arms tightening about her was the most wondrous sensation of safety. "I promise to be the most perfect wife," she whispered softly against his mouth.

Geoffrey breathed deeply of her lilac scent. She was an enticing child, tempting and promising as a partially opened rosebud. He reasoned that she was his wife, and by law available to him, but enticing or not, Rose was still of tender years and required protection now, not seduction. Perhaps one day, for after all, she was to be his wife for a long, long time. Yes, one day, and one day soon, he promised himself, he would take her as his body demanded...but not tonight. Tonight he must remain the gentleman.

Dear Reader,

Although this month's *The Essential Wife* is only Taylor Ryan's fourth book, she is fast becoming one of our most popular authors. Those who enjoy her lighthearted humor and emotion should be very pleased with her delightful new story of a dashing nobleman who finds himself falling in love with the penniless heiress whom he has arranged to marry out of pity.

Keep an eye out for Laurie Grant's new Western, *Lawman,* the fast-paced sequel to her 1996 release, *Devil's Dare,* about a lonely lawman who rediscovers love in the arms of his childhood sweetheart. And we are very pleased this month to be able to bring you Silhouette Yours Truly and Special Edition author Beth Henderson's first historical for Harlequin, *Reckless,* in which a young woman accused of being a jewel thief is rescued by a mysterious baron intent on clearing her name.

Nevada Territory is the setting for *All But the Queen of Hearts,* Rae Muir's heartwarming Western about a shy farm widow and the handsome stranger who was swindled in a poker game by her late husband, which rounds out our lineup.

Whatever your taste in reading, we hope you keep a lookout for all four titles wherever Harlequin Historicals are sold.

Sincerely,

Tracy Farrell
Senior Editor

Please address questions and book requests to:
Harlequin Reader Service
U.S.: 3010 Walden Ave., P.O. Box 1325, Buffalo, NY 14269
Canadian: P.O. Box 609, Fort Erie, Ont. L2A 5X3

the ESSENTIAL Wife

Taylor Ryan

Harlequin Books

TORONTO • NEW YORK • LONDON
AMSTERDAM • PARIS • SYDNEY • HAMBURG
STOCKHOLM • ATHENS • TOKYO • MILAN
MADRID • WARSAW • BUDAPEST • AUCKLAND

ISBN 0-373-28968-5

THE ESSENTIAL WIFE

Books by Taylor Ryan

Harlequin Historicals

Love's Wild Wager #262
Birdie #312
Beauty and the Beast #342
The Essential Wife #368

TAYLOR RYAN

A passion for solitary mountain trails, a love of restless cloudy skies and a propensity for long daydreams on rainy afternoons, led her to abandon a penthouse condo and hectic corporate life for romance in the golden hills of Northern California. Perched high in the vineyards, far above the mists, she feeds her soul with liberal portions of shimmering lakes, towering redwood trees and nature's wildlife.

To Major Jerry Lee...
who gives unstintingly of his love and broad shoulders,
and whose wisdom is inspired by a real life,
with all its cruelties, its joys and
its—sometimes not too subtle—lessons.

Chapter One

Yet another heavy spring storm raged down upon London with incessant violence. Reducing the streets to an impassable sea of mud, it set the filth of the sewers flowing throughout the slums of Haymarket, where sickness raged and deaths were reportedly in the hundreds. And yet, the only concern of the haute ton was that the season of 1836 was threatening to literally wash away.

Not a fortnight into the season, and the matrons with debutante daughters were wailing over groundwork, meticulously laid, gone sour. Their equally upset daughters despaired of making a good marriage their first year out, crying that they were ruined. For how was one to promenade in Rotten Row with the tracks a mire of mud? And how was one to shop Bond Street, strolling so that draperies swayed delectably from side to side to draw attention to one's curves, with the streets awash?

The vast majority of the ton was electing to remain indoors, much to the relief of their grooms and coachmen, and therefore, only the most inventive of minds could have arranged a seemingly innocent outing, between two of the most eligible of the haute ton, on the day of the foulest weather of the year, and actually see it come to fruition.

And that was exactly what Miss Sharon Bartley-Bacon had accomplished with apparently little effort on her part, while at the same time making it appear as if the whole idea had originated from the featherbrain of Lady Lavitia Wyse, Dowager Marquise of Hetherington.

Thus, it was supposedly upon his mother's wishes that Geoffrey, Lord Wyse, was sitting rather rigidly in the close confines of a stuffy chaise, jolting into Bond Street with the rain drumming a heathen beat upon the roof and the hapless coachman, pondering for the thousandth time the absurdity of this errand. The day was much more suited to holding a hand of piquet at White's, or pitting his foil against a worthy antagonist at the Royal Fencing Academy, than to this purpose. Yet, here he was, accommodating his insistent mother by accompanying Miss Sharon Bartley-Bacon on a decidedly wet and thoroughly discomforting mission of the most dire importance—a fitting appointment at the dressmaking establishment of Madame Howard.

But the marquis was, above all else, a gentleman and, as he regarded it, a gentleman was, whenever feasible, attentive to his mother's wishes. Unless that venerable lady's most impassioned wish, and seemingly primary occupation these days, was to see her only son married within the coming year. And attached to that wish, he must be hard set upon the heels of a well-established nursery in the shortest time allowed by nature's benevolence.

Fully cognizant of his mother's thus far abortive attempts to march him to the altar with this one miss in particular, Geoffrey studied Miss Sharon Bartley-Bacon guardedly from beneath hooded eyes. This being her second season, she was not new to his acquaintance. Nor was she particularly sought after company on his part, but he could only notice she was most persistent about seeking out *his* whenever possible. In pondering this fact Lord Wyse had reasoned, in his own mind at least, that he had not danced any particular attendance upon her the previous season that might have given her false hopes.

While not overly interested in pursuing a union of any sort, he would grant her an assured air of quality from the tip of her sodden bonnet to the toes of her muddied boots. Her attire, disregarding the damp, was flawless and her cape was fur lined and spoke of wealth in her own right. She was the only daughter of the Viscountess Bartley-Bacon and used to having every whim granted even as she opened her mouth. There was no hostess so notoriously high in the instep as to exclude her from a guest list and escape having her own self raked over the coals by her peers.

Geoffrey supposed she was pretty enough, possibly even declared beautiful in the circles in which they moved, with her wide china blue eyes in a small, heart-shaped face, but he would wish for more honesty in emotion from her, instead of the carefully orchestrated motions set to her own inner image of what a peeress was supposed to exhibit. For he had no doubts at all that Miss Sharon Bartley-Bacon had every intention, come hell or high water, of becoming his wife—and the next Marquise of Hetherington. Just as he had no illusions as to her top priority of those two.

"I do declare..." complained Sharon, flipping the brim of her weather-beaten bonnet away from her forehead. "If I did not need this gown for the Townsend tropical ball in a fortnight, I would not have ventured out on such a day. I swear, with the exorbitant price of such finery these days, one would think the dressmaker would have come to me rather than force me out into this deplorable wet."

Geoffrey tilted an eyebrow upward in boredom at such illogical, spoiled-missish nonsense. "I would quite imagine, Miss Bartley-Bacon, that Madame Howard has one too many patrons to make such services feasible. Besides, would you really prefer she drag a silk and satin ball gown about in the rain just to keep your feathers from becoming damp?''

Sharon did not deem to dignify the remark with an answer. Since she would be in obvious disagreement with the marquis's views, it was perhaps best to keep one's own counsel rather than initiate an argument. Not only was it never very propitious to bait Lord Wyse, as he was not one to ruffle easily, but this day his mood did seem uncharacteristically hard-pressed over today's outing. And while she herself would much rather be indoors on such a day, a girl with lofty ambitions must use every opportunity to her advantage. No, it wouldn't do to display foul temper before the object of her desires. And foul temper was exactly what she felt nipping at her brain at his absolute refusal to indulge her in any comment she wished to make.

Regarding the elegant man seated so nonchalantly upon the leather squabs, Sharon forced her lips into an upward curve contrary to their wishes. Her thoughts were tempered with ill humor. Must he appear so unaffected by the weather? It was just such a thing to set one's teeth on edge.

Even though his greatcoat with its twelve shoulder capes suggested the Bond Street fribble of the dandy set, no one could be in the marquis's presence overly long without noting he was an athletic Corinthian, reportedly wicked with the blade as well as with his fists, and possessing an admirable stable of blooded cattle that was the envy of his many friends.

Sharon swallowed her irritation at his inattention and chose another tack entirely. Flashing a larger, more melting smile at the distant marquis, she batted her eyelashes in a way she knew to be most becoming. ''I do thank you for your gallant show of kindness this afternoon, Lord Wyse, as I am quite certain no one else would have displayed such bravado—as to venture out as escort for me today," she simpered prettily.

"Oh, come now, Miss Bartley-Bacon, I am quite certain the Lord Carlton or Viscount Philpotts would have lent his arm on this urgent errand just as readily. But, alas, they were not marking attendance upon my mother at the time the urgency arose," Geoffrey remarked, casually contemplating the smart gold tassels decorating his shining Hessians, giving the distinct impression they held more interest to him than the lady whom he escorted.

Sharon gritted her teeth, then switched to a pretty pout before her eyes could narrow and give her thoughts away. "Now that sounds as if you are being mean to me. There was also no one in attendance, Lord Wyse, who would have twisted your arm if you had cried nay to the errand. No one of sufficient brawn to overturn you, that is."

Geoffrey snorted slightly. "Now there is a statement that puts me in doubt of your acquaintance with my esteemed mother, Miss Bartley-Bacon. She may appear to others as a fragile woman in doubtful health, but it has been my experience that it is not above her abilities to take a broom to my head for disobedience—even if it requires she perch upon a stool to do so," he replied. There was a slight twinkle of warmth in his eyes before he shuttered them, which was uncharacteristic of him in company, especially when the company was this particular vamp.

Sharon tittered a small laugh behind her hand and tilted her head just so to gaze with mystery and coyness at the object of her intentions. When she captured his warm, brown eyes, what she thought she saw made her heart beat faster with a pleasant surging of power. She was positive she detected a decided look of admiration on his face. It was certainly not above her ability to distinguish a look of interest in a man's eyes, for after all, weren't broken hearts a specialty of hers, having left a string of them in her wake this past year? It was well-known that a path strewn with weeping swains only added to a girl's consequence. This must certainly mean this miserable trip in the wet was to bear fruit after all. Rushing to ensnare him further, she batted her lashes suggestively at him and flipped her damp ribbons.

"Miss Bartley-Bacon, pray stop your flirting, or you will have me fearing myself compromised by the absence of your maid," suggested Geoffrey, with the edge of bored amusement slipping into his deep voice.

"Flirting?" gasped Sharon, turning a shoulder slightly toward him. "You do me an injustice, my lord. I *never* flirt!"

When he did not reply, she casted a glance at his face through her lashes. He was watching her with a stare, most speculative and direct, which gave her pause of uncertainty. Perhaps—just perhaps—this man might prove more than she could handle. She gave a minute shrug. There had not been many men, commencing with her father, whom she could not manipulate to her own benefit. And she did mean to have this one to husband. Her mind was quite set on that. Even to the extent that she had demanded her own mother retire to the country, for the entire season if required, pleading illness and infirmity, so her daughter might beg residency and protection from none other than Lord Wyse's own mother, Lady Lavitia.

Everyone knew of the marquis's devotion to his mother and she intended to ruthlessly use that devotion to further her intrigue. It was a masterful plot and one the dowager marquise had readily fallen in league with, as that lady was smitten as peaches on a Sunday morn with the thought of having Miss Sharon Bartley-Bacon as her daughter-in-law.

The carriage rattled to a halt before the Bond Street shop.

The drenched footman leaped down to snatch open the door, allowing a mighty gust of wind to shower rain over the occupants. He held aloft an umbrella that was proving totally inadequate against the bluster and driving wet. Lord Wyse stepped down first, holding his beaver topper against the thieving wind, and extended his hand to Sharon. Her skirts billowed out the door ahead of her, whipping in the wind like a full sail on a schooner running before the gale. Suppressing an oath, Geoffrey gathered her cloak tightly about her and, with a firm arm about her shoulders, rushed her inside.

The workroom of the dressmaking shop on Bond Street was fair likely to float away, if the wind-driven gale had its say. Water seeped into the brick facade of its cracked walls. It ran in little waterfalls from the small, tiered, flower beds bordering the tiny brick square that separated the building from the alley, creating rivers of muddy water that dared to push in beneath the threshold if left unattended for long.

The assistant dressmaker was down upon her knees, diligently contriving a dam by stuffing rag-bin scraps of silk, muslin and satin in every tint and hue of the rainbow into the cracks. She leaned back on her heels and planted fists firmly on slim hips to survey her colorful construction with satisfaction.

"Well, Orange Willy, that should hold the river at bay for the moment," she announced triumphantly.

An orange mackerel cat, perched well above the wet on a worktable pulled to the center of the small room, turned attentive yellow eyes toward his mistress but made no move to leave his perch. The girl rose from her knees to shake out damp skirts, surveying the destruction to her hems with a grimace. Even though it was no more than a faded tarlatan work gown, she hated to see it damaged. Her wardrobe was limited at best and even the worst of it must be pampered. As the nasty chore did seem, like this season's weather, to be never-ending, she carefully tucked the hem into her waistband to keep it away from the water and mud.

"Blasted weather! 'Tis no good for business, nor one's health either for that matter," she muttered, glancing toward the stairs.

This last she could well attest, for she was also serving as nurse to her employer and friend, Madame LaFee Howard. The little dressmaker was, at present, supine upon the sofa in her apartment of tiny rooms situated above the shop, laid low with sniffles and a scratchy throat. This had seemed a perfect opportunity for bed rest and recuperation, as the weather was so foul the ladies would unquestionably be deterred from venturing forth to ponder new gowns on this day.

That was why the tinkling of the bell startled the girl so. And why she quickly rushed into the shop with her damp skirts completely forgotten—and still tucked quite securely into her waistband—a goodly length of well-shaped calf visible above her cloth Adelaide boots. And it could only be laid at the door of shock, to see a fairly drenched lady whipping off her soaked bonnet and cloak to carelessly spray droplets upon a display of fine silk ribbons, gossamer tatted lace and soft kid gloves, that caused her to speak out so harshly.

"Oh, please! Do watch what you're about," the girl called, rushing to shield the fine things with her body and hands. "They will be water-spotted and totally unsellable!"

Sharon lifted an eyebrow at the shop girl's ill-mannered tone. Here was someone she could safely vent her foul temper upon. "And is that any concern of mine?" she snapped. "You had best be mindful of the manner in which you address me, girl."

"Perhaps I should take your wet things, Miss Bartley-Bacon," Geoffrey interjected, calmly relieving her of the offending cloak and bonnet. "They do seem to be in your way and causing a bit of trouble."

"Thank you for your kindness, Lord Wyse," Sharon simpered. She smiled at him sweetly, then turned a haughty glare upon the insolent shop girl. "Now, girl, where is your employer, Madame Howard?"

"I am terribly sorry, my lady. Madame Howard is quite ill and has retired to her bed for the day. May I be of assistance to you?"

Treating the girl with a long, arrogant perusal, Sharon narrowed her bright blue eyes and pursed the pink mouth primly before loudly demanding in a tone clearly meant to set the girl in her place, "And just what is your name, girl?"

Drawing herself up to the full height the Lord in heaven, and her rather diminutive father and mother, had allowed her, she introduced herself. "My name is Rose Lambe. And I shall be pleased to assist you with anything you desire in the shop, my lady."

"Well, the first thing I would desire is for you to summon Madame Howard forthwith. I must have a fitting on the pink and silver ball gown and I must have it today. Then *Rosie*," Sharon fairly sneered, taking in the rucked-up skirt and the exposed legs with disdain. "I would ask you to make yourself decent in front of myself and the marquis."

"Oh, m-my!" Rose stammered, hastily turning her back to jerk the skirt to the floor and cover herself. Totally mortified at her lapse, she blushed a rush of color to her cheeks and truly wished to fall straight through the floor. "I am so s-sorry! It's the water...in the back, you see...."

"Pray, do not stammer and stutter like a dolt. Just summon your employer. *Now!*" Sharon demanded.

Geoffrey stifled a sigh of dismay. Stepping forward, he introduced his version of male objectivity into the situation. "Miss Bartley-Bacon, if I may intercede here. I do believe you will catch more bees with honey than vinegar. Let's retrace our steps a bit here, shall we?"

Sharon turned with some surprise. Certainly that was a telling action, wasn't it? That he would rush to her aid in such a way? She turned a tight little smile upon the shop girl as if to say, See how he cares for me? "Well, of course, Lord Wyse," she cooed. "Your assistance is always welcome."

With a curt nod, Geoffrey paused a moment. Then, with deliberate motions, he draped Sharon's wet cloak on a coat tree beside the door and placed her bonnet atop it. Next he laid his topper carefully away from the ribbons and divested himself of his own wet greatcoat to reveal an impeccable, black swallowtail coat requiring no padding to display to advantage broad shoulders and a neatly nipped waist. That satisfactorily done, he turned to take charge of the situation. "Now, Miss Lambe," he began, then hesitated to ponder. "Lambe? I say, that name is very familiar to me. May I inquire of your father?"

Rose's eyes grew large in her face to be addressed by such a splendid tulip of the ton. The shop was an area normally occupied only by ladies and their attending maids. This noble seemed to fill the room, allowing no space remaining for air to replenish her lungs. His hair was quite curly, and a deep rich brown. The color of well-rubbed walnut, she romantically thought, and his eyes were softly brown and gentle upon her face. He was truly perfectly magnificent and only as perfect as he should have been for a young miss's dreams.

Sharon gave an exaggerated sigh of patience sorely tried, and tapped her foot upon the puddled tile floor. "My dear Lord Wyse, just who the girl's parents are, even if she might have knowledge of them, does not signify at present. Let us just get on about our business and be on our way. Are you going to summon Madame Howard, girl, or shall we simply stand here until we all catch a chill?"

Rose directed her gaze to the irritated lady in front of her and immediately discerned that she could not have done one thing to bring about such a unladylike snit, and therefore she saw no need to apologize to her. Nor would she rouse a feverish and coughing LaFee from her covers to mollify one rather spoilt miss of the haute ton. She carefully schooled her expression into one of polite helpfulness before widening her eyes into untarnished innocence and replying sweetly.

"I am truly sorry, my lady. Madame Howard is indeed quite ill. And, the doctor fears, possibly contagious. I will, of course, summon her as you request, for I am sure she will rise from her sickbed just for you."

Geoffrey quickly stepped forward to intervene before Miss Bartley-Bacon could flare into further rudeness, but his mouth did so want to curve into a smile at the audacity of this pint-size chit. Absolutely *nothing* would be served at this point for Miss Bartley-Bacon to see his mirth, and it most assuredly *would* succeed in adding fuel to her temper tantrum. Furthermore, he was beginning to harbor no doubts whatsoever that the diminutive shop girl could hold her own in this case.

"Contagious!" exclaimed Sharon. "Of course, I want the woman nowhere near me! Are you completely addled?"

Rose watched with satisfaction as the spoilt lady backed a full three steps from her.

"Then perhaps I might assist you. I assure you, as Madame Howard's senior assistant, I am quite capable of taking your fitting. As it is, I have in fact, been assigned the making of that particular gown." She gave another of her innocent looks, and drew the drape back to indicate the way to the workroom. "If you will come this way, my lady?"

Sharon swept past her in a huff. Suddenly, as the thought struck her, Rose spun back to the nobleman once more. Clasping her hands tightly together, she silently resolved not to stammer before the magnificence of him like a backward schoolgirl. "Forgive me, my lord. Might I bring you a cup of tea? I fear there is nothing stronger in the shop, as we very seldom have occasion to serve gentlemen."

Geoffrey eased his eyes over her face, bringing a soft peach blush to her complexion. Interestingly enough, she did not demurely drop her eyes as one would have expected, but in fact they grew even wider at his attention. They were quite enticing, he decided, a soft gray with a tinge of lavender, and surrounded by astonishingly thick, sooty lashes.

The girl was small, with smooth raven hair that fell unbound and straight to her waist. In his estimation, she could be no more than fourteen. He sought to reassure her and smiled that unconsciously tender smile reserved only for children and old ladies. It was a smile that brought forth a deep dimple on the right side of a generous mouth and had been known to melt the hearts of those few ladies who had been privileged enough to receive it.

"I thank you, Miss Lambe, but I do not wish to trouble you as you are alone in the shop today and—" he indicated the still swinging drape with a nod of his head "—have more than your hands full at the moment. If you will simply estimate a time for the completion of Miss Bartley-Bacon's fitting, I shall tarry here.''

"Th-the fitting will take no more than half an hour," Rose stammered, regardless of her resolve. Never in her sheltered upbringing had she occasion to be in the company of such as this toplofty lord. She dropped a curtsy to him in confusion before scurrying to the protection of the back room. Although she dreaded dealing with the fractious lady, attending a quarrelsome female seemed decidedly safer than remaining near such a stunningly handsome gentleman.

Sharon stood before the mirror in her smallclothes, preening this way and that, admiring her slim form. "I had thought to expire with chills while you *flirted* with the marquis, girl," Sharon insinuated nastily. "It will do you no good, you know, to bat your eyes at your betters. The Marquis of Hetherington is not the sort to pleasure himself with shop girls. So why not focus your attention on your duties and away from schemes to feather your nest with thoughts of gains through the use of your body."

Rose gritted her teeth at the crassness of the woman and gathered the skirt of the pink ball gown to drop it unceremoniously over the blond head. It would do no good to cross words with this vixen, she cautioned herself. It was impossible for her to utter the scolding set-down that trembled on her tongue at this moment, and no purpose whatsoever would be served by saying anything other than a politely murmured, "Of course, my lady."

Sharon pulled at a seam here and there, turning to view the back of the ball gown. It was a creation of fairy tales, with yards of dusty pink silk caught up in generous drapes over a quilted underskirt of silver satin. She twitched the skirt several times with obvious disapproval before flipping back to Rose. "This is poorly made," she stated quite calmly. "And I shan't take it. Remove it."

"I—I beg your pardon?" Rose sputtered, not believing her ears. The gown was perfection. Each stitch tiny and invisible. Each delicately laced edge was as fine as a wee spider's web. Nothing could have been more flawless than the fit of the bodice with its décolletage cut daringly low and designed to display the lady's meager bosom to best advantage. The skirt swayed with a promise of sensuous delights awaiting beneath with even the slightest step. The gown was beyond description. Totally exquisite.

"Do I not speak clearly?" Sharon snapped. She tugged the gown from her shoulder with a hard hand, tearing the fragile fabric in her anger. "Take it off, I said! It is ill-sewn and rubbish. You obviously do not understand! I am Miss Sharon Bartley-Bacon! And I do not wear rubbish!"

"Oh, please do not tear it! There's weeks and weeks in the stitching of it," cried Rose, in distress. She attempted to gather the skirt up over the lady's head before she further damaged the delicate fabric.

"And I should care?" shrilled Sharon. "Assist me to dress! And let me assure you, I will never enter this rancid little establishment again. I should have listened to the rumors of the shoddy work done here, but in my charity I thought to lift a second-rate seamstress to notoriety by my patronage. No doubt the disaster created by your stupidity and ineptness is beyond your limited comprehension, but *now* I have no gown for the ball! Trust me when I say that word of this would have been spread throughout the ton but for the fact that I would perish of humiliation if anyone even knew I had frequented this place!"

Rose quickly assisted the lady into her damp gown, wishing for nothing more than to see the back of her through the door before she spoke her mind and landed herself in deeper trouble. LaFee would be furious at her for losing this wealthy customer but for the life of her she could not see anything she had done wrong. Nor could she see what she might do to right the situation and make amends to this irrational lady, but somehow she must make an attempt. "Please my lady, I am so sorry. I shall do whatever you think required to adjust the gown, but I do not see—"

"Stop!" Sharon shouted, flinging her palm up in front of Rose's face. "Do not speak to me again, you ill-mannered girl! One more word and I shall see you dismissed from your position and thrown into the streets to starve. Now, get out of my way!" With great flair, she gathered her damp skirts and swept through the drape and into the front of the shop with her nose in the air.

The marquis was standing braced in the middle of the shop when she sailed out, head held high and cheeks flushed. A much paler Rose trailed after her, the offending pink gown still bundled in her arms. As he had overheard the unnecessarily harsh words, Geoffrey's mouth was firmly set and his anger barely controlled. Retrieving Sharon's wet cloak from the coat tree, he flung it about her shoulders. Abruptly thrusting her bonnet into her hand, he swept open the door. "Miss Bartley-Bacon, please wait for me in the chaise."

"But..."

"*The chaise*, Miss Bartley-Bacon."

Sharon stared at him in astonishment, but as his expression clearly left no ground for argument, she straightened her spine and gave a nearly imperceptible nod of her head. "As you wish, Lord Wyse, but do not be overly long, for I am quite chilled," she directed. Crushing the bonnet in her hand, she exited the shop with her head held high, despite the raging wind and rain that tore at her uncovered hair.

Closing the door rather firmly behind her, Geoffrey turned to face the child's sad and solemn face. Her even, white teeth worried a trembling bottom lip, and she looked for all the world ready to dissolve into tears. Moved by a kindly impulse, he stepped quite near to her. "I feel I must apologize for Miss Bartley-Bacon. And I wish to pay for the gown that she has rejected, as I am quite certain there can be nothing whatsoever wrong with it."

"I thank you for your kind words, my lord, but I am afraid the gown is ripped beyond repair and—and—quite ru-ruined," Rose said, sniffling. She displayed the silk bodice, rent from shoulder to waist in such a way that it could never be repaired invisibly. Hours and hours of work had gone into the gown and it was a costly piece of goods that the struggling LaFee could ill afford to waste, but it was ruined now. Large tears spilled over her thick lashes and traced down her cheeks.

Slipping a forefinger beneath her chin, Geoffrey raised the tearstained face. A wry smile of humor played over his sensual lips, and deepened the dimple in his right cheek. Dabbing at her cheeks with a snowy handkerchief, he murmured teasingly to her, "I assure you, Miss Lambe, I care nothing for the manner of its damage. I *truly* have no intention of wearing it to any function of import in the near future."

So unexpected was his remark that before she could help herself, Rose emitted a watery giggle with a small hiccuping sob at the end. His kindness was totally overwhelming and most comforting, but still she shook her head. It was a kind gesture, and one she should accept as the money was sorely needed, but after all, fair was fair and he had not been the one to rip the gown. "Nay, my lord. I cannot take your money for damaged goods. I fear Madame Howard would have my head for doing such a thing—even more so than somehow irritating one of her society customers to fractious behavior. But I thank you for your kindness, just the same,'' she said. Slowly, reluctantly, she moved away from the handkerchief, and the disturbing warmth of his fingers.

"Then it shall be as you wish, child," acceded Geoffrey with a sigh of acceptance. With a slight bow and a rakish wink, he replaced his beaver atop chocolate brown curls and exited the shop.

Rose could only stare after him. Such a display of manners and elegance! He was absolute perfection. Truly the stuff of every maiden's dreams. She dashed to the window to stare after the departing chaise with its elaborate crest emblazoned on the black, paneled door.

"But not dreams you may dream, Rose Lambe," she chided herself. "Although, while I have no desire to envy one as nasty as Miss Poor-Manners there, how I wish you were in love with me, my beautiful perfect marquis."

Chapter Two

"Well, that is that! There is no use crying over the milk that has been spilt, *chérie*. Rip it out, and we save what we save!" LaFee ordered. Dropping the rich stuff onto Rose's lap, she dusted her hands over the tail of the pink gown in an elaborate gesture. Even such little effort brought a fit of deep, racking coughs that doubled her over sharply.

"Oh, LaFee! You cannot go on like this!" admonished Rose, flinging the pink silk onto her worktable. "You should not be out of bed. Regardless of what you say, I think you should have the doctor in to listen to your chest."

LaFee rejected the glass of water Rose brought her with a shake of her head. Easing her frail body into a chair drawn dangerously close to the meager fire, she fought to draw adequate breath into her tortured, fluid-filled lungs. "And do you think he will cure me with only thank-yous for payment?" she rasped.

"Then let me bill for what's owed us, LaFee. That witch should pay for the pink silk, if not the work that went into the stitching of it," argued Rose. "Simply apply to her solicitors. I have no doubt *that one* never bothers to review her own accounts, and I just know the accounting would be settled without question."

"*Non, chérie,* I'll not charge for work that was not accepted." She stubbornly shook her head at the suggestion. "Besides, I would be either recovered or dancing in my grave before we saw coin on the bill."

"Oh, LaFee. I despair of you!" Rose gained her feet and moved back to her worktable to extract Orange Willy from beneath his canopy of pink silk. She knew what LaFee said was the truth. The nobles with the most fortune seemed the ones least concerned with the paltry sums owed to a dressmaker, never understanding their very livelihood might depend upon those small sums. Payment was often delayed months and months, long after the actual gown had been worn, admired, soiled and stashed away in the back of some musty wardrobe as nesting for baby mice.

Her brow furrowed with worry as she regretfully set about ripping out the careful stitching. "This beastly weather has made a sizable dent in business of late. It's only rational that ladies who have no occasion to parade their gowns have no need to order more. We must petition for every penny owed."

With the lift of her thin shoulders, LaFee Howard shrugged off her young protégée's concerns. She was inured to such worries and hardships, instructed early on by a turbulent life. A Frenchwoman of unnotable birth, she'd had the misfortune of falling madly and obsessively in love with a soft-spoken, poetry-spouting Englishman. But, upon following him across the channel, she had heartbreakingly discovered him quite satisfied with the wife he already had in residence. Born LaFee Turgot, she had appropriated the man's surname of Howard, to remind herself, she declared, never again to behave so stupidly in love. She studied her little friend now, bent so intently over the pink gown, determinedly taking out the stitches she had just as determinedly put in over the past fortnight.

"Do not worry your pretty little head, *chérie*. If we cannot collect what is owed us, and we cannot purchase more fabrics with which to sew our lovely creations, then we will do something else. Whatever we do, I do not think we will starve."

"I swear to you, LaFee, I did nothing untoward to bring her haughty ladyship's wrath ringing down upon our heads."

"Ah, *chérie,* have you learned nothing? These nobles—" she flipped her hand in the air "—they need only their imagination to set their hearts against us."

Rose nodded her head, but did not raise her eyes from her task. Having her employer's confidence, she was privy to the rumors that kept the haute ton from gracing LaFee's establishment. She reasoned LaFee must have run afoul of a lady of much higher station than the blond witch she herself had encountered, for it was the ugly rumors circulated among the ladies of the ton that kept the generous little Frenchwoman on the brink of starvation despite her tremendous talent.

The bell on the front door of the shop tinkled faintly. Rose glanced up from her stitching, but LaFee motioned her back to her work. She watched her push through the curtain with relief, for LaFee had such a knack for cajoling orders that Rose secretly suspected her of witchcraft. With her natural flamboyance and her earthy sensuality, she had a gypsy sense when it came to seeing inside a woman.

"Willy, my feline friend, after the last disaster it is best if we hide in the back room behind our needle." Rose sighed, shaking her head at the young cat. "We shall leave the customers to LaFee. At least that will assure food on our table, for there must be food on the table or there will be no scraps on the floor for little orange cats...."

LaFee burst into the room, waving her arms in an excited

manner and gasping for breath. "Quick, *chérie!*" she said in a stage whisper. "There is a gentleman—oh, la-la, what a gentleman! He wishes to order a gown for a young lady. And as you are exactly her size, he wishes you to be his mannequin. Come! Come! Be quick!"

Rose started to protest as the woman shoved the silk from her lap and dragged her to her feet. "But LaFee! Me?"

Disregarding the protests and the reluctant feet, LaFee pulled Rose through the drape separating the workroom from the front of the shop. "See, *monsieur?* Here she is?" she announced, pulling Rose into the best light for display. "Is your young lady the size and shape of my *ingenue?*"

"Exactly the shape, exactly the coloring and exactly the age. Yes, Madame Howard, exactly, and charmingly, so."

The voice snapped Rose's eyes up from her toes of her boots. She hastily brushed her hair from her face. No one else could have a voice that deep. That rich. That resonant. He smiled that tender smile that brought out his dimple, and sent Rose's heart into a dither, making it impossible for her to keep her eyes from growing huge in her astonishment. "It's you...." She gasped, disbelieving her eyes. "Why are you here?"

"Why, it's very simple, child. I wish to order a gown. There is a young lady, you see—one with hair as black and filled with lights as a starlit night, and gray eyes with the barest hint of lilacs in bloom—a young lady who, I somehow suspect, has the sweetest of natures to go with her looks, and who I feel should have a simply marvelous gown," teased Geoffrey.

LaFee's eyebrows rose abruptly in dawning. She swiveled her head to look long and hard at Rose, as if seeing her clearly for the first time. Ah, so. It was to be that way, was it? "And is your young lady small in stature?" she asked. "Such as this one here?"

"Yes, just so," Geoffrey admitted. Without turning his attention from Rose, he nodded just once. "I would like a gown suited to just such a young lady as this one here. The gown should be of...ah, blue, I think. Perhaps with a hint of lavender to match her eyes, and suitable for...say, a dinner party. Can that be arranged, Madame Howard?"

It was blatantly obvious that the marquis was improvising as he spoke. LaFee's mind worked quickly despite the fever that raged inside her body. She sensed the beginnings of an intrigue. It was not unusual for the bored nobility to seek amusement among the girls in the shops and taverns. And there was money to be made from such things. She clapped her hands sharply together to bring his attention back to her.

"Of course! And others? What of day dresses of sprigged muslin? A riding costume with a Spencer jacket of black-and-white checks and yellow piping? Perfect for her coloring, no? A ball gown of unadorned ivory satin cut low to compliment soft, ivory shoulders? Nightdresses with lace and ruffles? Oh, and the small, lacy unmentionables—" she tilted her head saucily at him with meaning "—that are so delectable for a bachelor gentleman to contemplate?"

"LaFee! Please!" Rose scolded. She could feel color racing to her cheeks and wished for nothing more than to sink through the floor. Never had she been so embarrassed, and in front of this man of all people.

Geoffrey grinned at the tone of her complaint. It pleased him to see her blushes. She was a delightful child, indeed, and the French dressmaker could only be described as truly outrageous. Both were entirely irresistible. He was not ignorant of their plight and, contrary to most of his rank, felt a certain sympathy for one who was simply attempting to keep body and soul together in hard times. He had no illusions concerning the damage the gossip of the waspish ladies of the haute ton occasioned and he could find no harm in this simple prank. The child would have a wardrobe beyond her wildest dreams, and the dressmaker would better her circumstances, and his well-padded pockets would not suffer noticeably in the process. He readily fell in with the plot.

"Of course! Why not? Yes, Madame Howard. Day dresses, and a ball gown and riding costume and the tender things best kept far from the imagination—with much lace and tiers of ruffled edging. Do an entire wardrobe for a young lady just the age and coloring of Miss Rose Lambe. Everything she should require...in the richest of jewel colors...uh, for socials and such. And as quickly as possible."

"Of course, *monsieur!* We shall commence immediately, making certain the one gown is ready in a fortnight and sent to your address," LaFee said with glee, making notes and adding figures as quickly as possible.

Geoffrey cleared his throat somewhat uncomfortably. This was something he had not anticipated. Wouldn't do to have a carriageload of little girls' dresses showing up at his bachelor apartments. "Ah...that will not be necessary, Madame Howard—" his face brightened "—I shall call for the gown personally on the third Thursday of next month, and I would like to see it fitted upon Miss Lambe. Just to be certain it is perfect, you understand."

"Yes! Yes!" LaFee exclaimed, with color high. Then she pondered a moment, tapping her tablet with the stub of a pencil. "Although I caution your choice of rich colors for such a young girl. If she is a *débutante, monsieur,* she will not be allowed darker colors and the gowns will be wasted. Although if she is of the demimonde..." she paused with emphasis, raising her eyebrows in open question.

Geoffrey was stunned for a moment at her directness, then cleared his throat self-consciously. "Perhaps I have given the wrong impression here, Madame Howard, but most definitely not the, er, demimonde. I am more than content to trust your judgment as to the correctness of fabrics and colors suitable for a young girl. I am certain your choices in all the wardrobe will be most appropriate in every way," he conceded. He was slightly embarrassed and beginning to feel he might be in over his head. Impulsive acts were entirely out of his character, and in truth, he wasn't quite sure why he was here on this mission, except that he happened to be in Bond Street, and well, it just seemed the thing to do after Miss Bartley-Bacon's rudeness and the young girl's tears. But there must not be any misunderstandings on the matter. "No, Madame Howard! Most definitely not the demimonde!" he emphasized.

"As you wish, *monsieur*," conceded LaFee with a slight incline of her head. Such a windfall, after the beginnings of a lagging season. *Carte blanche* with fashions, colors and costs! She glanced at Rose with a wink.

"Excellent, Madame Howard. I shall see you on the third Thursday of next month then," Geoffrey said. He sketched an abrupt bow to the dressmaker, and turned to do the same for Rose, but a warm parting smile spread over his face at her wide-eyed expression. He could not stem the tender feelings that came when he looked at her. She was, after all, a most beguiling child and surely in need of some kindness in her young life. "Miss Lambe, thank you for your assistance. You have been most helpful in this matter," he murmured.

Rose blinked several times beneath his smile, then, remembering her manners, bobbed a curtsy. "Of course, my lord. Anything for your pleasure."

Geoffrey considered this a moment, then abruptly plopped his topper on his head as if to restrict the unbidden thoughts her words brought to mind. "Ladies," he murmured, then stepped briskly out of the shop to continue on his business.

LaFee laughed and clapped her hands in excitement. "You see, *chérie!* God is always with LaFee! Now what do you think of that?"

Rose ran to the window to watch the elegant marquis until he had mounted his horse and disappeared from her sight into the surging traffic of Bond Street. "Who do you think she is?" she asked, pressing her face against the glass. "The lucky girl he is ordering a whole wardrobe for?"

"I have ideas prancing about my head, but that is not for us to question. All we need to know is that we are going to be very, very busy—commencing right this moment," she vowed. "Come! Come!" Grasping Rose's wrist, she headed for the workroom. "This job will be easy. Now off with the clothes. I would look at the body!"

"LaFee!" wailed Rose.

"Come!" LaFee demanded, flipping her hand at Rose's modesty.

Sensing complaints would serve no purpose, Rose stripped to her linen smallclothes and stepped before the mirror to turn as the dressmaker studied her figure and jotted measurements. Her face turned pink beneath the close scrutiny of the black eyes but her thoughts were with the marquis and his young lady. "He must like her a tremendous amount to buy so many lovely things for her. Don't you think so, LaFee?"

"I would expect so. Turn! Yes, yes! A good body! How

old are you, *chérie?*'' the quick voice asked, as the survey went on with a quick measurement here and there.

"Seventeen! You know that," admonished Rose.

"Yes. Yes, but I forget." LaFee raised her eyebrows as her eyes took in the ample bosom and slim hips. "I forget because I do not truly look at you, as I see you every day. Hmm, too large in the bosom for fashion perhaps, but your husband will worship you, no?"

"LaFee!" Rose exclaimed, crossing both arms over her bosom.

"Never be ashamed of God's gifts, *chérie.*" LaFee laughed. She tossed Rose's gown to her and spun toward the storeroom. "Come, pick out what you like so that we begin." Waving her arm over the fabrics, she declared, "Golds, bronzes, blues—most any color for your skin and hair. But no white! *Non!* White is for pale, insipid females. It will be creams and ivories for you."

"The gowns are not for me," Rose reminded the exuberant dressmaker. Stroking a careful hand over a length of bronze velvet, she sighed wistfully for the good fortune of the unknown girl so lucky as to have the perfect marquis in love with her. "Oh, I couldn't begin to select fabrics, not knowing the person they're intended for. Surely the girl's mother should—or perhaps, Lord Wyse's mother…"

"Bah on that one! She is a prune turned into a raisin that has never had a real man between those fat thighs, so we will not trust her to gild a lily."

"LaFee!" squealed Rose.

LaFee cut her off with a rude gesture of her many-ringed hand. "You shall learn what you do not know, for I will teach you. Stand up straight in pride, *chérie!* The gowns will not hang well if you try to hide inside your own body."

Rose self-consciously straightened her shoulders, but laughed at her employer and friend. "LaFee, you are totally outrageous and I give thanks every day that I found you. All right, let's pretend the gowns are for me.'' Striding purposefully down the line, she touched first one and then another of the luscious fabrics, choosing things she had coveted for herself. Beautiful, sumptuous satins, lightweight silks, dainty sprigged muslins and luscious velvets. "I like this—and this. And those three there…''

LaFee followed her down the line, pulling bolts forward on the shelves as Rose made her selections. It pleased LaFee to see the girl's face aglow with delight. If her suspicions were confirmed, the wardrobe they were commencing upon *was* for this very girl, but it was not for her to voice such suspicions. Though the marquis would deny his intent, quite possibly being unaware of it himself, he was irresistibly drawn to her youth and promise of real beauty.

LaFee paused to think seriously of just such a future for Rose. The demimonde wasn't such a terrible place when one was young and much desired. The less fear Rose had the better, as competition was fierce among the women of the demimonde for the attentions and pockets of the rich, bored husbands of the ton. "*Chérie,* tell me. You are afraid of nothing. *Non?* You may look like a timid little thing, but you are afraid of no one, are you?''

Rose frowned over LaFee's question. Was she afraid of anyone? A protected, quiet country life with two loving parents had not placed her in the way of many perils and dangers. But that was before homelessness and an uncertain future had intervened in an otherwise orderly life. It was only through sheer blind luck she had arrived, unexpected and uninvited, upon the doorstep of the generous Madame Howard to beg gainful employment. "No, LaFee, a worrier I may be, but I am not unnecessarily afraid. I feel I shall always survive whatever trials life brings my way.''

LaFee cupped Rose's chin in her hard hand to scan her

face. "Good! *Chérie,* you come from a world of people born with much silver in their mouths. Be proud that you are a survivor! Always remember that we survivors are not afraid of work! Carry yourself erect and proud, for you have survived things that those others are too foolish to know exist!" LaFee advised her in a raspy voice. "Now, to my design books! We haven't much time and there is much to do!"

The excitement and flurry of action proved too taxing for the dressmaker's poor health. She leaned back against the bolts of fabrics to cough deeply, holding her chest as if it pained her greatly.

Rose rushed to her side to support her. Placing the back of her hand against her flushed forehead, she grimaced. "Just as I suspected, your face is burning up!"

"Ah, the excitement..."

"No, LaFee! Raging fever, not excitement," Rose amended. "Enough of this! Back to bed with you. I shall bring the books upstairs and you can play with your designs there, and—money or no, I am going for the doctor!"

Chapter Three

Not a fortnight later, the Marquis of Hetherington strode forcibly into his lodgings just off Pall Mall Street and straight into the library, where he hurled his riding crop into the corner with a vengeance. His man followed closely to accept the hastily shrugged-off greatcoat and retrieve the offending crop from the floor with a suitably bland expression, as if such useless behavior was entirely in character for the staid marquis.

Lord Wyse's closest friend and confidant, Viscount Milton Philpotts, lifted his eyebrows in astonishment at this outward show of temper from one who seldom demonstrated his thoughts so effusively. "I say, old chap! 'Twas as rough an outing as all that?" he inquired. Ready to offer condolences and advice, Lord Philpotts hefted his bulk from the leather sofa. In the process he dislodged the head of a rather large Irish wolfhound from his thigh. The dog voiced his disappointment at the object of his adoration retiring from him with a long, piteous whine and a canting of soulful eyes.

Geoffrey splashed a bumper of brandy into a crystal glass, and firmly installed himself in the chair opposite the fire with a thundercloud marring his warm good looks.

Sourly he contemplated the dog's pitiful expression. "You are spoiling that dog, you know, Milty. I would swear he suffered lovesickness by the look of him. Balderdash, get off the damn furniture!"

"Spoiled! Balderdash—" Lord Philpotts waved a hand over the animal still sprawled upon the divan "—is one of God's finest hunters. 'Tis only town life that has him depressed. An animal of his strong killer instincts should actively hunt to sharpen the senses." The viscount poured a bumper of brandy for himself with the familiarity of long friendship, and returned to the divan. The dog rolled over to offer a lean, hairy belly for attention, which the large man obligingly scratched.

"Killer instincts?" Geoffrey snorted. He slanted a telling glance at his friend and the fawning dog.

"Now, Geoffrey, leave off with the complaints over my noble friend here, and expound upon the reason for such a foul display of temper," Milty admonished. "The fair Miss Bartley-Bacon again, I can only presume?"

Geoffrey snorted again and crossed one elegant leg over the knee of the other, smoothing the fit of his trousers with a slim, refined hand. "The situation is no longer amusing. In fact, it is becoming highly intolerable. She has began pressing her suit most ardently and I am no longer capable of a simple visit to my mother without her simpering, cloying presence. I tell you, Milty, Miss Sharon Bartley-Bacon is hanging out for a title and it's mine she intends to have, come hell or high water!"

"You are a contrary, Geoffrey. Only one of my acquaintance, don't you know, who perceives an irritating nature behind Miss Bartley-Bacon's astonishing beauty," mocked Milty. "Most I have cognizance of would pay dearly to be in your boots this very moment. Mayhaps you could sell her affections—" a flush crossed his round face as he realized the implication of his remark "—no, doubt that would fly. Bit like Chelsea Street. Not good to refer to a lady in that light."

The marquis looked at his friend with great affection. As light as the marquis was dark, Lord Milton Philpotts was a top-of-the-trees Corinthian and a bashing rider to the hounds, though he would insist upon hiding that fact beneath the paint and frippery of the dandy set all during the season. A sturdy young man with a broad, rosy, countrified face beneath his paint and patches, he possessed a bearlike figure and an extraordinary length of leg. Regardless of the damage he inflicted upon parlor glassware and such set about on tiny, fragile tables, the viscount was as gentle as the massive wolfhound that so adored him.

"Well, be that as it may, but the lady has begun to try my patience sorely, and the season is not aged past two months," grated Geoffrey, returning to the subject of his complaint. "Since Miss Bartley-Bacon has taken up residence at 1 Leicester Street, I would warrant she's embroiled my mother head over heels in her plots for my hide. It is enough to drive a man to the Continent. Season or no season!"

"I'm not much for the petticoat line," offered Milton generously. "But perhaps I should make a play for her, Geoffrey. I have the title she's after, and it would give you some breathing space. Do you think the girl has a yen for viscountess?"

"Well, Milty, you have the look she prefers. All ruffles, lace and red high heels. She greatly favors the Tulips and the Bond Street beaux, you know," Geoffrey teased fondly. "And I daresay viscountess might just be the thing to turn her head in your direction. Take her if you want her, for I truly do not."

A discreet cough from the doorway turned their attention

to Lord Wyse's gentleman's gentleman. "Yes, Deming? What is it?"

"There's, er, a young lady calling, my lord. I have placed her in the back parlor." The man's long nose fairly twitched with an air of disapproval. Ladies of quality did not call upon gentlemen at their place of residence. Either this one was not a lady of quality at all, or she was an infatuated young miss escaping her mama's sharp eye to moon after the object of her misguided affections. Both situations fathered Deming's disapproval, for a gentleman's gentleman was colored by the same paintbrush as his master, and it greatly pleased him that the marquis carried the reputation of one who kept his affairs in strictest confidence—and elsewhere. Deming cleared his throat and added, "A most respectable young lady, I feel, my lord. Although there is no maid with her...nor carriage waiting below."

"Good Lord! What now?" Geoffrey exploded. "No longer satisfied with destroying my leisure at 1 Leicester Street, has she tracked me to my lair? Forgive me a moment, Milty, while I see what's about."

Rose Lambe sat primly ensconced upon the horsehair sofa in the back parlor on Pall Mall Street. She had removed her bonnet, and the fall of her undressed hair down her back was smoothed by nervous hands that would tremble. She jumped to her feet when Lord Wyse entered, then clamped her red-rimmed eyes tightly closed, for to look into that beautiful, kind face was to lose all courage, and to lose all courage was to fall into utter despair. Drawing a deep breath, she announced her intention in a loud voice.

"My Lord Wyse, I have come to be your...your bird of paradise."

After a short moment of utter silence, Rose opened her eyes. The marquis was standing quite motionless in the doorway, staring at her in a great show of disbelief, as if he could no longer trust his hearing. Although Rose had not known exactly what to expect from a man who had just been offered the most precious thing she owned, she most definitely had not expected total speechlessness. Tears suddenly filled her huge lavender eyes and spilled over to trace down her pale cheeks.

Geoffrey cleared his throat. He could see nothing else to do but be polite and discover where this addle-brained notion had come from. While the child was a pretty little thing, a man did so like to choose his own flights of fancy.

"I, ahem, see. And what possibly could have brought about this sudden decision, Miss Lambe?"

"Oh, it's no use," Rose wailed. She plopped back down to the sofa as if her legs had turned to water. "You don't want me! I can see that readily enough. It's just that I'm too young to be anybody's g-g-governess, and I don't know any other gentlemen...."

Quickly overcome with remorse for causing her unhappiness, Geoffrey crouched beside the sofa to take her small hand in his. "Now, now, have over with the waterworks, child. Let's begin at the beginning," he urged in a soft, comforting voice. "And tell me what's brought about this sad state of affairs."

Before she could commence, Deming, bearing a heavily crusted silver service, strode forcefully into the room. He would not see his master compromised by an unchaperoned visit from a scheming young minx. He had his duty, after all. The sight of the weeping young lady, and the marquis practically on his knees before her, brought him up abruptly with eyes agog. He quickly masked his shock behind years of service to the nobles. "Ahem, I took the liberty of bringing some refreshments for the young lady, my lord."

"Yes, yes, excellent idea. Thank you, Deming," said

Geoffrey, without taking his eyes from the tear-streaked face. "Now, please, Miss Lambe, what terrible calamity has befallen you to produce such great distress?"

"I can't go back—ho-home. My cousin—once removed—has taken up residence. My father having passed, you see—from drink if you must know the awful truth—although I have always thought it was loneliness that killed him as he never before—I mean, before my mother's death…"

"Here, accept this cup of tea and try to compose yourself," offered Geoffrey, waving Deming away. "Perhaps the distraction will busy your hands and halt the flow of tears and stammers, so that the tale might be made clear."

Rose accepted the tea, but would only twist the cup in the saucer with a grate of china against china, which further set the marquis's nerves on edge. She raised sad eyes to his face. "But you do not understand, Lord Wyse. You see, I thought the gowns you ordered—I mean, obviously they are for someone, and as that someone is my size, I thought perhaps you'd accept me instead of… I realize I don't know much…but I hoped you would like me a little—well, enough to accept me as your bird of paradise, I mean."

Geoffrey shook his head in utter amazement at this muddled tirade. He stood to his full height and stepped away from her. "Really, Miss Lambe, what could a child like you possibly know of such things? Now I must insist that you drink your tea and return to Madame Howard directly. Should anyone have seen you arriving here at my lodgings, your reputation will be shredded quite beyond repair. Bird of paradise, indeed! My dear, I do not take children to bed!"

"No! No, I can't go back! It's just that—LaFee—Madame Howard has passed this very day. Pneumonia! And the landlord, who is acquainted with the doctor who tended her, says I must be gone by morning. And—and—I have nowhere to go! *Nowhere at all!*" she wailed afresh.

"Who's got nowhere to go?" hailed a cheerful voice from the doorway. Lord Philpotts strode into the room, his eyes brimming with avid curiosity to find a weeping female drinking tea in Geoffrey's back parlor and Deming hovering about the doorway boasting a thundercloud of disapproval upon his face.

Geoffrey waved Deming away from the door and moved to bar his friend's progress into the room. "Milty, my friend, I must ask you to excuse us. This is a private matter, and more than a bit delicate...."

To Geoffrey's utter surprise, his words went unheeded, for the confiding Miss Lambe, impressed by the large, friendly Corinthian with the merry eyes, immediately launched into the tearful tale all over again. It was not a great deal clearer this time than last, although the amiable Lord Philpotts seemed to have followed it beginning to end.

"I must say, that is indeed a pickle," conceded Milty, once she had finished her sad, sad story.

"It's just that I—well, I thought of the demimonde," she whispered, turning large eyes to the marquis once more. "And you were so kind the other day and..."

"And you thought of me!" demanded Geoffrey in astonishment. "What sort of loose screw do you take me for—to seduce children?"

Rose jumped to her feet and confronted both of them with a stamp of her small foot. "I am not a child! Just because I am slight in stature doesn't mean..." She stamped her foot again. "I would have you know I am seventeen and—and that is not a child!"

The two men looked at her doubtfully. She was attired in the shabby tarlatan dress, which was too short for her, and exposed the pair of much-worn cloth boots no bigger than a minute. Both reaching six feet, the men seemed to tower over her, filling the tiny parlor to bursting. In their impeccable swallowtail coats, intricate cravats and glossy Hessians, they were a glittering world away from a poor assistant dressmaker.

Rose caught her bottom lip with her small teeth. That which had seemed such a logical solution to an impossible problem only this morning now seemed utter madness. Although she would not mind being Lord Wyse's bird of paradise, as she did admire him greatly, and even if she was unsure of all the implications of that title, perhaps it had not been the thing to bluntly ask of him.

"I say, Geoffrey, seventeen is not all that young, and she is a deuced pretty little thing. Pray introduce us—" Milton began.

"Milton Philpotts!" Geoffrey exploded in outraged disgust at his friend's improper implication.

Rose bobbed a tiny curtsy to Milty as if the marquis had, in fact, performed the introduction. "Pleased to make your acquaintance, my lord. My name is Rose Lambe—of Sussex," she announced, raising large eyes to his face.

"Good God!" muttered Geoffrey. "Am I the only one in this room with a mind that hasn't flown? The two of you are going to be the end of me, I can just feel it."

Milty tapped a forefinger on his pursed lips in thought. "Lambe! I say, you wouldn't be the daughter of the Earl of Shenstone? Neighbor of mine, you know. Not that I ever venture to squireship. Neglect my property there most dreadfully. Can't seem to find a reliable steward...but I knew the earl. Decent enough fellow..."

"You knew my father?" demanded Rose, her eyes widened in disbelief at her good fortune.

"Yes! Yes! Did some hunting with the earl, don't you

know. As I say, decent enough fellow,'' Milton elaborated, much to Geoffrey's dismay. "Kept a fine stable, he did.''

Geoffrey frowned in thought, then rounded the sofa to confront him. "You say the girl's father is an earl? Shenstone?''

"Was, not is. Believe he's passed now. But yes, Earl of Shenstone. In fact, distant relation of yours,'' the large man agreed in the most congenial manner as if the news was common knowledge to all. "Oh, quite distant, of course. Way, way distant, in fact.''

"Relative!'' Geoffrey exclaimed in unison with Rose.

"Oh, yes. Yes, indeed. Sure of it,'' Milton muttered, glancing from one to the other in good humor, then brightened with an idea. "I say, old man, this could be your relief.''

Geoffrey blinked several times then stared hard at his friend. He was thoroughly confused and rapidly becoming nonplussed by this whole affair. "I do beg your pardon, Lord Philpotts, but I think you have quite lost your mind. I do not have the slightest notion what you are speaking of.'' He commenced pacing the floor, four steps to the door and four steps back to the sofa.

"Not only do I have a young lady of tender years installed in my back parlor begging to become my bird of paradise, of all things, but now you are telling me she is a relative *and* the daughter of a title? That makes me, as a relative *and* a member of the nobility, doubly responsible for her dubious welfare whether I wish it or not—and all this commenced from one ill-fated trip to a damn dressmaker!'' he finished with voice raised almost to a shout.

Lord Philpotts made a halfhearted attempt to pat his friend on the shoulder. Clearly exasperated and losing patience with the confusion, the normally unruffled marquis was rapidly exhibiting signs of becoming very ruffled indeed. This fact, rather than alarming his friend of long standing, seemed to increase his good humor to out-and-out mirth. He barely refrained from laughter but could not control the grin that spread wider and wider across his face—an expression that did little to alleviate the marquis's confusion, and nothing at all to decrease his increasing ill humor.

"Oh, come, Geoffrey. Surely you see—"

"See what, Philpotts! Out with it or I shall—"

"Easy, old man. I am referring to the problem of inconvenience we were speaking of just before this delightful young lady happened upon the scene," Milton explained. "I mean, as your mama is so insistent you buckle before this year is gone, regardless of the fact that she has chosen a real snake in the grass as her candidate, and while you desire only peace in which to continue your well-ordered existence, what better way to gain that peace than to announce your engagement to another?"

Geoffrey stared at him as if he had truly taken leave of all reason, then shook his head in defeat. "The way your mind works is amazing, Milty. Announce my engagement, indeed. What does that have to do with the—" he waved a hand toward Rose, who appeared as lost in the conversation as he was "—immediate situation?"

"Well, look at it this way," Milty calmly explained. "Here is a personage—young, impressionable, in need of housing and support—turns out she's even a relation. Lady Rose. Look it up in that bible your mother sports in the library at 1 Leicester Street. 'Tis all there, I assure you. Wyse, Leaven, Laird, Sewell, Lambe, if my memory serves and it usually does."

"Sewell! Elmo Sewell is my cousin—once removed, of course," Rose exclaimed, then shuddered at the thought of the man. "He succeeded to the title *and* deed to my home—when my father passed three years ago. Records were very scarce, with the fire at the abbey and all—most burned, you see. But they would claim him as heir, and I was put on his charity. But—'' she shuddered again ''—I ran away.''

''Yes, just so,'' Milton agreed, patting her gently on the shoulder. ''Should have done so, my dear. Understand the man's a bounder. Much given to corrupting young girls, if you will forgive my saying so.''

Waving Rose to a chair, Geoffrey sank to the sofa and pondered his two guests closely. He could never expect an expedient end to Milty's tales, but at least he was more than pleased to see the tears disappearing from the young girl's eyes. ''Ahem...'' Geoffrey prompted his friend to continue by clearing his throat loudly, as the hour grew late with little of this dilemma solved.

''Oh, yes, where was I?'' Milty began. ''As I was saying, what better thing than to announce your engagement to a newly discovered, and quite beautiful, might I add—'' he bowed toward Rose ''—relation of genteel quality? Mama's mollified, and our Miss Bartley-Bacon's tiffed, then rushes off in a different direction to seek her title. And you have your peace.''

''Peace? Peace, you say? And what of this young lady I am now promised to? Could it be possible that you have forgotten her?'' Geoffrey asked, waving a hand at Rose. He was torn between humor and exasperation, undecided as to whether he should return to the original problem, or satisfy his curiosity as to the direction of this absurd yet entertaining yarn his great buffoon of a friend was spinning.

''Why, install her in residence with your mama, of course. It's just the thing mothers dote upon, Geoffrey. Let Lady Wyse train Lady Rose for society, suitably outfit her—''

Rose, catching the gist of Lord Philpotts's direction, interrupted to exclaim, "Oh, I have a whole wardrobe of fashionable...well, almost a whole wardrobe...nearly completed...I mean, I think I could use them...." Rose tapered off, remembering suddenly that those gowns were indeed meant for another. Someone the marquis could very well be enamored of. That thought greatly saddened her. She did not want the marquis to be in love with anyone else.

"And introduce her into society," Milty concluded as if Rose hadn't spoken. "Just the thing mamas like to do. All you have to do is squire her to a few socials. Keep up the pretense for a suitable time, then quietly dissolve the engagement. Or hell, marry the child. Not bad to look at, and she will get older, you know. Could do worse. Need to buckle sometime at any rate."

Geoffrey's eyebrows lifted in surprise, then knit together in thought. Leaning forward, he placed a long finger beneath Rose's chin to turn her face toward him. Her expressive eyes spoke of uncertainty and worry, as if she were not at all sure what she'd gotten herself into. "I wonder—" Geoffrey mused aloud "—if it might just suit all concerned at that?" Then, as if the decision was quickly made, he added briskly, "Please leave us, Lord Philpotts."

"Wha...?" Milty sputtered to a halt. While he himself thought it a splendid idea, the perfect answer to Geoffrey's dilemma actually, he had never considered he'd be taken seriously by the staid marquis. Why, it wasn't even exactly on the up-and-up, and definitely wasn't like Geoffrey at all. "I say, Geoffrey, our Miss Bartley-Bacon must have you spooked more than even I imagined. Perhaps you should consider this thing just a bit more."

"Leave us, Lord Philpotts," Geoffrey repeated, more firmly this time.

The viscount cast a glance at Rose and winced a little,

as if he had started something that was going downhill without brakes. "Geoffrey, she's such a little thing. Best be gentle...."

"I will. I will," said Geoffrey impatiently. Rising quickly, he thrust his large friend from the room and firmly closed the door. Returning to stand in front of Rose, he stated his case. He would have no misunderstanding between them. "I do not know how much of that ramble you comprehended, but it so happens, my dear Lady Rose, that I am thirty years of age, and every matron, including my own mother, has decided that this is the year that I take the essential wife.

"Now, understand me! I do not particularly want a wife, but that does not signify anything to that party of rather ardent ladies. I tell you, I am fair beset on all sides by daughters being shoved beneath my nose. It is a most uncomfortable situation, and it would seem that the only way out is to yield and to marry. And trust me when I say I have given this due consideration. When I do contemplate marriage, I have decided I should like to be left to my own pursuits, while my wife, provided with a generous allowance, of course, is left to pursue her own fancies. Therefore, to my way of thinking, a *mariage de convenance* is the best solution. Now you, er, Lady Rose, on the other hand, need an escape from an equally unpleasant situation."

Rose drew down her eyebrows. It did seem a bit much to compare the inconvenience of starvation in the streets to avoiding ardent mamas with marriageable daughters. "It would seem to me the situations are not equal at all..." she began.

Geoffrey turned to pace the room, continuing as if she had not spoken. "You are—if it is indeed as Lord Philpotts states, and I must confess, he does have the memory for such things—a distant relative and a peeress. As I need a wife, however temporarily, it seems quite possible we might assist each other in these dilemmas.''

"But what of Miss Bartley-Bacon? If I was following Lord Philpotts correctly, your mother has selected her....'' Rose faltered. She shuddered at the thought of that one's revenge upon hearing that the shabby dressmaker's assistant had stolen the prize of the season from beneath her haughty nose.

Geoffrey's face hardened and he looked fiercely at Rose. "I do not wish to wed any lady who is only interested in my title.'' He squatted down before her to take her hands into his much larger ones. His voice softened as he smiled at her, with dimple flashing. "I am not forcing you, you know. It is quite simple to say no. I shall assist you either way. You will not be turned into the streets. But...would you like to be my wife? Announce an engagement to that fact, at any rate?''

Rose lowered her eyes to her hands held so tightly in his warm clasp. She suddenly realized that if she let this chance pass her by, she would be lost in the shadows of London society forever. She raised her eyes to that beautiful face watching her so intently, and barely suppressed a sigh. Yes, she would very much like to be his wife. In every sense of the word. But that was not what he was offering. As it were, at least here was a chance to remain in the society to which she was born. And perhaps the marquis would someday learn to love her a little. Stranger things had happened, hadn't they?

Rose fought to ignore the little warning nag in her mind that said that this was only a temporary sham, and she was never going to be Lord Wyse's wife in reality. He did not want a wife! And no matter how many times he squired her about society, how many times he turned that wonderful smile upon her, he would never fall in love with her. Her rational mind reasoned this out and knew it for fact. But then her romantic nature interjected to add, there was always the possibility of a miracle. But only if she took this chance.

She smiled a heartrending smile and answered bravely, "I would like it above all things. But what will your mother say?"

Geoffrey shrugged as if it were of no great worry. "If I know my mother, she will have a great deal to say. But she will take you under her wing and mother you as she does all manner of small, helpless things. The wedding announcement will no doubt come as a jolting surprise to many, but I think that we shall both profit by it. I propose we announce our forthcoming nuptials reasonably soon."

"If that is your wish," Rose whispered.

"Good," Geoffrey stated, then patted her hand. "Now, let us tell Milty the news. He is probably down upon his knees, pressing his ear to the keyhole at this very moment, and undoubtedly looking very silly from the other side."

Rose giggled as he flung the door open with a flourish, but Lord Philpotts was standing quite erect...and with a huge smile on his merry face. A frowning, concerned Deming peered anxiously around his bulk.

"Thought a celebration might be in order," Milty announced cheerfully. He stepped aside to display the tray Deming carried, with a chilled bottle of champagne and three stemmed crystal glasses. He unceremoniously brushed past the stunned marquis to seat himself across from Rose and offer tender best wishes in the heartiest of voices.

Chapter Four

At 1 Leicester Street, Miss Sharon Bartley-Bacon was yawning over a midmorning breakfast when the obviously flustered Dowager Marquise of Hetherington fluttered into the dining room. Her face was set and flushed, and her hands waved about in helplessness as she sought in each corner of the room something that might have slipped her mind. Sharon tilted an eyebrow upward, but chose to wait for the lady to broach the fact of her upset in her own sweet time. Sharon hadn't long to wait.

"Do tell me you have seen that Humphrey. I must find him at once. I am just beside myself," Lady Lavitia vowed. As if to demonstrate as much, she dropped heavily into the Chippendale chair opposite her young houseguest and tapped her fingers vigorously on the table.

"And just what is this latest tiff, dear Mama Lavitia?" Sharon queried, languidly flicking out her tongue to remove honey from her thumb. Her politeness was of the pretended sort, for she truly had no interest in the infractions of servants and such. And Lady Lavitia's latest quandary, and her reason for tracking the fearsome majordomo about the house this morning, could not be otherwise. As for herself, she was too busy in her head wondering why the bothersome marquis had not appeared for his customary Wednesday breakfast with his mother. It was the reason, the only reason, mind you, she was out of bed at this ungodly hour *and* attired in her best day dress. Blue, of course, to enhance her eyes to devastating brilliance.

Lady Lavitia lowered her voice and glanced over her shoulder to ensure privacy before she confided through clamped teeth, "That *man* has brought a child into my house, and furthermore, he is insisting that I properly bring her out into society!"

This bit of *on dit* stopped the honey-laden muffin halfway to Sharon's open mouth. "My word! Humphrey has?" she queried in disbelief.

"No, of course not Humphrey. Really, Sharon! I merely seek Humphrey to arrange a bedchamber. But a long-lost relative he claims, and true enough it's there in the family bible. Printed in black and white. Lambe!"

"Lambe! I've heard that name before," Sharon considered, a foreboding creeping up her spine. Her eyes narrowed. She leaned forward to prod the lady to confidences. "Who brought her? Where is she?"

"Why, Geoffrey, of course. It seems the child was forced from her home by a disreputable cousin, or some such—actually earning her living as a dressmaker—with that Madame Howard of all people! There will be no end to the tittle-tattle when *this* gets around town!" warned Lady Lavitia. She nodded her head and clicked her tongue for emphasis.

"That little chit! She's here?" Sharon demanded, snapping erect in her chair. "A *relative?* That can't be true. You say Lord Wyse brought her into *your* home for *you* to bring out? Outrageous!"

"Yes, well, actually his home if one wants to be technically accurate, but this is not the only place he had available to him. Hetherington Harrow would seem a better choice. She's too young to be seen about in society if you asked me, which of course, no one did. Why he must dispense such charity—well, apparently she threw herself upon his mercy. Seems quite taken with her too." She paused to ponder the strangeness of that thought.

"That does give me pause," she continued after a moment. "I do find it hard to judge when she is wearing such a shapeless gown...and that hair hanging like that, but I swear if the girl were dressed properly, she could take London, and perhaps Geoffrey as well, by the ears. Most extraordinary but he seems quite tender with her." Again she shifted focus in her conversation to exclaim. "I'm supposed to have her ready for the Townsend ball, and that's only a fortnight! Apparently she does have some gowns, although one can only wonder at the appropriateness of them. I mean—" she shuddered in disgust "—*Madame Howard!*"

"But she's here—" Sharon stabbed the table with her forefinger "—right here? In this very house?" She was rapidly losing patience with her babbling hostess and her slippery changes of subject.

"Yes, bold as brass, sitting in the drawing room. Saying her goodbyes to Geoffrey, then I'm to settle her...."

"Geoffrey's here too! And I wasn't informed?" Sharon exclaimed. She jumped from her seat and dashed down the hall without another word to Lady Lavitia, steam practically pouring from her ears. Damn those servants! She'd told them repeatedly that the marquis was not to set a foot on the front stoop without her being notified. They'd certainly have the back of her tongue for this day's work!

"Oh, Good Lord," said Lady Lavitia with a snort as she peered after Sharon. Then with a sigh of resignation, she levered her round, teakettle figure from the chair to follow her vexing houseguest down the hall. She had expected some support in this delicate matter, not all this mad dashing about without so much as a by-your-leave.

Rose, sitting quietly on the satin-striped sofa, nervously pleated and smoothed her worn skirt. She was unsure of her reception in this opulent residence, as Lady Lavitia Wyse did seem rather stiff and not at all welcoming as Lord Wyse had led her to expect. But she would make the best of the situation. She hazarded a glance at Lord Wyse. He was leaning casually against the mantel with one leg before the other, looking for every nonchalant inch of him to be totally unaware of the manner in which his mother had accepted the news that her son was fostering a complete stranger upon her hospitality.

The man was proving to be an enigma to her, quite out of the range of her experience. Although that experience could only be considered limited at best. With some relief, she did note that even though she had offered herself as bird of paradise, the marquis did not seem to have any intent of mischief toward her. After all, a less reputable man wouldn't have presented her to his mama, would he? Or taken such great pains to explain the nature of their family connection, even carrying in the huge family bible from the library to prove his point. No, she could only surmise that he was absolutely the most splendid man in the world, and she would gladly have given her life for him in gratitude.

Sharon rushed through the arched doorway, then paused dramatically to pose in pretty surprise, as if stunned to find the room occupied. "Lord Wyse!" she gasped delightfully. Her golden head tilted, and she postured with her hand pressed to her bosom as if to pull all eyes there to admire.

"Good morning, Miss Bartley-Bacon," acknowledged Geoffrey with a slight incline of his head, and a hooding of his eyes. Just the person he had no wish to see on this particular morning. "I am certain you will remember Miss Rose Lambe, although now we have discovered she is, in fact, Lady Rose. Lady Rose, may I present Miss Sharon Bartley-Bacon?"

"Yes, yes," said Sharon, with a disinterested flip of her hand. She turned her back on Rose and addressed the marquis. "Your mama and I missed you at breakfast this morning, my lord. Usually you are an early—and most welcome I might say—addition to our little family gathering. Your absence quite took the shine from the beginning of my day."

Rose stiffened beneath the blatant snub, and the open proprietary manner she demonstrated toward the marquis. Her eyes narrowed and glinted frostily. If looks could freeze, the blonde would have had icicles hanging from her nose.

Lady Lavitia puffed around the corner. "So there you are, Sharon. Allow me to introduce Lady Rose—oh, Geoffrey dear, you're still here?"

"Yes, Mother. I am still here," he affirmed in a teasing tone, then straightened and moved to extend a hand to Rose. "But now I must be off. Lady Rose, I shall dispatch Deming immediately to Bond Street to see to the removal of your belongings. All are sorted and packed?"

Rose placed her hand into his much larger one and smiled into his warm, brown gaze. How could she not have noticed the golden glints in the sherry brown? And the way the corners crinkled into small lines of merriment when he smiled that way? His dimple flashed deeply. Her heart filled to bursting and she could not help but respond to the merry sense of conspiracy that danced there.

"Yes, all is ready," she answered. At that moment, there came a plaintive squall of displeasure and complaint from the wicker case at her feet.

"Oh, my gracious! Something is dying!" squeaked Lady Lavitia. Her hand flew to protect her throat, and she swiveled her head madly about, fully expecting to find some poor, suffering creature being rent to shreds in her drawing room.

"Hush now, Willy," admonished Rose, tapping the case sharply. "I do apologize, Lady Wyse. It is only my cat. I wasn't sure of his welcome, but I just could not leave him behind." She quickly raised wide, pleading eyes to the marquis. "Surely you must see that I could not turn him into the street to starve."

"A cat!" sniffed Sharon. "That makes two strays."

Geoffrey straightened abruptly, and leveled a look upon Sharon that wasn't at all kind. "I am positive it is a very nice cat—" he turned back to Rose "—and, of course you could not leave it behind."

"But Geoffrey—a cat?" hedged Lady Lavitia. She glanced at Sharon's angry, set face. This was not going to be easy. Drat Geoffrey for being so stubborn and bringing such strife into her household. He seemed fully intent upon driving her to an early grave with this sudden unpredictable behavior.

"Oh, well, Mother. Number 1 Leicester Street is such a large mausoleum, after all. What trouble can one small cat be? Lady Rose, let's have it out of the basket, shall we? Might as well have introductions all around."

"His name is Orange Willy and I assure you, he can be very well behaved," said Rose, praying Willy chose this morning to exhibit the best of his manners. She lifted the irritated cat from the case and placed him on her lap, keeping a restraining hand on his collar, lest he decide to dart away from the strangers.

Sharon swished her skirts back as if the animal would foul her by its mere presence. "Well I, for one, have always thought cats to be sneaky. Up to no good most of the time," she insisted. "I much prefer dogs."

Rose's head came up to level her chin somewhat sternly, although she replied sweetly, "While I, on the other hand—" she paused for just a second to meet the hard, blue eyes before continuing "—have always found that people with whom cats refuse to associate, normally do prefer dogs."

Geoffrey's expression remained blank for a full minute as silence rang in the room. It took that long for the real intent of Rose's words to register. As they did, a delighted grin spread over his features, quite taking ten years from his age. The girl appeared such a meek little thing, but there was more than a bit of the minx about her. With a deep chuckle, he waved his hand toward the struggling animal to quickly redirect the conversation, and forestall any blue words from escaping Sharon's gaping mouth.

"So there you have it, one small cat. Come, Mother. You'd not be put off by Orange Willy, now would you?" he coaxed. "Not after the unruly wolfhounds your own son filled the place with? Not to mention the toads and snakes I used to keep secreted in my bedchamber?"

"Oh, I suppose not. We shall take him to Cook for milk, and Rose, you may place his basket in your room. I do not see that he is such a ferocious beast," conceded Lady Lavitia. After all, she did subscribe to the belief that the care of a pet increased any child's sense of responsibility.

Sharon's eyes narrowed. This was not a good thing. Such solicitous regard for this little chit and her flea-infested alley cat did not mesh with her plans. If the girl was coming to stay, and it very much seemed that she was, there must be some way to turn all this to her own advantage. Perhaps if she championed the girl? Would that possibly earn points with the elusive Lord Wyse? She stroked her smooth cheek with her forefinger in thought. This bore some momentous plotting and planning.

Geoffrey spread his hands and looked exceedingly pleased with himself. "There, Lady Rose, that is settled then. And now I shall be off. Mother?" He brushed a light kiss on his mother's cheek. "Miss Bartley-Bacon, Lady Rose, I shall take my leave of you then."

"Lord Wyse?" cooed Sharon, as she stepped to lay a possessive hand on his sleeve. "Are you positive we cannot persuade you to linger? No? Then I shall just walk you to the door."

Geoffrey deftly removed his arm from beneath her hand. "Having been born and reared in this house, Miss Bartley-Bacon, I am fairly certain I have learned the way to the front door." Then as an apparent afterthought, he turned to Rose again. "I say, Lady Rose, do you ride?"

Rose beamed at him with undisguised enthusiasm. "Oh, yes. I was placed on horseback practically before I could walk."

"Very good. We shall have to see about procuring a suitable mount for you in the near future."

"That would be delightful. I had the best warmblood at Shenstone. He was simply lovely, and a real goer. But—" she hesitated and the glow on her face dimmed and her teeth caught at her lower lip "—that was at home."

"Ah, yes," sympathized Geoffrey, nodding solemnly. "Well, we shall see about another. And once again…I'm off. Ladies?"

Glaring after the departed Lord Wyse, Sharon simmered. The gall! He had practically ignored her, while dancing attendance upon a little shop girl. Turning slowly, she moved leisurely around the sofa, studying the girl. Unkempt, unfashionable and uninteresting, she judged her. Her glance flicked contemptuously over the offending cat, then over the tiny figure from the head of undressed hair to the tiny feet in their shabby Adelaide boots.

"So! I see you did find a way to feather your nest after all, girl. Well, by your leave, it will do you no good here. Do you understand me?" gritted Sharon, planting hands on hips in an aggressive stance.

"I'm sure I do not know of what you are speaking, Miss Bartley-Bacon—" Rose began, only to be cut off by Sharon in the rudest manner possible.

"Why in such a pucker, Mama Lavitia?" Sharon asked, yawning broadly. "Surely you do not expect the shine to be taken out of me by *Rosie* here."

"Oh, my goodness, no. Of course not," interjected Lady Lavitia. She searched for something soothing to say to the volatile young woman. She had no desire to further fracture her morning with a disagreement with Sharon Bartley-Bacon. Besides, there was the matter of arranging a place for this uninvited young guest in her household, and then there was the Townsend ball....

"Nothing troubles me because I am beautiful," said Sharon in a bored voice. "There is no one in the whole of London as beautiful as I. Nor will there ever be." She delivered herself of this piece of self-praise with a calm vanity quite awful to behold. "Pull the chit's hair up in curls and I will lend her one of my old gowns for the Townsend ball. She'll do to attract some second son with no hopes of marrying anyone else."

"Oh, I am told she has gowns of her own...." Lady Lavitia's voice tapered off, then came back forcefully. "Although I did tell Geoffrey that he is not to leave her sitting with the old women. He must dance some attendance upon her or I shall give him a piece of my mind!"

"That might not be advantageous in *your* case, Mama Lavitia," chided Sharon in open insult, which quite sailed over Lady Lavitia's head. "Nothing will keep Geoffrey from my side—especially not this little nothing."

Rose gritted her teeth. How rude of them to speak of her as if she were not present. As if she were a—a thing! Rising from the sofa, she dumped Willy from her lap. "I would not be too sure of that," she declared, straightening her spine. How she wanted to fling the news of the betrothal into the spoiled girl's smug face, but the fact that it was nothing but a sham stilled her tongue. If only it were all true then she would blurt it straight out and laugh in their self-important faces.

"Listen to the little girl," jeered Sharon. She pinched Rose painfully on the cheek. "You are so backward, *Rosie.* You know you shall stammer and blush every time a gentleman so much as looks in your direction. Best be warned, stick close to the Lady Wyse. The marquis will not give you this much—" she snapped her fingers sharply beneath Rose's nose "—of his attention." She flipped around to sweep from the room, nearly stepping on Willy in the process. "Out of my way, cat!"

"Oh, heaven help us," snorted Lady Lavitia. She looked after Sharon with consternation, then back to study Rose intently. She did not fear that Sharon would be overshadowed by this untutored little girl, but there was something in the way Geoffrey treated her that caused her concern. It was not that she feared her son would do something stupid in relation to this girl, it was just that she did not wish him to be distracted from her purpose. "Rose, if you will wait here, I shall locate someone to take you to your room so that you might become settled."

Rose gritted her teeth in silent fury. So, it became painfully clear. There was to be no peace for her in this house. Lady Lavitia was blatantly uninterested in having her here, and would not stand up for an unwanted houseguest against the favored Miss Bartley-Bacon. And that one was a witch who meant to have her marquis, even if it meant running roughshod over anyone she felt might stand in her way. Turning to scoop Willy into her arms, Rose sat back down to wait for someone to remember she was here and show her to her bedchamber.

"I must use my head, Willy—" she stroked his soft head "—for this is only an ephemeral fix to a perilous situation. And I had best have a care for my heart to boot. Already it is in danger of being broken, for I am quite taken with a man who might just be the worse kind of rakehell of all."

Chapter Five

Number 1 Leicester Street enfolded Rose in its arms as lovingly as a mother does a child. Not at all echoing and forbidding, as one would expect of a place so large, the mansion had mellowed and softened with age, providing welcoming surroundings to a homeless young girl.

It was designed in a St. Andrew's cross, with two wings reserved for guests and servants and two wings for the family's residence. Much attention had been given to a proper setting, with elaborate gardens and patterned walks comprising surprisingly expansive grounds for a town residence. The stone facade, ivy-covered, boasted towering windows on either side of enormous doors, which opened to the house's most outstanding feature, the reception hall. Its dome was skillfully frescoed with a colorful Diana at the Hunt, and numerous mirrors in heavy ornate frames reflected light and space, making the hall resemble a grand theater.

Tall columns stood guard at the entrances to the four hallways, each elaborately scrolled with gilded clusters of flowers and fruit. Numerous doors, carved and draped, marched in order down the long corridors. There were cavernous drawing rooms, delightful little salons, romantic alcoves tucked here and there, each one inviting exploration and discovery. And if one tired of architecture, there was a vast portrait gallery to explore, cheerfully christened the Court of Honor, which hinted broadly at an ancestry spent in service to the Crown. It was here that the young maid-in-training, assigned by Humphrey to see to Rose's needs, found her charge.

"Lady Rose? Lady Rose?"

At the sound of urgency in the maid's voice, Rose spun away from the painting she had been studying. "I'm here, Lettie," she called.

Lettie rushed through the doorway with her blue skirt and white apron flapping, nearly colliding with Rose as she hastened to the door. "Oh, miss, I thought never to find you. Mr. Humphrey says his lordship's waiting for you in the library," she gasped, fanning her flushed face with her apron tail. "Says for you to dress for riding, and to make haste."

"Riding! Oh, no! I haven't finished sewing my riding costume yet!" cried Rose. She leaped to pull the door wide and rushed into the hallway. "Oh, Lettie, I shouldn't have been dawdling about here, looking at portraits. I should have been sewing. There's no hem yet and the capelettes aren't attached to the Spencer jacket."

"I already thought of everything, miss. We'll just make do," Lettie announced, shooing her charge up the stairs and toward her bedchamber. "I found a serviceable brown skirt. That and a white shirtwaist under that deep green pilot jacket will be just fine. I'll even tie you a coachman's cravat just like the gents wear. A proper valet I'd be, miss. We'll pin a feather to that saucy little rust-colored cap, and there's those half boots...."

Soon attired thus in her haphazard riding costume, Rose ran lightly down the staircase. She hurried across the vast entry, fully expecting an impatient Lord Wyse to be pacing about with a scowl on his face. Rounding the corner into the library, she slipped on the polished floor and was forced to clutch the doorjamb to keep from losing her balance and landing a bump on her bottom in the hall.

Humphrey, coming out the doorway at that time, was startled and thumped his massive staff sharply on the floor. "Humph!" he grunted, giving her a stern look down the considerable length of his nose, clearly expressing his disapproval of such rambunctious behavior in children.

"Oh, do forgive me, Humphrey." Rose panted, barely refraining from bobbing a knee to the imposing majordomo. When he did not seem disposed to grant leniency she gingerly edged past him into the library.

"Here now, we aren't in that much of a hurry," called Geoffrey, with cheerful laughter in his voice. He advanced toward Rose, smiling that wonderful, warm smile, and holding out his hand to her.

Attired in tight buckskins, much-rubbed Marlborough boots and a black jacket of superfine, and displayed against the rich red backdrop of the linen-fold mahogany paneling of the library, he was too breathtakingly beautiful for words. Rose, suddenly very shy before the magnificence of him, slipped her hand hesitantly into his. "I am sorry to keep you so long, my lord, but I haven't anything proper for riding as yet, and some improvisation was necessary," she apologized, looking down at herself.

"It's of no consequence, child," he reassured her. "We are riding to take the exercise, not to impress the ton. What say you? Are you game?" He smiled down at her tenderly, tapping a forefinger on the tip of her nose.

"Yes, of course," said Rose, gently drawing back her hand. *He treats me as one would a toddler from the nursery,* she thought with dismay. She straightened her spine and leveled her chin to achieve more height and perhaps a year or two on her age. "Yes, Lord Wyse, I should like nothing better than to venture out. But what of—" She paused, then finished more definitely, as an adult would. "I *shall* request a maid."

"Milty, er, Lord Philpotts, awaits without. And there will be no less than two grooms. I suppose if we confine our jaunt to the main paths, and remain in plain view of anyone who cares to watch, you will be quite safe. Surely the four of us can repel any threat that might step forth."

Rose laughed at the immediate picture leaping into her mind, of four burly men rushing to protect her from pigeon-plump matrons knocking their heads together to whisper behind gilded chicken-wing fans. "I sadly fear, Lord Wyse, even with the brawn you mention, I would not be protected from the gossips of the ton, should I do something improper in public."

"Truer words were never spoken, Lady Rose," agreed Geoffrey, shaking his head as if it were a sad, sad thing indeed. "But, as your relation and your protector, I shall attend my duty and see that you are aboveboard at all times. No rambunctious galloping now! Do you hear, miss?" He frowned menacingly and shook a finger beneath her nose.

Rose laughed again at his sally and moved away to draw on tight leather gloves. "I shall heed your instruction. Now, shall we be off before our mounts lather at a standstill? I'm eager to see what bit of blood and bone you have brought for me this glorious morning."

Settling his topper, the marquis moved rapidly toward the front door, Marlborough boots striking firmly on the marble squares. "I will say this. While he is a finely put-together hunter, and seems to be a gentleman of the first rank as to his manners, I must admit to some shock this morning to call forth such a clown from my very own mews," he called over his shoulder. Reaching the doorway, he stepped back to bow her through with an elaborate flourish of his hand.

Rose rushed to catch up, frowning in bafflement at his meaning...and his teasing manner. Easing past him to the stoop, her eyes grew enormous at the sight of her beloved childhood mount standing placidly under saddle in the front drive, attended by one of the two grooms mentioned. Lord Philpotts, restraining hand on Balderdash's collar, stepped forward, eager to catch her expression over the intended surprise.

"Perplexity! Can it truly be?" Rose squealed. Without a word for Lord Wyse, she flung herself down the steps and against the wildly spotted, black-and-white pinto. The gelding flung his head high and danced away from her excitement, but not quickly enough to escape the arms thrown around his neck in an exuberant hug.

"And pray, who else could it be? Surely there cannot be two such animals in all of England," challenged Milty. He beamed in delight at her obvious joy and tilted his topper to the marquis in a salute. "I say, old chap, well done. The young lady is pleased as a good child on Christmas morn!"

Geoffrey acknowledged the salute with a grin and a forefinger touched to his topper brim. He, too, was pleased. Rose's reaction was precisely what he had been seeking when he had made the decision to attempt the purchase of the horse. He went down the massive granite steps to stand beside her.

"He was, as I said, certainly a shock when I first laid eyes upon him. Having purchased him sight unseen and arranged transport to London through my agent, I confess to having no idea of his somewhat remarkable coloring. What was it you called him? Perplexity?"

"Yes, of course," confirmed Rose, as if it were the obvious choice. "When I first saw him, it was quite obvious to *me* that no clear decision had been made as to a color for him, and then suddenly—" she shrugged her shoulders and gave a delightful giggle "—it was entirely too late to decide."

Milty, quicker at catching the jest, chuckled and shook his head. "Oh, that's capital, Lady Rose! Too late to decide. That's capital, indeed."

Rose glanced from Lord Philpotts to Lord Wyse with a stern face. "Although I would ask you not to make such a pickle of it, for it does stir his feelings of inadequacy somewhat. Though one might hope, after all this time, he would have become inured of teasing, but I fear it just doesn't seem to be so."

Geoffrey stood for a moment, a frown etching his brow, before the full implication of her remarks became clear. Then, quite out of character, he threw back his head and burst forth with a resounding laugh.

Milty lifted astonished eyebrows and pursed his lips in thought. Never had he seen the Marquis of Hetherington respond with such open enjoyment of anyone or anything in all their twenty-odd years of carousing about together. This was proving to be the best of all seasons, and all because of one small girl.

Rose belatedly remembered her manners and spun toward the large man. "Good morning, my Lord Philpotts. It is a genuine pleasure to see you again."

"And for me to see you, my dear Lady Rose," Milty said, tipping his topper to her and beaming a smile to end all smiles down upon her. "Are you settling in nicely?"

"Fair enough," she answered, honestly. "The time has been short yet."

"Enough of the chitchat," Geoffrey said in good humor. Slipping his hands about Rose's slim waist, he easily lifted her to the saddle. "Let us be out in the park while the traffic is sparse enough for a lengthy gallop. I will wager you are eager to stretch this one's legs after so long without him. Am I right, child?"

"Oh, yes!" Rose exclaimed, bending to slip her foot into the stirrup iron.

For a moment, their eyes met and so close was her face to his, that Geoffrey could feel her feather breath against his cheek, sweet and warm. A rush of desire, instant and insistent, washed over him, flushing his face somewhat. He sucked in a deep, ragged breath in surprise. But the air he drew in was scented with her body warmth, and faintly with lilacs, which only intensified the feeling. He quickly jerked back as if having stepped too near a flame. A look of discomfort crossed his face and he slapped the pinto on the shoulder to hide his confusion. Whatever could be wrong with him to be blushing like a schoolboy over an untutored infant barely out of short skirts?

Although a man of limited success with women, Lord Philpotts had noted, with considerable interest, Geoffrey's jagged, indrawn breath. It was just possible, he thought with a wry grin, that his infallible friend might not be so infallible after all. Watching the elegant man swing upon his blooded mount, he could only determine that there could most certainly be worse things for the marquis than tumbling head over heels for such a lovely child as the diminutive Lady Rose Lambe. In fact, now that he thought of it, it seemed a very good thing at that.

Rotten Row was blessedly deserted as the small company arrived. Taking advantage of this, they had a bracing gallop off the beaten track, which developed into a contest of sorts. A contest easily won by Rose, as she was seemingly fearless in the saddle, and did not hesitate to challenge hurdles the size of which caused concern for her safety in both gentlemen.

Milty drew rein beside her as they neared the far end of Hyde Park. "I say, Lady Rose, you are a bang-up rider. Best in skirts I've ever seen," he exclaimed. Allowing his mount his wind, he drew forth an enormous white handkerchief to mop over his moist brow.

"Thank you, Lord Philpotts. It's marvelous to be aboard Perplexity again. Isn't he just the smoothest jumper? Nothing causes him to falter for his heart is as large and game as ever was seen."

"The same could be said of his indomitable rider," the large man teased. "Jolly good show. That last jump must have been easily five feet."

Geoffrey reined in the spanking black stallion he rode and whistled shrilly to bring Balderdash careering to his side. "Perhaps a dose of good common sense should be prescribed in this matter. Really, Rose, you take too many risks," he admonished sternly. "Now come, it's time we were starting back."

Rose's happy face slipped somewhat. Was she to be punished for unruly behavior by being sent home like the child he repeatedly called her. "I'm so sorry, Lord Wyse. I shall restrain myself in the future. Must we cut our ride short?"

Geoffrey glanced at her in surprise. Had he truly sounded so reprimanding? "No need for apologies, Rose. You've done nothing wrong," he said, pleased to see her face clear of concern and her smile return. "It's simply that traffic will be picking up soon and too many of the ladies' mounts take exception to Balderdash."

"I can certainly see why. He's probably larger than most of them," Rose declared, pointing her crop at the dog sitting in front of them with his tongue lolling out of his giant mouth. "And I must never hear one more remark about

Perplexity's name, especially not from one—'' she gave a teasing scowl at Lord Wyse ''—who would burden a dog with *Balderdash*, of all things.''

Geoffrey grinned at her and swept his topper from his head gallantly. ''It shall be as the lady wishes. I shall never again besmear your dear Perplexity, but I would have you know, the wolfhound was named in honor of my esteemed grandfather.''

Rose could only stare at him for a moment. She did not wish to offend him by laughing, but surely he was attempting a witticism. As his expression did not give him away and her curiosity would not allow her to remain quiet, she inquired of him finally, in as polite a manner as possible, ''That's very nice, er, your grandfather's name was Balderdash? Most unusual.''

Milty hooted with laughter, slapping his thigh with his palm. Geoffrey grinned at her and urged the company on the track back through the park. They rode at a leisurely pace, three abreast with Rose between the two. As Lord Philpotts seemed unable to control his glee, it was left to Geoffrey to explain.

''Actually, my grandfather was Lord Nelson Chesterfield Wyse. After my father's death, my mother and I retired for a time to Hetherington Harrow, where my grandparents maintained a permanent residence. My grandfather was a man of great stature, with a drooping walrus mustache and glinting steel blue eyes that could see through walls and into one's thoughts if they were not pure enough,'' he said, with a teasing smile for Rose.

''He stomped about the Harrow with a heavy-footed gait aided by a cane, as he suffered terribly with gout. There are those who maintain his foul outlook on life was caused by that pain, but then there are others who say it must be laid squarely at the door of my beautiful, philandering grandmother. But, for whatever the reason, as a boy, I was terrified of him. And while I do not remember being such a hellion, perhaps I was, for the one thing I recall most clearly of my grandfather was his rapping that cane violently on the floor and bellowing *'Balderdash!'* at the top of his voice whenever I would attempt to render an acceptable excuse for inexcusable behavior.''

"How terrible for a small boy," sympathized Rose. Her heart was tender for the small boy so frightened by a terrible ogre of a grandfather, that she drew rein and impulsively reached out her hand to lay it over his in comfort.

Geoffrey smiled softly toward her, and raised that hand to plant a kiss on her leather-covered knuckles. "Ah, well, I have quite recovered. And as I grew older, I soon realized he yelled the same at the servants, at the dogs and at my grandmother, usually whenever events did not move in the exact direction that pleased him. But we became quite close before his death. I actually like to think that his ghost haunts the rooms of Hetherington Harrow, and when the winds are just right you can hear him up and down the long hallways—" he leaned toward Rose, using her hand to draw her closer, and lowered his voice to a near whisper "—Balderdash! Balderdash!" To his utter delight, she shivered mightily at the thought of lurking ghosts.

Milty burst forth with an exhilarated laugh. The sight of his dear friend pranking with the young lady was just the thing to make his day. And it fairly brought his tender heart to singing to see the young lady in giggles. "Jolly good show, old chap."

Geoffrey released Rose's hand and tipped his hat to Milty. "Perhaps before we return to 1 Leicester Street, or encounter traffic that requires polite convention be observed, we should speak of our plot. I have decided, in sorting out plans in a logical fashion, that the Townsend ball is the opportune time to announce the engagement.''

''Engagement?'' Rose squeaked. She had been enjoying herself so thoroughly, she had forgotten her reason for being at 1 Leicester Street. Now, hearing the words spoken so calmly in the light of day, was akin to having ice water dashed into her face. Both Lord Wyse and Lord Philpotts glanced at her in question. She quickly schooled her expression. She must not give them concern that she was thinking of reneging on the arrangement, although she could not help but ponder just how wonderful it would feel to have the announcement made in earnest. But, while it would be something she might desire above all else, it was also something she was never to know, and therefore it did no good to even bring it to mind. She slid a finger over the knuckles where Geoffrey had pressed his lips. As if the desire ever left her mind in the first place, she thought ruefully.

''Most agreeable timing, I would say,'' agreed Milty. ''One little announcement and all your worries will cease. No more pressures to wed until you want to be pressured. And there's no saying how long an engagement can run. Why, you could remain engaged for *years* and never actually marry, if that is your wish!''

Rose's head snapped up to stare in disbelief at such reasoning. Of all the absurd notions. ''What's this I hear? You would have me grow old and gray with only an engagement ring upon my hand? Then, once the prank is finished, you'd toss me aside as if I had displeased you? No one of consequence would offer for one so long in the tooth, nor one so long promised to another.'' She looked from one to the other of the stunned faces. What was the matter with them? Were they both dense as tree trunks? ''What of my future? What of *me?*'' she cried out in earnest.

Geoffrey pulled up short, stunned at this outburst. While it was true he had no desire for a wife, and he had fallen into this harebrained scheme as nothing more than a way out of an irritating situation, he had never stated plans for an indefinite engagement. One look at Rose's stricken face brought forth a rush of reassurances on his part. "Do not despair, child. I would not let you languish and shrivel on the vine. You shall be compensated most admirably for your part in this farce.

"I shall see to it that you are brought out in society with great pomp and circumstance. I shall dance attendance upon you most ardently at each and every social. And I promise not be miffed if you flirt outrageously with the young Tulips of the ton as opportunity presents itself." He nudged his mount closer to hers and smiled tenderly down into her worried face. "And if you find yourself forming a *tendre* for someone, pray inform me and I shall release you from our engagement immediately—" he reached over to pat her hand "—with an appropriate show of irreparable loss, of course. Does that satisfy you?"

Rose sat quietly for a moment. Yes, that should satisfy her. And yet, why was it that she felt no satisfaction in the thought of his releasing her from anything? She dropped her head to murmur, "I suppose it will have to, won't it?"

Milty's eyes met those of Geoffrey over Rose's head, both sets of eyebrows lifted in question. Milty gave a slight shake of his head to the unanswered question. He could think of nothing that could have put the girl to sorrows and tears.

Geoffrey leaned forward and tilted Rose's face upward with fingertips beneath her chin. "Rose, I assure you when it comes time to call the engagement quits, it will be done with a great show of pain on my part. I will gladly gnash my teeth and rent my clothing so the ton can think nothing else than I am the one cast off, not you," he promised softly.

As Lord Wyse rode without gloves, his fingertips were warm against her flesh. The very nearness of him was enough to bring a shiver from her. She dropped her eyes and barely resisted the urge to turn her face into his palm and press her lips there. Instead she straightened and moved away from his touch, announcing primly, "Thank you, my lord, that will be most satisfactory."

Milty's frown cleared and he gave a long sigh as her unhappiness seemed diverted. "Splendid then! Now that you are all reassured, Rose, let's have a smile and regain our frivolity in this day, shall we?"

Touching a heel to Perplexity, Rose gave a weak smile before moving past both Lord Wyse and Lord Philpotts. Once ahead of them, she sobered somewhat. She was more than a little nonplussed to find herself in the position of an amusement for these two gentlemen. What was to happen to her when boredom replaced the amusement?

Chapter Six

Rain again poured down upon London, dampening the spirits of the elite of London society. But if the wet did not necessarily dampen Rose's enthusiasm for her first ball, the same could not be said of Sharon or Lady Lavitia. Both ladies were straining beneath the confinements of the house, and tempers flared. Tea served as more of a sparring event than congenial enjoyment and Rose, although she felt it was her duty to attend her hostess at these times, dreaded the hour spent in the company of one or both of the women.

"And tell me, Rose—" Lady Lavitia paused to stare over her teacup and down her rather sharp nose at the girl "—how is it that your father did not make provisions for you before his death? I mean, a match of some sort...."

Wed, wed, wed, Rose thought irritably. Was she never to escape that subject? It seemed to be everyone's primary topic of conversation, particularly for Lady Lavitia and Sharon. It was addressed in one manner or another each and every day. As for herself, it was by far the most tedious, disconcerting, vastly irritating subject. She smiled sweetly at Lady Lavitia.

"Perhaps my father did not realize that the end of his life was to be so soon, Lady Lavitia," she answered.

"You were, what did you say—fourteen at the time of his demise? Hardly toward marriageable age, yet it is never too soon to begin advancing a girl. Certainly he had that comprehension—being an educated and titled man. I mean, you were not likely to grow any younger, now were you?" Lady Lavitia dolefully reminded her.

Sharon tittered. It did her heart good to watch Lady Lavitia take little nips out of the upstart. As for herself, she would never forgive Rose for waltzing into 1 Leicester Street with her sad little tale. The chit had thrust her nose into affairs that did not concern her. She established an unwanted distraction whenever Lord Wyse was in attendance. And, in general, she was making a muddle of an already murky puddle.

Rose settled her teacup and smoothed the finely sprigged muslin ruffle over her wrist. She greatly wanted to return to her sewing. There was much to do yet.

"Rose, did you hear me?" Lady Lavitia prompted.

"Yes, Lady Lavitia, and no, I doubt Papa expected me to accomplish the unaccomplishable feat of growing younger," she confirmed. She searched her mind for some way to divert the conversation from her family. It was entirely too painful a topic to make social chitchat of for teatime entertainment.

But Lady Lavitia was not to let her off easily. "Well, I suppose, though presumably he did, of course, leave to you, his only daughter, that part of his estate that was not passed to the heir." She paused to receive the affirming nod from Rose. "But I doubt there are resources enough to see you through your declining years."

Rose, even in her most pessimistic moments, could hardly regard seventeen as the beginning of her declining years, but she would only dutifully reply, "Yes, Lady Lavitia, I did receive some funds, but I do not think to survive the remainder of my life on that small amount." This was quite true, for if the funds left her comprised the bulk of her father's wealth, then he must have subsisted at the very edge of poverty.

"Didn't he instruct you to be even a trifle encouraging to the young men of your surrounding county? Surely, with your mother's passing, he didn't expect you to take London by storm—unchaperoned by relative or family friend?" Lady Lavitia prodded, then continued with no pause for Rose to respond. "Although I doubt he would have expected you to do better than a local clergyman or country squire, as you have no dowry at all, and you certainly cannot be called a *remarkable* girl."

"Really, Mama Lavitia, I think you are being too unkind. See? She has turned quite pale," Sharon admonished, with a sly smile that belied her concern for the younger girl's feelings.

Rose's head snapped up in defiance. She would certainly not stand for defense to come from that quarter. And while she might not be considered *remarkable*, she certainly could do better than some black-clad, pulpit-pounding, country clergyman. Just what she *was* going to do was another thing entirely. Since her father's bequests to her had proved to be the clothes on her back and a few mementos hardly worth carrying away with her, her choices were limited.

She'd had enough coin to pay for transportation to London and had been hard on an empty stomach when she'd had the good fortune to seek employment on LaFee's doorstep. From there her circumstances had certainly taken a sharp turn into uncharted waters, and all in the guise of a kindly marquis escaping a harpy mother and the unwanted attentions of a debutante with the same personality.

"I truly do not see what any of this signifies now. The

truth of it is that I *am* impoverished and forced to live off the generosity of virtual strangers, distantly related though they may be,'' she commented in an offhand manner. ''I can only promise you, Lady Lavitia, that I shall do my best, even with my unfortunate lack of looks, to make a decent match in the most expedient manner possible. Then it shall be upon someone else's head to support my *declining years,* shan't it?

''And now if you will excuse me, I shall retire above stairs to continue work on the gown designed for me by Madame Howard. In just two days, Lord Wyse is to call for me at exactly nine o'clock, and has requested that I be prompt. I would rather assume he expects me properly attired as well.''

Lady Lavitia frowned and pursed her lips in a prim, disapproving fashion at the girl's cheekiness, as well as at the reminder that Geoffrey was personally escorting Rose, instead of Sharon as was her wish. When she had demanded that Geoffrey dance some attendance upon the girl, she had not intended it to be this extensive. Nor was it her wish that he should appear so devoted as to offer to act as the girl's escort for the entire evening. Whatever was the ton to think? To see him so diligent over the girl? Rose's sweet smile in return for the frown brought about a glower of intense displeasure.

Sharon smiled derisively and set her teacup into its saucer with a loud clatter. ''All those airs you put on, pretending you are something you are not. You're a spineless dishrag of a girl, that's all you are. It is absolutely disgraceful the way you leap at Lord Wyse's every word. Tell me, Rose, have you displaced His Lordship's valet and taken to shining His Lordship's boots also?''

''No, but only because he has yet to ask it of me,'' Rose answered sweetly, as she rose to leave the room. ''And if

I were you, my dear Miss Bartley-Bacon, I should contrive
to cover my feelings more cleverly, or it will be rumored
throughout society that you are jealous of a girl described
by some as less than remarkable.''

"Jealous of you? How absurd!" Sharon trilled a false
laugh. "I have no need to be jealous of anyone. I have a
perfectly marvelous escort for the ball."

"Precisely," Rose stated and swept from the room with
her head held high, leaving both ladies staring after her with
gaping mouths.

Rose raced up the three flights of stairs to work off the
angry tension of the confrontation. Retiring to the sewing
room, she gathered the ball gown of muted rose and
plopped down upon the hearth rug. They might bait her
with their cruel words now, but all that would soon
change...when they realized it was she, and nobody else,
who was to be Geoffrey's wife and the Marquise of Hetherington. But, oh, if only it were true. If only...she traced
a finger over her knuckles just once before shaking herself
away from those thoughts.

Losing herself in the luscious feel of the fragile silk,
Rose busily applied her needle on the seemingly endless
hemline of the voluptuous skirt and slowly felt herself
calm. All of the gowns ordered by the marquis had been
carefully transported from the dressmaker's shop, without
any apparent consideration, and so far no mention, of the
imaginary person they had originally been intended for. The
few that were complete were now arranged in the giant
wardrobes of her dressing room. As Rose was to be presented to society in an indecently short time, Lady Lavitia
had suggested installing a seamstress to complete the vol-
ume of sewing that still remained, but Rose had repeatedly
refused, until Lady Lavitia had finally thrown up her hands
in despair, declaring her as headstrong as a mule. Rose

could not have explained without inflicting insult upon the lady, but in loving memory of LaFee, she could not bear to have another dressmaker complete the lovely designs. The ton had slighted the dear woman for most of her life and, in some small way, Rose felt these last gowns were to be a tribute to her.

"I thought to find you here. Why does it not surprise me that you should be busy with your little needle?" Sharon chided from the doorway. She clicked her tongue and shook her head at the sight of Rose sitting on the hearth rug, half-buried beneath silk.

Rose looked up sharply, irritated beyond all belief at having what she had come to consider her private sanctuary invaded. Hadn't she taken enough abuse over tea? The frown on her face was probably the exact purpose of Sharon's cutting remark, Rose considered sourly, but it had appeared before she had time to school her face. She watched the blond girl saunter about the room, fingering fabrics and flipping packets of lace about on the table. She'd seen enough of this one's personality to know that there was no pleasing her, and therefore she resolved to expend no effort toward that end.

"And what could possibly have brought you to the sewing room, Sharon? Did you forget to count the floors as you climbed the staircase?"

"Meow," mimicked Sharon, curling her fingers into imaginary cat claws. "Actually, I came out of the generosity of friendship, be that as it may. I cannot help but feel some sympathy for your situation. I mean, to be homeless and penniless places a girl in a perilous position, does it not?"

"One could say that," Rose conceded, dropping her head over the tiny stitches again. "And what advice would you have to offer me?"

"I'm not sure I am in a position to *advise* you, Rosie,"
Sharon admitted, with a charming smile. "But toward that
end, I suppose I would ask what is your purpose in coming
here?"

Rose glanced up at Sharon. She could think of no good
to come of this little conversation, nor could she believe
Sharon Bartley-Bacon capable of placing anyone's interest
beyond her own. "Purpose?"

"Well, yes. I cannot believe that you intend to simply
establish yourself as a permanent houseguest. I mean, you
can't expect Lady Lavitia to crush you to her bosom as a
long-lost, beloved relative, now can you?"

Rose dropped her head over her sewing again. Could
Lady Lavitia possibly have asked Sharon to broach this
subject with her? The thought nagged at her. For it was
readily apparent that they both considered her an interloper
in the house, and a burr beneath the saddle of the horse,
namely one Lord Geoffrey Wyse, that they were attempting
to break to their own command. "Of course, I intend no
such thing."

"At any rate, what course *do* you propose to follow?"

"Course?"

"Yes. Surely you have some plan somewhere in that
dizzy little head of yours?" Sharon insisted.

"I am not dull-witted, you know." She paused to search
her heart. What did she intend? What had been her purpose
when she had thrown herself upon Lord Wyse's doorstep?
To become his bird of paradise, to have him become her
protector? To obtain housing, clothing and sustenance when
she could think of no other way of gaining them on such
frightfully short notice? What would she have done if
granted more time to plan? There really was only one answer. "I shall use this gift of time and sanctuary as a means
to procure a suitable offer for my hand," she stated flatly.

"Failing that, I shall seek a position, as governess or some such, and immediately thereafter, I shall locate alternate accommodations."

"Well stated. But securing an offer of marriage is not so easy—" Sharon stepped back and studied Rose as if assessing her value on the marriage market "—without a great deal of advance preparation. Although I shouldn't wish you to feel that you are not welcome to live with Geoffrey and me after we wed...."

Rose glanced up, startled. That was an extremely distasteful prospect...residing with Lord Wyse as husband to another woman, and this one woman in particular. Even with the pretense of Lord Wyse's engagement to her, there was always the possibility of his marrying someone in the future. At a loss for anything better to say, she stammered, "Th-thank you."

"However, in point of fact, you would *not* be welcome," Sharon continued with a sly smile. She did not appear to detect the slightest contradiction in her remarks. "Geoffrey is generous to a fault, as you have already seen, but I am sure you understand that I cannot request too many favors of him."

Rose stared at her in disbelief. The gall of the woman! To imply that Lord Wyse's generosity to her would come only as a favor to Sharon. "I think..."

"Consequently," Sharon continued with an arched look at the intended interruption, "you must arrange to be out of the house by season's end. I anticipate an announcement of Geoffrey's and my engagement before long and I shall want the marriage to take place by the end of the year. Even Lady Lavitia has generously agreed to move her household elsewhere, so that I may take my rightful place as mistress of 1 Leicester Street with the new year."

Fed to the teeth with the high-handed manners of the

blond girl, Rose tossed the rose silk from her lap and stood. Orange Willy, taking the action as a much too convenient opportunity for mischief, dashed beneath the pile in a flurry. "Willy! No!" cried Rose, leaping to extract the cat before he could do damage to the fragile stuff.

Sharon turned toward the door. "Ah, well, with that settled I shall be off. I do wish you good fortune in your quest." She knit her brow again. "If you like, failing an acceptable offer for your hand, I could be prevailed upon to search my friends for…a…" She was apparently unable to conceive a single position for which Rose might qualify. "Well, you know."

"Thank you," Rose grated. "But I shall not require anything from you in that quarter."

Sharon, satisfied she had planted her seeds in fertile soil, sauntered from the room, forestalling the scalding retort that Rose had been prepared to deliver. Willy's attack was fortunate, actually, as she had been on the brink of blurting out the news of her own engagement to Lord Wyse, just to render the blond vixen speechless…for her words were too painfully close to the truth of the matter.

As the chaise rattled over Westminster Bridge the evening of the Townsend ball, Geoffrey watched the emotions play over Rose's excited face with appreciation, and a great deal of genuine affection. Something, possibly the simple dress of her hair, coiled at the base of her neck in a black, liquid chignon, had added years to her face, masking the child that she was. The simple style left the perfect oval of her face elegantly exposed and displayed her amazing lavender eyes with their sooty lashes to great advantage. The gown of sherry pink tissue silk with its bodice of intricate pleats and cutouts, was a work of art and set off Rose's satiny shoulders wonderfully well.

Shifting his gaze to her animated face, he pondered again this situation in which he had placed her. He admitted to having harbored severe second thoughts following the girl's outburst in the park. Was he behaving like the worst sort of cad, embroiling her in such a scheme? Until her outburst, neither he nor Milty had anticipated she might harbor false hopes in that pretty little head—that she might somehow create fairy-tale dreams of his actually marrying her in the end—and it was this notion of leaping from the pan directly into the fire that had generated in him thoughts of calling the whole affair quits before it commenced. He came back from his woolgathering to note that she was studying him as closely as apparently he had been her.

"Is there something amiss, my dear?" he asked. "I do hope my neckcloth is not coming undone, for Deming spent hours in the tying of this *A la sentimentale*."

His grin was wry, and there was absolutely no reason for Rose to blush, but blush she did. Her cheeks felt quite warm, and she dropped her eyes. "I was merely thinking that you are exceedingly handsome tonight. I—I realize it is not the thing for a lady to tell her escort but—" she raised her eyes to grin at him with a minute shrug "—I really do think you are marvelously turned out."

"Well, thank you. And while perhaps it is not the thing, it is always pleasant to receive a compliment," Geoffrey conceded. "But it has been said that the black and white of formal attire would make a pig into a prig."

Rose tipped her head to one side and laughed at him, her lavender eyes snapping fire. Seeing the happy mischief dancing upon her face, he again felt sure of his generous impulse. He had to admit, the girl's happiness was infectious, creating an air of gaiety and adventure that he had not felt in a long time. No, he did not feel, considering the shine in her lovely eyes, that he was in the wrong elevating

her into society as his intended bride. She was a sweet child
and deserved to always be as happy as she was this night.

In another surge of generosity, he swore a silent oath to
himself, and one he would repeat to her at first chance, that
he would do whatever it took to keep that look of happiness
on her small face for all time. He must reassure her also,
that she need never fear a physical side of their alliance,
for this was an arrangement of convenience, and he could
be depended upon to keep his word to her—and his distance from her.

"You know, Rose," he began. "I did want to assure you
that you need have no fear of me...."

"Goodness gracious!" Rose exclaimed, startled by his
statement. "I could never be afraid of you. Why, you are
kindness itself...."

Geoffrey smiled indulgently. "Still, you are very young,
and in an extremely vulnerable situation, if you but had
experience enough to recognize it. I merely wish to assure
you that I shall take no unfair advantage of—"

"You would *never* take advantage of me, Lord Wyse,"
she interrupted again to exclaim. "You are much too kind
and generous and—and..."

"Please, Rose." He held up his hand to halt her denials.
"Hear me out. I merely wish to impress upon you that I
view this as nothing more than a proposition that will serve
as benefit to both of us, for I am prepared to openly confess
that I am in a bit of a hobble."

"Yes, having lived beneath the same roof with Miss
Bartley-Bacon, I can understand why you should wish to
avoid..." Rose halted herself, appalled that she'd slander
another person so readily. Even someone so horrid as
Sharon.

"It is more than that. It's family, name and obliga-
tions..." Geoffrey muttered, pausing to gaze out the side

window of the chaise. When he spoke again, it was distinctly, giving an unusual clarity of every syllable, as if reciting something of import that had been repeatedly drummed into his consciousness from infancy. "The heirs of Hetherington Harrow have been an unbroken line of first sons, who knew how to bear the title of marquis and the name of Wyse. It has long been a tradition of this family that the man to disgrace that title and name would be the heir who died leaving the fortune no greater than he received it."

"And do you feel that you will be that heir?" Rose asked softly, wishing to discern the cause of his pensiveness so that she might alleviate it.

"No, I have greatly surpassed the so-called requirements as a successful heir," he confirmed. "But..."

"But?" Rose echoed. His hobble continued to elude her. "Is it your mother's insistence that you wed that is causing you such concern? Surely a simple statement of your concerns to your mother about this marriage business, and perhaps..."

Geoffrey gave a dry little laugh. "My mother has—for all her delicate health, what should I call it—a strong personality?"

"Yes, that I have noticed," Rose agreed, nodding her head in sympathy and pulling a face before she thought of the insult he might take.

Geoffrey laughed at her contorted face and leaned over to tweak her nose. "Well, be that as it may, I merely wish you to understand that you are safe from me, Tiger's Breath. I have no untold designs upon you."

"Yes, I do understand. I understand very well, thank you," Rose muttered, shifting her gaze out the window.

The London scenery was wasted on her as she blinked rapidly to still the tears that threatened to spill over. So he would press her further to understand that he was not in the least interested in a permanent union of any kind. While he did seem to like her at least, it was only as one would a child, or a pet dog one is particularly fond of. A deep sigh escaped her for, silly as it must seem, she was decidedly in love with the marvelous marquis, and it hurt something awful in her heart to want something so badly that would never be hers.

Chapter Seven

Lord Townsend had chosen a tropical theme for his ball, and uprooted every palm, fern and lily in his own garden, as well as at all available commercial nurseries, to transform his ballroom into an overflow of flora. Musicians played arrangements of drifting melodies to remind one of soft tidal waves and sea breezes. Footmen strolled about with spiced teas and spiked fruit drinks placed upon wicker trays decorated with giant palm leaves and lilies. The ballroom's alcoves and corners had been papered in soothing ocean scenes, and impulsively banked with sand to simulate inviting beaches. An impulse Lord Townsend was to regret as the evening wore on, for the sand was carried about on the dancing slippers of his guests, quite effectively removing the finish from a large portion of his varnished ballroom floor.

Sharon nimbly executed the steps of the first dance set of the evening, glancing under her upraised arm to search down the line for Lord Wyse. He had not arrived to collect little Rosie before Sharon's escort had called for her, but she knew them not to be too far behind. She reasoned, with no small feelings of satisfaction, that even when Rose did arrive, the chit would not be allowed the dance floor until she had been presented at court, *and* received her vouchers from the three patronesses of Almacks. By all that was proper, she should be left situated beside Lady Lavitia and the rest of the dowagers while she, golden Sharon, ruled the dance floor as always.

Poor dear, Sharon thought with a smirk, tipping her torso forward to enthrall the hapless young man who chanced to be partnering her with a generous show of bosom. Although it only served the chit right, to think she could use some distant blood connection to move up in the world. But her worst mistake was to presume to stand equal with me. Sharon preened. To think Rose could redirect the marquis's interest in her own direction. Such folly!

The dance came to a breathless end and, as the couples separated to locate their next signed partners, the chamberlain's announcement rang from the top of the stairs. "His Lordship, the Marquis of Hetherington, and Lady Rose Lambe."

All heads turned. Everyone stared. Sharon whirled round and gasped as if she could not believe her eyes. Why was Lord Wyse making such a grand entrance with that little nobody? By rights, he should have simply brought her to the side of his mother and left her. Why, she hadn't even bent her knee to the queen yet!

The handsome pair descended the staircase in stately silence. The marquis was overwhelmingly handsome in his black-and-white formal attire and even little Rose was spectacular in the candlelight. Her gown of tissue silk moved in just the most perfect sway to capture every light in the room. It was breathtakingly alluring. Rose was breathtakingly alluring. Too damned alluring, in fact. Sharon's mouth turned down unkindly at the sight of them.

"Hetherington and his little Rose make a magnificent pair, do they not?" murmured a voice at her elbow.

Sharon whirled to see who would address her in this manner. A slightly built, bland-featured gentleman, not of her acquaintance, was standing uncomfortably close behind her. She curled her lip into a snarl to deliver a blistering reply, but having delivered this sharp barb, he stepped back into the company before she could openly snub him. Returning her foul-tempered glare to the pair coming slowly down the stairs, she could feel her heart hammering against her chest. Something did not seem right this evening.

First, Rose would manage to arrive, fashionably attired in an absolutely exquisite ball gown that, had she deemed to admit it, put her own in the pale of the shade. And now, to add insult to injury, Lord Wyse was being entirely too attentive to her, drawing her deferentially close to his side in a show that was almost possessive in manner. Something was amiss. Deep in thought, Sharon caressed fingertips over the porcelain of her cheek. Just what was it that generated this bad feeling of premonition?

When she could not draw forth a single, logical reason, she gave a little shake to relax the tension from her shoulders. What could possibly be amiss? The marquis was only making a public show to introduce Rose as his relation, and therefore placing a stamp of approval on the girl for all to see. Of course he was as interested in seeing her settled and out of his residence as Mama Lavitia was. Furthermore, it was only because of who he was, and his excellent standing with the king and queen, that he could lead the little idiot onto the dance floor without her vouchers...which he was now doing. And she would give no credence whatsoever to the disturbing, nagging thought that now that Lord Wyse had made his appearance, he should have pledged this first dance to her. She seemed unable to remove her jealous eyes from the sight of Lord Wyse holding Rose

lightly in his arms, circling in a dreamlike trance to the
lilting waltz.

"Would you dance, Miss Bartley-Bacon?" asked Lord
Philpotts, sketching a short stiff bow before her.

"I do not believe your name graces my dance card...er,
Lord Philpotts, isn't it?" Sharon sniffed, then turned her
back rather rudely before he could answer.

Milty shrugged minutely and turned aside but did not
venture too far away. He would want to have a clear view
of her face when the announcement came. It was always a
pleasure to observe a cat having her claws trimmed. Although he had quite thought she could at least have looked
at him. Perhaps to admire the slimming cut of his new
wasp-waisted cutaway coat. Such an admirable shade of
apricot, too. The very latest thing among the dandy set it
was. He smoothed a hand almost lovingly over his sleeve,
thoroughly pleased with himself and his appearance, if not
so with his reception by the ladies.

After the first and the second set, Sharon feared the marquis might never stand up with her, for he was obviously
taking his mother's instructions to heart, dutifully moving
about the assembly, presenting the girl to those of his acquaintance. Now he was again standing up with a beaming
Rose for a set of country dances. Well, nothing would
thwart Sharon overly long. She was a master at this game.
Quickly seeking a partner from her ever-present group of
fawning gallants, she joined the set. Resorting to old tactics,
she contrived to slip quite convincingly just as she took
Lord Wyse's hand and stumbled against him so heavily that
he was forced to put his arms about her to prevent both of
them going nose down on the floor.

To Rose, her breath stopping dead in her chest, it looked
as if he had seized the opportunity to take hold of the beautiful girl in an affectionate embrace, and her heart sank

down to her little embroidered slippers. She had so looked
forward to this evening. And now it was spoiled with one
scene of Lord Wyse holding another in his arms. She closed
her eyes and allowed her partner swing her away. She could
not bear to see him bending so solicitously to another, especially to have that other be spiteful, snipping Sharon
Bartley-Bacon. But when she opened her eyes again,
Sharon was seated with a dark, pouty face next to Lady
Lavitia. The dance was proceeding as if nothing had happened, and Lord Wyse was returning to her round the chain
of the dance. Suddenly the beam came back to her face.

Just as Geoffrey reached her with a teasing grin and a
decided wink, there was a fanfare of trumpets, calling attention to their host. Lord Townsend mounted a small riser
in front of the musicians and held up his hands for attention. He huffed and puffed importantly, calling out to the
company to quieten down, taking obvious relish in being
so fortunate as to deliver the choicest bit of *on dit* of the
season to the exalted crowd. The lord and ladies of the
haute ton murmured and stirred, speculating behind shielding fans into the ears of bent heads.

Once Lord Townsend felt assured of every ear, he
cleared his throat and called out his news in a loud voice.
"Ladies and gentlemen, my friends, this evening is full of
surprises. It seems an announcement is in order and...er,
consider myself fortunate, actually, to be the one chosen to
do the honors...er, startled even me when I first heard of
it...."

"Come on, George! Out with it!" called a ribald voice
from the room. A titter followed.

Again, Lord Townsend lifted his hands. "All right now,
quieten down and I shall get on with it. Ladies and gentlemen, I have the grand pleasure of making it known to this
company even before the banns are posted. One of our most

eligible eligibles has chosen his bride! The Marquis of Hetherington is to wed!''

A generalized gasp preceded stunned silence, which quickly gave way to a great, unison snap as gilded chicken-wing fans popped open to flap vigorously. The hiss of whispers gave way to murmurs, then a great wave of applause went up. More than one hand slapped Lord Wyse on the back, and many chucked Rose under the chin, rightly assuming she was the object of his affections as she blushed most prettily and smiled shyly into the marquis's face.

Sharon let out a squeak of protest and shock. This just could not be happening! A buzzing took over her hearing and she thought for a second to call for a chair as she did feel faint. But then, as always, her vanity came to her aid. With a deep sigh, she shook herself. There was nothing to fret about. Who could that old toady, Lord Townsend, be referring to except herself? The marquis had danced attendance on no other all of last season, nor had there been one lady singled out from the masses as special in his affection this season. And of course, if he *had* been harboring a secret *tendre* for anyone, she would have known it instantly, for she had spies everywhere. Despite his deplorable treatment of her this evening, he could only be thinking to surprise her with a ring and a bended knee here—in front of all her friends. A marquise! She was to have her title after all.

Sharon had the enviable talent of believing her own lies as soon as she uttered them. She fixed Lord Wyse with an excited and expectant gaze and began to make her way delicately toward the riser. The company did not readily part for her, which made her smile more than a little brittle as she was forced to shove through tightly knotted groups of people more than once.

Lord Townsend clapped his hands loudly, to draw attention back to him. "Lords and ladies, my friends...may I present our future Marquise of Hetherington. Lady Rose Lambe!" Lord Townsend exclaimed, holding out his hand to Lord Wyse, who in turn held out his hand to Rose. Blushing furiously at the cries of surprise and energetic applause, Rose stepped toward her now fiancé, only to have her arm gripped tightly and jerked backward.

Sharon moved past Rose to clutch at Lord Wyse's arm, with fingers like claws digging into his evening coat. "What a silly mistake, Lord Townsend," she cried shrilly. "Everyone knows it is I who is Lord Wyse's affianced bride. This...this person is nobody. Surely you must understand...."

Geoffrey looked down at her with something between loathing and shock. "Miss Bartley-Bacon, you are making a scene where there should be none." He pried her fingers from his arm. "Control yourself, or I shall request you be removed from the gathering. Rose?" Extending a hand to Rose, he turned his back unceremoniously upon Sharon.

Rose mounted the riser beside Lord Wyse. His friends—she could not count them as her friends but certainly the marquis could—clapped and whistled as rowdy as a common crowd at a country fair at the unexpected turn of events. There were catcalls and ribald remarks lamenting the marquis falling into the marital trap at last, which brought gilded fans sharply down upon more than one husband's knuckles as wives took pretended offense. Any further remarks were forestalled by the arrival of King William and his company. With the ease of long social practice, the company formed itself into two long reception lines in order of rank.

As the daughter of a viscount, Sharon stood along the middle, and at the very top stood Rose. His Highness was laughing and clapping Lord Wyse on the back with congratulations, and patting fingertips upon a glowing Rose's cheek. Sharon writhed in misery and jealousy. But His Royal Highness would surely notice her, for it was well-known that the king loved beautiful women, and wasn't she the most beautiful here? But she was destined for yet another disappointment, for the royals did not continue down the line, instead veering off into the card room without taking note of the blond beauty.

Sharon's bitter cup was full. She carried murder in her heart. Murder, yes, but she'd see her rival disgraced horribly first. She would see Rose humiliated, just as she'd been humiliated by Lord Wyse's public rejection. She'd see the day every back would be presented to Rose's face in blatant snub. Sharon shivered with the violence of her emotions. Notice from the company at large was being taken of her behavior, and hard glances directed in her direction. Matrons whispered behind their fans and even her gallants backed away with downcast eyes. Sharon knew she was behaving poorly but could not seem to stop herself.

"Control your anger and school your face, Miss Bartley-Bacon. You'll accomplish nothing by making yourself a tidbit of every matron's parlor gossip," advised an amused voice at her back, properly verbalizing her very thoughts.

Sharon spun to confront the smug face of the same man as before. Here was someone to vent her hurt and anger upon. "Who *are you?*" she demanded, in a black mood. "And what business could you possibly have with me?"

"The business of getting even, I should think. Revenge, sweet revenge, my dear Miss Bartley-Bacon."

"Again, I must ask, who *are you?*" she insisted, intrigued in spite of herself with the audacity of this man to approach her without an introduction. And to speak to her of the very thing that burned in her mind.

"Elmo Sewell, Earl of Shenstone, at your service," he said, sweeping a low, mocking bow.

Sharon flipped open her fan and applied it vigorously. Taking a moment to study this small, yet stylishly attired man, she could imagine he was new to London as she had never seen him at any gathering. He was not unpleasant to look upon, merely a nondescript, rather dull personage. Reddish skin, thinning reddish hair and weak blue eyes made him perfectly forgettable. Although when he directed those eyes to stare boldly into her face, there was a decidedly unrefined, dangerous look about him.

"I have never been introduced to you," she snapped.

"Yes, most unfortunate, isn't it?" Lord Sewell said with a smirk, interrupting her in the rudest manner. "But in some circumstances, I suppose pleasantries can be overlooked. It would appear our paths are aimed in similar directions. If our goals could be combined, the end could be all that much sweeter, for you see, I too wish revenge upon the bridal pair."

Sharon gasped slightly and glanced quickly around. No one seemed to be paying them the slightest attention, and for once, she was entirely alone—a position in which she seldom found herself and disliked instantly. She slowed her fan and yawned to indicate ladylike boredom. "I really do not know why you would speak of this to me. You could not be farther from the truth. Being the dearest friend to both, I wish the Marquis of Hetherington—and Lady Rose—the very best. But your tale of woe piques my curiosity, and I might find it amusing. Pray continue. But please do not fly into the boughs if I choose to end our conversation should I become bored."

Lord Sewell smirked at having read the jealous cat correctly, and again sketched a small bow. "I have my own reasons for not wishing to see this marriage prosper."

"What will you do?" asked Sharon, leaning forward eagerly. "Stop the wedding? Do injury to one or both of them?"

"No, my little bloodthirsty miss. I simply wish the union to be childless. You see, a son costs me my title and my inheritance."

"I do not understand. How would a son of Lord Wyse's affect your situation in the least?" she questioned. She glanced over her shoulder to see if they were receiving undue attention for having such a lengthy private conversation in such a public place. But alas, the ball continued its frantic pace behind her, distressingly unchanged by her absence.

"I shall keep that part of the business to myself. It suffices for you to know that I only wish them to be as unhappy as two people can be. I would see them estranged in the least possible time," he retorted smoothly, unconcerned that his reluctance to elaborate only piqued her curiosity that much more. He watched her caress her cheek with her fingertips and knew her mind was racing. He did not interrupt her thoughts, for he judged her to be best won over by the misguided belief that she had some control in the matter. Finally she frowned at him, then irritated him greatly by openly sneering.

"So, Lord Sewell, you would live year after year hoping they did not conciliate? As with an ax suspended over your head, just waiting to fall? Not the best solution, I think. There is no satisfaction in that, nor any security of position, either."

"Ah, but there is a sweetness in prolonged revenge. I merely wish to maintain my position. And to do that is relatively simple. *My* position can be secured simply by seeing that the new Marquise of Hetherington is vastly un-

happy in *hers*. And that is where you come in, Miss Bartley-Bacon.''

"*Me?* What could I possibly do? Assuming that I would
enter into league with such as you in the first place,"
Sharon demanded, narrowing her eyes at this man. She
could not believe she was even entertaining this discussion.
He was decidedly dangerous, or perhaps merely a fool.
Rose was nothing, but Lord Wyse was another thing entirely. In plotting to keep Rose unhappy, this man was plotting against Lord Wyse as well. And Lord Wyse was a very
powerful man, indeed.

"I would require very little of you actually. Simply begin
by developing a friendship with the girl. Offer your support...your friendship. It would not do at this time to have
you sent packing home to mama, now would it?"

"And that is all you would have me to do?" Sharon
eyed him with no small amount of skepticism. She could
not believe revenge was to be had this easily. With someone else volunteering to do the dirty work? There was
something bad, almost evil, about this man. She had no
knowledge of him and might be doing herself irreparable
damage just by talking to him. Again, she glanced around
to see if they were drawing attention.

Lord Sewell smirked to see her caution. "That is the first
part," he said, bringing her eyes back to him. "The only
other part you should play is a delight on my part. Allow
me to squire you about—" he watched her chin rise stubbornly "—to a minor degree only. So that it is not considered gossip for us to be seen talking thus." He watched her
face closely. Watched the greed, the humiliated pride, the
absolute selfishness of her personality flit over her expression. She clearly cared for no one but herself, and such a
one was always easy to use for another's own benefit.

"And that is all? Nothing else?" Sharon countered. She

had an uneasy feeling there was to be more, and she would be smart to back away at this moment. Possibly even inform Lord Wyse that there was a plot of sorts against him. Perhaps points of favor would be gained by that alone.

Seeing the girl was not to be drawn into his scheme so easily, Lord Sewell suddenly gripped her arm and spun her toward the dance floor. Directing her eyes to the sight of the marquis whirling a laughing Rose about in his arms, he hissed in her ear, "See how lovingly they gaze into each other's eyes? How closely he holds her in his arms? That should have been *you* he so obviously adores. Instead it is she who is the future Marquise of Hetherington. Not you!"

Anger, pain and helplessness welled up in Sharon's chest at the sight of them. "Yes, it all should be mine!" she gritted, before tearing her eyes back to Elmo Sewell. "All right. I shall do as you say." She jerked her arm from his grasp. "Now take your hands off me!"

Lord Sewell sketched a shallow bow to hide his look of satisfaction and triumph, and backed away from her, appropriately enough, into the shadows.

Chapter Eight

Orange Willy crouched behind the potted palm, tail swaying gently to and fro in anticipation of the attack. His prey advanced down the hall, unaware of imminent danger. Willy dropped lower, his hindquarters coming up. The tail twitched faster...any second now. His hind legs began to dance in readiness. Then with a flash of orange fur he streaked across the parlor and through the doorway. Under the skirts, through the froth of petticoats, a nip on the ankle and a successful escape out the other side. It was a perfect attack.

"Eeeek!" Lady Lavitia shrieked, spinning about to see the orange-striped tail disappearing around the corner. "*Rose!* Rose, come here this instant!"

"I'm right here, Lady Lavitia," Rose called. Hurrying from the library to see the lady fanning herself diligently, Rose dropped the book she carried on the hall table and rushed to put her arms about the older woman's shoulders. "My goodness! Are you ill? I'm here. Just tell me what I might do...."

"That cat of yours!" Lady Lavitia huffed and clutched at her chest. "He attacked me again! Oh, my—I feel faint. My heart! I think it's my heart!"

Rose solicitously eased the woman onto the divan in the hallway. Dropping to her knees before her, she patted her hand comfortingly, and made soothing noises of concern. She was more worried for Willy's fate than for the woman's health. She had quickly discovered Lady Lavitia to be as strong as a horse, yet she seemed determined to maintain a lifelong habit of treating her imagined physical ailments as high drama. Yet, she must placate the woman somehow, and correct Willy's bad behavior a great deal, before he was dispatched to the furriers to be skinned for earmuffs.

"Lady Lavitia, please allow me to apologize for Willy. He is just a youngster, and you must know how youngsters like to play..." she began, only to quickly change tactics when Lady Lavitia frowned down upon her most discouragingly. "But you are certainly correct to think he should be punished for unseemly behavior. If you are quite recovered, I shall find him immediately and, I promise, deal him a terrible reprimand. Shall I ring for your maid? Perhaps a nice cup of tea to help you recover yourself?"

"Yes, yes dear, ring for her," grated Lady Lavitia. She frowned at Rose as she stepped to the bellpull, pursing her lips in disapproval. It was so difficult to be angry with the girl, for she was such a small thing and always eager to please, but Rose was not the daughter-in-law she had wished for and she could not appear pleased at what she could only refer to as Geoffrey's open defiance to her wishes. Fortunately, there remained the fact that the marriage had yet to be performed, and that meant there remained time to right a terrible wrong. If only Geoffrey could be made to see reason. And the sad fact of that was the awful truth that Geoffrey was not responding very sensibly these days.

"Lady Lavitia?" Rose prompted.

Lady Lavitia glanced down to see Rose watching her

with sweet concern. With a flip of her hand she released the girl. "Yes, yes, run along now and find your cat, like a good little girl. Such excitement—" she paused to draw a hand over her eyes "—and at my age can be very dangerous, you know."

Released by the arrival of Lady Lavitia's maid, Rose quickly escaped to her chambers with her book. Now, reclining on the silk pillows piled upon the window seat, she plunked at the embroidery of rose vines and tangled red blossoms absently. A self-satisfied Orange Willy came to plop down beside her.

"You are a very bad cat, Willy," she admonished, tapping a forefinger on his head. "And if you do not cease bedeviling Lady Lavitia, I shall be forced to confine you to this room, and then you will be a very unhappy little cat, indeed. What do you have to say about that?" The purring cat rolled over and batted at her hand. Rose could only laugh at his kittenish pranks. "Wouldn't be such a bad prison at that. A bit fussy for a killer like you, all these Cupids and curlicues racing about the woodwork. Come, my feline friend. Let's take this energy out to the jungle, shall we?"

Number 1 Leicester Street boasted a jungle composed of neatly swept paths bordered by orderly, well-behaved flower beds and enclosed by clipped trees, all of which ended at the main axis with a circular carp pond without one leaf of debris anywhere in sight. Bundled into a cloak of sapphire wool against the chill, Rose wandered down the path while Willy dashed into the shrubs to attack wayward leaves that had the audacity to frolic merrily in the wind. She was feeling somewhat closed in and pensive today. For some unexplainable reason, she wanted to shout with restlessness, but that might disturb the quiet of the orderly world of London society. And that just was not done.

She was at a loss to explain her feelings. It was not as if the Townsend ball of the night before hadn't been a triumph, for it had. The excitement of the announcement and the heart-stopping thrill of being whirled about the dance floor in Lord Wyse's arms. Then the acceptance of the ton rushing to surround her, meeting the king...it all had made her feel elated. So elated that even the necessity of reviving Lady Lavitia, who had swooned in obvious shock, had not marred the evening. But this morning, Rose felt cold and alone, for it was all playacting and nothing more.

The facts remained that she was penniless and very much on her own, with only one angry word spoken by the marquis and a finger pointed sternly toward the front door between herself and homelessness. And worst of all, she was beginning to fear that, while she had her fiancé's permission to fall in love with whomever she pleased, it was not going to be easy, for in all truthfulness, her heart was already engaged. Completely, painfully and agonizingly so, and by the very man who would create such an outrageous sham, just to escape the very thing she desired of him. Marriage! What a fix.

Safely, and blindly secure, at Shenstone with a loving and devoted family about her, she had often debated with her father over the manner in which women did nothing to shape their own lives, but now, out in the world and supported by the generosity of others, she was rapidly learning how fate would seem to constantly intervene, effectively binding her hands behind her. Her options were limited. For her it was service in someone else's house, hand herself over to a marriage broker to be sold to some aged nobleman in search of a wife of tender years, or perhaps go to the poorhouse for indigent women. She smiled at that thought. Reside there to dress in cast-off gowns and hem gray woolen blankets for the hospitals from dawn to dusk? Better that she would open her own dressmaking establishment if she was to earn her bread by sewing.

"You must do something, Rose Lambe," she admonished herself. "At least, make plans for a future of sorts, as this is nothing more than a temporary plug in a very leaky dam."

"What dire things are you plotting with yourself here in the garden, Little One?"

Startled, Rose jerked up her head to see Lord Wyse striding forcefully toward her. Here was a man who marched through life, firmly in charge and confident of his position. She greatly envied him that. His was such a purposeful stride, straight and true, as if nothing could deter him from his mission, whatever that might be on this chilly morning.

"Good morning, Lord Wyse," she called, unable to keep the smile of delight from spreading over her face. He was dressed all in brown today, she observed, in dark brown pantaloons, a coat of rusty bronze superfine, a biscuit-colored waistcoat edged in almond and an ecru neckcloth simply arranged. His choice of attire enhanced his coloring superbly.

"And good morning to you. I figured you to be hard abed with the covers pulled over your head after such a late night," he teased, tapping a finger beneath her chin.

So near to her, his presence was almost overwhelming. Rose could smell the woodsy scent he used and there was a warmth coming from him that made her want to lean against him. She moved a step back and tempered her smile, which she was sure spoke besotted female to him.

"So much excitement doesn't make for a restful night, my lord," she said. "Besides, I am afraid Willy has been banned from polite society and I could not, in all good conscience, allow him to bear his disgrace alone."

"Ah, Tiger's Breath, you are ferociously loyal," Geoffrey declared. Tucking her hand in the crook of his arm, he sought to move her on down the path, as there was more warmth in movement than being stationary.

"Why do you call me that? Tiger's Breath?" Rose asked. It seemed a bit juvenile to be assigned a pet name, and yet there was a tenderness in it, too.

"Because, my dear Lady Rose, while you are as tender and fragrant as a newly opened rosebud, your nature is much more explosive and aggressive. More reminiscent of a tiger's breath blossom, I think."

She laughed at his observation. "I see that I am much too transparent. My father repeatedly told me I had been dubbed Rose at birth simply because he could tell at that very moment I would be as beautiful as my mother, but he knew if I had anything of himself in my nature, I would produce thorns."

Geoffrey smiled and inclined his head. "A very astute observation for a celebrating father to make of a tiny newborn babe. Tell me of your father. What do you remember most of him?"

Rose glanced up at him in surprise that he would pursue such a personal topic. "Poppy? He was a sweet, simple man. Much given to horses and hunting. And books. He read everything—always studying this and that. Expounding on a variety of things at the dinner table we had set in my mother's apartments. Very loving and completely devoted to my mother throughout her illness." She hesitated, then continued in a voice softened with emotion. "It was very difficult for him when she died. He never recovered from the shock of losing her although she had been ill from the first moment I remember her. He always believed she would get well, no matter that the doctors gave her no hope. He passed not long after she did."

She turned her head away from the marquis, not wishing

him to see the loneliness she felt after losing her family and home. How could she explain her feelings to someone who was surrounded by accepting friends and doted on by a loving mother?

The marquis, sensing her sadness, cleared his throat and sought to distract her from sad memories. "The daughter of a man so given to books and learning must have soaked up a fair amount of knowledge. Perhaps that is where the supposed thorns come from. Knowing more than polite society would feel a young girl of breeding needed to know?"

"Oh, Mummy would have agreed with you. She despaired of me, and eventually insisted I attend finishing school in the hopes I would acquire some measure of grace...as well as the right sort of friends. She never forgave herself for being so ill that I was sequestered in the country at Shenstone, instead of moving about the beau monde. Not that I was unhappy as a country hoyden, mind you. With playmates from the servants' quarters, I fished and swam in the creek. I hiked in the woods. I sledded and skated in the winter. And proved an absolute nuisance in the workshops and sheds. In spring, I marched out with the servants in the early mornings to pick strawberries from plants still wet with dew. It was a delightful childhood," she admitted, laughing up at him.

Geoffrey greatly enjoyed the rapidly changing expressions playing over her face. She was a delight, with her satin hair escaping its knot and ribbons to blow about her head in charming disorder. He captured a lock and tucked it tenderly behind her ear. "And then you were sent to a school for young ladies?" he prompted.

"Yes. As you can imagine, school was a bit confining after that," she answered, slightly breathless at his attentions. "Although I must say I did receive a most useful education there. Embroidery, paper-cutting, watercolors, moss works. You can never imagine the picture I can paint using a mere feather as a paintbrush. Oh, and polite conversation. Very enlightening topic. No, my lord marquis, I sadly fear I was the rebel of the classroom, as I'm sure you probably suspected.''

Geoffrey directed her along the path toward the carp pond. Never would he have imagined such enjoyment could be discovered in the company of such a young miss. Or that he would have remained so entertained by her vivid descriptions of her life as a country child, or by the way her wonderfully expressive eyes appeared to alter hues with each emotion. It pleased him in some undefined manner that her cheeks alternately paled then flushed with a delicate pink when she smiled up at him, sometimes openly and with unabashed delight, and sometimes with shy self-consciousness as if she was acutely aware of him as a man.

''Sounds to be a disagreeable place,'' Geoffrey said, encouraging her confidences, wishing the enjoyment to continue.

''I imagine, in its own way, it was no better and no worse than others,'' Rose conceded. ''I remember it mostly by smell—cottage stew and pease porridge, little girl perfume, chalk dust. Oh, and sound—malicious gossip in shrill, piping voices.''

''You are most descriptive. I can almost imagine myself there. I doubt you fit in very well, Tiger's Breath, with your exuberant nature.''

''I, my lord? Exuberant?'' countered Rose, pulling a face at the thought of herself at that age. ''I fear I was a shy, serious girl with stringy, straight hair, when all the fashion was ringlets and curls, who spent most of her allowance on inappropriate books.''

Geoffrey threw back his head to laugh heartily at the picture she painted. Suddenly he wanted to sweep her into his arms and swing her around in a circle and hear her squeals. And he wanted to kiss her. She made him feel good. No, actually, she made him feel great. Oh, yes, he wanted to kiss her very much.

The sight of his fine head tipped back, baring his strong throat, took Rose's breath away. How she wanted Lord Wyse to fall in love with her and make this engagement one that ended in marriage. To have him turn those warm, brown eyes upon her with the same intimacy that her father used to look at her mother. If that would happen, life would stretch out before her in a long, happy road, filled with love and children and security. Oh, she wanted him to kiss her in the worst way.

Instead he beamed down upon her with great affection, and drew her hand more firmly into the crook of his arm. "Come, we'd best keep moving as it is chilly. Tell me of your mother. I am most interested and entertained."

The warmth of his hand seeped into Rose's cool flesh and raced up her arm to strike at her heart. She wanted him to touch her forever. She wanted him to hold her tightly to him. She fought the urge to lean in to his body, searching her mind for details to entertain him so that he would remain with her. "Re-regardless of what Poppy called her," Rose continued breathlessly. "Mummy was a plain, sweet woman with a pale thin face. So thin, in fact, that her chin was quite pointed. I always thought he must be seeing her as she was before the illness. That's how great his love for her was.

"I remember best the smell of lavender. She was very feminine and dressed like a little girl in flounces, ribbons and frills, puffed sleeves and lace, always scented with lavender. Poppy adored her, and treated her like priceless porcelain. They were together a great deal of the time. Her illness was a wasting one, and she tired easily, so my memories of her are bits and snatches of conversations and admonishments on my deplorable behavior. She would have thrilled to see me last night, elegantly attired for the ball, and acting like a proper lady.''

"Ah, yes, the ball. What a cursed dull evening that was.''

For a second Rose felt as if someone had struck her across the face. The glittering evening, her glorious gown, meeting King William, all shattered at her feet like a fragile glass bubble. Her fairy-tale evening had, for him, been tedious and boring? She eased her hand away from his arm and moved quickly to bend over the pond. Perhaps if she appeared to inspect the carp there most diligently, he would not see the hurt and disappointment in her face.

Startled for a moment at her abrupt withdrawal, Geoffrey looked thoughtfully at his pretended fiancée. She was seemingly engrossed in the carp, but the tension in her body belied that. Suddenly he was at a loss as to what to say. Were the memories too tender for her? Or, as they had been discussing her parents' obviously close relationship, perhaps she was uneasy about their alliance now that they were supposedly engaged. He was clear in his own mind about that, and though they had touched on the subject in a general way, perhaps he should set her mind at ease in greater detail. He truly did not want her to be uncomfortable in his presence. Actually the exact opposite was true.

"Rose…'' he began. He cleared his throat in discomfort, yet he felt he must forge on. "Rose, I do want to assure you that you need not fear the forcing of any unwanted attentions upon your person. As I mentioned last evening, I shall respect that this is an arrangement between us, and I can be trusted to keep my distance. You may have your friends and amusements, and I promise not to interfere. I am sincere when I say that you may seek a permanent protector as you will.'' He paused, but Rose gave no indication that she had heard, or if she had, was prepared to give an answer.

There was just enough maturity about Rose for her to realize there was nothing whatsoever she could do to encourage this man to fall in love with her. She could only behave lightly and happily, and hope somehow the heavens would open and a miracle would happen. For it might well take a miracle for this man to stop treating her as a child, and see her as a woman, a desirable woman that he wished to take to wife in every way.

"Tiger's Breath?'' Geoffrey ventured again.

Rose forced a brilliant smile to her face and turned to him. "How serious you sound, my lord. Being chucked under the chin by King William may be an everyday event for you—cursed dull, I believe you called it—but for me the experience was thrilling. You must remember, I am but a country bumpkin.''

Geoffrey gave a snort at his ineptness. He was making a muddle of this with her. He had not meant to insult her, but merely to put her at ease. "I did not mean.... Please don't misunderstand my intent, Rose. We are to be friends, are we not, Tiger's Breath? The very best of friends?''

"Of course. And please do not despair of me, my lord. While I might sound for the most part like a rambunctious tomboy, I readily admit to possessing all the romantic thoughts of most females. Though I assure you, I shall curb such thoughts and feelings as best I can. I am aware as none other that this is simply the first act in a very imaginative drama,'' she countered. She even went so far as to give him one of her bravest smiles.

Geoffrey breathed more easily when he saw her good humor restored. She was truly a dear little thing and he did feel such strange responsibility when he saw her sad or unhappy. "We have an agreement then," he announced, then as an afterthought, added, "although I would have you know, child, that if I were to truly wed, I would as well be buckled to you as to any other in the whole of London."

When Rose did not come back with a ready quip, Geoffrey pulled her around to face him. Tilting her face upward to the light with fingertips beneath her chin, he attempted to read her expression.

Rose held quiet for his appraisal, although she did make every attempt to control the look of longing that must surely shine in her eyes. He gazed unwaveringly down at her, and she was helpless to tear her eyes away. His fingertips moved to caress her cheek, his touch as light as the feather brush of a moth's wing. Despite her statement of just a moment before that she would control her romantic fantasies concerning Geoffrey, her heart crashed against her ribs and her knees grew alarmingly weak.

Geoffrey's eyes darkened to a chocolate brown, then almost to black, as if he too were operating under strong emotions. He gently pushed a wayward lock away from her face. Then with a sigh, as if catching himself woolgathering, he shook her chin gently and released her. Rose watched his handsome face flush beneath his sun-browned flesh and sensed his discomfort, which she immediately set about easing. With a smile, she replaced her hand on his arm and tugged him toward the house in a playful manner.

"Now come. I must find Willy before he does something disgraceful to your mother's gardens and we are again in the doghouse. And that, as you can well imagine, is a most discomforting place for a cat to be."

"Yes, I quite think it would be so," Geoffrey agreed, following her lead toward the front of the garden. He lapsed into a thoughtfulness that she did not disturb.

Under the guise of smoothing her wayward hair, Rose

touched her cheek where his fingers had stroked. Again, she admonished herself that she absolutely must cease dreaming that one day he would view her as a woman instead of a child. For, although he was totally unaware of it, she was a woman, a woman with all the feelings, desires and yearnings of most women for the man who had captured her heart. If he ever came to recognize that, perhaps—just perhaps—he would yearn in his heart for her, as she did for him.

Chapter Nine

"I do understand your point, Mother. Miss Bartley-Bacon is a guest in this house, and without a chaperon as her mother is in ill health. I also concede that Lady Margaret Bartley-Bacon is your friend of long acquaintance and I applaud your willingness to shelter her daughter for the entire season!" Geoffrey's voice rose in exasperation.

"Geoffrey! I will not stand for you raising your voice to me," challenged Lady Lavitia, looking him straight in the eye with an expression clearly meant to intimidate him into doing her bidding.

Geoffrey refused to drop his eyes or resort to schoolboy feelings of guilt over a reprimand. And refused to be pressured by his own mother into doing something he had no wish to do. "And while I have agreed with you on those points, Mother, I would still state emphatically that Miss Sharon Bartley-Bacon remains a deuced nonsense. And furthermore, she exhibits an unpleasantly aggressive nature that makes a man like myself, who has no wish to be bothered, guard his crotch with both hands."

"Geoffrey! Do not bring your barroom language into this house! And that's a terrible thing to say of Sharon," Lady Lavitia admonished. "It is simply that she has developed a genuine *tendre* for you. Your regrettable engagement, totally out of the blue like that, and to a complete stranger—an *engagement*, I might add, that you kept secret even from your own mother, has broken her heart. I am merely asking you to be particularly solicitous of her.''

Geoffrey, in an uncharacteristically agitated move, raked his hand through his hair, disarraying his curls and sending his mother's eyebrows upward in surprise. ''Mother, I seriously doubt Miss Bartley-Bacon has a heart to break. *And* I am always kind to everyone. It is deemed by all the matrons to be one of my most charming attributes. As to paying her extra attention, I assure you, that will only serve to encourage her to further outrageous flights of fancy concerning me, my title and my fortune. I can almost place a wager on that!''

''Oh, Geoffrey, do not be melodramatic. I'm merely mentioning that she is so dreadfully unhappy at present.''

''As well I can imagine, having seen her plan go awry and my title slip through her greedy little fingers. I would quite imagine she is *most* unhappy, and as you must concede, when Sharon Bartley-Bacon is unhappy, Sharon Bartley-Bacon is never unhappy alone.''

''Really, Geoffrey, you are being very tedious this morning. If you cannot see your way to honor a simple request from your own mother I do not have any hope for you in the future. What has come over you lately? First, you bring forth a girl no one has heard of—'' her eyes swept strongly over him with her stern glare ''—then you announce your plans to wed her, and now this. I am truly vexed beyond reason by you lately!''

Geoffrey was spared the need to answer his fractious mother by a flurry of skirts charging into the dining room. Fully expecting the persistent Sharon Bartley-Bacon to disturb his already disturbed morning with her unwanted presence, he had the blackest look he could effect firmly set upon his face when he glanced up at Rose.

Rose skidded to a halt. "Oh, I am sorry. I simply did not realize anyone else was about this early. I do not wish to intrude...."

Lady Lavitia looked up with a set face fully as disagreeable as her son's. She did not wish to have her discussion cut short by the distraction of anyone, least of all this girl. Something must be said, and said this very morning, to make Geoffrey reconsider this rash step. He must, simply must, cancel this engagement. "I am sorry, my dear, but if I were you, I would take my breakfast elsewhere," Lady Lavitia advised. "The clouds are so thick here, I expect lightning bolts and rainstorms at any moment."

"As I can see," Rose said, taking in the thunderclouds on Lord Wyse's face. "But please do not feel you must apologize, Lady Lavitia. It was a sad affliction suffered by many in my family also."

"Affliction? What affliction?" Lady Lavitia demanded, confused and irritated by her confusion.

"Why, morning bears, my lady," Rose commented, with a significantly lifted eyebrow at the marquis. Then, with an impish grin and a gay little wiggle of her fingers, she backed from the room and disappeared down the hall.

"Morning bears? *Morning bears?* Now whatever does that mean?" Lady Lavitia demanded. She frowned deeply. "That girl! While not actually doing anything to irritate, somehow she manages to do just that. Perhaps it is merely the exuberance of her youth that grates upon my nerves. Why must she always be charging about? So much energy for such a small person." Never would Lady Lavitia admit to herself that her feelings toward Rose just might be displaced frustration for her son's blatant refusal to fall in line with her plans.

Geoffrey stared at the doorway, stunned to silence. His face cleared of its thundercloud, then broke into a delighted smile. The minx! Ever ready with a quip to bring out the absurdity of the moment. Abruptly, he slapped a palm flat on the table, threw back his head and roared with laughter.

His mother spun in her chair to stare at him, with her hand clasped to her throat. "Geoffrey! Whatever has come over you?" she demanded. "I just do not know what to make of you! You have not been acting yourself at all lately."

"I quite fear, Mother, that I am becoming more myself than I have ever been in my life. If you will please excuse me," he announced, shoving back his chair. He rose, tossed his napkin onto his barely touched plate and, with a little wiggle of his fingers at his gaping mother, strode purposefully from the breakfast room to seek out Rose.

Upstairs, a proud Orange Willy stalked through the doorway of Rose's bedchamber, his pouter pigeon chest puffed out, dragging a mauled magenta plume with its jeweled clasp tapping loudly on the wooden floor. Rose's eyes grew large as she recognized the plume that accented Sharon's newly arrived ball gown. It was the very same plume, mysteriously missing since last night, that had caused an uproar of major proportions throughout the entire house. Before her horrified eyes, the mighty orange hunter disappeared into his lair beneath the bed to demolish his latest kill.

Rose dived under the bed after him, crying out, "Willy! Oh, you horrid, horrid cat! You would make a liar out of me? After I proclaimed your innocence to all who would listen?"

"Ahem!" Appearing in the open doorway, Geoffrey cleared his throat uncomfortably. Having been through the main rooms, then out into the garden in search of Rose, he had finally gained her direction from a housemaid and followed her up the stairs. Now, finding her head and shoulders beneath her bed with rump in the air and legs flailing about, he was unsure if he should offer assistance, or merely back out of the room unobserved.

"Oh, don't just stand there. Please help me!" Rose wailed from the depths of her under-bed cave.

His presence being discovered before he could come to a decision, Geoffrey resigned himself and inquired in good humor, "And what would you have me do to assist? Should I join you under the bed, or attempt to extract you by dragging you out by the heels?"

"Oh, Lord Wyse!" Rose gasped. Sticking her head out, she could only stare up into his wonderful face. His smile was so sweet, so genuine, and the dimple in his right cheek winking so merrily, she could almost forget what an undignified picture she must present. "I thought you were Lettie."

"As I am not, may I assume you would accept my assistance in her absence?"

"Oh, it is just Willy. He's filched Sharon's—I mean, Miss Bartley-Bacon's—plume and I cannot reach him. He moves just out of reach each time I try."

"Well, I shall attack from the other side and we will quickly corner the rascal. How about that?" he generously offered. Passing quickly to the opposite side of the bed, he bent down on one knee and raised the bedskirt. Willy, hunched over his prize, remained in the center, just out of reach from either side. The cat crouched lower and placed protective paws over the plume to prevent its escape while his attention was diverted by threat from this new direction.

"Oh, Willy," Rose admonished, wiggling farther under the bed. "Must you be such a bad cat?"

Geoffrey bent the other knee and stuck his head under the bed, then lacking space, lowered himself to his stomach and reached in farther. Willy, sensing real danger from that direction, moved quickly away from his extended hand and inadvertently into Rose's clutches. She quickly swiped the plume away from him.

"Aha! Got it!" she exclaimed, waving it triumphantly at the marquis.

Geoffrey could only grin at her, for she was so childishly outrageous.

"My goodness, Rose! Whatever are you doing now?" Lady Lavitia demanded, halting in the hallway to stare into the bedchamber. Rose hurriedly wriggled from beneath the bed to regain her feet. Hastily secreting the wet, damaged plume in the folds of her skirt, she turned to sweetly smile at the older woman. The marquis rose from the other side, dusting off his knees with a nonchalant hand. Shocked to her very toes to discover her son rising from beneath Rose's bed, with his hair mussed and neckcloth disarrayed, she could only clasp a hand to her bosom and exclaim. "My Lord! Geoffrey! What on earth are *you* doing beneath Rose's bed!"

"It is nothing, Mother. I was merely assisting Rose. You see, Willy…" he began, uncomfortably aware of the guilty look that must be settling over his face.

"Oh…" Rose gasped. Quickly shaking her head at him in warning, she sought to keep the mauled plume a secret. At least until Lettie could attempt some salvage of the poor, mangled thing.

"I mean, ahem, that is to say…" Geoffrey stammered. Incomparably eloquent on the floor of Parliament, he was at a total loss for words to explain away a situation where he had no experience to draw upon.

"Oh, never mind! I do fear for your senses, Geoffrey. And if your father were here, I vow I'd accuse him of lying to my face when he swore on our wedding day that there was no weakness of mind in his family. It is either that or—'' she paused to level a stern look at Rose ''—unruly influences in your life. Either way, Geoffrey, I shall wash my hands of you unless you choose to apologize to me for your unforgivably rude behavior at breakfast. I shall be in my room while you consider your actions, and their repercussions.''

Stunned silence remained after the lady had swept from the room. Rose worried her bottom lip with small, white teeth, then hazarded a glance through her lashes at the chastised son. Lord Wyse had such an expression of stark disbelief on his face that she fought the sudden urge to laugh. Had he truly never been in trouble with his mother before? He brought his eyes to hers, then a shameless grin spread over his face, the dimple winking in and out. Rose giggled in delight.

Moving quickly to close the door lest his mother hear their merriment, Geoffrey shook his head at Rose. She could contain herself no longer and began to laugh in earnest. He stepped to her to shake a finger in front of her face. ''You are outrageous, Tiger's Breath. You've landed me in hot water with my mother, and for that you must make amends,'' he warned, grasping her arms and giving her a playful shake. ''Hush now, or she'll be back to paddle both of us for impertinence.''

Rose could only giggle helplessly. The sight of the two of them protruding from beneath her bed must have conjured unmentionable lewd images in that righteous lady's mind. She only giggled harder, quickly wiggling free of his hands. A wicked gleam appeared in Lord Wyse's eyes and he approached her threateningly, forcing her retreat until the bed bumped the back of her knees.

''You should be taught an important lesson. And I can only think of one way to school a naughty child, Miss Rose

Lambe," he threatened. Snatching her wrist, he drew her slowly toward him.

"No, you wouldn't..." Rose squeaked, thinking he meant to paddle her soundly, then dissolved into giggles again.

Geoffrey's original thought had been to threaten a spanking that any naughty child deserved, but when he bent close to her, her soft lilac scent wafted up to him and her merry, pink mouth beckoned so invitingly that he could not resist. His firm, cool lips claimed hers in a light kiss instead. Her mouth was warm, pliant and totally inexperienced. A fact that only made the stolen kiss all the sweeter. He folded her more tightly into his arms, strengthening the kiss until she was quite breathless. When he did raise his head again, it was to look down at her with a dawning wonder.

Rose, with a startled look of surprise on her face, attempted to step back from him and plopped down on the bed instead. Her abrupt shift in weight pulled him down atop her.

Geoffrey deftly claimed her lips once more in long, sensual kisses as his weight bore her back into the pillows. Desire seared through his blood. He gently arranged himself on top of her, reveling in the lush feel of her breasts against his chest. He longed to cup that fullness in his hands and feel the nipples rise beneath his thumbs in excitement. He wanted to teach his little tiger's breath the taste and feel of a man in the heat of passion. He wanted to strip the clothes from her body and taste her pale flesh, drive her to whimpers with awakening sensations. He wanted to hear her beg for something she had no name for. He wanted... Suddenly, he released her mouth and shoved himself away from her to regain his feet.

"Oh God, Rose, that was abominable of me and I do beg your forgiveness. I remember saying I'd never force myself on you, and here I've betrayed your trust at the drop of a hat. Rose, I am so very sorry. That was reprehensible of me, to say the least,'' he apologized, raking a hand through his curls and clearing his throat guiltily. Whatever could he have been thinking to ravish the child that way? Damn, perhaps his mother was correct. Maybe he was demonstrating a weakness of mind.

Rose sat up quickly and smoothed her hair in embarrassment. "No, it was me.... I sh-should be the one to apologize. I am so sorry to have caused you problems with your mother. And then to laugh at you…''

"Ah, yes, there's that.'' He quickly smoothed his neckcloth and dragged a hand through his hair again. "I suppose I should go along like a good little boy and make amends with Mother. Receive my tongue-lashing and all that.''

Geoffrey moved to gently open the door, then paused to look at Rose with such intense speculation that she flushed deeply and hurriedly rose from the bed. He noted her hands were unsteady as she self-consciously smoothed her skirts. Then, as if unable to resist, she pressed trembling fingers to her bruised mouth, a move that brought his eyes to linger there. He very much wanted to return and taste her lips again. Even more thoroughly this time. Instead, he nodded once and eased his frame out the door, closing it gently behind him.

Rose sank back onto the bed, clasping her hands hard in her lap. Her heart pounded erratically, and she seemed unable to draw enough air into her lungs. Never in all her dreams could she have imagined that being kissed by Lord Wyse could be—so perfect, so entrancing, so…

Suddenly, the door was wrenched open again, causing Rose to startle with a small cry. Geoffrey loomed large and authoritatively in the doorway. He stared at her with a rather stunned expression for a moment, then, as if the decision had been made a long time before but had never been verbalized, he calmly announced, "Tiger's Breath, I do think you and I should make good on this engagement thing. Follow it through to the end, you know? What say you?"

Rose could only stare at him in astonishment. Could he possibly be offering for her hand in marriage? No playacting? No sham? A real marriage, with babies and everything? Please, dear Lord, let that be his meaning, she silently begged. "I'm n-not sure if I follow your meaning, Lord Wyse," she stammered, afraid to hope, yet unable to stop the rush of expectancy.

"It's just that, when one thinks of it logically, I mean, I do have to wed someone sometime. It's not something I can put off for the rest of my life, now, is it? And I suppose I'd rather be buckled to you than to any other I know. We do deal remarkably well together, don't you agree?" Geoffrey asked. He watched her face for a moment, then discomfited by her silence, he cleared his throat and edged back through the door. "Er…give it a bit of thought and I shall see you, perhaps downstairs in the library, before I leave."

"No," Rose cried, leaping from the bed to hold out her hand to stop him.

Geoffrey jerked his head around to stare at her, stunned disbelief at her blunt refusal written over his face.

Rose moved to the door hesitantly. She started to touch his hand on the shiny brass doorknob, but held herself back. "I mean, no—I don't need time to think of it. I shall marry you, Lord Wyse. At any time and at any place you should specify."

Happiness burst over Geoffrey's face in a wide grin and deepening of dimples. He exhaled a great breath, which he had not even been aware he was retaining. "That's splendid. Splendid, indeed. I shall tell Mother to start her planning. We'll be married as quickly as society rules dictate. I'm certain there is a time frame that must be heeded. To avoid gossip and all that. Pact then?''

"Pact!" Rose agreed, gratified at the look of happiness on his face.

Geoffrey reached out and ruffled her hair in the manner one uses on a favored child. "Pact then, Tiger's Breath. Now I must go atone for my sins with Mother before she strikes my name from the family bible."

Gently closing the door behind him, Rose leaned her forehead against the panel and listened to his jaunty footsteps disappearing down the hall. She raised fingers to press against her lips. Lord Wyse had kissed her. He had pressed her down on the bed and kissed her most thoroughly. Then he had asked her to be his wife. Couldn't that mean there was some depth of feeling there that perhaps *he* did not even recognize? True enough, it was hardly flattering that he'd said he liked her as well as any other. And to have one's hair ruffled as a child was not the most desired caress she would wish for, but one did take one's affections however they were offered these days. And she could only reason that this was a giant step in the direction she wished with her whole heart to go.

"Today his wife—tomorrow the mother of his children," she swore to herself, twirling across the room to fall upon the bed. "Willy, I will make him love me!"

Chapter Ten

"I simply do not understand you, Sharon. For months you have bent my ear over the sad, sad condition of your broken heart. But now that the wedding is done and over with, you profess to missing the company of little Rose!" Lady Lavitia declared disagreeably. "I would have thought she was the last person you would be pining for."

"Well, you must admit the house is decidedly quiet now that she has gone. And one can mourn one's losses for only so long before the future must be faced. I am still a young and beautiful woman, aren't I? I will not declare my heart forever broken and take to the nun's garb over the marquis's marriage. I merely thought a visit to Hetherington Harrow would be in order." Sharon pouted her lips slightly and made a thorough investigation of a perfectly oval fingernail, shrugging as if it truly weren't anything to her. "After all, you *are* her mother-in-law and she *is* quite young. Perhaps you should see that the chit is doing right by your son. I very much doubt, regardless of her mother's prolonged illness, that she has managed such a large house before, do you?"

"Ah, there, you see. No one is supposed to know, but they haven't gone to Hetherington Harrow at all," Lady

Lavitia announced triumphantly, "but to Shenstone. Geoffrey has been to the solicitor's, and it would seem he is above that second cousin or whoever he is, and has stood heir to the Earl of Shenstone, Rose's father, all along. Without even knowing it! Amazing the way things worked out, don't you think?"

Sharon turned her back on the woman and paced to the fireplace. How well she did know it. Wasn't that why she was being sent to the damn country by *Mr.* Elmo Sewell? He was furious at being ousted from his title and estates by the marquis. And, she rather feared, he meant to do someone bodily harm to regain control. It was to be her task to drive a wedge of unhappiness between the newlyweds and force them back to London. Such a nasty affair, and coming at a terrible time. Who wanted to be cooped in the country when everyone of import was in town? She had no desire to leave the season, but of course, with the state of affairs, she had no choice but do as he bade.

Foul man, that Elmo Sewell. And one she would see herself rid of as soon as the opportunity presented itself. But then, if he could bring about a permanent separation, perhaps even a dissolution of the marriage, she could only hope to gain from it even if that gain was only to see Rose disgraced.

Lady Lavitia, assuming the rigid set of Sharon's back to mean the onset of one of her famous and tedious tantrums, decided capitulation was the best course of action. She was growing tired of the season anyway, and it would do no harm to retire to the country for a brief rest. And perhaps there was some truth in what the girl said. It was her place, in absence of Rose's mother, to see the girl started on the right foot.

"All right, Sharon. If you have your heart set upon it, we shall take a sojourn down to Sussex and see what is what. I do not believe it will be seen amiss by either my son or society if we visit. I mean, the way Geoffrey described it, the trip to Shenstone was more of an inspection of newly acquired property than a *honeymoon.*"

Sharon spun around to clap her hands with pleasure. She had no idea it was going to be so easy to get the old lady to leave the comfort of her position and travel to the country. "Oh, thank you, Mama Lavitia. That pleases me no end."

Sharon's pleasure would have disappeared in a vapor, had she known at that moment her quarry was in the raptures of joy. Not having been privy to the matter of the misdirected inheritance, Rose had naturally assumed the estate at Shenstone lost to her forever. And now, here she was, departing the chaise in the driveway, and commencing her life as the new Marquise of Hetherington with the very act of reclaiming her beloved home.

"Oh, Geoffrey, you have no idea how thrilled this makes me. There could not have been a more fitting wedding gift in the entire world."

"I will say, the solicitors at Bailey, Banks and Biddle were most apologetic about the oversight, but as you mentioned, adequate records were scarce with the fire and all. I shall never again make disparaging remarks to my mother about her meticulous attention to detail over the family bible, nor of Milty and that damnable propensity of his for trivia," Geoffrey conceded, gazing with interest at the old hall.

Meticulously rebuilt following the fire in the seventeenth century, Shenstone looked for all the world like a huge sprawling Gothic castle with its multitude of towers and battlements in mellow yellow stone. On the ground floor, the main block was mostly occupied by living rooms for the family, drawing rooms, dining rooms and library, all on a scale to dwarf its occupants and make anyone less important than the marquis feel small and insignificant. A huge conservatory led west from the dining room to the chapel, concealing the servants' wing from the driveway. The northwest wing was the family's private apartments, and after introducing her new husband to the staff—from the main butler to the most insignificant knife boy—it was there Rose led Geoffrey to freshen themselves from their journey. The master's and mistress's bedchambers were separated by a dressing room of ornate and regal purple and gold.

Allowing Lettie the briefest moment to remove her travel wear and tidy her hair, Rose burst through the room not only to find her new husband absent, but startling Deming into an unmanly squeak of surprise, which changed to a frown of humiliated disapproval at her back when she contritely apologized and quietly retraced her steps in dainty ladylike fashion.

Ferreting out Geoffrey in the library, she smiled to see him already poring over estate ledgers. She paused for a moment to study him sitting there in her father's chair, outlined in the last golden rays of the late-afternoon sunlight. If she squinted her eyes ever so slightly, it could have been Poppy there, just as she remembered him. But, as much as she wished for her father, she wished more for her husband. Sweeping her eyes over the room, she shook her head at the sight of it. The library was clearly a gentleman's library, with a ceiling as tall as a cathedral's and spiderwebs everywhere. Unused and desolate, out of the way, it was too damp to be a library, and all the leather bindings had a greenish tinge. It was a room obviously sadly neglected these past three years, but that would soon be rectified. She turned eyes filled with love back to ponder the engrossed

Geoffrey. With a glimmer of mischief, she set about distracting him.

"And is this the way a marquis spends his honeymoon, my lord? Poring over ledgers and ignoring his beautiful, talented, charming wife?" she asked.

Geoffrey glanced up with a smile. "I do not have any idea at all, dear wife, of the manner in which a marquis spends his honeymoon, never having partaken of one myself. I suppose we shall have to invent as we go along, unless there might be a tome of sorts on these many shelves containing pearls of wisdom on the subject."

Rose moved farther into the room, swaying in what she hoped was a fair imitation of a seductress. Her gown of sea green taffeta set off the creaminess of her neck with its neckline of minute scallops and intricate embroidery of seashells. And while she had hoped for something in the way of a compliment, it would seem her new husband was much too preoccupied for his own good. She wrinkled her nose at his inattention to her, and changed tactics in her attempt to draw his interest.

"I can't imagine three years could make this much difference in the cleanliness of a place," she said. "Or do you think it was always in this deplorable condition and I was too inured to notice?"

Geoffrey glanced up at his new wife with a sigh at the interruption. But, there would be time enough later for this, he thought, and regretfully closed the ledgers. He was a man who enjoyed straightening out muddles, and this was going to be a fine muddle to correct. "It is no matter which it is, now, is it? All this will be remedied soon enough, and our bedchambers, if not perfect, are at least adequately habitable. It is only these unused rooms that need a great deal of attention." He grinned at the wrinkled state of her small nose. "Come then, let's move into the drawing room. You will be much more comfortable there."

The drawing room was furnished, just as Rose remembered it, in sumptuous brocades and rosewoods, with carpets woven in mauve and salmon, cream and beige wool. The familiar sight of it filled her with such emotion that her eyes teemed with tears. Not wishing Geoffrey to see her silliness, she moved through French doors to the terrace. Formal flower gardens, bordered with neatly trimmed hedges, stretched out before her. A park, beyond the gardens, was dotted with temples, obelisks, and inviting stone seats beside an ornamental lake fed by a meandering creek. Beyond that lay secret swimming holes and ideal fishing spots.

Rose experienced an overwhelming feeling of pride as she inhaled a deep breath of country air scented with newly mown grass. A sudden longing struck her to fill the gardens and park with happy faces and liven the formal rooms with music and dancing. She was so carried away with this vision that she swung around to rush at Geoffrey as he came along the terrace, and threw her arms exuberantly about his neck. This was noted by the steward's boy, who told the third footman, who told the under butler, who told the cook, who merely smiled at the thought of the old abbey being alive again with laughter, love and babies.

"Oh, Geoffrey," Rose cried. "Do let us have a party!"

Geoffrey ruffled her hair absently and moved away from her with a frown creasing his forehead. "We shall see, Tiger's Breath. First we must move in an army to clean and air the place from top to bottom. Plus make a list of essentials—oh, linens and such—that require replacement. The accounts have been sadly neglected. I fear the steward…what's his name? Jessups? I fear he will have to be replaced."

Rose looked after him with a sigh. "Oh, Geoffrey. Must all that be seen to right this very moment?"

Geoffrey turned at the wistful tone of her voice and studied the pleading expression on her face. She looked so forlorn that he felt a pang of guilt, for after all she was such a young thing. He shrugged and grinned at her. "I suppose not this exact moment. Come, have a glass of sherry with me, Tiger's Breath. Not a very romantic honeymoon for a young girl but perhaps once the place is refurbished and you've had your party, we can contrive to be merry."

Rose followed her husband back into the drawing room. Contrive to be merry? She felt quite merry enough at this very moment. It saddened her to think that he did not. This feeling prevailed over a light supper laid out in the cavernous dining room. Ever contrary to custom, she had directed her place setting be moved to Geoffrey's right rather than sit the great length of the table from him where no conversation might be possible. Then to her consernation, she found him very distracted and preoccupied with estate matters and rushing through the meal with little thought to Cook's creations. Not her idea of a proper honeymoon supper. Nor was it her idea of a wedding night to be sent to bed alone, like a naughty child deserving punishment, while he retired back to the library and his ledgers.

She followed him into the library to wander about the room and finally shoved the ledgers aside to perch on the edge of the desk. "Geoffrey, must you attend estate business tonight of all nights?"

Geoffrey leaned back in his chair to study Rose. She was young, soft and vulnerable, with her lavender eyes and teasing mouth. His wife. To love, honor and cherish for the rest of his life. Thinking the words, but looking at Rose, he did not feel the familiar garrote of enclosure on his lungs. Instead he felt a rush of warm affection.

Rose, puzzled by his searching look, but encouraged that at least his attention had been drawn from the papers on the desk, leaned forward, brazenly close, inviting his kiss. She very much wanted to entice a repeat of the time he had lain over her body and kissed her breathless, for after all, that was what married people did and that was what made babies. She wanted lots of babies.

With a grin, Geoffrey obligingly pecked her on the lips. When she wrinkled her nose at the inadequate response, he laughed and drew her to his lap. "Now, Tiger's Breath, do not become a scolding wife at the very beginning of our marriage, or we shall have nowhere to progress to, now, shall we?" he teased, pecking her again, lightly. Then again, not so lightly.

Rose melted into him, tilting her head and offering her lips for a more thorough plunder. The feel of his arms tightening about her was the most wondrous sensation of safety, and thrilling to the extent that her heart felt as if it were leaping from her body. "I will never scold or nag, my husband. I promise to be the most perfect wife," she whispered softly against his mouth.

Geoffrey breathed deeply of her lilac scent, and watched her eyes sparkle for a moment before she blinked lush sooty lashes downward. He smoothed a forefinger over her pouty lips. She was an enticing child, tempting and promising as a partially opened rosebud. He reasoned that she was his wife, and by law available to him, but—he shifted uncomfortably with the quickening of his body—immediately chastised himself for lecherous thoughts. Enticing or not, Rose was still of tender years and required protection now, not seduction. Perhaps one day, for after all, she was to be his wife for a long, long time. Yes, one day, and one day soon, he promised himself, he would take her as his body demanded...but not tonight. Tonight he must remain the gentleman.

Geoffrey quickly pecked her on her cute upturned nose and levered himself to his feet, setting her on her own feet in the process. "Come along, little one—" he took her by the shoulders and propelled her toward the door "—it's been a long day and time you were abed. I shall see you for breakfast in the morning." Pushing her gently through the door, he firmly shut it behind her. Drawing a deep sigh, he ran his hand through his walnut curls. He had every desire to follow her up the stairs and teach her all the delights he sensed hidden in the depths of her innocent soul. No. While it was difficult being the responsible one, she was safer out of sight, for then his normally good sense could overcome the rampage of his desire to take her as his wife, thoroughly and repeatedly.

Rose allowed Lettie to settle her into the great canopied bed that had been her mother's. She was feeling very small and very alone tonight. Pulling Orange Willy up next to her, she snuggled her face into the warm fur. She had not given it a great deal of thought when her husband had avoided her bed for the first three weeks of their marriage, for she herself had felt quite constrained at 1 Leicester Street, with Sharon moping around with dejected eyes and her new mother-in-law frowning damnation upon her head at each opportunity. But here, at Shenstone, she had thought it would be different. She rightly considered this to be her true wedding night. And she wanted her husband.

She wondered sadly if Geoffrey was sitting, staring into the fire, thinking of her on this night as she was thinking of him? Or, once having disposed of her, had he promptly put her from his mind and buried his nose in the accountings? He had seemed so incredibly handsome in the candlelight tonight, she mused dreamily, then grimaced. Was she always to be treated by him as sort of a younger sister?

"No!" she muttered vehemently. Tomorrow was a brand-new day in which to try for his love. Nothing must come in her way. They would be alone—all alone—to wander the estate on horseback, to explore, to share her childhood haunts with him. It would be wonderful. Too wonderful to imagine.

Their wedding, although lovely, had not turned out to be the wedding of her dreams. Even though she had pleaded for Lord Philpotts to be given the honor, Lady Lavitia had demanded otherwise, and a distant relative of Lord Wyse's had begrudgingly escorted her down the aisle. Quite elderly and decidedly hard of hearing, he had tottered the length of the church aisle, all the while expounding loudly and enthusiastically his disapproval for the union. The bride was too young and too inexperienced, he deemed. And he had never known a marriage between a schoolgirl and a rake of adult years to make a go of it. Having never before heard Lord Wyse described as a rake, Rose very much doubted the validity of the declaration, but that aside, she had wondered most ardently just how long in the tooth one must be before society at large considered one a grown-up.

The only memorable moment of the short affair had come when Geoffrey had turned to watch her progress down the aisle, radiant and beautiful in her ivory gown. He had given her one of those tender smiles that brought out the dimple in his cheek and softened his eyes. It was a look that melted her heart and made it difficult to draw air into her lungs. It was the look she yearned so for every moment of every day. It was the thought that this might somehow be possible that she took with her into sleep to sweeten her dreams.

Breakfast brought another obstacle to Rose's plans.

Geoffrey was at the table when she entered. He appeared distracted and rumpled, as if he had spent the night at the ledgers instead of in his bed. He glanced up at her with a deep frown, then nodded toward a parchment leaning against his crystal service. "It would seem my mother is on her way here," he stated flatly.

"Oh, Geoffrey," Rose cried out. "Is there no way to stop her? I have no wish for company descending upon us at this time."

"Doesn't seem to be. This is an express from her to that fact, so I am left to assume she has already departed London. We can only hope against hope that she is coming alone—" he lifted eyebrows with meaning "—and *others* best left in London *are* left in London."

"Oh, surely so, but…" Rose began, then fumed inwardly, for after all it would do no service to defame a new mother-in-law to her son. But how thoughtless of Lady Lavitia to think that they would want houseguests underfoot on their honeymoon. Slipping into her seat, she plopped her elbow on the table and her chin in her hand to look at Geoffrey. He had resumed his breakfast, and had poked his nose back into the papers propped against the vase of roses placed there by a servant who assumed such was appropriate on a honeymoon.

Not that this was any ordinary honeymoon, where the groom could not keep his hands from beneath his bride's petticoats, she mused. No, this was a test of wills. His to ignore her and hers to tempt him to thoughts of nothing else. And, as for the imminent arrival of Lady Lavitia, there was nothing she could do except acknowledge that her mother-in-law was rude and meddlesome, and used to having her son dance attendance upon her at any time she chose.

Geoffrey pushed his plate back and drained his teacup.

"I would assume the local gentry will be calling this morning. As I would rather take this time to tour the estate, I shall leave it to you to greet them, and arrange a convenient time for me to meet with them. Perhaps at this country party you would like to have," he announced. "Do not wait luncheon for me. I shall grab something from Cook. See you at dinner, Tiger's Breath." And with this, he departed with yet another of his pats on the head as if she were an obedient spaniel.

Rose pushed her plate abruptly back on the table in a foul humor. Well, he'd best beware or she might take to biting! She, too, expected half the county to call this morning, and had so looked forward to greeting acquaintances of her childhood with her handsome husband at her side. But, ever optimistic, she set about planning a romantic dinner and a seductive gown of forest green that was shamelessly low in the décolletage. Lady Lavitia could not possibly gain Shenstone today, unless she drove her horses to exhaustion between every changing station. So she had at least tonight to be alone with Geoffrey. And once she had her way with him, he would be the one sending his meddlesome mother packing back to London and following her about the house like a lovesick boy.

Chapter Eleven

The evening air in the garden was cool and pleasant as Rose strolled along the graveled path. A faint light was left of the dying day and a splendid moon threatened that would turn the glassy water of the lake to beaten silver. Rose tipped her face back to the sky and counted stars as they peeped shyly into view until there were too many to track. The silence of the countryside was dotted with the energetic sawing of crickets and the croaking serenade of frogs. Soft music drifted from somewhere in the house. Delaying the necessity of returning inside, she leaned against the garden wall and imagined the spacious lawns on sunny afternoons filled with laughing, romping children. Geoffrey's and her children. Many, many laughing, chubby, tumbling, children with locks of walnut brown.

Having not seen Geoffrey since breakfast, she was uncertain if he had quit his bedchambers as of yet. Wishing to share the delight of this evening stroll with him, and deciding it advantageous to rout him before he became mired in yet another project to keep his attention distracted, she detoured around the house to the drawing room terrace. Carefully holding her voluminous taffeta skirts away from the shrubs lining the walk, she mounted the wide stone steps to the terrace and passed before the brightly lit windows. A glance through the swept-back velvet draperies brought her to a stunned halt, and a grimace of painful distaste crossed her face.

Her handsome husband was standing before the stone hearth, deep in conversation with none other than Miss Sharon Bartley-Bacon. Rose pressed her fingers over her lips to still their trembling. So, it would seem those best left in London hadn't been left in London after all.

Diamonds sparkled on Sharon's white bosom and at her ears, and winked from the intricate embroidery of her high bodice. On a lesser beauty, the effect would have been ostentatious and vulgar, especially in a country setting, but Sharon looked magnificent. She was laughing at some vastly amusing remark Geoffrey had apparently made, and playfully reached up both hands to straighten his already immaculate cravat. Lady Lavitia reigned in a proprietary manner over the small group from a salmon pink satin divan, with a blatant expression of approval upon her face as she viewed the two together. Rose spun away in a rustle of stiff taffeta, balling her hands into fists.

"That old witch must have driven more than one team into the ground to make Shenstone in time for dinner," she muttered. "Well, Geoffrey most certainly is downstairs! And most certainly not distracted by paperwork now! He's also not one whit concerned that his *wife* has yet to appear."

Tears stung her eyes. She suddenly felt like a child playing at grown-up in her new forest green taffeta, donned such a short time ago with the idea of seduction in mind. She self-consciously tugged the plunging neckline higher over her breasts. These lords and ladies of the haute ton! They were all so sure of themselves and the rights given to them by society and title. So much so that they lost no time at all looking down their aristocratic noses at anyone they considered to be the least bit beneath them, she fumed.

With her confidence in shreds and her heart like lead, Rose trailed off the terrace and sought a small side door that would let her into the house without discovery. She had neither the desire, nor the courage, to join the unwanted company. So much for a sensual honeymoon and the rare chance to be alone with Geoffrey. So much for being allowed the time to instill love and devotion deep in her husband's heart. Her reluctant husband, she might add. He might state over and over how he despaired of Sharon's company, but he did not display such when his wife was not in attendance. No, he merely wanted respite from his mother's insistent demands. And he merely wanted relief from Sharon's presumptive claims on his title and fortune, not from her amorous attentions.

Rose slowly climbed the back stairs to her bedchamber. With each step her anger built. "Well, he can just have her, if he wants her. I have exactly what I want also. I have security of name, title and fortune. I have Shenstone back in my possession. And I have his word that this is an agreement between us and nothing more, with license to go our own ways. Well, two can play at these games. He has already said I may live my life as I find agreeable. And so I shall!" All this she declared to herself, without giving consideration that her husband might not take lightly to her proclaimed independence.

Without summoning Lettie, she slowly undressed, tossing the now offensive gown over a chair, and crawled into her bed with Willy. She lay in the dark, listening with anguish to the faraway sounds of laughter from the drawing room. Well into the night, and not yet having accomplished sleep, she heard the connecting door from the dressing room squeak open and gently click closed. The face of her husband seemed to swim above her in the weak light from his candle. Seeing her eyes open, he set the candlestick on the nightstand and confronted her in a tone that was laden with schoolmaster censure.

"Well, Rose," Geoffrey admonished grimly. "I think perhaps it was not altogether the most agreeable behavior for you to slight my mother by refusing to descend the staircase for dinner on the very night of her arrival."

Suddenly Rose's misery fled before a wave of suffocating fury. Fury at her own helplessness before the depth of her love for a man who so obviously wanted none of her. Fury for the audacity of his mother, who would even consider descending upon them at this time, and fury for her husband's total lack of concern that she, his wife, might have been hurt over such a thoughtless thing. "And am I not to feel slighted that my husband did not even notice that I was absent from the gathering? Or that my—*our* honeymoon has been invaded so soon after the pledging of our vows?"

Geoffrey looked shocked, then skeptical. "And *that* was reason enough for you to hide away in your room like a pouting child?"

Before she quite knew how it had happened, Rose had picked up the pillow from behind her head and flung it straight in the marquis's stunned face. "How dare you!" she screamed, beating at the coverlet with her fists and sending Willy scurrying beneath the bed to safety. "I will not be treated as if I am a misbehaving brat. I am *mistress* of my own house and I will invite houseguests only when I want houseguests! It shall not be the other way around."

Geoffrey tossed the pillow back on the bed and straightened his cravat. He stood calmly before his furious young wife, pondering her through hooded eyes. She was sitting up in bed looking so deliciously tossed and tumbled with her thin cambric-and-lace nightdress slipping down to bare one creamy, smooth shoulder and her liquid, black hair fanned sensuously over her shoulders. Her rapid breath drew his attention to her full breasts and his body quickened in response. His sense of outrage over her tantrum would not allow his baser instincts to register such tempting sights at present, but his thoughts would return to them again and again as he courted slumber in the coming sleepless night.

But now he merely remarked in that unforgivably remote tone of his, "Rose, you will be treated like a spoiled child as long as you insist upon acting like a spoiled child."

Never in her life had Rose been so livid. "You—you unfair cad..." she stormed, kicking the covers from her legs. Flying from her bed to her dressing table, she picked up the first thing of weight that reached her hand. Being a sizable bottle of scent, it flew across the room to smash against the door with satisfactory force.

Geoffrey effectively ducked the erringly aimed weapon and reached her in three forceful strides. He seized her wrists and twisted her arms behind her back as she would attempt to grasp anything within reach to fling at his head. Finally having subdued her, he stared down into her infuriated face. He felt such intense irritation at her uncontrolled display of childishness that he was at a loss as to express it, especially in the face of what he thought was a simple request for a reasonable explanation of her earlier behavior.

"Rose, I'm distressed to find that you have the temper of a tiger as well," he gritted through clinched teeth. "I feel it prudent to remind you that you are my wife now, and as *my wife,* you will learn to behave."

Rose could only glare up at her equally angry husband. Then her eyes narrowed and she appeared to calm somewhat. "As your wife, may I remind you that by your own wishes ours is a *mariage de convenance?* And as such, in accordance with your own rules, you are to live your life and allow me to live mine. Well, my lord husband, I am *distressed* to find that you force me to inform you that I choose to live my life without your brutal hands upon my person."

Geoffrey abruptly dropped his hands, but did not step back from her. He glared down at this surprising spitfire that was his wife and pondered a moment. This was not the way he had imagined marriage with her to be. She had always displayed such a sweet, pleasing temperament prior to the vows. Could there actually be a calculating, scheming Sharon-like personality buried beneath her impish demeanor? Had she also married him for title and position? And having accomplished that, was she now telling him she wanted nothing more to do with him, even to the point of insulting his mother? He was not at all pleased with that prospect, for he suddenly did not want that to be true. His jaw tensed and his brown eyes narrowed coldly. But there was truth in the fact that it had been his rules they had wed under, and if that was the way she wished it there was little he could do about it.

"As you say, my lady," he said stiffly. "And that is the way it will be. But do grant me liberty to give you adequate warning of one thing. Before you embark on this so-called life of yours, you may rest assured that I will never knowingly play the *mari complaisant,* and therefore you will conduct yourself as the Marquise of Hetherington at all times, which is to say, in a manner that I deem proper for my wife. I will not stand for scandal. Do I make myself clear?"

Rose could only glare up at him, her lavender eyes shooting golden sparks of varied emotions. This was not what she wanted from him at all, but pride would not allow her to back down. The picture of him smiling down into Sharon's simpering face was too fresh in her mind, and too painful in her heart. The very intimacy of the vixen daring to straighten his cravat in public was too telling. And that his mother would merely act as audience without one word of admonishment to her son for allowing such intimacies from one not his wife, spoke volumes on that lady's true feelings toward the little nobody her son had taken as wife.

Geoffrey, seeing no advantage to remaining in Rose's room unless he could lay hands upon her shoulders to shake her soundly, moved rigidly to the connecting dressing room door. Turning once more, he waved his hand over the heap of broken glass and pooling scent. "Call someone to clean up this mess," he ordered. "It smells like a Covent Garden brothel in here."

Rose, suddenly alert, glared at him. "And my lord marquis," she demanded coldly. "Just what do you know of Covent Garden brothels?"

Geoffrey stood rigid beside the six-panel door, scowling at her from his great height, looking every inch a nobleman, and icily replied in that damned withdrawn, absolutely correct, tone of his, "I assure you, it was nothing more than an expression. But I agree it should not be used in front of a lady. Please forgive my brashness, my lady. And now I shall bid you good-night."

Rose jumped as he closed the dressing room door behind him far more firmly than was necessary. She stared after him with her teeth worrying her lower lip. His countenance had been so stern, his tone so cold, that it was incontestable, should she dare try the handle, the six-panel door would have been securely locked, and probably double-bolted from the other side. Considering the amount of irritation Geoffrey was clearly feeling toward her at this very moment, it was also quite possible a weighty chest of drawers had been shoved against it.

And that was a fitting portrayal of her husband. Aloof and locked away, distant and unapproachable. She sobbed gently in self-pity. She was so misunderstood. And she could think of nothing to do to make things right. Then, giving in to her insurmountable unhappiness, she flung herself full-length upon the bed to soak her pillow with tears.

Within a fortnight, 1 Leicester Street saw the marquis and his diminutive young marquise back in residence. Geoffrey had readily complied with his wife's request to immediately return to London and the season, and had escorted a strained and stilted trio of ladies back to London in a chaise of enclosed tension. It was enough to wear upon the vitality, and stress the tempers, of at least three of the four estranged occupants. Sharon, although she admirably covered her smug glee with an expression of boredom, was well pleased with her part in estranging the newlyweds. An estrangement she would take full credit for with Sewell, even though the deed had apparently been accomplished before she'd even set eyes upon the new marquise.

Once reestablished at 1 Leicester Street, Geoffrey, infinitely weary of the strained silence and stilted glances between the three ladies in his life, decreed it necessary that the dowager marquise, accompanied by her young houseguest, remove themselves from the residence forthwith. This was done with great flourish and fanfare on the part of his mother, and she and Sharon Bartley-Bacon retired to a town house on Grosvenor Square. While their new abode, an appendage to one of the numerous lesser titles Lord Wyse sported, was opulent and finely appointed, 1 Leicester Street remained the jewel of the marquis's households and therefore was deemed by Lady Lavitia to be hardly appropriate for its new mistress with her rather common

ineage. Being painfully aware of this widely held opinion
among those with whom she must now associate, Rose immediately set about establishing herself as the reigning mistress. Although firmly beneath the iron rule of Humphrey,
the servants were quick, deferential and polite, and Rose
eventually left the army of staff to run things themselves
since they seemed able to cope efficiently whether she was
attentive to them or not.

The ton watched with some delight as the marquis resumed his previous life-style, seeming neither encumbered
nor inconvenienced by the addition of a wife to his household. It was duly noted, however, with great interest that
he did appear to scrutinize her actions rather closely as she
flitted from one gay, social engagement to another. And he
did frown rather darkly as she whirled from one gallant to
another across innumerable ballrooms, with seemingly
reckless abandon. Then, contrary to his customarily me-
thodical agenda for this time of year, he set about planning
an out-of-season expedition to Ireland, supposedly to view
his estates and partake of the hunting. And, as he announced to Milty at a later date, although he had anticipated
Rose would accompany him without question, his astonishment was plainly registered on his face when she offhand-
edly announced her intention of remaining in England…alone.

"I am afraid I did not understand you correctly. You
intend to remain here?" Geoffrey had quizzed, clinching
the sharpened quill tightly in his fingers. Studying her down
the length of the library, he regretfully saw little left of the
dash-about child with a disarming zest for living whom he
had plucked from the poorhouse. Days spent shopping in
the company of sophisticated acquaintances and nights
spent in one frenzied entertainment or another had applied

a town bronze that was as finely varnished as that of any
seasoned matron on the scene.

"Yes, I intend to remain here," Rose answered. She
smoothed her lemon-colored kid gloves over her fingers
one by one, as if impatient to be off to her next planned
engagement.

"And what is this, Tiger's Breath? Another act of defi
ance?" Geoffrey challenged. He was at a loss for othe
words that might bring forth the tomboyish, tree-climbing
hoyden from beneath the cover of this stylish, aloof, ye
dashing young matron.

"Defiance? Of course not. It is simply not convenient t
me to traipse about the wilds of Ireland at this time," Ros
retaliated, placing both hands on the head of her parasol
She fought the urge to rail at his head. He would neglec
her all this time, sometimes not even speaking to her fo
days on end, then tyrannically assume she would accom
pany him on an extended trek, without even the courtes
of being consulted beforehand? "I did not imagine it woul
necessitate reminding you once again, my lord, that our—"
she waved one hand elegantly through the air as if search
ing for a word "—*union* is a *mariage de convenance.*
have quite effectively established my life around a circl
of friends who are zealously demanding of my time. I
would take easily months to free my schedule to accom
modate a separation the length you are proposing." Agai
she paused to level a straightforward stare in his direction
"Even if I should desire to accompany you in the firs
place."

The quill in Geoffrey's hands snapped in two with a lou
crack. He jerked in surprise, then rose from the desk t
stalk to the hearth. He hurled the two halves in the genera
direction of the fireplace in derision, before directing hi
speculative gaze upon her for the longest time. "As yo

wish, my lady," he finally conceded. He sketched a tight bow and turned his back on her in as dismissing a posture as he could muster. He heard the swish of her skirts as she turned to leave the library, shutting the door behind her quietly.

Resting an arm on the mantel, Geoffrey stared down into the flames. He did not have to turn to know that she was no longer in the room for, aside from a hint of her floral scent, the very air had lost most of its warmth. He felt hurt and angry, but was forced to accede to her statements as the terms she so aptly reminded him of had indeed been his own blasted covenant. As she had not made a gossip morsel of herself with outrageous behavior, he had no complaints to lay at her feet. She had simply forged a life for herself, and there was nothing he could do at this time to remedy a situation that he found to be completely dissatisfying in some obscure manner that he had yet to identify to himself.

So, Lord Wyse, the Marquis of Hetherington, packed himself into the traveling coach and departed 1 Leicester Street, totally without awareness that Lady Wyse, the Marquise of Hetherington, had thrown herself facedown upon her bed as soon as the coach had turned the corner and wept herself to exhaustion and finally to sleep.

Not a fortnight had passed with the marquis absent from home and hearth than Mr. Elmo Sewell, having been stripped of both title and estates, made an abrupt call on Sharon Bartley-Bacon at the Grosvenor Square town house. She rudely, and perhaps unwisely, kept him pacing the drawing room for an inordinate length of time, then sauntered down the stairs in a leisurely, confident manner. She saw no reason to be solicitous of Mr. Elmo Sewell's feelings any longer. But, as nonchalant as she might appear, her heart skipped a beat upon entering the drawing room

and observing the object of her loathing pacing about like
a caged animal, obviously seething with impatience and
rage.

Becoming aware of her presence, he whirled and snarled
"There you are at last! Listen, we must advance our cause
while the marquis is absent," he gritted without greeting
or preamble. Snatching her arm, he forcibly shoved her into
a chair before the cold fireplace.

"We?" queried Sharon faintly, rubbing the mark she
could only imagine now marred her arm. She refused to
consider this misgotten alliance as a partnership. While it
was true she wished for Rose to be set down sharply, and
as publicly as possible, she did not have much more to gain
from any revenge Mr. Sewell might exact. Only Rose's
untimely demise would place Geoffrey, Lord Wyse, on the
petticoat line again, and even with that, she very much
doubted she could bring him up to the mark. He simply did
not like her, as much as it pained her to admit it. And
Rose's disappearance from the scene would do nothing to
alter Elmo's situation, as the marquis held legal claim to
Shenstone and the title in either event.

"All right, not *we* but you alone," he said with a sneer,
bending uncomfortably close to her. "Since Rose refuses
to even receive me, it must be left to *you*."

"Me!" Sharon squeaked, leaning as far as possible from
him. "I can do nothing!"

"Just listen and listen closely. There is a Frenchman I
know, Henri Bonheur, not of noble birth, but sufficiently
charming and with the right looks to carry off the show I
have planned. He is low both on blunt and moral fiber,
which readily places him at our disposal. We will say he
is related in some manner to that dressmaker, LaFee Howard, that Rose was so taken with. That will assure a speedy,
congenial reception for him."

Sharon snorted in disgust and flipped her skirts into a more perfect arrangement, while Elmo resumed his pacing. "Bah! That is a singularly stupid idea! As Madame Howard's relative, he would be—well, just too common. While that would not stop Rosie from throwing hugs and kisses his way, polite society would never receive him."

"Precisely the point, you nit. What could be more appropriate for our purposes? The Marquise of Hetherington taking up with a common Frenchman of obscure origin? Lord Wyse will be livid at the insult. We must supply Bonheur with the necessary funds to keep up the demeanor of affluence. He will require attire befitting his station—a carriage, perhaps a mount—as there must not be too many obstacles to their appearing in society together."

"I haven't that kind of blunt!" Sharon exclaimed in horror at the amount he was apparently requesting of her. "Besides, I do not understand—"

"You never do, you peahen—" he paused to expel an exasperated sigh "—Monsieur Bonheur shall lay siege to Rose's little heart. She is young, totally inexperienced in the way of the world. There is no way she could have established a *tendre* for the marquis, as they are apart too much of the time." He spun to advance upon Sharon menacingly. "You are absolutely certain there's been little contact between them since their return from Shenstone?"

"For the last time, *yes,* I am quite certain!" hissed Sharon. "His mother tells me they are estranged. That should be apparent, even to you, when Rose refused to accompany him to Ireland. Besides, what have I to do with this Frenchman? My part is simply to flirt with Lord Wyse, which I cannot do at the present. So you see, there is nothing more I can, or *will,* do for you."

"Don't you see? Rose will meet him through *your* introduction. And you will do it promptly—and nicely, or I will make you regret the unfortunate day you were born. Just introduce him. He will advance the play from there. But be careful! Lord Philpotts is back in London and dancing avid attendance upon Rose. I do not want him suspicious. He may look a buffoon, but I do not think we should underestimate him."

Sharon turned slightly and sniffed. She was through with this mess, and she was through with this upstart. "No, I think not," she stated.

Her calm refusal to do as he directed brought the agitated Elmo's control to an end. "You nitwit female!" he roared, snatching her shoulders to shake her roughly. "You damn well *will* do as I say!"

Sharon shoved him away from her and leaped to her feet. "No! I do not think I *shall* do what you say. I do not like it when you call me names, and I will not allow any man, especially you, to lay rough hands upon my person. Besides, I have nothing else to gain with this." Sharon pouted, turning her back and moving away from him, only to round on him with a loud, shrill voice, cruelly emphasizing his lack of title. "And now, *Mr.* Sewell, I think you should leave. Oh, my God! What are you doing?"

Elmo, desperate to bring the situation back under his control, had drawn a pistol from the pocket of his jacket and was pointing it straight at her heart. "I do not think just yet. Drop your bodice."

"I will do no such thing!" Sharon shrieked, turning white with anger and fear. She backed away from him as if the distance would make her safer.

But he followed her, careful step by careful step. And by way of an answer, he pressed the pistol firmly between her eyes. She shuddered at the hard, cold feel of it, and could not help but turn her eyes inward to look down the long, dull, gray barrel. Tears of fright began to spill over her cheeks, and she drew a shuddering breath. "No, please!" she cried, still attempting to back away from the pistol. "Why are you doing this? Haven't I helped you thus far?"

"But it should be obvious to even you, flea brain that you are, that it is not yet enough. I am homeless. I am nameless. I am penniless. And all because of that ass, Hetherington. He has thousands and thousands, and all I want is hundreds. But do you think he would let me keep just the small portion that is Shenstone? Hell, no! Well, by God, now I will take it! I repeat, drop your bodice or I shall rip it from you."

Sharon looked into his pitiless, pale eyes and realized he would do as he threatened, or far worse. Turning her back to him, she tugged at the fastenings of her robin's-egg blue muslin with trembling fingers. Easing it from her shoulders, she let it drop to her waist. "What are you going to do to me?" she pleaded.

"And that other too," he demanded, waving the pistol to indicate her chemise. "I would have you bare before me. And turn around!"

The chemise followed and Sharon modestly folded her arms over her bare bosom. Turning slowly, she kept her head down in humiliation. It had never been her intention that the first man to lay eyes upon her bare body would be a murderer and a common thief.

His cold eyes raked over her body. "Ah, just as I had hoped. A birthmark! And a very distinctive mole there and there." The pistol, cold and lethal, touched each mark in turn, causing her to flinch away. "Now listen to me and listen well. You will do as I instruct or I shall tell the world that you and I have shared the most intimate of acts. I will be able to describe each one of these little marks—" again the pistol marked off the spots on her tender skin "—and your mother will not be able to deny their existence. You will be labeled the Haymarket ware I know you to be. There will never be a title in your future if my tale gets out. Now dress yourself!''

Sharon swung away from him and tugged her chemise up to cover herself before he changed his mind and inflicted physical affronts upon her person. Elmo Sewell walked around the shivering girl and surveyed her from head to toe in disgust. Then he shook his head and laughed rudely as he slammed out the door. Sharon's face burned with humiliation and fury. She slowly fastened her bodice with trembling, icy fingers.

"Damn you, Rose Lambe! Had you just lived out your miserable little life in that dressmaker's shop, I would be the Marquise of Hetherington by now,'' she whispered. Tears of helplessness spilled over her eyes and streaked down her cheeks. She daubed at them with her hankie and made a solemn oath to herself in the fireplace mirror. "I swear, once I am finished with you, *Rosie,* I will marry the next man of wealth that bends a knee to me. Then, with his money, I shall have Elmo Sewell eradicated from the face of this earth in the most painful manner possible.''

Chapter Twelve

The opera had already begun when Rose entered her box. Spreading her taffeta skirts about her, she sank into the tufted chair with a sigh. Perfectly contented that she had excluded herself from the normal rowdy company that crowded her life, she sought to soothe herself peacefully in the swell of the music. Milty, serving as escort, appeared to sense her pensive mood, and sat quietly at her side. It pained him greatly to see her little face sad and the rosy mouth without its smile. While he was not a man much given to the entanglements of the heart, he could plainly see what apparently Geoffrey was blinded to. The dear girl was hopelessly in love with her husband, and pining over his inattention. And, unless he was missing his mark, Geoffrey was in love with her too, would he but open his eyes enough to recognize it.

What had, at first anyway, seemed merely a romp, watching the marquis behaving with such frivolity that even those closest to him were stunned, was now a sad state of affairs for all. Milty wasn't clear what had transpired between the two to bring about such a state of misunderstanding, but he would have wagered his new swansdown vest that a misunderstanding was all that kept them apart. And, meddlesome though he might appear, he intended to clear the air in as straightforward a manner as possible as soon as Geoffrey returned from his ill-planned trek to Ireland. Hunting, indeed! At this time of year? Contumacious dolt was most probably shivering before some drafty, ill-vented hearth right at this moment, in miserable discomfort, too stubborn to return to the solace of 1 Leicester Street, confront his wife and straighten out the muddle his life had become since his marriage.

The thing that worried Milty most was that little Rose might transfer her affections to one of the innumerable gallants beating the bushes to her door on a nonstop basis. He turned his gaze from the entertainment to regard Rose and her stunning gown of midnight blue heavily laden with sparkles. Never had there been such a popular girl, especially one that was so unaware of the stir she was causing. In fact, it elevated his own standing in society to be seen so often as her escort. And in gratitude for that as well, he would gladly accept it as his mission to see that she remained unfocused on another until Geoffrey had the good sense to return to his own hearth and home, and have a care for his wife's happiness.

When the houselights went up, announcing an intermission, Rose was still under the music's spell and focused dimly on the people milling about below.

"I say, Rose, shall we pop out into the mix and see what's what this evening?" Milty offered eagerly. It pained him to see her so withdrawn from her admirers. She was truly a sad little muffin tonight.

"Oh, Milty—" she turned large, pleading eyes toward him "—would you mind terribly if I just sat here? I truly am not in the mood for company tonight. Probably should have stayed before my own fires, but..."

"Stay at home! Never!" Milty exclaimed at the thought

of her languishing at home. "Hardly the thing, old girl, to not be seen about. But I, too, have had those days when it is, er, difficult to be with people. What's say I fetch us a libation, and you just stay tucked in here? I shall return in a trice and tell you all about everyone I bump into on the way."

Rose laughed at his absurdities, which seemed to please him no end. "That would be excellent. And, Milty—" she placed a hand on his arm with great affection "—thank you for being just the most bang-up friend a girl ever had."

All smiles and flusters, Milty stumbled his way out of the box. Rose shook her head at his clumsiness. She had no doubt he would bump into a great many people, and in the literal sense of the word. If only she could tempt him out of his absurd high heels and what she chose to call war paint. He truly was a remarkably attractive gent and would be swarmed with ladies if only he would present himself better.

"Lady Wyse, I see you are deserted. Has your escort fled? Or merely been misplaced in all the crush?"

Sharon Bartley-Bacon's unwelcome voice tapped into her consciousness. If she had been asked for the least desirable company ever, this was the one she would have named. She turned to see her rival taking over the chair so recently vacated by Lord Philpotts. Rose's eyebrow lifted to see that the simpering blonde was escorted by a most admirable man, and someone not already of her acquaintance, when she would have sworn to know everyone who was someone in society.

"No, Miss Bartley-Bacon, I am alone by choice—the music being more important to me than conversation on this night," Rose announced. With this rather broad hint, she had hoped Sharon would move on to stick verbal pins into some other unfortunate, but Sharon merely settled herself more comfortably as if she meant to remain the entire intermission. Rose swallowed a rather large sigh of resignation.

"May I introduce Monsieur Henri Bonheur to you. I believe he has, in some way, an acquaintanceship of your friend from the dress shop. Once I heard that, I just knew you would wish to make his acquaintance also." Flipping her fan open to act as a shield, she leaned forward to whisper confidentially to Rose, "I fear he has not yet received the tragic announcement of Madame Howard's demise, and felt it was not the sort of thing one should heard from a stranger."

Rose stared at Sharon but could see no prank or apparent mischief in the beautiful face. Could this be true? Turning fully to acknowledge the gentleman, she looked up into the most incredibly blue eyes she had ever encountered. The white, thin face was almost effeminately smooth with thick, black lashes shadowing the tender flesh beneath his eyes. "Monsieur Bonheur, I am thrilled to make your acquaintance. Pray be seated. Is it true you are connected to my dear LaFee?"

Henri Bonheur flipped coattails elegantly out of his way and seated himself beneath the wall sconce, where he believed the candlelight upon his oiled blue-black locks was to advantage. "Yes, it is so. There is a family connection on my mama's side. I have been sent by my mama to persuade LaFee to retire home to the country of her birth."

"Oh dear! Then it is so, you truly do not know," Rose uttered, with a sad shake of her head. "I am so sorry, Monsieur Bonheur, but—" she impulsively placed her hand over his "—dear LaFee passed to heaven…pneumonia, you see, quite early in the year."

"Oh, that is most distressing," Henri said. Tearing large eyes from her, he hung his head beneath a display of apparent grief, and placed his hand over hers in a tight grip of overwrought feelings.

Rose leaned forward in concern for the man's obvious distress. The French were said to feel things much more deeply than the staid English. Having no knowledge of the French other than LaFee—and she had been decidedly excitable—Rose could only respond sympathetically. "She did not suffer overly long. And I was there with her until the end. I am so very, very sorry, *monsieur*. She was a dear, dear friend to me."

Henri raised tear-filled eyes to hers. "I do not weep for myself, *madame*. I was very small when she went away. But I weep for my mama, you see. I weep for her despair when I must tell her LaFee has perished and been buried in foreign soil where she may never place flowers upon her grave."

"Ah, yes," Rose murmured. "So tragic."

Sharon raised eyes heavenward at such a sad sight. She truly did not know which to laugh at first, Henri's horrid playacting or Rose's gullibility. She was so bored, and now, when all society was gaily strolling the halls and lobbies, she must sit and pretend sympathy for a damn dead dressmaker. She could absolutely kill. And at this moment, it made no difference whom—Elmo, Rose or Geoffrey. To her own mind, all three were equally responsible for her unhappiness.

"You have such kindness for a grieving stranger, madame," Henri urged, allowing pain to flow into his voice and into his entreating eyes. "And I must request of you a large imposition. I must know everything of our LaFee. For mama's sake, you see." The dimming of the lights for the second act halted the confidences he requested. "May I beg permission to call upon you, *madame?*"

"Of course, Monsieur Bonheur. I shall be most pleased to speak of LaFee with you," Rose rushed to reassure him.

"Oh, thank you. Thank you, kind *madame*."

Milty blundered back into the box, spilling a goodly amount of the iced champagne he carried for Rose over the silver satin of his knee breeches when he came up short to see his seat occupied. Rose hurriedly, and in a stage whisper, made introductions all around. Monsieur Bonheur rose slightly and sketched a bow before resuming his seat slightly behind Rose. Sharon, having appropriated Lord Philpotts's seat beside the rail, forced poor Milty to sink into the back row where he gulped the champagne intended for Rose, and frowned over the fact that this Frenchie quite openly held Geoffrey's wife's hand.

The young man's gratitude was overwhelming and his grief too plainly written on his handsome face for Rose to take exception to the fact that he had yet to release her hand. But she was no longer able to concentrate on the music. She was aware of a new and powerful personality beside her. She was also aware that Monsieur Bonheur was studying her quite closely in the semidarkness. And sometime during the second act, the music, his admiration and the warmth of his flesh against hers became utterly delightful to her lonely soul.

When the opera ended and the lights again were raised, Rose gently withdrew her hand. Henri smiled deeply at her and gave a small bow, establishing a subtle atmosphere of intimacy between them with his laughing eyes and his smile, which illuminated his face with charm. Rose could not resist returning his smile and she facilely realized that if she weren't so completely in love with Geoffrey, her heart would be in danger with this man.

Rose covered her confusion at this discovery with the activity of allowing a scowling Lord Philpotts to assist her with her cloak and dissuading Sharon from accompanying them on a round of the more popular haunts for the after-theater crowd. Then it was Milty's turn to persuade a prettily pleading Sharon that he, too, must decline her invitation to join the crowds, and under absolutely no terms could he be compelled to neglect his duty as escort to Lady Wyse to do so, even if Monsieur Bonheur did so *gallantly* offer to escort the marquise safely back to 1 Leicester Street.

"Oh, Lord Philpotts, you are so—" Sharon leaned closer to lay a hand on his broad chest and lift melting eyes to him, taking flagrant advantage of him as he became flustered over her fluttering eyelashes "—trustworthy. That does make a girl feel so safe and protected."

"Well, now—" He stepped back, tripped over a chair and only managed to right himself with a great show of dancing about. Once steady again, he turned a scowl upon Henri Bonheur, who made no effort to conceal the grin of amusement at the viscount's expense.

Sharon watched the flush creep from beneath the man's stiff neckcloth and advance to his cheeks. While she had the viscount's acquaintance, she had never given him more than a second of her notice. But now, considering the alarming manner in which he was glaring upon poor Monsieur Bonheur, she thought it best to hasten their exit before he demonstrated the extreme exception he was apparently feeling. Besides, Elmo had been most specific on the fact that Lord Philpotts was to be avoided, and here she was in a face-to-face confrontation. Drat and double drat! He would most certainly take her to task over it at first opportunity.

Rose smiled encouragingly at the great bear of a man and gestured toward Henri. "Lord Philpotts, Monsieur Henri Bonheur is newly arrived from France. He is a distant relation to my benefactor, Madame Howard."

"My lord." Henri bowed as gallantly as the limited space in the theater box allowed, with one lace-adorned hand elegantly pressed to his chest.

"Monsieur." Milty returned the honor with a great deal less grace. "And now if you are ready, Lady Wyse? I just know that *your husband*—" he emphasized the last word, raising a questioning eyebrow at Rose, then redirected his gaze, which would lapse into a dreadful scowl again, at Henri "—would have my head if I allow you to stand about in this drafty place. Could catch a chill, don't you know."

"Ah well, if you can't be tempted…" Sharon concluded, edging toward the doorway, suddenly anxious to be gone. "We shall make our goodbyes."

"*Au revoir,* my perfect lady," Henri said, bowing over her hand and placing a lingering kiss upon her wrist. "With your permission, I shall call in the afternoon on the morrow?"

Rose blushed prettily and nodded. Lord Philpotts's frown deepened.

Upon their arrival at 1 Leicester Street, it took a stern refusal on Rose's part to make her escape from his dubious protection. Despite her repeated reassurances, he seemed determined to secure her safely behind closed doors and post a guard against imagined dangers of a French origin. Waving him off, Rose finally tripped lightly into the mansion and leaned back against the door as it was closed on his sputtered reprimands. She ignored the tilted eyebrow from Humphrey, and made her way up the staircase deep in thought.

The evening had proved more diverting than she had hoped. Who was to say, it might be pleasant to have a charming escort dancing attendance upon her. He was more than presentable, and had the added attraction of being related, no matter how distantly, to someone who had been very dear to her. He represented family in some small way. And as family, Henri quite possibly could be relied upon to behave as a gentleman in all circumstances...and she was almost positive that was what she wanted of him.

Rose sighed as Lettie began removing her evening clothes. She might as well admit it. She was lonely, and more times than could be counted she wished, with a longing that was a physical ache, that she had accompanied Geoffrey. But then the memories of his coldness, his neglect, his seeming unconcern for what she did and whom she did it with, were too painful. She slid beneath the covers with only her cat for company and snuggled down. No, she would never plead for Geoffrey's love, even though she could not help but wonder if he thought of her at all.

Geoffrey did indeed think of her. Sitting a chilly distance from the smoking fire of a rather second-rate traveling inn, he prodded his dinner of cooling mutton and boiled potatoes around in their congealing gravy with little appetite. He was engaged in a serious conversation with himself, determined to reach a workable solution for winning the affection and devotion of none other than his very own wife. Another hard fortnight of travel and he would be home, and home was where he wanted to be.

He freely admitted to having been confused and more than a little disappointed when Rose had declined to accompany him on this journey. In fact, her outright refusal had sparked no small import of mounting irritation, and that was an uncomfortable pathos more and more common to his personality these days. Now, in a frame of mind greatly gentled after his long absence from her, he realized that he had never actually courted his wife. She had simply taken him by surprise...overwhelmed him with her outrageousness, enthralled him with her exuberance for life, and unconsciously seduced him with her soft sweetness…and then suddenly, she was his wife.

He had thought he knew her intimately, but in view of the changes she had wrought in herself during his inattentiveness, he no longer could say what did or did not please her. Exasperated with himself and the pickle he found he had inadvertently created, Geoffrey turned from the past and attempted to lay a course for the future. He was not inexperienced with the tempting of the fair gender, but even courting Rose did not necessarily signify that she would readily fall into his arms, especially as this whole *mariage de convenance* had been his idea from the beginning. That had been a vastly stupid idea on his part. Totally out of reason if he'd only taken the time to properly view Rose. True enough, he'd readily recognized his affection for her, and had more than once denied his desire for her out of consideration of her youth and inexperience, but blast it all, she might have been of tender age, but not unwilling or frightened. The image of her sitting upon the edge of his desk, inviting his kisses, flitted uncomfortably through his mind. Yes, the *mariage de convenance* had been a stupid idea, and a stupid idea he wished to modify immediately.

Damn the whole thing to hell! He wanted his wife to be his wife! He would begin afresh as soon as he reached 1 Leicester Street. She would be wooed as no other ever had been. The thought that her affections might have been turned elsewhere during his absence plagued him. For hadn't he practically given her *carte blanche* to look for love anywhere but in his direction? And one so tender in the heart and with so little experience, might fall in love most unsuitably. He had no illusions of the numbers of men with little morals who would find an inexperienced, shy miss such as his Rose a tasty morsel indeed.

* * *

It was as well for his peace of mind that Geoffrey was blessedly unaware that a particular man was indeed abroad in society, and busily plotting a rather harsh downfall for his wife. During that fortnight, Henri Bonheur became a familiar fixture before the drawing room fire at 1 Leicester Street. A fast friendship developed between Rose and the young Frenchman that was falsely filled with confidences and shared feelings of loss over LaFee, a woman Henri had never even met. It was a friendship greatly frowned upon by Lord Philpotts, who made his presence known at every possible opportunity in the role of diligent watchdog, much to Rose's amusement and Henri's disgust.

Today, having repeatedly explained to Elmo Sewell that the plan to take Lady Rose Wyse for her final drive in the country had gone awry by that lady's having pleaded a prior engagement, Henri settled back before the meager fire in that man's suite of cheaply rented rooms, to sip his cognac with eyes closed in pleasure. Henri was such a one to enjoy to the fullest extent any pleasure to be found in drink, music, food and women.

"Already engaged! And you could not summon enough charm to overshadow a damned afternoon musical at Standiford?" Elmo Sewell loudly challenged. There was a decided air of tension about the man that bordered on desperation. Possibly generated by his sense of time growing short in which to dispatch the bothersome marquise before the return of her husband and the imminent threat of eviction from his present abode. He paced the length of the room, muttering in agitation. His brow furrowed deeply, then suddenly cleared. "I have it! I shall send the marquise a note supposedly from Standiford canceling the afternoon's amusement. You will appear upon her stoop at exactly the right moment with a renewed offer to drive. After all, it would be a shame to waste such a remarkable afternoon of sunny weather by staying indoors, now wouldn't it?''

Henri stretched lazily in his chair and surveyed Elmo Sewell with distaste. ''I do not for the life of me understand why you plot against such a sweet lady as the little Rose. She is harmless enough. Totally guileless, although—'' he wisely switched directions as Elmo Sewell rounded on him in a fury ''—it is no concern of mine and I do so appreciate the generosities in which you have conducted your plot, but my curiosity, my dear sir, gets the best of me sometimes.''

Elmo advanced to snatch the glass of amber liquid from Henri's hand. Glaring at him with a dangerous snarl to his mouth, he gritted through clinched teeth, ''In that, you are correct. My affairs are no concern of yours. Do as you are instructed or crawl back beneath your rock to end your life on cheap swill for all I care.''

''No, no! It shall be as you wish,'' Henri quickly amended. ''Pen your note and I shall be off to carry out the dear little marquise's destruction. It is just a pity it is her and not the other. Now, *that* one I would enjoy taking down a peg. Our Miss Bartley-Bacon is not a woman of pleasant nature.''

Elmo Sewell sat down at the unsteady desk to take pen in hand. Carefully wording the note, he signed it M. Janna Standiford with hopefully a feminine flourish. Searching frantically through his desk, he pulled forth a seal reasonably close to the Standiford crest and stamped it down upon the hot wax as if it were the Marquis of Hetherington's very neck. Holding it aloft, he was fairly certain that Rose even if she did examine the seal closely, would not recognize the fraud.

Satisfied with the dispatch of the note of cancellation and

timing its arrival, Henri doffed his hat without another word of protest and strolled off to reluctantly carry out what he considered the final step to their plot.

Elmo Sewell continued to pace up and down and back and forth. His plan must succeed. With the assurance of no heirs to the title, he would be granted the time he required to plot the death of the marquis—leaving the title of Earl of Shenstone, and possibly much more, his for the taking. The idea of a lion's share of the marquis's holdings coming his way was enough to create delirium in the man's brain.

How he had overlooked someone as prominent as the Marquis of Hetherington was beyond him. He had studied the family tree closely for years, watching as one successor after another dropped off the line, some with more assistance than others. Until finally came the day he could step forward to claim the identity of the last. No one had questioned him or his credentials—until the marquis had been so unfortunate as to champion Rose, and make her his wife.

Again Elmo plucked the crest from the desk to study it closely. The match was near perfect, and he was not worried that Rose would suspect foul play...even if she bothered to look closely.

And she did not. Rose merely read the note and took its contents as fact. But, upon his arrival at 1 Leicester Street, Henri found an unexpected and vastly unwelcome obstacle to his plan. Lord Milton Philpotts, larger than life, was installed before the drawing room fireplace in advance of him, and voicing amazement at the note of cancellation for Lady Standiford's musical afternoon Rose held in her hand, when Monsieur Bonheur was announced.

"I do believe I saw Lady Standiford last night," Milty protested. "Surely she would have said something to me if the amusement had been canceled by necessity. I say, Rose, if I may just have a look at the note...."

Henri neatly intercepted the note as Rose willingly handed it over. "Ah, you, my rather large friend, are only jealous, as I have arrived at the most opportune moment, and shall snatch the lady's attendance for the afternoon drive to Bellingham. You see, the cancellation was simply the heavens above taking mercy upon me and my sad, sad plight, for I was desolate at the loss of the lady's company for such an afternoon of unexpectedly clement weather."

Rose laughed at his sally, but Milty huffed and puffed in irritation. As he still held out his hand for the note, he clicked his fingers in demand. Even faced with a black scowl on Lord Philpotts's brow, Henri merely smiled an infuriating smile and firmly crumpled the note in his slender fingers and tossed it toward the fire. Turning to Rose, he spread his hands beseechingly. "Come, my lady, the sun is shining and we are wasting time. And I am the most correct of escorts. I have procured an open carriage so you do not even need your groom. Quickly now," he instructed in a teasing tone, "before your errant husband returns home to gloat over his sad little wife languishing at home on such an afternoon, pining away from missing him."

This was exactly the right prod to send Rose flying up the stairs to change. Drawing on the new sapphire blue driving costume, with an ingenious display of overskirts in layers, she set her pouty mouth into a firm line of determination. It was not that she was so desirous of a drive in the country, but never would she want Geoffrey to think she pined for a husband who could not be bothered to give her the time of day...or even send a note of courtesy during such an extended absence.

Left alone with the disagreeable viscount, Henri leaned back at his ease. He did not deign to make conversation

with one of Lord Philpotts's overdressed foppish attitude
and ineffectual huffing. He slid hooded eyes over the viscount's strawberry wine waistcoat. Although if asked, he
would have admitted to an admiration for the man's tailor,
but he refused to grant the viscount any credit, other than
an open, well-heeled pocket, for the excellence of his attire.
As others in society had mistakenly done, he was too busy
feeling disdain for the foppishly dressed Lord Philpotts to
notice the unusually shrewd and speculative look in his
companion's eyes.

Milty pursed his lips in a disapproving line. He did not
like the fact that Rose was to venture out driving, without
a groom no less, in the company of a fellow like this one.
He couldn't be sure, of course, but he truly did not think
Geoffrey would approve. This thought rapidly solidified
into a certainty in his mind, and drove him to demand,
"And just where are you taking the marquise?"

Henri pointedly ignored him, giving his manicure a thorough examination. Milty was just opening his mouth to
make his demand again, much more forcefully this time,
when Rose dashed back into the room. Henri cast him another mocking glance, then gallantly offered Rose his arm.
Poor Milty was left with no alternative than to bend over
her hand and wish her a pleasant outing.

Some minutes later, the Marquis of Hetherington strode
forcefully into the decorous entry hall of 1 Leicester Street.
He acknowledged Humphrey's welcome and relinquished
his hat and gloves. "Is her ladyship at home?"

Humphrey shook his head in obvious disapproval. "No,
my lord. Her ladyship has gone driving. I believe the gentleman mentioned Bellingham as the destination."

Geoffrey frowned inwardly. He had actually hoped to
surprise Rose with his unexpected return, but now he felt

a fool for not having notified her of his imminent arrival. "Who is escorting her?" he asked, striding across the hall.

"Humph! Monsieur Bonheur, my lord." The majordomo almost sneered.

"Never heard of him," Geoffrey stated flatly. Had he been so remiss in this marriage that his wife gallivanted about the countryside with men not of his acquaintance? He turned toward the library, planning to sort through his correspondence and wait.

Humphrey quickly forestalled him. "My lord, Lord Philpotts is in the drawing room."

"Milty's here? That's strange," Geoffrey muttered, changing directions. Good grief, whatever could all this mean? He strode quickly into the drawing room to find his friend down upon his knees in front of the fireplace, armed with a poker and muttering beneath his breath.

"Whatever are you doing, Milty?"

"Oh, Geoffrey! Thank God!" Milty exclaimed, jerking upright. "I am so glad you are home at last. Wives are just the damnest nuisances. Take ever so much looking after. And this one's not even mine!" He returned his attention to the fire again and resumed his poking through the ashes. "Not that I'd ever want one after seeing the attention they require. Not that your lady is the worst of the lot, of course, or so I've been told...."

"Milty, you are not making yourself clear!" Geoffrey threw up his hands and grinned down upon his friend. "Why ever are you down on your knees, raking through the ashes in my drawing room? And with Rose off driving? Is she expected back momentarily? You are, perhaps, awaiting her return?"

"I was worried, you see," admitted Milty, hefting his bulk to his feet and attempting to straighten out a singed piece of paper. "I was wondering about our Rose going off with that suspicious Frenchie and—"

"Suspicious Frenchie!" Geoffrey exclaimed, his attention suddenly riveted upon Lord Philpotts's obvious concern.

"Yes, Monsieur Bonheur. Don't think you've had the pleasure, if pleasure could be stated," Milty said, turning the paper this way and that to catch more light. "No, actually think he came on the scene after you left...."

"Damn! Explain yourself, man." Geoffrey advanced to brace himself before his friend. "And do it slowly and clearly!"

"Now, now," Milty said, soothingly patting Geoffrey's shoulder, leaving black fingermarks on the brown superfine. "Won't do you any credit to show temper with me, you know."

"Milton Philpotts!"

Milty quickly shoved the crumpled notepaper toward Geoffrey. "Oh, all right! I can tell nothing from the melted wax now, but I would swear *that* is not Lady Standiford's signature."

Geoffrey snatched it in confusion. Flipping it over, he scanned the words still readable, then flipped it over to inspect the melted seal. "No, it is not her signature!" he declared, with the beginnings of dread in the pit of his stomach.

"There, you see!" Milty cried out in triumph. "Knew there was something out of sorts about the fella. 'Course, one can never really tell with the French. Damned lots of spies if you ask me. Suspects, the lot of 'em."

"Milty," said Geoffrey in a slow, measured tone. "Strange that it may seem, I am all of a sudden anxious for the safety of my wife. Think, Milty, think. Just how did she come to meet this French dandy?"

Milty frowned in concentration. "'Twas at the opera, I believe. I walked in on them, and *Miss Bartley-Bacon...*" His face lit and he snapped his fingers. "There you have it! Miss Bartley-Bacon introduced them."

"Sharon! I shall call on her immediately. Come or stay, Milty, but either way, I'm off!" Geoffrey said, striding back into the hall.

Humphrey, surprisingly, was standing there with cloaks and hats ready. Geoffrey tilted an eyebrow in query, but did not waste time or breath with questions. Was everyone of his acquaintance taking care for his wife...except for him?

"I'm in for the fray!" stated Milty plaintively, sweeping his topper from Humphrey's hand. "A man can't have too many friends at his back at a time like this!"

Geoffrey glanced back at him with great affection. "And you are a true friend, Milty. But I will point out that you have no obligation here."

"Well, I do in a way," said Milty good-naturedly. "Deuced fond of the little thing, you know? Besides, owe it to her in a way. Your lady is all the crack this season, and I am no end pleased to be able to cut a dash with her in front of the Tulips. Rose likes me, you know," he added simply.

"As do I, my friend," Geoffrey admitted, clapping a hand on his friend's shoulder to shove him through the door. "Now, let us be off to the rescue."

Fortunately Sharon Bartley-Bacon was at home, and just as fortunately Geoffrey's mother was not, so he was granted the reprieve from lengthy explanations. He cut through the pleasantries and came straight to the point, regardless of the enthusiastic welcome Sharon would show him. "Who is this Frenchman you have introduced to my wife? And where has he taken her?"

Sharon stepped back with feigned shock at being addressed so abruptly, gaining time for her mind to work feverishly. She knew that Rose was being taken east of London to some obscure little inn in Ellensburg, to be held overnight, or at least until she was thoroughly compromised. Or at least that was what she thought the plot was. Of course she could only speculate, as Elmo Sewell was decidedly closemouthed with such details. But her dilemma at this moment was to turn all this confrontation in another's direction. And from the scowl on Lord Wyse's face, she was not to be allowed time to think it through with any thoroughness. Should she simply tell what she knew of the plot? Or should she plead ignorance of the whole charade?

Geoffrey glared at the silent woman. "I do not care for the fact that you must consider your answer at length, Sharon. If anything happens to Rose, I will hold you personally responsible. And I shall use my considerable power to make sure all of importance have knowledge of your part in any dire deeds done to her."

Sharon bit her lip in sudden fear. This was more than she had bargained for. Her mind raced, quickly bringing up possible lies, and just as quickly discarding them. She suddenly hit on a plan to extricate herself and still smear Rose's character in some way. "They have gone to Ellensburg," she burst out. "Something was said about visiting a sick aunt of Henri's. But they did not tell me much—" she paused to tilt pleading eyes up to Lord Wyse "—oh, Geoffrey, I *am* sorry. I didn't want to be a party to deception, but you see, Rose would swear me to absolute secrecy and I thought...." She let her voice trail off with suggestive guilt and dropped her head prettily, canting eyes upward through her lashes.

Dismayed at the blatant lie on the blonde's lips, Milty burst forth, "By God, Geoffrey, she's implying that..." He stepped forward to gain Geoffrey's eye. "I swear to you, Rose would never! Do you hear me, Geoffrey? Not Rose! Not in a million years! Rose would *never!*"

Geoffrey was none too sure if Rose would or Rose would not. Suddenly he was feeling quite the fool. Obviously he did not know the least thing about his wife, or her affairs, and that was a sad state for a husband to admit to. Without another word for Sharon, he turned and pushed through the door. "Come Milty. We're off to Ellensburg. They have a good hour head start on us."

The two dashed pell-mell across the English countryside. "I hope we are still in time," Geoffrey yelled as they raced neck and neck through North Bend village, scattering geese, chickens, children and dust on either side.

Milty's heart sank. So his friend was thinking the same as he—that the ailing aunt did not exist. With any luck, Rose would realize that she was not on the northern, well-traveled road to Bellingham before it was too late. He gritted his teeth and put spurs to his willing mount.

Chapter Thirteen

Rose, not being familiar with the outskirts of London, was blissfully unaware that the direction the curricle was bowling along was taking her farther and farther from Bellingham, and her expected destination. At present, she was enjoying the speed and the wind in her face. It was exhilarating to be out in the countryside. The crisp, clean smells brought home to her that she was a country girl through and through. While she enjoyed the town life for a spell, her heart was happiest when she was trudging through vast fields with rampant wildflowers rather than strolling down manicured walks in sculptured rose gardens.

Once clear of the streets and houses and traffic of London, Henri had not wasted time or breath on polite conversation, but kept his attention on the rented team, maintaining a goodly pace. He was thankful that the lady did not complain of the speed at which they traveled, for he suddenly had no other desire than to finish the task at hand, collect the remainder of his payment, a payment he was beginning to find totally inadequate for the deed, and escape to the safety of the Continent. He was more and more uneasy about doing this blameless lady serious harm...and about Sewell playing fair with him in the end.

When they had traveled for more than two hours, Rose reached up to tuck a stray lock beneath her hat and turned to Henri. "You are not one for conversation this afternoon, Monsieur Bonheur? Are your thoughts more entertaining than my company?" she teased.

"Non, non!" Henri rushed to reassure her. "I am merely attending to your safety. This is a new team for me—" he turned a swift smile upon her "—and being ladies themselves, I fear they bear some close attention."

Rose, suddenly tired and slightly bored, and beginning to feel more than a little travel ill with all the lurching and bumping of the lightweight curricle, was just about to request he diminish his frantic pace when he slowed and turned off the main road. "Just where are we, Monsieur Bonheur? I am more than ready to be done with this rough ride. If I had imagined we would be coming this far and over such a rutted track, I would have suggested we ride," Rose complained.

"Ah, Lady Wyse. That would have never done, as I do not ride astride these contrary beasts," Henri confided with a soothing smile down at her. Before she had chance to rebut, he pulled up before a small inn that looked to Rose to have seen far better days than these. He secured the leather ribbons, and made as if to leap down.

"This is it?" Rose stared around her in disbelief. "This is the fabulous inn you praised so highly and at such great length?" The alarming sway in the roofline threatened a fair chance of having it down upon one's head should one be foolish enough to enter such an establishment. A chill of foreboding crept up her spine. She suddenly realized she was a great distance from home with a man she really knew almost nothing about.

"Yes, this is it. Are you not surprised?" Henri answered. Rose glanced quickly at him. Whatever was she doing here when she only wanted to be at home, with a loving, caring husband? "Henri, I wish to return to London immediately."

"Ah, non chérie," the handsome Frenchman soothed. He came around to the side of the curricle and held up his arms to assist her descent. "Not after coming so far."

Rose did not move toward him, and in fact, forcibly held her body still as it wanted to lean as far away from the inviting arms as possible. Suddenly, she did not like him very much, nor did she like his free use of such an endearment when addressing her. "I am feeling unwell. All the bumping from the fast pace," she said tartly. "Where is Bellingham? I thought it was located on the water and I see no water here. Just what are you about, Henri?"

To her surprise, Henri smiled with such ease at her, and with no small amount of amusement. Propping his hands on the high side of the curricle, he shook his head at her with a charming smile. "I declare you are making sounds like a little frightened bunny rabbit," he teased. "Come! Admit you are wondering why this so strange Frenchman is taking you to a small out-of-the-way place in the country? Do you think I, Henri Bonheur, would bring you to such a place to seduce you? Is that what you think? Not so! It is only that the food is so excellent here. So very French, not pallid like this English fare. That is all."

Looking down into his familiar face and his easy smile, Rose had the grace to blush at her fears. The young man did not seem so dangerous or threatening now with the teasing light in his blue eyes and the wind ruffling his black locks. After all, it wasn't as if she did not know him. Hadn't she spent an exorbitant amount of time in his presence these past weeks? And hadn't he always behaved like a gentleman?

"I am sorry, Henri," she apologized, feeling very foolish. "Merely a spell of wayward instincts, I suppose. Truly, I'm sure I shall be famished again, once my stomach has a chance to settle a bit. And——" she allowed him to assist her descent from the curricle and lead her toward the door of the inn "——I did not mean to imply that I thought you capable of devious acts upon my person."

"Ah, one should perhaps pay heed to their instincts." He smiled sadly down at her as he held the door open for her to pass before him.

Rose stepped into the dark, low-raftered taproom, only to come to an abrupt halt as the smell of mice, wood rot, stale ale and flawed sewer drainage assailed her senses. She wrinkled her nose at the unpleasantness and made to hastily retrace her steps through the door, but Henri's hand, placed squarely between her shoulder blades, shoved her pell-mell into the room. She slammed hard against a wobbly table and lay stunned for a moment, trying to understand what was happening, then recoiled with a sick lurching of her stomach when she did comprehend the whole of her perilous situation.

Rose shoved herself upright, brushing her troublesome hat to the floor, and smoothed her hair as a way to calm herself. The thundering of her heart was loud in her ears. Taking a deep breath, she quickly scanned the dark, dank room for another means of escape. "But why, Henri? What do you hope to gain with this bit of foul work?"

"What can I say?" he shrugged his shoulders as if he were a product of something beyond his control.

Rose refused to accept that. "Henri, please reconsider this. We could leave right now and no one would have to be the wiser."

"Ah, *chérie*, I fear that is not possible, though I wish it were...."

"If you say it is out of your control, then someone must

be pulling the strings to your actions. Who has ordered you to do this to me? Who, Henri?'' she insisted. She must know who could possibly hate her so much as to wish her this much harm.

The barkeep came through a loosely hinged door in the back before Henri had an opportunity to answer, assuming he might have done so if granted time. Instead he raised an elegant hand in a limp salute to the proprietor of the disgraceful inn. ''Ah, here is our host now.''

The burly man came forward, grinning and bowing in an insulting, mocking courtliness. ''Welcome, yer ladyship. 'Tis not often we gets quality here.'' He spit upon the floor at her feet, wiping his mouth with the back of his beefy hand and laughing as she rapidly stepped back to protect her shoes and hemline. '''Tis through there, sir,'' he advised Henri, waving toward a second door in the back of the sad dwelling.

''Come now, *chérie*,'' Henri cajoled. ''It will do no good to make things difficult. Our host has readied accommodations in anticipation of our arrival.''

''You motherless sot!'' Rose shouted. Shoving abruptly away from the table, she made a mad dash toward the door. One second faster and her flight attempt might have been successful, but a quick, hard hand snatching her flying draperies jerked her roughly backward. Henri quickly folded her into his arms, trapping her arms against her sides, and lifted her from her feet. He did no more than grunt as her heels drummed against his shins.

''Ah, mine host!'' cried the Frenchman gaily, carrying Rose forward. ''The bird's wings are clipped. Lead the way, if you please.''

''Yer room, yer ladyship,'' the foul man said with a sneer, throwing the door open and stepping back. He bowed deeply to Rose and tugged his forelock in mock deference to her as Henri set her jarringly upon her feet. A hearty shove in the small of the back sent her catapulting into the room to fall headlong on the floor. The door was slammed behind her and the grate of a bar dropping into slots to hinder her escape sounded with a sickening finality.

Leaping to her feet, Rose rushed to pull at the door. As expected, it refused to budge even an inch. She pressed her ear to the crack, desperate to know what was to become of her. She heard the chink of money exchanging hands in the taproom and then the burly barkeep demanding in a peeved voice. "Can't ye let me watch ye do her in? Mayhap have a spot of fun with her first? Not many chances like this come along, ye know, gov."

This rude suggestion was met with the sound of a slap and such rapid phrases in French that Rose was unable to follow and could only ascertain were curses. She was relieved to hear the sound of wooden clogs trudging off in the distance and the angry slam of a door. That was a short-lived relief though. Her situation was still dire. Spinning about with a frantic look, Rose assessed her dim prison. Apart from an iron bed, covered with a greasy quilt of sorts, and an upright wooden chair in the corner, there was no other furniture in the room. The only light came from a small window on the far wall, apparently so crusted over with filth that it admitted scant light. With a cry of hope, she ran to the wall and reached for the frame. It was high over her head and even on tiptoe, her fingertips could only touch the lower sill. Stepping back, she could see that the frame held only shards of broken glass and someone, possibly the barkeep in anticipation of his prisoner, had nailed several boards across the frame.

The sound of the bolt being drawn from its cradle over the door brought Rose back to the center of the room. Frantically, she sought anything that could be used as a weapon. There was nothing. She whirled to face her captor.

Henri cautiously opened the door. Seeing her stanced a good ten feet from him, he leaned against the doorframe to look solemnly into her frightened eyes. "I am truly sorry, Rose," he said bluntly. "But it is a terrible burden to be without money, and—" he shrugged in a manner of resignation that made Rose want to scream at him "—the revolution, you understand, took everything. *Mon père*...well..." Again he shrugged.

"Who is paying you to do this?" demanded Rose. "Whatever it is, I can pay more—double, no, triple what they are paying!"

"I would gladly take your money, but to do so would, I fear, bring about my death as well. So you see..."

"No! You are going to *murder* me?" Rose screamed. "But why? Who hates me so much that I must die?"

"It is not a matter of hate, *chérie*. It is no more than the sad fact that you are in another's way. At first the intention was merely to stain your reputation and make you retire to the country in disgrace, but now—" the shrug came again "—it is simply best for someone that you no longer exist."

"Y-you are even more despicable than the cad who conceived such a nefarious plot—to take another's life for no other reason than to line your pockets? Henri, my friend—" she held her hands out toward him to plead for her life "—how can you do this to me?"

Henri avoided her eyes and her questions in shame. "I am going for a while. I cannot do such as this in the light of day, nor with a clear head. Lie back, rest. Make your peace with God, for there is nothing you can do."

"No!" she screamed again, leaping for the door. He slammed it quickly in her face. Rose leaned against the rough wood, listening to his footsteps die away in despair.

The light of day he had said. Could that mean she had until night to find a way out of this predicament? Judging by the hour at which they had left 1 Leicester Street, she could calculate no more than two or three hours until dark. Such a short time to live. But she would not simply lie down and wait for his return.

Rose stood still and tried to breathe slowly to calm her panic. She must think. Fighting the overwhelming desire to wail and gnash her teeth, she righted the chair and sank down upon it. Dear God, was there truly nothing to do but offer her prayers to heaven and hope for a quick end?

Raising her eyes upward, the tiny winking diamond of light coming through the boarded-up window taunted her with a glimmer of freedom. If only she could reach that window, she could break free the boards and wiggle through. True the frame was small, but then so was she. If the window had been boarded up recently, it would be too strong for her to break through, but if it was an ancient repair, rotten and weathered like the rest of the place, then...

She leaped to her feet and stared intently at the window. Sliding the chair forward, she carefully lit a candle stub to supply as much light as possible. Then standing on the chair, she held her hand aloft to illuminate the broken glass. The boards did not look overly new and that gave her hope. For want of any other tool, she pried at the rotted frame with her finger, flicking pieces of broken glass down upon her shoulders. With diligent work, she was able to clear the opening of broken glass. Now, she must find something to pry at the boards.

Jumping down from the chair, she grasped the iron bed frame. Slamming it against the floor repeatedly, she tried to separate the pieces. Everything was still firmly attached. Exasperated, she grasped the chair and flung it with all her strength at the window, but only succeeded in nearly braining herself as it bounced back into the room. Leaping back, she slipped and banged her shoulder sharply on the bed frame. Sinking to her knees, she allowed tears of despair to fill her eyes.

"No!" she admonished herself, striking the tears away. "There is no time for self-pity!"

Jumping to her feet, she grabbed the chair and flung it against the wall with such a descriptive curse that she was shocked at herself. As if intimidated into submission, the chair leg broke away. Grasping the rounded tool, Rose shoved the bed frame against the wall and climbed atop the curved back. Perching precariously, she hammered laboriously at the boards for what seemed the longest time imaginable, pausing only to listen for the sounds of returning footsteps. Finally despairing of any success, she grasped the boards and threw her weight backward in an effort to pull them loose. With a deafening crack, they tore loose from the rotting frame. Caught unaware, Rose pitched backward, her arms windmilling for a second before she fell heavily to the floor, knocking the air from her lungs and sending stars dancing about her head. When at last the pain in her chest began to ease, she realized she was looking at the sky through the clear opening of the window. It was enough to bring her shakily to her feet again.

With desperate strength, she dragged the iron bedstead up on end and braced it against the wall. Carefully climbing the unsteady ladder, she gently stepped upon the headboard rail, grasping the edges of the window. Twice she and the bed slid to the floor with a disappointing crash. But on the third attempt, she squatted and leaped through the window just as the bed crashed down again. With her head and upper torso through the opening, she braced her hands on the frame and wiggled her hips through the tight fit.

Perspiring, and near to sobbing, she hung there for a moment, staring down the wall, and farther down a rather steep hill. Her heart nearly stopped. Disastrously, the inn was built precariously close to a ravine, appearing to have one story from the front where she had entered, but actually having three or more stories from the rear. Escape from this position was to be a challenge indeed. Balancing herself on the narrow window ledge, she plotted her next move. It was entirely too far to drop, especially as she was hanging head down at present.

She craned her head back to look upward, to the roof. The roof thatch hung down to tickle the back of her neck, but there was a lath trim-strip, at least one inch wide, running the length of the wall. Just wide enough for a toehold. If she could lever her legs through the window without falling headfirst into the ravine below, she could climb to the roof, and across to the front of the inn. There she could easily drop to the ground.

Raking her fingers through the slippery thatch, she sought a support beam to steady herself as she levered her legs through the window. She grasped the rotted wood rafter, balanced her weight and pulled a leg through, cursing the bundle of overskirts on her driving costume. Once through she gingerly set her toe on the thin trim-strip, praying it was not too rotten to support her slight weight. Still, better to die of a broken neck attempting escape than at the hands of a hired killer.

Holding her breath, Rose slowly twisted her body until she was facing the wall. From there it was easy to step on the windowsill and haul herself upon the roof. Lying on her stomach, she looked across the fields where little wisps of smoke rose from the houses of what she hoped was Bellingham. Somewhere a thrush was pouring out his heart in a song of love to the darkening sky, seemingly so in-

nocent for her situation. It was just when she was plotting
her course across the thatch, her toes scraping on the gutter,
that she heard the sound of horses' hooves on the hardpack
drive. Henri was back! Her heart sank and she had to bite
down on her hand to resist the urge to scream in terror.

Panic-driven, Rose twisted her head and looked downward. The ground seemed to fall away at an awesome rate
from the high-pitched roof. There was no way she could
drop to the ground from this side without the risk of snapping her neck in the process. And there was not time to
climb the slippery thatch, over the peak of the roof, and
down the front. Besides, Henri would only be waiting for
her there when she did. No, she must try for the side, and
pray that the drop was no more than two stories there.

Still lying on her stomach, Rose began to pull herself
forward by grabbing handfuls of rotting thatch. The thatch,
worm-eaten and weak, gave alarmingly with her weight,
creating yet another seemingly insurmountable obstacle.
She feared she would fall through it, and end up back in
the room she had just escaped. But there was no time for
care for she must get to the side and down before Henri
could snatch her again. To her horror, she heard quick footsteps in the room below her, then silence as Henri apparently took stock of the situation, then retreating footsteps.
She heard her name being called from directly below her.

"Little Rose, you surprise me. I did not think such a
little thing as you would have such a lion's courage," he
called, his words slurred with drink. "But you cannot escape your fate, *chérie*. You must not make this more difficult than it is."

With a sinking heart, Rose heard the thud of a ladder
being slammed against the side of the building. She twisted
her head, and stared across the roof, fully expecting to see
his head appear any moment. He was going to climb up

and get her, she thought. Or perhaps shoot her where she lay. Well, to hell with fate. To hell with taking what life seemed to deal. If she was going to die, it was going to be after the fight. Wrapping her arms tightly against her, she found the thatch did not give nearly as much if she rolled straight across it. It was in this manner that she reached the side of the roof and the ladder before Henri's head emerged over the eaves.

Gone were the proprieties of the London salon. Gingerly rolling onto her back and sitting up, her ladyship, Marquise of Hetherington, hitched up her skirt and drew her knees up to her chin. She focused her attention, channeling every bit of her fright, on the ladder, just as Henri's head broke over the eaves. He did not even have time to look surprised before she forcefully drove both feet into his face. He teetered for a moment with his sensuous mouth in a small circle, his arms windmilling in midair, then he arched backward and disappeared from her sight without a cry.

There was a loud crash from below, and then silence, except for Rose's labored breathing. Wasting no time, she gathered her skirts above her knees and swung over the edge, trying to ignore the feeling that at any moment her ankle would be grabbed and she would be jerked backward. With the speed of a country tomboy, she hurried down the ladder. Only when her feet touched the ground did she look for the fallen Frenchman. He lay tangled in a pile of wood against the side of the building, his head at an angle that strongly suggested a snapped neck.

With little feeling of remorse, Rose rushed around the building. Unfortunately Henri had taken the time to unhitch the team and secure them to the side of the inn. Apparently he had meant to spend some time tormenting her as a prelude to the dirty deed. The spirits he'd consumed must have given him false courage. Moving quickly, she slipped the bridle on the fastest-looking of the two horses and led him to the front stoop, fearing any moment to be snatched by the horrid barkeep. Tucking her skirt into her waistband, she swung aboard and set a spanking pace toward the town in the distance.

When Rose had put a reasonable distance between herself and the inn, she drew in her horse and allowed him to blow. There was a tall wooden signpost with two arrows, one pointing off toward the little town she had seen and spelling out Ellensburg. So they were nowhere near Bellingham. Luckily for her, the second arrow pointed to London, so she at least had a direction, if not a measure of distance. She set the horse in that direction at a brisk pace.

She had been such a little fool. Blindly trusting. So much so that she had come close to departing this life before she had even begun to live it. Someone wanted her dead and moldering in a grave. But who? She had no enemies that she could readily identify. Who would benefit from her death? Sharon Bartley-Bacon? No, she might whine and complain, but she did not have the backbone to do murder. Besides, she would gain nothing—except possibly another chance at Geoffrey? That brought to mind the only other who might benefit from her death. Her husband! He had never wanted a wife in the first place. And he had made it very apparent in many ways after the wedding, that he had no use for a wife whatsoever. But to do murder! What obstacle was she to him in his chosen life?

Could it be that he had finally succumbed to the heart and developed a *tendre* for someone he truly did wish to wed? If that were true, then she supposed a wife would be a most unwelcome obstacle. But murder? In all honesty, what did she truly know of the man she called husband? While he seemed one thing, was it possible that he was an entirely different thing altogether? They had hardly ever been alone in the short months of their union. And what times there had been, he had practically ignored her. But if her husband felt that strongly about having a wife he did not want, best she just run away.

Tears filled her eyes and spilled over to trail down her dusty cheeks. But where could she run to this time? Everyone who had ever loved her was dead. All she had ever wanted was a home with a husband to love her and lots of babies. Was that too much to ask of him? Apparently so, for the fact remained that she was very much alone, and someone had serious intent to end her life. Only she could save herself. She determinedly dashed her hands over her face. Well, then she would do just that! She would save herself, even if it meant placing Geoffrey in the fire. Better him than her.

Pushing anger to overcome fear and sorrow, she urged the horse to a greater speed. Plans formed in rapid fashion now. She would ride within a goodly distance to 1 Leicester Street, then turn the horse loose. There must be no questions about the horse, nor a charge of horse theft and murder laid at her door. Then she would return home in a hackney, just praying no one of import was there to question her bedraggled appearance. She would merely say she had become bored with driving and requested to be set down in Bond Street. No one would question a young matron shopping without a maid in Bond Street. Furthermore, she was expected at Almack's Assembly tonight and be there she would. Come hell or high water, she would dance at Almack's tonight—and with rings on her fingers and bells on her toes and a gay tilt of her head, just as the ton would expect of the dashing Marquise of Hetherington. But she would be a much wiser marquise than before.

* * *

Geoffrey and Milty had made exhaustive inquiries en route to Ellensburg. But all they had gained for their efforts were shaken heads and shrugged shoulders. The few that spoke said that lots of carriages passed them and who had time to notice what nobs and their ladies were about? There were even those who would chance a grin at the lord who could not keep track of his lady wife, and must inquire of strangers for her whereabouts. Tired and dusty, the pair finally halted at a posting house to rest their weary mounts, and bolster their spirits with toddies of double strength.

Lord Philpotts watched his friend's long face and shook his head. "You know what I am beginning to think, old chap?" he hazarded.

"I could not even fathom, Milty. Pray tell?" Geoffrey asked. He was feeling quite low in spirits at present. He tilted his glass and emptied it in one gulp, signaling for another.

"I think our Rose never came to Ellensburg," Milty declared. He slammed his hand down on the bar for emphasis. "That's what I think! Lay you better than even odds, she's sitting at home right now. Or shopping for ribbons at Grafton House. I think we have been sent on a Banbury chase."

Geoffrey's stern face lightened at his friend's avowal, as it mirrored his own thoughts. "I am beginning to think you may be right," he said slowly. He very much wanted that to be true. He very much wanted to think that Rose was blameless of any fault and perhaps wiser in her choice of escorts than it had appeared she might be. He did not like to think she was easily duped by some sweet-talking Frenchman, especially as her husband was so negligent at taking care of her.

"And," Milty continued with strengthening determination that he was right, "the Frenchie probably made up that fake letter from Lady Standiford so's to create the opportunity to drive out with our Rose. Probably didn't have anything more sinister than that in mind."

"Well, the letter was most assuredly a fake," Geoffrey conceded. "But it seems a great deal of trouble to go to for a drive. Why on earth go to such lengths?"

Milty looked at him in the most particular way. "Well really, Geoffrey, open your damned eyes. Our Rose is a deuced pretty little thing. All the crack, you know. Her attire is a constant item of gossip. Why, if Madame Howard was still alive, she would be besieged by the ladies of the ton. Everyone's copying Rose's style. If she appeared in rags, the ladies would track the rag sellers to the bowels of London to raid their wagons in a trice. Quite the darling of the ton actually, our Rose."

Geoffrey stood back and stared at him in surprise. "Tiger's Breath? I do agree that—" a frown creased his forehead "—well, I mean, she does look remarkably well on occasion but..."

"Remarkably well? Good Lord!" Milty snorted. He cast his eyes heavenward and ruefully shook his head. "What a cursed rum marriage you two have!"

Geoffrey returned his attention to his libation. What a rum marriage indeed! But that was something he had every intention of altering. He did not intend for this farce of a marriage to continue in its current path any longer. The picture he had in his head was of breakfasting together, planning their days to include mutual outings...and intimate dinners before the fire to share thoughts and dreams. And hours...no, days...at a stretch beneath the blankets together, with food trays slipped through the door to be shared over giggles. Time to explore, to teach, to love...damn, but he was impatient to see his wife. And to make her his wife in every way. But first, he must run her to ground.

"Ah, Milty," he muttered. "You have absolutely no idea just how many torments reside within the circle of a wedding ring."

It was upon her entry to 1 Leicester Street that Rose learned from Humphrey of Geoffrey's return from Ireland. It did not take his sternly set lips to know that she looked a fright. But, think what he might, she considered herself fortunate to be alive. She rushed upstairs, ignoring the stares of the servants over her disheveled state, and rang for a bath. She was more than ever determined to keep up appearances. Long gloves would hide the scratches on her arms, and a liberal application of rouge would disguise the pallor of her cheeks. Although there was nothing at all to be done about the pain in her heart. From this moment on, she must never let down her guard until she discovered who was behind this foul plot against her life.

Lying back in the steaming water, she allowed the sadness to touch her heart. She was frightened...badly frightened...and so very alone. Suddenly it felt as if a very old soul lived in her body and she was so tired. It was only through grim determination that she faced frivolity tonight.

Chapter Fourteen

What the assembly rooms of Almack's lacked in appearance was more than made up for by the sparkling glamour of its inhabitants. The gaiety of the gathering was portrayed in the frantic pace of the dancers, the rushing about of footmen bearing trays of refreshments, and the rapid beating of the matrons' fans along the sidelines. The exciting news of the Marquis of Hetherington's return had already been whispered from one end of the ballroom to the other, and curious eyes followed the little marquise as she danced with admirer after admirer with a reckless glint in her eyes.

There were some who wondered at her appearance at Almack's upon the arm of Lord Abernathy, instead of Lord Wyse. Others, with lifted eyebrows and coy grins, wondered why she was out and about in society at all, instead of at home awaiting her husband's pleasure. Still there were those who acted as Rose's supporters, reminding the company of the marquis's and marquise's separate life-styles, and avowing that all was well in the marriage, while others declared the marriage had been doomed from the start. Elmo Sewell was among the first to witness Rose's grand entrance and, being the most unobtrusive of gentlemen, slipped stealthily away from the gathering with none being the sadder for his absence.

Rose might have heard of her husband's frantic search for her had Lord Philpotts managed to arrive at Almack's before Geoffrey. But that stalwart gentleman had dropped in at White's to chat with cronies and to display the glory of the new swansdown waistcoat, and when he finally did make his appearance at Almack's, he found himself too late to scribble a line upon Rose's crowded dance card. In fact, so popular was she that he was unable even to request a moment of her time for an audience. It was good to see her there, and as far as Milty was concerned, her presence brightened all things in the room. She did not seem in the least distracted, so he concluded that Geoffrey had adequately handled matters upon his arrival back at 1 Leicester Street.

Lord Philpotts contented himself by rocking back and forth on his preposterously high heels at the edge of the ballroom floor. The crush was abominable and he eagerly searched the faces and figures swirling madly about the dance floor for Geoffrey. It was the best thing to have his friend back in the country. Finally, catching sight of the elegant figure as he entered through the arched doorway, Milty gave a long sigh. Now, he would discover the resolution of the day's dilemma. Eager to approach him, the large fellow zealously stepped forward, missed his footing on the polished floor and prostrated himself at the feet of one of the patronesses, Sally, Lady Jersey.

"There is no need to go to such extremes, Lord Philpotts," trilled Lady Jersey. "A simple bow would be quite enough, I can assure you." Then she moved away, flitting from group to group, her high voice carrying back to the red ears of the poor, unfortunate Milty. "And, my dear, I then said, 'A simple bow will be quite enough....'"

Poor Milty quickly picked himself up, totally and unconditionally humiliated. He desperately wanted to fall through the floor to escape the laughter, or pour his troubles out on a friendly ear. Looking for Lord Wyse, he could see the marquis was now waltzing with his wife, thus effectively removing the four most sympathetic ears of his acquaintance. He stared after them with a great deal of longing. Both were waltzing beautifully, both were looking at each other with hard, glittering smiles and both were obviously furious, a sight that distressed poor Milty more than his paramount humiliation of the evening.

Geoffrey, upon entering Almack's, had sought Rose in the throng. Having returned home to find his wife was indeed safely in residence, or at least *had been,* before dashing off on the arm of Lord Abernathy, had done his temper little benefit. And the necessity of having to extract her from the reluctant arms of a proprietary admirer had only topped off the head of steam.

"Well, my dear," he admonished her. "And did you not consider it important to wait at home for my arrival? I believe Humphrey informed you of my return."

Rose retained her brittle smile and refused to turn eyes in his direction. "He did, but I did not feel you placed any importance upon my presence as you did not even care to write and tell me of your arrival," she snapped.

Geoffrey took the reprimand well. He did not miss a step in the intricate dance, althought he was now doubly angry for she had made him feel guilty. "I do believe I gave you a duration for my travels. Surely there is a calendar at 1 Leicester Street. If one were interested, one might have noted the date of departure and calculated, within a fair estimate, a date of return."

"Perhaps you expect too much of one, my lord."

Expect too much? Could a husband expect too much of

his wife? Geoffrey's eyes narrowed and he glared down at the top of her glossy head. She still refused to meet his eyes. "And what about this Frenchman you have been parading about town with?" he demanded.

"Oh, Henri?" said Rose faintly. She had a sudden vision of Henri Bonheur lying against the woodpile with his head canted sideways and his wonderful blue eyes open and staring at nothing. She shuddered violently. The horrid reality that she had a dangerous enemy who would certainly strike again, as he had not obtained his end the last time, pierced her heart with icy fingers. And that it was also most probably her own husband who was that enemy only made it more unbearable. He had been gone the longest time, and now that he had returned it was more than evident to everyone within the room that he was not in the least pleased to be near her. Suddenly she felt very young, very alone and very vulnerable. Her face washed of color and she swayed, missing a step in the dance.

Geoffrey caught her in his arms, supporting her. "Rose, what is it?"

Rose clutched his arms and just for a moment leaned against the strength of his chest. His scent assailed her senses and brought forth the most awful yearning. Awful, because he only wanted her dead. Jerking away from him, she forced her spine stiff. "I am not feeling well, Geoffrey. I am going home," she announced.

Geoffrey bit back the angry remarks on his lips. Whatever could there be about this Frenchman that had upset her so? It had not passed his notice that she called him by his first name, setting off warning bells in his head. Could he be too late? Had her heart been engaged elsewhere? But, plagued as he was by these questions, the fact of the matter was—she did look quite ill. And it was quite obvious she wished to have nothing whatsoever to do with him. The miserable feeling that his marriage was dead in its tracks even before it had begun to live sat heavy on his heart. He led her silently from the ballroom.

"I shall see you home," he said. He flung her cape over her shoulders and took her arm firmly in his hand.

Rose drew her elbow from his hand. The last thing she wanted at present was to be alone with Geoffrey. "That will not be necessary."

Geoffrey did not say a word, just signaled for his carriage and handed her inside as if she had not spoken. As Rose could not see any way of avoidance, short of making a dreadful scene, she settled herself on one side, arranging her skirts to cover the entire width. If Geoffrey noticed the blatant move, he did not respond but took the opposing seat. They swayed side by side through the dark London streets, both lost in their own thoughts.

Rose slipped sly glances toward Geoffrey's set face as he stared moodily out the window, wondering if he were indeed capable of hiring a thug to court her, then do her bodily harm. He had seemed not in the least pleased to see her, and immediately pounced upon her acquaintance with Henri Bonheur. Probably wondering where his assassin was and why he had failed in his mission, she thought miserably.

Geoffrey stared into the night, his thoughts as dark as the alleys between the buildings and as dangerous. There did not seem to be any way to approach the subject that burned in his heart, for Rose so obviously harbored no feelings for him aside from the tolerance required to remain the Marquise of Hetherington. It would seem that he had unwittingly entered into the exact marriage he had been attempting to avoid all along.

He had been tricked by a schoolgirl with an unruly mouth and lavender eyes. Perhaps it was best he remain where his talents were assured...in business of Parliament, and management of his holdings. To bloody hell with marriage and wives! Although, there would come a day when he would demand she fulfill her obligation to produce an heir for the name of Hetherington. But just how would he be assured that the babe actually carried his blood and not the blood of one of her admirers? By damn he'd not stand for scandal. And he'd be alert for the first hint of it!

Upon reaching 1 Leicester Street, they silently separated. Rose retired to her bedchamber to cry herself to sleep, and Geoffrey left the house again, bound for his club. They could not have been further apart had Elmo Sewell's plot succeeded in putting Rose six feet under the flowers.

The long summer passed, the Little Season began, and three people were absent from the social scene. Noticeably, the Marquis of Hetherington had thrown himself into Parliament with his usual zeal, resuming his weekly Wednesday breakfasts with his mother and spending most evenings at one club or another.

Much less noticed, the displaced earl, Mr. Elmo Sewell, had ridden hard to Ellensburg the night of the ball to find Monsieur Bonheur laid out on the table in the dilapidated inn and the barkeep avidly going through his pockets. There was nothing for Elmo Sewell to do but retire to his own suite of shabby rooms and plot his next move. Hounded and harassed by the threat of exposure and the ruination of her life, by twice-weekly post Sharon Bartley-Bacon reluctantly kept him informed of the continued coldness of the Hetherington union.

And Rose, having discovered a second, much smaller library on the third floor, had laid claim to the delightful room. She set about refurbishing it to her own taste, with warm golds, spicy cinnamons and Chinese reds to complement the mahogany linen-fold paneling. Now instead of boxes from the dressmaker and milliner, crates of books appeared weekly from Hatchard's in Piccadilly.

The worlds held between book covers removed Rose temporarily from the bitter reality of her lonely existence and loveless marriage. As time passed and the nightmare of Henri's attack had begun to recede, she relaxed more and more. The little she saw of her husband was at least enough to convince her that he perhaps did not hate her. And while he might have exhibited extreme irritation with her upon two separate occasions, it did not seem that having her as wife affected his life overly much. In fact, he rarely appeared to take note of her at all. It soon became her opinion that he had absolutely no need of her one way or the other.

Rose began to wish she had confided in Geoffrey about the incident with Henri, but having since realized ladies of the ton did not casually accept invitations to drive out unescorted unless they were setting up a new flirt, she knew she could only expect a stern lecture for her confidence. Geoffrey had been very explicit on the perimeters of her behavior at the onset of their marriage, and she did not see any benefit in bringing her lapse to his attention. Besides, the more she reviewed her actions, the crazier a plot against her life seemed. Perhaps there had been no plot at all, and Henri Bonheur had been merely telling a tall tale. The possibility that she had been mistaken in Henri's intent and the probability that the abduction had been for no more nefarious purpose than a blundering seduction attempt took root in her mind.

In her tranquil world of eating, sleeping, reading and long, well-escorted rides upon Perplexity, Rose barely saw a soul, although sometimes Lord Philpotts dropped by to take tea with her, patently sad that the dashing marquise showed little signs of dash these days. One wintry afternoon it was he who threatened to destroy her peace of mind by refusing to believe she was entirely content ensconced in front of a blazing fire in her small library, with only a book for company. He bustled about the room, picking up knickknacks to study and poring over book titles on her shelves, as restless as he declared she should be with it all.

"You know, of course, that all this reading will make your eyes begin to squint," he warned. "Besides, it will make you a social outcast. Your mind and conversation will become all cluttered with this stuff. No one will know what you are speaking about, and as everyone hates being made to appear dense, why whoever will you converse with?"

"Oh, Milty," Rose said. She could only smile affectionately at her bear of a friend. "It is just that nothing seems to tempt me from my comfort these days."

Milty watched her pensive little face for a moment, then snapped his fingers. "I have it! Do not move! I shall return forthwith. Of course, you shan't move. You've just told me you have absolutely no desire...."

Rose could only stare at his departing back as his words trailed down the hall. Shaking her head at him, she retrieved her book from her lap and settled down with a sigh. Not an hour had passed when he returned to positively burst into the room, triumphantly waving two tickets over his head.

"Now you have got to come out of seclusion," he cried. "I have purchased, at a very great expense, mind you, two box seat tickets to see the Baroness Catts!"

"Who on earth is the Baroness Catts?" asked Rose,

dropping her book on her lap with a reluctant sigh. "A woman of fisticuffs, I presume by your enthusiasm?"

Milty raised his eyebrows and his hands in horror. "My Lord! You *have* been rusticating for too long. Baroness Beatrice Catts is *only* the most renowned actress to grace the stage in our time. Baroness Catts? The French enchantress? The Gifted Amateur? Catts *à l'amour?*"

"What a lot of names the poor woman has acquired," Rose remarked with a sweet smile for her excited friend.

"Rose, I despair of you! She's the latest rage," cried Milty. "She is playing in *Romeo and Juliet* at the Haymarket tonight. And you *must* come. Really, Rose, I have gone to terrible lengths to procure these tickets. Quite possibly the only two tickets left in the whole of London...costs me more than my new waistcoat...."

Rose hesitated. Milty did have the look of a puppy that had been unfairly beaten. And she had never seen Shakespeare performed on the stage although she had read almost all his plays during the past few months. With a newfound awareness of the plays, it might be enlightening. "I do not know whether I should accept. Geoffrey is at home, I think, and..."

"Oh, that's right," said Milty, remembering. "Slipped my mind totally. Met Geoffrey on my way in and told him about it. He said he had no objections to me squiring you. He was just on his way out anyway."

"Really? I am certainly the most fortunate of women, to have such a sweet and understanding husband," said Rose acidly. Swinging her legs off the chaise, she tossed her book on the seat in an excellent exhibition of controlled vexation. "All right, Lord Philpotts. I shall dress to the nines and await your pleasure. We'll set the town on its ear tonight."

Lord Philpotts seemed impervious to her sarcasm. "Marvelous! That's settled. I have the most amazing new outfit for the occasion. You won't believe your eyes."

He was right! Rose could not believe her eyes when he presented himself in the drawing room that evening. Attired from head to toe in flaming orange silk, he resembled a bejeweled pumpkin, but to say so would have been to wound the tender man unnecessarily. Therefore, Rose could only shake her head and allow him to hand her into the carriage. He made her own gown of luscious purple satin seem dowdy by comparison, and it was a sad thing for a lady of her standing to be so overshadowed by her escort.

But as startling as was Lord Philpotts's attire, London society was not far behind. The little theater was ablaze with jewels sparkling on men and women alike. It was packed to capacity, and Rose noticed with surprise that the rowdier of the Corinthian set had turned out in full force. Only five minutes after Baroness Catts's first appearance, which was greeted with tumultuous cheers and catcalls, Rose began to understand her reputation. The woman was a most ridiculous, if somewhat magnificently dressed, buffoon. Heavy-set and many-jowled, she had swathed her upper body in dazzling silver silk, laden with diamonds, and as she appeared particularly enamored of her legs, she had encased them in shocking pink silk stockings and left them scandalously exposed. She kept holding up the action of the play by walking to the front of the stage to present her legs to their best advantage. Such of the lines as Rose was able to hear above the catcalls and laughter were new to her, and quite possibly, would have been to Shakespeare also.

The actress was mercilessly heckled from the boxes, and would single out the noisiest of her tormentors by pointing straight at their box and delivering the next speech to them, thus egging everyone on. Rose was beginning to wish she had not come. The noise became deafening as a chorus of cock crows arose from the pits, and rotten fruit rained upon the stage with enough force to drive the actors back and halt the play while it was shoveled away.

Rose was restrained from leaving the box during intermission by Lord Philpotts, as he deemed the crowd was too rowdy. "I just do not understand the reception here tonight. I fear I have been mistaken to bring you here. They are so rude! Baroness Catts is one of the finest actresses—" he drew forth a silken handkerchief of lime green with which he proceeded to mop his brow "—extremely well received on the Continent. Why, look there! It's Geoffrey! Oh, no, I was mistaken. Why, it couldn't be him...I mean, er, after all...." Poor Milty could have bitten off his tongue. His attempt to take back his words proved unsuccessful, for Rose had already spied her husband in one of the lower boxes along with a fair charmer at his side.

Rose felt her heart leap to her throat then plummet back to the pit of her stomach at the sight of Geoffrey with another woman. The girl was no older than Rose, but as blond and beautiful as Sharon. There seemed to be a large number in his rowdy party and a large share of the din in the theater this performance could be laid squarely at their door. She hastily moved her chair farther from the edge of the box, desperately wishing to escape Geoffrey's notice. As he had been well aware of her destination, his affront could only have been intentional. The lights dimmed as the curtain mercifully arose again, and she kept her face rigidly toward the stage although her thoughts were not on the ill-spoken words.

Milty's guilt felt insurmountable. In his attempt to draw his sad, little friend from her doldrums, he had only succeeded in adding to her sorrow. He truly could not understand why Geoffrey would escort his bird of paradise to the same theater where he knew his wife would be attending. If the blond chit was actually his bird of paradise, that is, for in all the years of his acquaintance with the marquis, he could not say Geoffrey had been one to flaunt his light-skirts.

The play amazingly survived to the sixth act when the sight of the Baroness's overacted, outrageously hilarious death scene became too much for most of the audience. Some women laughed so much they became hysterical and had to be carried out. Milty, seeing that Rose was not amused, insisted they not wait for the last curtain to swing down and the houselights to be lit, but make their escape in the dark. As they wound their way to 1 Leicester Street, he was riddled with guilt. He watched Rose's set face from the corner of his eye, not having the courage to confront her openly. He pondered the good of a heartfelt apology but did not have any idea how to commence. He had inadvertently caused pain to one of the few people he admired most in the world.

Rose was terribly incensed. It wasn't so much that Geoffrey would appear at a performance with another woman on his arm, but that he presented such a nonchalant manner—a perfect portrayal of selfishness. He never once gave a thought to her feelings in any matter. It was as if she did not exist for him. When she considered the incredible effort it had taken her to go about after her abduction, and near demise, at Henri's hands—keeping quiet to protect the house of Hetherington from gossip—and when she considered the long restless nights of nightmares in which Henri's blue eyes haunted her—all to be suffered alone, she felt like strangling her handsome husband. Upon reaching 1 Leicester Street, she gave poor, suffering Milty an abrupt good-night, and swept into the mansion to confront Humphrey.

"Please inform the marquis that I shall await his arrival in the library," she instructed. Still dressed in her finery, she ordered the fire in the library to be made up and sat down before it, prepared to wait all night if necessary to confront her husband. This was not the life she wished for herself. True enough, she was clothed and housed in absolute luxury. But better to live in a hovel, surrounded by a loving husband and a tribe of rowdy children, than be sealed alive in this tomb of isolation. Friends aplenty she had, but they filled only a small portion of her heart. She wanted—needed love. And if she could not obtain it in her own home, then she was prepared to seek elsewhere.

It was hard on first light before Geoffrey fumbled his way into the hallway of his home. Humphrey, not trusting the message from the furious marquise to a footman, greeted him at the door, and informed him in hushed tones that her ladyship was waiting for him. He watched with anxious eyes as his lordship tacked erratically across the hall in the general direction of the library. Seeing him safely through the door, Humphrey took himself off to the kitchens to demand coffee. Even if the marquis refused the sobering stuff, his own tired, old body would benefit from it.

If asked to confess, Geoffrey would have admitted to never being so drunk in his life, nor so angry. While he had never consciously harbored any plan of retaliation against his young wife for tricking him into a loveless marriage, the liquor he consumed at White's had appeared to bend him in that direction. At the time, it had seemed an excellent plan to avenge his loneliness and punish Rose for her cold silences and snubs by appearing at the play with that particular bit of muslin on his arm. But the quick glimpse of her horrified face across the theater had all but sobered him. It had not felt as good to slight her as he had originally thought. But, damn her, she could not expect him to live like a monk! That annoying, nagging voice of conscience that had plagued him most of the night came again, reminding him that, as his wife, she had every right to expect him to keep his *amours* from the public eye. Perhaps it was the guilt that made him so defensive.

He pushed open the library door and went in. Rose was lying asleep in a chair before the fire. Her small face looked very young in her sleep. The smudged traces of dried tears on her cheeks added vulnerability. "More deception on her part," he muttered. "Just about as vulnerable as a rattlesnake." He grasped the poker to stir up the fire.

The noise awoke Rose and she opened scratching eyes to see Geoffrey. He looked very handsome and debonair, just as he'd looked in her dreams, and she smiled at him sleepily. She stretched like a lazy cat and pushed herself upright. Then her eyes seemed to focus and she remembered why she was here. Why she had spent an extremely uncomfortable night waiting for him. Brushing her tangled hair from her face, she stared quite sternly at him.

"I would have an explanation of your behavior this evening, my lord," she demanded. "And some assurance of what I can expect in the future. It is most discomforting to see you parading your tarts about at social events."

"Yes, I imagine it is," Geoffrey said casually, tapping his fingers lightly on the mantel, making diligent effort to keep his words from running together like warmed molasses. "But, regardless of your decision to behave like a nun, my dear, I will tell you that I certainly do not intend to live like a monk."

Rose felt numb for a moment. Then she was shaken by pain. A nun, was she? When had he ever given her any choice in that matter? She trembled with rage, and fought for control of her voice. It would serve no purpose to scream and rail at his head. "It is as well I found out about your—" she floundered for the right words "—your flights of fancy, Geoffrey, in good time. Only think what might have happened to me had I decided to share your bed."

"What are you talking about? What could have happened to you?"

"The pox!"

Shock sobered him momentarily, then he protested. "I will have you know, dear wife, that the ladies I consort with are diamonds of the first water and, above all, *clean.* And—and furthermore, you have no right to know about such things!"

"Ha!" Rose sneered. "It is just as well I do!"

"And might I inquire which of your gallants has seen to your education in these matters?" he said, at a loss as to how he should rebut this attack. "For I shall have no truck with Haymarket wares."

"Nonsense!" replied his little wife, looking him up and down in the most direct fashion. "That might be the only type of female you know how to deal with! As you have demonstrated quite well tonight."

The hard and bitter words were building a wall between them but both were too proud to try to soothe the other. The marquis weaved slightly and clutched at the mantel for support.

"You are bosky," said Rose disgustedly. She rose to stand before him, looking at him with a mixture of disgust and pity. Geoffrey stood glaring down at her, the red lights from the fire glinting in his eyes, or was it from an indulgence in spirits? Whatever had happened to her handsome, correct Lord Wyse?

Geoffrey did not like the feelings he was experiencing at this moment. He felt guilt for hurting her—remorse for the loss of the childish admiration he used to see in her eyes—and a sudden hunger, deeper than anything he had ever imagined, for her to love him. He needed her to save him from this prison of indifference he felt about most things in his life. But, at this time, it seemed impossible for him to express it all to her. Instead, he took refuge in stubborn defiance and male bluster.

"On the other hand," he announced, "I might as well give you a sample of what you have been missing with your cold and distant ways."

Before Rose could understand what he meant, he abruptly pulled her to him and kissed her hard on the mouth. He tasted of spirits and tobacco. She tore herself free and wiped her hand over her mouth. Turning to the door, she tried to keep her voice from exhibiting the tears that threatened to overcome her. "I am going to bed! You are too drunk to monitor your own behavior."

"Better I had accepted your first offer..." he said with a snort.

"What offer was that?" Rose flared back at him.

"As my bird of paradise, you might have shown me some tenderness at least. More so than you have as my wife."

Rose felt as if she had been slapped sharply. Hurt and anger at his unfairness made her words sharp. "Perhaps you are kinder to your birds of paradise than you have been to your wife, my lord. Now I bid you good-night!"

"You are always running away, damn it!" exclaimed Geoffrey, lunging after her. His intent was to grasp her firmly in his arms. To feel her against him again...and to keep her with him until something could be settled between them.

Rose twisted, eluding his grasp, and then ran as hard as she could up the stairs. Avoiding her own rooms, for surely that would be the first place he would search, she continued up the curved staircase to the third floor. Locking herself in the small library, she sank into the upholstered chair before the dead fireplace. She heard him roaring her name. She heard doors being thrown open and slammed closed on the second floor. Then there was blessed silence.

Rose sat for the longest time, until she was certain he was not going to resume his search. She found she was trembling with cold and shock, and made her way on shaky legs to the bellpull. She ordered a fire from the gaping footman, and wrapped a woolly throw about her to pace to the window. From the gossip at the tea tables, she had gathered that a drunken husband was a common occurrence in this hard-drinking society. Ladies of her acquaintance seemed to cope with an elegant shrug. Men, it would seem, were not men unless they crawled home in the small hours on their hands and knees. But Rose had considered her husband to be far above such behavior. Perhaps she did not truly know this man she had married on such a lark. Perhaps the love she thought was true on her side was nothing but schoolgirl infatuation and a fleeting thing. Well, one thing for certain, she would consider herself well out of the agonies called love. Tomorrow, her coldness toward Geoffrey would no longer be playacting. It would be a part of her soul.

Chapter Fifteen

Rose started the next day with a cold courage. Confident that, after his rowdy behavior of the night before, she would be spared her husband's presence at the breakfast table, she dressed and ventured listlessly downstairs. But, to her horror, Geoffrey was already at the breakfast table and obviously waiting to speak to her before he went out. He was spotlessly attired in a cinnamon frock coat of superfine, a boldly patterned brown-and-saffron waistcoat and biscuit-colored pantaloons.

His cravat was impeccably tied and the very sight of him made her heart ache. Was she to moon for the rest of her life after a man who did not want her? With a small sigh, she allowed the footman to seat her, wishing that she had not set the silly practice of always dining at her husband's right, instead of at the opposite end of the long table.

Geoffrey cleared his throat and straightened. There was much he needed to say to her. As it was certainly impossible to converse with any privacy in front of so many servants, he could only bide his time, studying his young wife as her plate was being filled and arranged with great flair.

Rose no longer resembled the child he once knew, and

he could only ponder who this stylish young matron was. The hair that used to hang to her waist in a liquid fall had been arranged in a sleek, severe style that was entirely her own. Her slim, girlish figure was able to carry out the fashion of the day in a most admirable way, and he realized for perhaps the first time that where once she had been pretty, very pretty in fact, she was now stunningly beautiful. He waited until he was confident she had been adequately served, and then brusquely waved the servants from the room with a dismissing hand. When at last they were alone, Geoffrey cleared his throat again, suddenly unsure how to approach the apology.

Rose choked down a bite of dry toast and desperately wished he would just go away. She did not wish for arguments and recriminations this morning. She reached forward for the jam pot and his long fingers closed over her wrist, forcing her eyes up to his. She could not hold his intent gaze and dropped her eyes to his smooth, long-fingered hand caressing the back of her hand with his thumb as he drew her toward him slightly.

"Please look at me, Rose," Geoffrey said in a soft voice. "I must apologize.... I am truly sorry for my behavior last night. If it's any consolation to you, I feel I shall most assuredly expire of the aftereffects this morning. I—I do not offer it as an excuse, but I connected with a pretty hard-drinking set at Watier's yesterday, and won the damned tickets to that farce at Haymarket Theatre. Some were much further gone than I and began baiting me about my wife's many gallants. They began to imply that I was a cuckold and I am ashamed to admit I challenged them to a duel. Don't worry—" he held up his hand as Rose gave a gasp of horror "—I was not taken up as I am accounted a pretty fair shot."

"There is some small relief in that, I suppose," she conceded and gently withdrew her wrist from his stroking fingers. His touch was far too distracting to one who was no longer in love with her husband.

Geoffrey allowed her hand to go reluctantly. Then he twisted his cup around and around in its saucer with nervousness. He pushed on with his repentance. "I decided to walk from Watier's to the theater, and the fresh air, combined with the spirits, only further addled my wits, instead of clearing my head. There can be no other way to put it. I began to become furious with you, my dear—for illusory slights and fancied improper behavior. I unjustly laid the humiliation I had suffered at your door. And I...I guess I wanted to humiliate you in return. I called on a certain lady bird I used to know and carried her along with me to the theater. Once there I only succeeded in heaping further mortification upon myself. I sent the lady home untouched, I promise. But instead of seeking my own bed as sanity would have dictated, I repaired to Brook's, where I made myself extremely obnoxious by insulting the entire gathering—"

"Oh, Geoffrey..." Rose began, only to have him hold up his hand and continue.

"Whereupon Milty rather forcefully took me aside, and told me to go home. I challenged him to a duel, to which he replied, 'Good God, certainly not!' and I thought my abasement could not be more complete. But then—" he shook his head sadly "—what did I do but come home to abuse you in the most unforgivable manner. Thank heavens, I finally ruffled Humphrey's dignity sufficiently to be ordered to bed like a misbehaving schoolboy. I know I have no right to ask it of you, but I am extremely sorry. Please say you will forgive me, Tiger's Breath."

Frosty gray eyes met warm, brown eyes and poor little Rose fell more in love with her husband than ever. Seeing the soft look in his eyes, she thought suddenly that she was wrong about his lack of emotion. He was just very guarded much of the time. But as a hidden undertone, there was—what? Sorrow? Sincere regret for actions that could not be taken back? He reminded her of a small boy who knew he'd been bad, but was truly sorry for his deeds. "Of course, I shall forgive you," she remarked truthfully, then retorted lightly, "you are truly a terrible man, you know."

"So I have regrettably discovered," he admitted, only somewhat mollified by her forgiveness. Then, in an attempt to return somewhat to normalcy, he asked, "And what are your plans for the day?"

Rose looked deep into the warm, brown eyes with the little gold flecks, which held her own with such an expression of...of what? Whatever it was, it seemed different than usual. "I had planned to drive with Lord Philpotts—" Rose hesitated a little "—but if you would rather I not..."

"No, no." He laughed. "Milty is the best of men, and a true friend to us both. Please, you must forgive my jealousy of last night."

Rose looked at him with a gleam of hope. Jealousy? "Yes, but..."

"You know what men are like," he teased. "When it comes to their wives, they can be like a dog with a bone."

"Oh!" said Rose in a small voice. Hardly the comment she was hoping for, but still it might mean something if she thought about it.

"We shall be attending a ball together tonight?" When she nodded her head, Geoffrey rose from the table to take his leave. He started to ruffle her hair affectionately, but stopped in confusion with his hand above the coiffure. Suddenly he bent and kissed her lightly on the check. "Until then," he said on his way out the door.

When Milty arrived, Rose was still holding her fingers

to her cheek and staring at the door with an expression halfway between bemusement and longing. She hurriedly made her apologies and ran to retrieve her outdoor things. When she returned, she was wearing a burgundy velvet carriage coat with a fur-lined hood and carried an enormous swansdown muff that quite sent her escort into raptures of appreciation.

London was gray and black, and much of it lost in swirling fog. And more bitterly cold than Rose had thought it would be. Milty handed her into the curricle and settled the lap robe securely about them. "I say, it's frightfully cold out here. What say we restrict our outing to a short swing around St. James's Park and no more. Then perhaps retire back to 1 Leicester Street for toddies and biscuits before the fire?" he suggested, edging his curricle in that direction through the press of traffic. "I fear Geoffrey will have my head if I allow you to take a chill, as he did admonish me sternly about that very thing on his way out the door."

"I am quite warm, thank you," Rose reassured him with a smile. She was feeling such hope for realizing her dreams after Geoffrey's confessions, and now to hear that he was solicitous of her health enlarged that hope. She touched her cheek again and smiled to herself.

Lord Philpotts gave an exasperated snort and moved his restless team over to allow a large traveling brougham room to maneuver. "I swear, London is fair bursting at the seams, and today it would seem that nearly half the inhabitants are bent upon moving from one place to another. Makes one wonder, with the weather and all, why they aren't home by the fires, don't you know."

Rose smiled to herself, thinking the occupants of the other carriages just might be murmuring the same about them. But she only nodded, her mind shifting to review every word, every expression of Geoffrey's as she sought reassurance for her hopes. When at last they reached St. James's Park, Milty set his team to a spanking pace, rounding the corners in an exhilarating brace of icy wind. Before they could break a sweat in the cold air, Rose pulled his arm to gain his attention.

"Could we stop just for a moment? Perhaps pull over there," she asked, pointing to a slight rise overlooking the park. "I would dearly love to just sit quietly for a moment."

"Of course, but only for a moment. Deuced cold out here," Milty agreed, drawing the curricle onto the rise as she had indicated. He glanced down at her, concerned to find her so pensive. She sat so still, so lost in thought, he hated to disturb her but he was chilled to the bone and desirous of a warming toddy. He looked vaguely out over the deserted park. Fog was beginning to creep toward them as if pale ghosts were emanating from behind trees. Long, dismal lawns stretched in front of them, toward the king's house at the far end of the park, gray and hauntingly beautiful in the mist.

Rose gave a long deep sigh. Milty shivered and turned to her. "I do say, Rose, have you had enough? I haven't seen a day this miserable since—oh, let's see—yes, I can think of one more miserable. And what a terrible day that was! I suppose you heard of my tripping and landing a facer on the floor at Lady Jersey's feet? That was only the topper—commenced with that thundering ride to Ellensburg. But good old Mary...even Geoffrey remarked on her stamina. I quite suspect he thought the old girl couldn't—"

"What?" Rose rudely interrupted. The word *Ellensburg* seared through her thoughts. Twisting sharply, she stared at Lord Philpotts as if her hearing were faulty.

"Mary. You do remember my gray mare? Had her since I was in short pants—don't ordinarily take her on long, hard rides, you know. Just happened to be riding her that day. But as I said, Geoffrey couldn't believe the way she charged up that last hill before Ellensburg—when we came looking for you."

A cold hand clutched Rose's heart. "When were you looking for me?"

"Didn't I tell you? Suppose not, though I meant to—" He paused to stroke his chin in thought. "It must have been driven clear out of my head when I prostrated myself in front of Lady Jersey. Damned if everything else wasn't driven out of my head. It hurts a chap deep, when such embarrassing things like that happ—"

"Yes, but Milty—" she laid her hand on his arm to shake him "—tell me why did you go to Ellensburg?"

"Looking for you," Milty said, surprised. "When Geoffrey came back from Ireland, he said, 'Where is my wife?' I said, 'I don't know. Think she's gone to Bellingham with that Frenchie.' He said, 'What Frenchie?' I said, 'Monsieur Bonheur.' He said, 'Never heard of him.' I said..."

"Oh, do get to the point!" yelled Rose, balling her hand into a fist and bopping him sharply on the shoulder.

Milty looked at her in bewilderment, then puppy-dog hurt etched over his face. "I was getting to the point but if you're going to shout at me..."

"I am not shouting!" shouted Rose, and then visibly calmed herself. "Dear Milty, it is of utmost importance that you tell me, simply and clearly, just why you and Geoffrey went to Ellensburg."

"Well, to look for you, of course," remarked Milty, in a measured tone. "I told Geoffrey I thought the *monsieur* looked a rake, and that I thought he had faked that letter from Lady Standiford. Canceling the engagement, you remember? And we went off, helter-skelter, to Ellensburg, but couldn't find you."

"How did you know I had gone to Ellensburg, when you just said you told him I had gone to Bellingham?" she asked quietly. She did not want the large man to see her concern, or make him think she feared something amiss. She must learn as much as possible from him, which was not always the easiest thing with Milty.

"I can't remember. I suppose Geoffrey guessed somehow," said Milty. He shivered violently, the cold momentarily driving all memory of the visit to Sharon Bartley-Bacon from his mind.

Rose sat as if turned to stone. If her husband had known she had gone to Ellensburg, then he must have known about Henri—perhaps even paid Henri...

"But as I was saying, you should have seen old Mary." Milty returned to his tale, then glanced about with concern. "Hey, it's getting deuced foggy. Can't you feel the damp? Perhaps we should get back." Glancing down, he saw tears sparkling on Rose's pale cheeks. "Oh, I say." Milty gasped in distress. "Whatever have I said? I quite thought you *liked* horses, Rose?"

Rose smiled wanly through her tears. "Oh, Milty, you are such a dear. But could we stay just a moment longer? Please? I truly don't want to go h-home just yet."

Milty shivered in the damp, but was too much a gentleman and thought too much of the lady to protest. Great white clouds of fog were blotting out the trees, and his hands under their York tan gloves seemed to be frozen to the reins, but he swore silently to himself that he would hold his ground against all odds to please her. Suddenly he spied wavering lights approaching them in the fog. The ominous sight brought a curse under his breath. One should never make rash oaths, even to oneself, for they were sure to be tested every time.

Sawing at the leathers, Milty sought to turn the team into

a better position to whip them up to speed, but in the blink of an eye the gang of ruffians was upon them. The horses were seized by the reins and the curricle encircled by a group of five of the most evil street thieves he had ever witnessed. They were crudely armed with cudgels and their faces, brightly reflected in their torches, were alight with savage glee. Milty felt Rose cringe down behind him, and wished greatly for someone large enough for him to hide behind. While he was no coward, being faced with over-whelming numbers and himself armed with nothing more lethal than a dress sword, he was not liking the odds of coming out the other side of such an altercation in good stead. But he would give his life before he allowed them to touch Rose.

"Here's a fine pair of gentry folks jest sitting fer the plucking!" cried the leader. His red eyes glinted in a pock-marked face and his clothes, as were those of the others, were no better than rags held together by crusted dirt and years of grime.

"Let's get rid of the fat bloke, and then we'll have our fun with the lady," said another, placing his hand on the fine cloth of Lord Philpotts's coat sleeve.

Milty gallantly shook the hand from his arm, and held up his hand. "Now, look here, my good man," he said calmly. "Obviously you have never seen a coat such as this in your miserable life, or you would not be manhandling the cloth. And such is your ignorance, I can only assume you are incapable of imagining the warmth of such a garment as this. But here, I can be most generous. Perhaps you should see for yourself."

Without waiting for a reply, he started to calmly divest himself of his sixteen-caped driving coat. The rabble watched with disbelief on their faces. Such reason from one who should be crying for leniency and wetting his trousers was a strange sight. Milty abruptly stood tall in the curricle and twirled the coat about his head, releasing it to fly high over their heads. Except for the weasel-faced man holding the horses and the tall man as elected speaker, the rabble rushed en masse to retrieve it, causing a scrabble to break out among them. Milty was more than a little disappointed at that, as he had certainly hoped all would make a dash for the coat. Thinking fast, he withdrew his silken purse and tossed coins after the coat. This drew the weasel from the horses' heads to join the melee, whereupon Milty attempted to whip up the team.

The crafty leader of the bunch jumped up on the step, wrested the reins from his hands and jerked the horses to a standstill. "No, ye don't, gov. We ain't quite done with ye yet."

"And who is to say that I am done with you, bastard!" shouted Milty. Moving with an incredible speed for a man so large, he drew his dress sword and leaped down on the leader. With little effort, he ran him through. Rose watched in horror as the man's scream drew the others back upon the viscount as he fought to pull his thin blade free. Even with his massive size, Rose knew he could not stand off the whole pack of rabble. The tall man's torch burned weakly on the ground. Leaping from the curricle, she seized it in both hands. Swinging it in a great blazing arc, she held off the ring of faces that wanted to close in upon them. When they would circle behind her, Milty managed to badly wound two of them, before being brought down by a cruel blow from a cudgel.

Rose was left alone. She bravely swung the torch at the two men remaining on their feet. They circled around her as if a pack of wolves. She backed against the curricle, feeling it shift with the uneasy team. She knew she could not keep them off for long, as her arm was throbbing from the weight of the torch.

"Milty!" she called, hoping against hope he was still conscious. Her glance down at him was the move the ruffians had been waiting for. One swiftly nipped under the fiery arc and hooked his hand around her neck to pull her to the ground. Rose screamed and screamed until the grip became so tight, she could barely breathe. She closed her eyes and prayed for a quick death. The stink of the man's body as he pressed over her was unbearable. As his grip loosened about her throat, she quickly turned her head to sink her teeth into the fleshy part of his hand. His roar of pain and anger fanned out through the fog. She hung on with the diligence of a terrier as he fought to free his hand, only letting go when he pinched her nostrils closed with foul-smelling fingers.

There was a sound of thudding hooves and Rose felt the ground tremble with their force. Geoffrey, looking every bit as magnificent as any fairy-tale prince riding to the damsel's rescue, burst through the fog, closely followed by two grooms. He leaped from his horse with his sword in hand, but the two remaining toughs proved faint of heart before his charge and ran pell-mell into the fog. Rushing to Rose as she struggled to sit up, he lifted her very gently to her feet. His heart stopped to see the blood on her cheeks and mouth. Pulling a linen handkerchief from his sleeve, he held it tenderly to her mouth.

"Rose, where are you hurt?" he asked, almost fearing to hear the answer.

"N-nowhere, I think," she stammered, then paused when he drew the handkerchief, stained with blood, away from her face. "Oh, that blood belongs to my attacker—not to me," she declared, grasping the cloth to scrub vigorously at her tongue with a disgusted expression on her face.

"Oh, Rose, I should have known, shouldn't I? Thank God, you are not hurt." He gasped with relief, gathering her tightly to him. Then, as his relief was replaced with anger at their carelessness, he shook her gently. "What in hell's name were you and Milty thinking of? Driving in St. James's Park in the fog? I would never have known where to look if something had not been dropped by chance in front of Humphrey."

"I was sitting...uh, thinking," Rose started to explain, when a low groan made them both turn.

The grooms hefted a muddied Lord Philpotts to his feet, where he swayed weakly with his hand to his head. Then with a polite "If you will please excuse me," he tottered round the far side of the curricle where he was heard to be violently ill.

"We will have this out at home in front of the fire," declared Geoffrey. Then he instructed the grooms. "Help the viscount onto my horse. I'll drive my wife."

Geoffrey climbed into the curricle and snapped the reins to drive out briskly toward 1 Leicester Street. His self-control was such that he did not begin his interrogation until the viscount's head wound had been bathed and dressed, and Rose had washed and changed her clothes. But once all were gathered in the drawing room, he pushed a bumper of brandy into Milty's hand and addressed him sternly. "Now, an explanation, if you please."

"It was nothing really, Geoffrey. Our Rose merely said she wanted to think about something," offered Milty, looking very guilty even with his white bandage over one eye. "And she was crying. Hope it wasn't anything I said. I was only talking about horses and I know that can bore some ladies to tears, but our Rose is such a horsewoman, as you know...."

"Will you please get to the point, Milty?" Geoffrey instructed rather testily.

"You know something?" Milty announced suddenly with a decided air of indignation. "You are very much like your wife, damned if you aren't. Well, as I *am* explaining if you would only listen, Rose wanted to think, and well, we just sat there in the fog until that band of ruffians overtook us, and—" he spun to Rose in appraisal "—by gad, Rose, you were splendid! The way you flogged right in the fray. Would have bashed my head in if it hadn't been for you."

"Oh, no, Milty," Rose denied, gazing at him over her teacup with shining eyes. "It was *you* who was marvelous. I couldn't believe it the way you sprang upon that odious man and ran him right through."

"If I may interrupt this mutual admiration society," said Geoffrey coldly, "I should like to point out that you both behaved as if you had air between your ears. I fully expect Rose to be flighty and inexperienced, but you, Milty! I must say I expected better sense. If any other man were involved in this madcap event, I would have thought him too far gone in love to notice there might be danger."

Milty look stricken for a moment, then pensive, and finally he asked rather plaintively, "But you wouldn't think that of me?"

Geoffrey looked at his long face, then capitulated with a grin and a shake of his fine head. With a sign of resignation at his hopeless friend, he placed a hand on the big man's shoulder. "Milty, my dear friend, I swear, one of these days someone will think just such a thing of you, for not everyone is so blind. I thank you for what you did. I have always known you to be a man of action, and for that you have my respect.''

Rose watched the two of them with anything but amusement. It was as if Milty, the man of action, was to be commended for bravery, while she, as the addlebrained female with air between her ears, only received a pat on the head for acting in just the addlebrained manner they seemed to expect of one so *flighty*. It was entirely too much!

''If I were one given to envy, I should envy men. They are so wise and so strong—'' she sighed prettily, placing her hands beneath her chin in a meek, adoring pose ''—and if you will excuse me, this addlebrained female will retire to her room to partake of salts, for I do feel weak from the entire experience. Please forgive me my feminine frailties.'' She spoke with a great deal of sarcasm, then haughtily swept from the room before either man could reply, or for that matter even close his gaping mouth.

Rose's anger quickly diminished as she climbed the stairs to her library, and was replaced with a great deal of exhaustion. She was all sixes and sevens about her life. Deep inside she truly did not believe Geoffrey wished her out of his life. If he had wished so greatly to be rid of her as to do her bodily harm, would he have tenderly kissed her at breakfast? To do so with duplicity would have required an audience to give testimony to his loving treatment of her, wouldn't it? There were no witnesses, and therefore she felt justified in taking it for a genuine show of affection. Moving to sink down before the fire, she drew the lap robe, and likewise a disturbed, yawning Orange Willy, upon her lap.

''And what of his timely arrival to save me from that murderous band in the park? What of that, Willy?'' she asked, idly scratching the orange head. Of course, once she thought of it, there wasn't much else he could have done once he had ridden into the melee, not with two grooms pounding behind him to bear witness. But then, he did not have to come searching in the first place. No, he had ridden out in the foul weather because he was worried for her safety in the fog. Remembered the feel of his arms tightening about her, Rose decided to hug that to her breast, along with the breakfast kiss, like talismans for the rest of the day.

Chapter Sixteen

The fog Milty and Rose had experienced during the morning was paltry compared to the great fog that rolled around London in huge billowing, choking clouds later that night. It was only after a great deal of debate that the Marquis and Marquise of Hetherington set out from 1 Leicester Street to attend the ball at the Countess Attaberry's. Arrayed in their finery, they sat across from each other as their chaise rolled tentatively through the fog, with the footman calling out sharply at each intersection before they ventured forth. The lanterns hung on the side of the carriage cast a warm, golden glow in the interior though the postilion's foghorn sounded dismally every few minutes.

Rose shivered and drew her ermine wrap closer about her as she watched her handsome husband's face across the chaise. She wished for some way to return their relationship to the closeness of the beginning, but that seemed such a long, long time ago.

From time to time, Geoffrey would ease his neck in its high starched cravat and curse the necessity of making this appearance. "Damn this fog! Makes a miserable night to be about." He ran his finger around the neckcloth again.

"Geoffrey, what does Deming call that arrangement? It

is fairly complicated and looks to be most uncomfortable," Rose inquired, thinking to distract him from his irritation, and perhaps start a conversation that might lead to a discussion and end with shared confidences, giggles and a speedy return to their own hearth for the beginning of their marriage for real. Such a small thing to expect from a simple question, but one could hope nevertheless.

"This, my dear," said Geoffrey, with a wry smile, "is a hellish invention, a cross between the Irish and the Mathematical, do you see—two collateral dents and two horizontal ones—and it is deuced uncomfortable unless one holds the chin very still. Ah, life would be much easier without the nuisance of fashion, don't you think?"

"Most definitely. What an incredible amount of power fashion has upon the ton." She was reminded of LaFee. "And for those who serve the ton." She turned to stare out the window. "I truly wish we could have stayed home this evening. It is not a fit night for man, nor beast, to be out and about."

"It is a nuisance, I realize. But...ah, it was especially requested that we attend—" he ran his forefinger under the cravat again "—and so here we are. And I fear there is nothing else for it but to endure. We are quite close now."

Rose turned an uplifted eyebrow in his direction and decided to be very bold. "At least it will be a fashionable gathering," she said lightly. "I trust none of your birds of paradise will be present?"

"Outrageous Tiger's Breath," he countered just as lightly. "My days of bird-watching are most definitely a thing of the past, I assure you."

Rose greatly wished to query him as to who had taken over the duties of seeing to his physical needs, but there modesty drew the line. Not only did she not know quite how to phrase such a question, but also their arrival at the Countess Attaberry's estate diverted his attention.

As the line was long to gain entry, Geoffrey bustled her out of the chaise, to dash the last small distance and into the villa. In keeping with the foul weather outside, the King's Road villa was equally damp and cold. The female guests were arrayed in light fluttering muslins and lawns, accented by acres of gooseflesh. Rose, being more for comfort than fashion, was attired in a deep sapphire silk, artfully crafted with many drapes and layers, beneath which she wore flannel knickers most unbecoming but very warm. It seemed she alone was appropriately dressed for the weather, and the only one who had anticipated the draftiness of the villa, she noted as they eased through the reception line.

Although this was the first ball Rose had attended for some time, she was instantly surrounded by admirers and was never short of partners for dancing. And dance she did, for it was the most effective manner in which to warm oneself. Returned to the sidelines by one gallant, she found Sharon Bartley-Bacon at her side. Determined that it should never be said that the Marquise of Hetherington was anything other than a perfect lady, she gritted her teeth into a semblance of a smile and turned to offer a greeting of sorts.

"Good evening, Miss Bartley-Bacon. I trust you are enjoying yourself?" she asked in an awfully polite voice.

Sharon inclined her head slightly in acknowledgment, then waved her spangled fan languidly in the direction of the marquis, who was speaking earnestly to Milty. "So glad Geoffrey decided to heed my advice and attend this evening," she murmured. She then spread her fan for privacy and stage-whispered to Rose. "He did, of course, inform me that you had planned a little *soirée* at home, but I said, 'My dear, dear Geoffrey, all the ton will be there. You simply must come.' And he answered in that funny way of his, 'And will you be there?' And when I said I most certainly would—'' she canted her large, blue eyes sideways to see the effect of her barbed words on Rose ''—he replied, 'Then nothing can keep me away!' Isn't that just the funniest thing?''

Rose stiffened and tried to control her face. It wouldn't do to look positively stricken in front of this cat. She too readily remembered the look of guilt on Geoffrey's face when he had commented that they must attend this entertainment on someone's request. The implication had been that the countess had made the special request, but now that she thought of it, that lady had paid them no undue attention. She watched Geoffrey bend his head to hear something Milty was saying.

Rose, determined not to be undone by someone as catty as Sharon Bartley-Bacon, turned calculating eyes to Sharon's thin, aquamarine muslin, which had been dampened slightly to accent her curves, and deftly changed the subject. ''Aren't you afraid you shall take your death in that wet gown, Sharon?''

''No, not at all,'' Sharon retorted, with a shiver that would not be denied. With a bold insult, she cut Rose by turning her back to saunter over toward Geoffrey. Rose was claimed by yet another dance partner and swung away to the dance floor with a heavy heart.

Geoffrey gave a slight bow to Sharon and moved away before he could be engaged in conversation with her. Glancing about to locate his wife, he was not surprised to find her on the dance floor in yet another man's arms. At first he had looked on her popularity with tolerant amusement, and then with slowly growing irritation as he strongly suspected she was avoiding him. Try as he might, it just would not leave him that his wife could not abide being in his presence. His pride would not allow it to seem that he merely stood about on the sidelines with the dowagers awaiting his wife's pleasure.

Abruptly, he sought Milty. "Milty, I have remembered another engagement," he said. "Please convey my apologies to the marquise and be good enough to escort her home?"

As Milty nodded his head, Elmo Sewell, who had been shamelessly eavesdropping, slipped away to ferret out Sharon. "You must disappear at the same time," he told her. "I shall see that it is whispered that you left with the marquis."

"But I do not want to leave yet," whined Sharon, stamping her foot in anger. "You are abominable to make me!"

"Go!" he warned. "Or suffer the consequences. I shall inform Lord Wyse's mother of your departure, and name your escort."

Fretting under his authority, yet fearing to disobey him, Sharon moved quickly from the conservatory, rushing after the disappearing Geoffrey.

"My Lord Wyse," she called after him. "May I please beg a favor, and request you see me home? I think I have caught a cold in this place. My head aches terribly and I have quite misplaced your mother."

He turned round and surveyed her with weary boredom. "I suppose I can make a detour. I shall dispatch a note to Mother. Pray retrieve your cloak and I shall be only a moment."

"I have already left an explanation and this—" she indicated the fluffy capelette of muslin to match her gown "—is all I have brought with me."

Geoffrey nodded his head wearily and led her out to the carriage. He could not help but think that somehow this innocent act of kindness was going to grow teeth and bite him when he least expected it.

While the marquis would have maintained absolute silence the whole of the ride, Sharon deftly laid little pieces of gossip on his anger to fan the flame. "Amazing, don't you think, how our little Rose has blossomed? Have you noticed how popular she has become with the gentlemen? Oh, perhaps not. You have been out of country...." She peered at him in the dim light, attempting to gauge his reaction, and observed the tension in his jaw that spoke of teeth being ground in irritation. Pleased with that, she pressed on. "I must tell you, although Rose and I have not been overly close, I did take her to task for having so many admirers."

"And what did she reply?" asked Geoffrey, unable to contain himself.

"Oh, you know Rose," said Sharon with a tinkling little laugh. "She just laughed and said she had a very modern marriage. That surprised me somewhat as I did not imagine you to be a husband in such a marriage. But then what do I know?"

Geoffrey returned his attention to the bleak weather outside the window. A modern marriage, indeed. For the first time, he began seriously to consider his wife in a new light. All her innocence and blushes now appeared to be the manners of a designing minx, exactly as he had thought of her once before. It was only after he had set Sharon down in Grosvenor Square, and had given the coachman instructions to drop him at White's, that he remembered the long days Rose spent in her little library. He also remembered Sharon's obvious dislike and palpable envy of Rose, plus the banbury chase she had sent him on to Ellensburg, while Rose had been safe and sound at home. He felt a small pang of guilt. Perhaps he would simply retire home and wait up for Rose to return. There must be some honest conversation between them. He, for one, wanted a wife in every sense of the word. And he wanted Rose as that wife.

But Rose, her feet as sore as her heart from determinedly dancing all through the night, did not return until six the following morning, by which time the marquis had fallen asleep in the library. Filled past her tolerance with the gossip of Geoffrey and Sharon leaving the ball together, she was determined to have things out with him. Marching through the connecting sitting room into his bedchamber, she despaired to find it empty and his bed unslept in. She was too hurt and too angry to cry. She could only swear that Geoffrey would find no further opportunities to break her heart. She had enough cards and invitations to keep herself fully occupied. It was a *mariage de convenance*. Nothing more. And the sooner she began to treat it as such, the better.

Geoffrey, waking late in the morning, stiff and sore from sleeping in the armchair, went in search of his wife, only to be informed that she had gone out shopping and would not return until after luncheon. It had never been more obvious to him that she had built her life and clearly wanted none of him in it. He decided, at that point, to immerse himself in estate work to avoid watching his wife flitting about the salons and ballrooms of the ton, forever in sight and forever out of reach. He ordered his bags to be hastily packed and resolutely departed for Hetherington.

As the weeks passed, the only news Geoffrey received from London was in the form of various notes from his mother telling of his wife's racketing around society, and teasing little notes from Sharon, offering sage advice on the same subject. At last, he posted up to London with the intent of bringing his wife to Hetherington Harrow for the

Christmas holidays, only to find that she had already left for Chandler Hall, the Philpotts's country home in Hartford. For the first time, he seriously began to consider divorce.

Chandler Hall was a large stone mansion designed from ancient blueprints unearthed in the abbey, perhaps dating back to the early fifteenth century. It was unprepossessing from the outside, having no grand facade, but as Lord Philpotts cleverly pointed out, it was an essentially English house and looked very good in the rain. What that had to do with serviceability and comfort, Rose did not know, but she was pleased to be invited to spend the lonely holiday with friends who cared about her, as it appeared she had no family.

What the mansion lacked on the outside, it compensated for on the inside with richness and elegance in the apartments. Sensibly planned, the main rooms on the ground floor led into each other on a sort of circular plan. It was possible to reach the downstairs by a fairly direct route from one's bedroom rather than wander through a labyrinth of stairs and passages as one did at Shenstone. Milty had planned to celebrate Christmas in the traditional English fashion, and the gallery was decorated with holly greens and red berries, spicing the air with seasonal smells. In the center was a huge Christmas tree loaded with oranges, sweetmeats and gingerbread cutouts, iced in decorative colors. It was planned, as amusement, to allow the tenants' children loose on the tree on Christmas morn.

Even with the large gathering of guests for the holiday, Rose was lonely, and while she did take pains to hide her true feelings, they were sensed by those closest to her. Milty, in his attempt to be a good host and to boost her morale, introduced her to the delights of gambling and praised her skill extravagantly. In the long winter evenings Rose began to look forward to the card tables, where she could forget her sorrows in the skill of the game. He teased her gently about her gambling, and warned of its being habit-forming, but Rose shrugged off the warning and remained unconcerned. They were only playing for pennies after all.

A thaw set in on Christmas morning with a great gusty wind driving sheets of rain against the windowpanes. The planned skating party was canceled. A parcel arrived for the Marquise of Hetherington and Rose tore open the wrappings with the excited fingers of a child. Inside it was an exquisite necklace of rubies and pearls, which she tossed aside to search for a note. With her breath held, she opened the thin slip of embossed paper to read the neat handwriting.

His Lordship, the Marquis of Hetherington, presents his compliments to his wife, the Marquise of Hetherington, with many wishes for a pleasant holiday season.

The note was signed by some obscure solicitor from the firm of Bailey, Banks and Biddle. Rose dropped the note into her lap and buried her face in her hands. She had sent Geoffrey a wonderful Sèvres snuffbox from Gray's and had hoped against hope that he would understand the thought that went into the gift, as his collection was extensive. Poor Rose's misery was complete.

The noisy Christmas festivities washed past her as she stood in a small circle of loneliness and despair. Only in the intricacies of piquet or whist did she manage to escape her tortured thoughts. And she took her newfound gambling fever back to the loveless rooms of 1 Leicester Street. But to Elmo Sewell's eternal disappointment, and Sharon's unhappiness as he would rage at her about it as if there were anything at all she could do to encourage otherwise, the marquise drew the line at visiting gambling clubs, however select. The stakes were too high, she protested, and it was not her own money she might lose. She contented herself with ladylike games of whist or silver loo, when the card tables were set up after dinner in the households of her friends.

Elmo Sewell, despairing of ever extracting his prey from the safety of her friends' presence, began circulating rumors of irreparable problems between the marquis and his dashing wife. A favorite pastime of the ton was to rip and tear at its own members, and Geoffrey's extended stay at Hetherington fed their speculation. The whispers of divorce floated about the ballrooms and eventually reached Milty's ears. Always one to confront an issue head-on, he wasted no time, but rushed around to 1 Leicester Street and asked Rose bluntly if the news were true.

"*I* am not considering a divorce," stated Rose. "If it's being bandied about, then it must mean that it is *your* friend who is considering it."

"Then it's nothing more than a piece of idle gossip," declared Milty, with a great show of relief. "If, by any chance, Geoffrey were considering such a thing, then *no one* would know of it. He never discusses his marriage. Not even with me. As far as I am aware, I am the only one, other than yourselves of course, to know it was a *mariage de convenance*. And the two of you seem to have been rubbing along tolerably well. I mean, it's not as if either of you was in the habit of having lovers' quarrels!"

Perhaps if Milty had not been so robust and matter-of-fact, Rose might have confided to him her love for Geoffrey and her unhappiness in her marriage. But she had received so many hurts and humiliations since her marriage that she cringed inwardly from another rebuff. And after all, Milty was Geoffrey's friend first. And as he was her *only* true friend, that did not speak well of her. Besides, he would only point out the obvious——that she should never have married Geoffrey unless she was willing to meet the terms of the agreement.

So Rose plunged once more into the social round and, when Geoffrey returned to town, she found herself accepting no less than three or four invitations a day to stay out of his way. The marquis returned to his Parliament activities, actively partaking of the Corinthian sports of boxing, curricle racing and other manly pursuits, and spending most evenings in either White's, Watier's or Brook's. Thus the unhappy union continued.

Elmo Sewell's diligent work died a quiet death as the couple continued to share the same roof and more tantalizing *on dits* began to circulate. While it was fairly certain the couple would remain childless, the marquis thus leaving no heir, Elmo was still without his title and his fortune. It would do him no good to dispatch Lord Wyse to hell, because, as Lady Wyse was still able-bodied, she inherited everything. And undoubtedly, just to spite him, she would marry again, this time whelping a dozen or so brats to stand before him in line for succeeding. No, Rose must be done in first, then perhaps a quaint little suicide for the grieving widower.

Finally, in desperation, he called upon his unwilling cohort. To his immense irritation, he was rudely informed that Miss Bartley-Bacon was not at home, although he could hear her silly little laugh echoing from the drawing room. Elmo returned to his carriage outside the house and waited impatiently. Half an hour later, the rotund figure of a noted lord of immense wealth descended the stairs and was loaded, with much pushing and pulling by his grooms, into his carriage. Elmo narrowed his eyes in vengeful pleasure. So, it would seem the dear Miss Bartley-Bacon was re-

sorting to the bottom of the petticoat line in her search for
a title, he thought wickedly. Waiting until the carriage
turned the corner, he again raised the knocker on the town
house door. When the door opened, he pushed past the
startled butler and strode purposefully into the drawing
room. Sharon and Lady Lavitia were in a great flutter about
something and both turned to stare at him, Sharon with
haughty displeasure, and Lady Lavitia with a startled little
cry at this stranger who had burst in on them unannounced.

"A word with you in private, Miss Bartley-Bacon," said
Elmo Sewell, holding open the door with clear meaning for
Lady Lavitia. The lady started to bridle and protest at being
asked to leave her own drawing room, but Sharon rushed
to cut her off before she could express her outrage, and
perhaps refuse to budge at all.

"Please do as he requests, Mama Lavitia. I am quite
capable of dealing with this...ah, gentleman," she assured
her.

Both waited in silence for the older lady to storm through
the door, which Elmo shut none too softly behind her. "I
gather you are to be congratulated?" he asked with a mocking bow.

"Yes," hissed Sharon, standing defiantly in front of the
mantel. She had had enough of this game that went nowhere.

"Oh, Sharon, Sharon." He shook his head as if greatly
disappointed in her. "Must I remind you that this marriage
will never take place if you continue to give me such a cold
shoulder?"

"Do your worst," mocked Sharon. "Lord Abernathy is
much too enthralled with the thought of a young, beautiful
wife to believe anything you say."

"He may not, but the rest of London society will. And
Lord Abernathy may lust after young flesh, but he does

have a very old name to protect. I can assure you that you
will never reach the altar once I am through with you.''

Sharon turned white as a ghost and sank into a chair with
a trembling hand pressed to her mouth. "You wouldn't
dare!" she whispered urgently.

"You know I would," he said. "But to be lenient, I shall
ask only one more small chore of you."

Sharon hung her head in apparent defeat, and to hide the
absolute hatred in her eyes. "What now?"

"You are to go to the marquis with concern for your
little friend. You will tell him that little Rose has been
keeping low company, and is in the habit of frequenting a
certain Martha Raffle's establishment. You will say as a
clincher that she is to be there tonight. *Late tonight.* And
you will leave the rest to me."

"You are too stupid," Sharon hissed. "This is a dead
point. Can't you see he cares nothing about what she does?
You will never gain what you want through such nonsense.
And I for one am heartily sick of the whole mess."

"Don't waste your viper tongue on me," he snapped
brutally. "I am not one of your gallants, hanging on to your
petticoats. You will do this one last thing, or you will never
be Lady Abernathy. Do I make myself clear?" She did not
reply but stared at him with fury and a white face. "Answer
me," he commanded, gripping her wrist and twisting her
arm.

"Yes...yes," whispered Sharon. "But, by God, I hate
you more than anyone on this earth!"

"As if I care what you think of me," he said with a
sneer, flinging her arm away from him. "Just do it. Remember, it is Martha Raffle, and it is late tonight. Go to
the marquis this morning."

Sharon watched him stride from the room through a mist-
ing of tears, although her mind was racing. She resolved to

make the hateful call while she was still distressed and frightened and angry. Geoffrey had an uncomfortably shrewd way of seeing through her playacting. "If I ever get out of this mess," she swore to herself, "Geoffrey can marry Queen Adelaide for all I care!"

Rushing up the stairs to collect her outdoor things, she almost collided with Lady Lavitia in the hallway. "A moment of your time, my dear," Lady Lavitia requested with unwonted severity. "I would question your good sense, Sharon. Are you trying to throw your engagement to Lord Abernathy to the winds by receiving that man, Mr. Sewell, unchaperoned?"

"Why, Mama Lavitia, he is an old friend!" Sharon cooed.

"Bah!" Lady Lavitia expounded, with an abrupt wave of her hand. "An unmarried man who whispers in corners with an unmarried girl is no friend. I do have an obligation to your mother, you know. Now what was the purpose of this call? And no more of your lies!"

"Lies!" gasped Sharon, buying time to think. "I would never lie to you! It is just that it was Mr. Sewell who fostered my engagement to Lord Abernathy. That is all."

"Indeed! Was that all?" cried Lady Lavitia, much mollified to have had the confrontation go so smoothly and a plausible excuse laid before her. "I can see then that you are very much beholden to him. Lord! I'd love to see Geoffrey's face when he realizes he has lost you forever. As much as I love my son, he has made a true muddle of his life by not listening to me. All these rumors flying about his wife."

Sharon looked at the lady with some surprise. Could not Lady Lavitia understand that her son truly would not care one way or the other? With her engagement set to be announced and her initial campaign to marry the Marquis of

Hetherington dead ashes, she saw no reason to hold her tongue.

"You know, Lady Lavitia," she remarked in a conversational tone, "you are a remarkably stupid woman."

"How dare you!" gasped Lady Lavitia. The two began an argument with all the enthusiasm of two wet cats, when Sharon suddenly recollected her appointment and left a startled Lady Lavitia in midscream.

Geoffrey had not yet left for his club. Sharon was ushered into the walnut-and-crimson-silk drawing room, and left to await him. A cheerful fire was crackling on the hearth, sending little sparkles of light glinting from the gilded scrollwork on the pilasters of the fireplace. The marquise, fortunately for Sharon's purposes, was absent. Through the long windows, she could see glimpses of the leaden sky outside. Her purpose began to take on an air of unreality, and Sharon fervently wished that she could simply get up and walk out, thus forgetting the whole thing. But as that was not possible, she pinched herself sharply on the soft flesh of her underarm to bring tears to her eyes.

The door opened and Geoffrey strolled in. He was attired to go out, in blue fitted swallowtail coat, striped waistcoat, buckskins and highly polished Hessians with blue tassels. His face was still deeply sun-browned from his extended stay at Hetherington Harrow, and yet there was a weary sadness in his eyes. Or perhaps it was just the severe set of his face, as if he wished to dispatch with this bit of unpleasantness and be off. To Sharon, he looked a formidable opponent. Her nerves and distress returned, and she burst into most convincing tears. Despite her very obvious distress, Geoffrey felt nothing more than a pang of boredom until through her blubbering he caught his wife's name.

Three quick strides took him to her side and he jerked

her to her feet. "Rose! What about Rose?" he demanded, holding the sobbing girl by the shoulders and resisting the impulse to shake her until she became rational.

With an effort, Sharon pulled herself together. She might as well get it over with quickly and be out of here. "Poor Rose," she stammered, holding a wisp of a handkerchief to her eyes. "She has got into bad habits and bad company and spends her nights gambling in low dives."

Geoffrey released her so abruptly that she plopped back into her chair. "Absolute rubbish," he remarked coldly.

Sharon was suddenly afraid he would not believe her. Then Elmo Sewell would ruin her engagement and she would shrivel an old maid on the vine with her reputation destroyed. "It is true! I *swear* it!" she cried. "Why, I know that tonight you will be able to find her at her usual table...at M-Martha Raffle's establishment."

"Ma Raffle's! Come, come. Do you take me for an addlebrained fool? My wife may not yet be up to all the ways of the world, but she certainly would not attend a gambling hell frequented by cardsharps and the demimonde."

"But it is *true!*" wailed Sharon, almost believing it herself in her desperation.

Geoffrey sat down and crossed one muscular leg over the other. He surveyed her coldly. "It occurs to me that if Rose were disgracing herself by frequenting such a place, it would surely be a source of joy to you, rather than otherwise. You can act very coy with me, but I am persuaded that there is not one whit of truth in all this fa-ra-diddle. Why this sudden concern for poor, little Rose, Sharon?"

Sharon played her trump card. She swiped her cheeks, and opened her beautiful eyes wide, giving him a direct look. "I see I cannot fool you, Geoffrey. The fact of the matter is I have become engaged to Lord Abernathy this very morning. Any breath of scandal attached to you will affect me, because of my connection with your mother, and..."

She did not need to finish. Geoffrey vividly recalled her desire for a title and the lengths she would go to to obtain one. Suddenly her tale was made more believable by her selfish statement. He leaned forward threateningly. "All right, Sharon. I shall go to Ma Raffle's tonight. If Rose is there, God help her. And if she is not...then God help you, Sharon."

Sharon recoiled before his threat. His eyes were blazing and she realized with a thrill that this man was likely to be a much more formidable enemy than Elmo Sewell. She had been right all along to think that he was more than she could manage. A sudden impulse to tell him the truth came over her, but he had risen to his feet and rung the bell for the servant to show her out before she could summon the courage.

Chapter Seventeen

Rose's carriage turned into Leicester Street just in time to see her husband's smart yellow curricle bowling out the other end. Perhaps it was just as well. Whenever they did chance to meet, he either treated her with a chilling formality or simply looked at her with a somewhat bewildered expression that she could not comprehend.

As she stepped carefully from the carriage, a fine, light snow was beginning to fall from the leaden sky. She tilted her face upward to the wet and gave a deep sigh. She was bone-weary from the hectic round of social engagements, always hoping by some miracle Geoffrey would attend one of them and smile upon her, or hold her in his arms to spin across the dance floor. But on those few times he did attend, he afforded her no more than a curt bow, and promptly retired to the card room. Of course, Rose did not know how bitterly he loathed her crowd of admirers, nor how desperately he wished he could snatch her away from them. If she had, perhaps she would have confronted him and put an end to their needless pining.

Humphrey presented her with a note folded in the shape of a cocked hat. Rose assumed it to be yet another invitation, and slowly relinquished her outdoor things to the hovering footman before accepting the note. Upon opening the missive, the definitely feminine penmanship seemed to leap out of the page at her.

If you wish to know where your husband spends his evenings...and with whom...pay a visit late tonight to Martha Raffle's gaming house, 333 Cockly Street.

It was unsigned. Rose rounded on Humphrey so abruptly, he took a surprised step back. "Who brought this, Humphrey?"

"A footman, your ladyship. He was in plain livery and I do not know from which household he came."

"Oh. Well, thank you, Humphrey," she said faintly. She slowly crumpled the note and stared into space. She would not go. She would not be affronted by her husband's latest lightskirt. But then the thought of this agonizingly distant marriage dragging its painful, weary way through the winter days was too much. No, she had to know the worst, and she must find out herself. Then perhaps she could make an informed decision whether to continue or take another track. Although what other track was there open for her? Retire to Shenstone to live alone? Divorce? She wanted no divorce. She wanted love, children...companionship. She wanted a real marriage. And only with the one man who carried her heart so carelessly in his breast pocket.

The dreary day dragged on as the steadily falling snow transformed London into a black-and-white etching. Rose dined in her suite of rooms, alone except for Willy, and then rang for Lettie. Taking extra care with her toilette, she dawdled until she caught Lettie's questioning glances. She was in no hurry to commence this evening, for deep inside herself, she knew somehow it was going to force her to a decision that she had no desire to make. More than once, she thought to change her destination altogether. Or to just retire back to her bed and pull the covers over her head. But as inviting as that thought was, she continued to dress.

Attired in a warm gown of gold merino, adorned with tiny ruby satin stripes intricately woven into the wool, and a ruby velvet cloak lined with ermine, she trailed slowly down the stairs. She reached the bottom, only to come face-to-face with Geoffrey. Dressed to go out, he was elegant in formal black and white. The candlelight gleamed off his chocolate brown curls and her heart ached at the very sight of him. She wished to walk close to him and lay her cheek against that strong chest. She wondered what he would do if she did just that? What would he do if she begged him to love her? Probably set her aside with a ruffle of her hair. Rose was so lonely at that moment, and dreading what she might discover with this evening's spying that she would have welcomed even that parental gesture.

Geoffrey took in her elegant appearance with a scowl of obvious ill humor. "May I escort you somewhere, my lady?"

Rose, with her thoughts toward him so warm, felt stunned for a moment at his sharp statement. "I do not want to trouble you. I—I'm picking up a friend on my way, and I fear that might inconvenience you."

At her guilty stammer, Geoffrey frowned even deeper. "Ah, I had forgotten. My wife does prefer other escorts." He studied her for one moment longer, then, inclining his head slightly, departed out the door.

Rose allowed anger to overcome hurt at his tone. So, he would place her somewhere of his knowledge, before he would take up his light of love, would he? Well, he was in for a surprise this night. She pulled the hood over her head and allowed Humphrey to open the door for her. She had taken the precaution of arranging for two burly footmen to accompany her on this mission. There would never be a repeat of the Ellensburg incident. As she climbed into her carriage, a little of the unhappiness left her. Of course, it was all a hum! She would make her appearances at one or two engagements, then just look in at the gaming house. Martha Raffle, indeed! Geoffrey would most probably go to one of his clubs, to while away such a miserable night with his cronies.

As the night wore on, Rose felt tension creeping into her shoulders and up her neck, bringing with it a head pain of awesome strength. She smiled and nodded at friends and acquaintances, yet would remember little of whom she saw and what she heard of the earlier part of the evening. At half past eleven, she again drew on her ermine cloak and entered her coach to direct the surprised coachman to the address on the note.

Martha Raffle's gaming house was a three-story town house that sported a neat redbrick facade and a glossy, dark green door with a well-polished brass knocker. It did not seem to Rose to be the type of establishment she would have associated with the demimonde, although if asked to describe such an establishment, she would have been hard-pressed to put words to her expectations. Drawing a deep, strengthening breath, and directing her two footmen to accompany her, she picked her way up the steps, which had been freshly cleared of snow.

Mrs. Raffle placed one eye to the crack in the drape and watched Rose's slight figure as she mounted the steps outside. She lifted an eyebrow in wonder. "A crest, no less," she murmured, surveying the carriage. "Some lord has sent his fancy piece along in fine style."

"That, my dear Martha, is no fancy piece. That is none other than the Marquise of Hetherington."

"Lud!" Mrs. Raffle swung her massive figure around

and stared at Elmo Sewell over her several chins and awesome bosom. "What the hell does her ladyship want here?"

"You underestimate the charms of your establishment," he said smoothly. "Do not be put off by the marquise's youthful appearance and innocent air. She is a dedicated gambler."

"So? Many a toff and his lady that likes to sport with games of chance. There's fancier card houses in Mayfair to cater to the likes of her," Mrs. Raffle declared. "The really hoity-toity gentry make me uneasy with some of their ways, but by God, there's money to be made from them."

"The marquise," Elmo Sewell went on, "has a certain little-known penchant for wild young men. Her elderly husband is very strict so she cannot satisfy her...er, rather bizarre needs in her immediate circle. She is also exceedingly rich in her own right."

"Oh-ho!" She rubbed her hands together in glee. "Well, since she knows what she's about, 'tis up to me to supply such a plump little chicken with what she desires...fer a hefty price, of course!"

Mrs. Raffle moved rapidly among the tables, stopping here and there to speak with certain young men. With a snap of her fingers, a new table was set up just as Rose made her entrance. Elmo Sewell had melted from view. Mrs. Raffle sailed regally forward, enveloping Rose in a cloud of cloying cheap scent before she was ten feet from her. Sinking into a low curtsy, one that required assistance from one of her dealers before she could gain her feet, she panted and wheezed her greeting. "A great honor, my lady. I have all ready fer ye."

Rose decided against asking for her husband, but sweeping her eyes over the dim interior, she quickly ascertained that he was not in the room. She would play one game to while away a half hour, then if he had not appeared, she would make her departure. Signaling the footmen to wait by the door, she followed Mrs. Raffle to the back of the room. She noted with nervousness that everyone seemed to have stopped their play in order to follow her progress with interest. Many of the women wore necklines so low that the tops of their nipples were displayed, and their transparent gowns showed off as much of their form as they indecently could.

"Here we are, dearie," said Mrs. Raffle, pulling out a chair for Rose. There were five young bucks, all the worse for spirits, sprawled at their ease around the table.

"I do not care to join this company..." Rose started to say when things began to happen very quickly.

One of the young bucks pulled Rose down onto his knee and pawed at her bodice while his friends roared and cheered. Mrs. Raffle realized immediately, from the shock on Rose's face, that a dreadful mistake had been made. Too smart to wade into the five young toffs herself in an attempt to extricate Rose, she called loudly for assistance from her bouncers just as Rose's two footmen leaped forward. The opening of the front door to a sharp draft set the lanterns to dancing crazily, drawing all eyes and halting all action in the room as if a painter had captured the moment with his brush for all to contemplate.

The Marquis of Hetherington stood there, formidable in his formal attire and his brown eyes, like flat pieces of slate in his face, taking in the whole room in a sweep. Mrs. Raffle had one hand stretched toward Rose and the other toward the marquis, serving to direct his focus on his wife instantly. Rose's skirt was rucked up as far as her garters and Geoffrey was to remember long afterward that the thing that made his temper snap was the fact that this was the first time he had so much as seen his wife's limbs, and it had to be in the middle of a gaming house...and under another man's hand.

Shoving past the surprised footmen, Geoffrey bounded forward and delivered a smashing left straight into the face of the buck holding Rose. Then with one arm, he jerked her to her feet like a rag doll. "Time to take your leave, my lady," he snapped.

To Rose, it was a nightmare. She opened her mouth to protest his rough treatment, or perhaps to thank him for saving her, or possibly to demand to know of his presence at such a place, but no sound came. She was unceremoniously pulled from the room, bundled into her cloak and forcefully dragged out into the snow.

The whole miserable scene was burned into Rose's mind like a brand for a long time afterward...the marquis with his angry face...and Mrs. Raffle's great white bosom spilling over the window ledge of the club, surrounded by every face in the room, as everyone stared down at them. She was so humiliated, but still words would not come.

Geoffrey snatched her roughly toward him. "You will be removed from London to Hetherington Harrow immediately. You will remain situated there until I present suitable grounds to the queen for divorce. The servants at Hetherington Harrow will be informed that you are not to leave the grounds for any reason whatsoever, nor are you to receive anyone whosoever. I wish to hell I had never married you, Rose Lambe. And I most certainly never want to set eyes on you again."

With an imperious wave of his hand at the two footmen accompanying Rose, he entered his own coach and disappeared into the swirling snow, leaving her in their care.

"Geoffrey, wait. You don't understand!" Rose wailed, but she had found her voice too late. There was nothing she could do but climb into the carriage and cry her heart out the entire ride to 1 Leicester Street. Once there, she found the house in an uproar and Geoffrey departed again. She knew it was useless to plead with the servants. Her husband had reached 1 Leicester Street first with very explicit orders, and her husband was lord and master. They would not listen to a word she said, nor would they go against him.

Humphrey, although with a touch of moisture in his eyes and a propensity for turning his back to blow his nose, was meticulously correct as to the arranging and dispatching of her trunks. Lettie openly broke down and wailed as she hurriedly sorted and packed essentials. Ordered to accompany her mistress, she squalled as though she shared her mistress's disgrace. Rose was not even to be allowed to wait for morning, or for a break in the dismal weather. As soon as she had changed into her traveling gown, she was escorted to the coach waiting outside the door, with her trunks corded on the back, and the horses of the outriders stamping and snuffling in the snow. Without ceremony, she was bundled inside in dishonor, and the coach rumbled off.

Rose burrowed into her fur and pressed tears from her eyes with the heels of her hands. Extracting a complaining Willy from his basket, she snuggled him into her furs as the only comfort she could expect this night. She thought of the servants of Hetherington Harrow, meeting their mistress for the first time with a cloud of shame over her head. How she wished she could tell the coachman to veer off to Shenstone instead, but she was not to have any say in any of this. She was entirely at their mercy. The feeling of helplessness brought strongly to mind the attempt on her life at Ellensburg. It was very apparent now that Geoffrey, Lord Wyse, truly did wish to be rid of her. She had the horrible feeling she was riding to her death.

If only she had had the chance to explain, but he had

issued his orders and departed the house while she was being banished to the country. Pride had stopped her from writing an explanation to him. He had not trusted her. And in any case, she could not have produced the letter that had lured her to Martha Raffle's because, when she had searched her reticle for it, it had disappeared.

A livid dawn spread over snow-covered London as Mrs. Raffle waddled round the now-empty gaming room snuffing out candles. She stood on tiptoe, stretching to apply the brass snuffer to the last and tallest candelabra without success. She reached round for the nearest chair to stand on, even though to do so with her bulk would be taking her very life in her hands. Dragging the chair forward, she saw a piece of crumpled paper on the floor. Wheezing for breath, she bent over to pick it up. Never leave a piece of paper lying, she thought. It just might be an I.O.U. She smoothed the parchment with her swollen and mottled fingers, and then carried it over to the light of the one remaining candle. She read aloud, "If ye wish to know where yer husband spends his evenings…and with whom…pay a visit late tonight ter Martha Raffle's gaming house, 333 Cockly Street."

Mrs. Raffle shook her head over it. It must have something to do with the little marquise, for the note had been lying by the chair where the young toff had hauled the girl to his lap. She pursed her lips in thought. That piece of work just might bring the authorities down on her neck, and that always meant closures and fines, and a loss of money for old Ma. One had to be careful how one dealt with the nobles.

And that Elmo? Unless memory failed her, the man didn't owe her any blunt, so he shouldn't be harboring grudges. But, somewhere and somehow, the two were connected. And that just might mean unexpected coins for an old woman's pocket. A yawn took over her face. It was so complete and so satisfying that she gave it full range, deciding that she was too old and too weary to cope with the problem at that moment. Standing on the protesting chair, she snuffed the last wavering candle and waddled off to bed.

The crimson dawn awoke Rose from a fitful sleep. She was chilled to the bone and cramped in every muscle. The coach swung into the long drive leading to Hetherington Harrow, and as they approached the great house, the red glow faded, leaving the massive stone structure silhouetted threateningly against the heavy sky.

The majordomo, resplendent in crimson livery and carrying the staff of his office, emerged onto the entrance steps to meet the carriage. As if surprised to see the marquise instead of the marquis, he registered bewilderment before erasing his expression. Sketching Rose a low, stiff bow, he pasted a smile on his features that resembled more a grimace and carried no humor to his eyes. "My lady, Hetherington Harrow is pleased at last to greet the new mistress. I am Mr. Gresham, my lady."

One of the footmen who had traveled with Rose came hesitantly forward, carefully keeping his face averted from Rose. "Excuse me, Mr. Gresham, his lordship, Lord Wyse has directed me to present you with this missive and...er, instructions for it to be read immediately upon our arrival."

Rose, only too sure what the letter contained, moved past the majordomo and entered the great chilly hall. A shivering Lettie crowded close behind her. There was no long line of servants waiting to greet the mistress, nor was anyone waiting to direct her to her apartments. Clearly, Geoffrey had not sent a rider ahead of the chaise to warn the staff of her imminent arrival. That alone could account for Gresham's chilly welcome. It was not considered polite to descend upon one's own house without first announcing the intent. Rose gave a deep, weary sigh, as it would seem she was to be kept waiting in the drafty hall for some attention to be paid her, for she could not be expected to rattle about this great place, seeking the mistress's apartments.

Something about the thick quality of the silence made Rose turn around. Gresham was looking straight at her. He had just finished reading the letter with the marquis's instructions, and his face was twisted with malevolent glee. Rose steeled her expression, but could feel the color drain from her face nevertheless. She drew herself straight and assumed a haughty expression.

"Mr. Gresham, if you will direct me to my apartments, I wish to freshen myself. Please have tea brought up also," she requested. "With two cups, as my maid and I both are chilled to the bone."

"I am afraid that will not be possible," Gresham said with a mockingly shallow bow. "The servants are still abed."

Rose was too fatigued to argue. Retrieving Willy's basket, she turned her back on him and mounted the stairs. "I suppose then, since the marquis employs such inefficient staff at Hetherington Harrow, I am left to seek my own way to my apartments. Lettie, bring just my personal case. After we have rested, we shall carry the remainder of the luggage up the stairs. Is that what you would have me do, Mr. Gresham?"

With a snap of his fat fingers, the majordomo called a small footman who had been sitting night watch, possibly the lowest employee in the ring of staff, to his side. With a flip of his hand, he indicated the lad was to accommodate the marquise. Ducking his head in awe, the boy gathered as much of the luggage as his size would permit and scurried ahead of Rose up the stairs. Although politeness itself, and attempting to do his best to perform the duty of showing the new marquise her rooms with the courtesy he felt it deserved, the boy seem to bump into every table along the way and his uttered apologies soon began to run into one another. It was a relief to finally close the door after him.

"Well, Lettie. I do not like our welcome here. Not at all. And I do not see it getting any better, do you?" Rose asked, pulling the pins from her hat.

"No, my lady." Lettie sniffled.

Rose turned to study the girl with a stern face. "You know, Lettie, this imposed banishment on my part will not affect your position in the house in the least. Pray, do stop the tears."

"Yes, my lady," the maid said. Wiping her eyes and blowing her nose noisily, Lettie attempted a watery smile, for she truly did like the marquise, and she just could not believe any of the rumors flying around below stairs about her.

"That's better," Rose said. Flipping the latch on Willy's basket, she allowed him his freedom. "I think we are all three just overtired. See if there is a bed of any comfort in the dressing room, will you? If there is, let's retire for a bit. I think everything will look most different once we've rested."

"Yes, my lady."

Rose slept heavily for three hours and awoke hungry despite her misery. She rang the bell and waited…and waited. Growing impatient, she sent Lettie to see what was the situation with the servants.

Lettie bustled back after quarter of an hour, her mouth in a thin, furious line. "Well, my lady," she snapped, "that fat slug Gresham says the servants are too *busy* to attend to your needs. I told him that the marquis would hear of his behavior, and he said...he said..." Here Lettie burst into tears. "Oh, my lady," she sobbed. "He says his lordship wouldn't care one whit what became of you or how you were treated."

Rose's face washed as white as the powdery snow drifting and ebbing on the terrace outside. The letter Geoffrey sent must have blistered her character soundly, for the majordomo to be acting so rudely. Whatever was she to do? She shivered and drew the coverlet tighter about her. But, as unhappy as she was, she was still driven by anger at the very unfairness of Geoffrey to treat her this way. Her eyes narrowed and her teeth ground together.

"So he means to starve us? Where is the steward?" she demanded.

"Gone to London to see the marquis," faltered Lettie. "Oh, what on earth are we to do now?"

Rose suddenly flung back the covers and gained her feet. She was not going to spend the rest of her life being bullied. Enough was enough! She wrapped herself in an enveloping robe of crimson velvet and slid her feet into embroidered scuffs. "You shall see, Lettie! You shall see."

The sobbing maid followed closely behind her young mistress as she stalked out into the hall and up to the first landing of the grand staircase. Rose seized the rope of the fire alarm and gave it a mighty pull. The clang-clang-clanging echoed through the great house. Loud excited cries quickly rang out—"Fire! Fire! Fire!"—accompanied by the sound of running feet. Figures scurried to and fro in the hallway below, and on the stairs.

"You there!" Rose shouted. One by one, they looked up to see who had been ringing the fire bell and who called to them. The small figure of the marquise, in her Chinese crimson robe, stood on the landing, clutching the balustrade and looking down into the hall. One by one they fell silent. One by one they stopped. Rose waited until she guessed practically every servant employed by the Harrow had gathered in the hall below her before speaking. Gresham mounted the staircase three steps so that he stood above the rest. He looked insolently amused from Rose to several footmen, and made a rude gesture. The footmen closest to him sniggered, but the rest waited in silence. Rose could only guess what rumors were flying about the Harrow this morning, but whatever they were, they must be faced and faced now.

Her voice was as chilly, and as unwelcoming, as her arrival had been. It echoed throughout the musty air in the hall with great authority. "You have all, as far as I know," she began, "been guilty of the most insolent and disloyal behavior. Whatever the situation between myself and my husband may be at present, I feel you should know him well enough to know that he would not tolerate such treatment of any member of his family." Gresham merely grinned and gave a fat wink to those closest to him. Rose chose to ignore the man. Him, she knew she could not win over with intimidation, but there was hope for some of the others, as she noted more than one set of eyes shifting away in shame.

"I am certain, however, that there are some among you who realize the enormity of your behavior. I can assure you that there are positions in this household that will soon be vacant and offered to others who might be more than pleased to receive a good wage in these hard times. If there are any among you who would serve me as befits my rank, and as the marquis would wish…stand to one side, as I would know my friends in this place."

There was a long heavy silence. At first, Rose feared no

one was going to move. Then, amid jeers and catcalls, the
small footman who had led her to her room moved to the
far right. He stood with his hands behind his back, looking
up at Rose. Then the under butler, a man named Bonner,
moved to join him. He was slowly followed by several
housemaids and six footmen, including the two from London who had traveled with her and knew her better than
the rest. The smile began to leave Gresham's face. The
stillroom maid suddenly scampered to join Rose's side. A
pretty, mischievous-looking girl with a mop of fair curls,
she seemed a favorite, as that encouraged three more young
footmen to move to the right.

When the ranks were divided and no more moved to
Rose's side of the hall, she spoke again. "I applaud you
people for your good character. All those who have shown
loyalty to the marquis and myself this morning will be
handsomely rewarded. The rest of you—" she paused to
sneer openly at them "—will be released from your positions as soon as my husband hears of this affair." Pausing,
she ran lightly down the stairs to stand one step higher than
the fat, slumping figure of Mr. Gresham. She reached out
quickly and snatched the staff of authority from his hand.
He stepped back a bit in surprise before he could halt himself.

"Mr. Gresham, a great number of good, hardworking
people have lost their positions today, and it is all your
doing. You are a great, fat *useless* man." And before anyone realized her intent, she had stamped the staff down
sharply on first one set of toes, then as that foot was picked
up, stamped the other set, until the man was dancing about
the hall. "As of this very moment, you are relieved of your
duties, Mr. Gresham...."

She broke off as the great doors burst open with a force
to crash it back against the wall. A man and woman, both

tall and rangy, stood on the threshold. The man's dress immediately identified him as the local rector, and Rose guessed the woman was his wife. It was a toss-up as to who was the more startled, Rose or the couple, but their mouths hung open in astonishment to see the Marquise of Hetherington in her crimson dressing gown laying about the majordomo with his own staff of authority.

Being a merry soul, the rector's wife recovered first and broke into a grin from ear to ear with candid humor. "Mutiny in the ranks, your ladyship?" she teased, pleased to see an instantaneous lessening of the strain on the young woman's face.

Her husband, the rector, suddenly embarrassed, attempted to smooth over their sudden appearance and his reaction to such goings-on. "We heard the fire bell and came to assist. Pray excuse us, my lady, for barging in...."

Rose moved to extend her hand to the dear man and his wife, for they could clearly be viewed as the king's soldiers in this instant. "If there is any apology needed, it is from myself for having alarmed you unnecessarily. Oh, please do come in out of the cold."

The rector's wife stepped forward to take Rose's hand in both of hers. "Mr. and Mrs. Sunday, that's who we are. Rector and spouse from the village, my lady." With introductions complete, Mrs. Sunday rounded on the gathering of servants, and ordered in a loud stern voice, "Leave us and go about your duties. And bring us some hot tea, do you hear?" The servants sheepishly filed out, those that had elected to stand by Gresham feeling as if they had made a terrible mistake.

When breakfast had been served by a smooth, confident Mr. Bonner, Rose found herself alone in the drawing room with the rector's wife. The rector, being a sensitive and kind man who readily recognized his formidable wife's talent for drawing out the troubles from his parishioners, had tactfully taken himself off to the library. Without meaning to, and without conscious thought, Rose found herself pouring out her troubles into Mrs. Sunday's sympathetic ear. It was such a relief to talk to someone, to have a confidante of the same gender, that she felt she might never stop the overflow of words and tears.

Mrs. Sunday, well used to hearing tales of woe, listened with a clicking of her tongue for the foolishness of youth. When Rose had finished her long tale, and mopped up her tears, Mrs. Sunday leaned back in her chair and surveyed her with amazement. "*Mariage de convenance*, be damned!" she cried, and glanced about to make sure her husband was not around to reprimand her for the lapse. "It seems to me as if you two ninnyhammers are head over heels in love with each other, and don't even know it. And pride, my dear. Such pride! Not to tell your husband of your terrible experience with that Frenchman, and then to think that poor Geoffrey might have had anything to do with that is beyond belief. Why, I've known him since he was just a pup himself."

Rose sighed. "You make it sound so simple. But it was not like that at the time. If Monsieur Bonheur were to be believed then *someone* was trying to harm me and still is. And...and I believed Geoffrey...well, might be in love with someone else."

"Bah!" snorted Mrs. Sunday. "He does not speak of, nor has he ever spoken of, anyone the way he does of you."

"Me?" faltered Rose.

"Yes, you! I think every conversation we had during that long spell he was in residence, was begun, filled with and ended with Rose this and Rose that."

"Oh, if only that were the truth," cried Rose. Her eyes implored the older woman to be speaking the truth.

"Of course it's the truth!" Mrs. Sunday declared. "I am a rector's wife. We're not allowed to tell fibs, you know."

"Oh, I've been so stupid! What if I have lost him forever? What am I to do?" begged Rose, fresh tears threatening.

"Wait until the roads are clear," advised Mrs. Sunday. "And write a letter...a long, detailed letter...and send it to London. Frank my name on it if you think he might return a missive from you unopened. Explain everything to him. Leave nothing out. Tell him everything...*especially* of your deep love for him. It will be all right, you'll see. One of you has to break down this wall of hurt pride and I am afraid, my dear, that even in this modern world, that chore is usually left to the wife. Besides, by now, the marquis will surely have realized his terrible mistake! Mark my words! Geoffrey is no fool, although it's apparent he has been giving a fair imitation of one lately."

Chapter Eighteen

In issuing that statement, Mrs. Sunday was wrong, because the marquis had not yet realized a mistake had been made, although he was beginning to worry excessively. At present, he was fairly well prostrate in his library at 1 Leicester Street, attempting recovery from an exhausting breakfast at which his mother had been harassing him. That lady had bent his ear for well over an hour about the deplorable behavior, the shrewish manners and the unbelievable falsehoods of Sharon Bartley-Bacon. As consummation, she had announced triumphantly that she had sent the deceiving girl packing home to her mama. And then, she had uncharacteristically declared herself to have been in the wrong, while Geoffrey had exhibited the most marked good sense in the matter, and assured him that in the future she would attend more closely to his opinions.

While he was mollified somewhat by her admission and her compliment, it had done little to accelerate the wearisome interview to parry her repeated inquiries as to Rose's whereabouts. Finally, in exasperation, Geoffrey had poured out the whole of the tangled story, and to give the lady her due, Lady Lavitia had listened with an amazing clarity of mind he had seldom seen in her. He had been quite taken aback when she abruptly remarked, with her straightforward manner aimed unmistakably in his direction, "Good Lord, Geoffrey! Are you blind? That girl's besotted with you. And always has been."

By the time Lord Philpotts was announced, Geoffrey was pacing up and down the length of the library, closely followed by a decidedly worried Balderdash. When his large friend filled the doorway, Geoffrey looked up distractedly, then frowned disagreeably at the cheerful look of him. This might not have been the perfect moment for joviality, although Balderdash leaped forward with a reverberating woof of welcome, before cowering back with a whine and resuming his worried expression.

For his part, Lord Philpotts had a rather cheery, healthy glow and looked remarkably similar to a large cat that had just swallowed a particularly delicious canary. "I say, what's the matter with Balderdash?" he demanded, waving a hand at the worried dog. "He looks depressingly beaten down, you know."

"He's been thoroughly put in his place by that damn cat of Rose's," growled Geoffrey, with a disgusted look at the dog.

"Oh, is that all! Cats will do that to a good dog, you know. A good chase will right it. You'll see. But, where's our Rose? I've got tremendous news," Milty cried.

"She's in the country, and trust me when I say that there she will remain for some time," Geoffrey growled again, then resumed his pacing.

Milty's face noticeably fell. "What a disappointment. She would be so thrilled at my news." He looked hopefully at the marquis, who was still pacing up and down. When he did not seem to be at all curious, Milty sighed and asked plaintively, "Well, Geoffrey, aren't you even going to ask me what my news might be?"

Geoffrey stopped his pacing and regarded him with some vexation. "Oh, very well. What is your news?"

Milty took a step backward from the irritated tone. "I don't know as I want to tell you now," he said, sulking a bit. "I come in here quite happy, and all you can do is march up and down like a damned Friday-faced Bengal tiger."

That brought an unwilling smile to Geoffrey's face and he fell obligingly into a chair. "I have been called a lot of things in my time, Milty, but never, until now, a Friday-faced Bengal tiger. Out with your news, man."

"Having retired to my country estates for more than a month, I have reached a monumental decision. As you can see, I have discarded the dandy dress!" he burst out proudly. "I have tired of the malice of the dandy set. Out-and-out rude they can be. Never mindful of a chap's feelings, you see."

The viscount stood straight and proud before the mantel, displaying his decision before the marquis. Rigid days of sports and exercise had reduced his paunchy stomach to comfortable proportions and his rosy face beamed with sun and health. Having just come from Weston and Meyer in Conduit Street, he was free of stays and high heels forever. He felt and acted a new man.

"I will say, you are looking the top of trees, Milty. I think you've hit on the right place for you at last. And I shall be enough of a friend not to say 'I told you so' even once." Geoffrey laughed. He rose to clap his dear friend on the back. "I've always said you were a Corinthian, the way you sit a horse."

"Fact is, I was looking forward to telling Rose about it all. Why is she in the country? Deuced uncomfortable there this time of year, you know?"

"Because I sent her there," admitted Geoffrey wearily.

He plopped back into his seat, and for a second time that morning found himself telling the whole of his miserable story.

Milty looked at him goggle-eyed. "Our Rose? Consorting with a lot of bucks at Ma Raffle's? That's absolutely ludicrous! There must be something else behind it all. Why, Rose is Mrs. Propriety herself! That's why she liked me as an escort. Knew I was safe and that no one would take it seriously, what with my friendship with you and my ridiculous clothes."

Geoffrey seemed to be far away. Milty pursed his lips and narrowed his eyes, then spoke his mind. "Geoffrey, listen to me. There was something havey-cavey about that Ellensburg business," said Milty. He sat down opposite the marquis, leaning forward earnestly. "Remember that day when Rose was crying in St. James's Park and I thought it was because I was boring her to tears with tales of old Mary? You see, some ladies don't *like* horses. Now, that may seem downright strange to you and me, but some women..."

"Oh, Milty," Geoffrey said with a sigh, looking at his dear friend with tried patience. "Just get on with it."

"Oh, yes, where was I? Ah, I've got it. Well, you see, I think she was crying about you and me chasing to Ellensburg, and not about horses."

"That doesn't help me, Milty! On the contrary that leads me to believe that there was something deeper in her relationship with the Frenchman than I had been led to believe," Geoffrey said.

"What a pair you are!" declared Milty in exasperation. "Never seen a marriage like it!"

Geoffrey was just opening his mouth to make an angry retort when Humphrey appeared in the doorway. He cleared his throat not once but three times, obviously making a concerted effort to school his face into the proper, unaffected demeanor before making his announcement.

"Please excuse me, my lord. But there is a... a...*woman*...to see you." He cleared his throat again, obviously intending to imply rather strongly that it was a woman such as he'd not seen before, nor ever wished to again.

"A lady, Humphrey?"

"A *person* who calls herself...er, Mrs. Raffle."

"She does, does she?" said Geoffrey grimly, then tilted eyebrows at his friend. "Well, Milty, here is one seeking blackmail for silence, if I've ever see one. Might as well show her in, Humphrey."

"Of course, my lord," Humphrey answered, clearly not pleased with the decision. He would have much preferred to show her the door, then dispatch no less than three maids to scour the entry hall stem to stern with steaming water.

Mrs. Raffle brushed past poor Humphrey and sailed into the library. Before anyone could advise against it, she sank into a deep curtsy, from which she was unable to rise without the reluctant assistance of Lord Philpotts, for Humphrey would make no move toward her.

A great wave of cloying scent wafted across the room, reminding Geoffrey strongly of Rose's disgrace. "Why have you come?" he asked, leveling his dark eyes at the huge bulk of the gaming house owner.

"I've come about yer dear wife," she wheezed. "I've got something here—" she patted a huge reticule "—that I believe will show there was a plot afoot to discredit the marquise."

"Hand it over!" snapped Geoffrey.

"Not so fast," said Mrs. Raffle, clutching her reticule tightly to her massive bosom. "I come out in this dreadful dirty snow all for the sake of yer good lady's name. I paid for the hire of that there hackney outside. I..."

"You shall be amply rewarded. Now hand it over."

"One thousand guineas," she bargained, naming twice what she had intended to ask for, but a quick inventory of the furnishings and the size of the house demanded she try for more.

"Five hundred and not a penny more."

"I am a poor woman, my lord..." she wheedled.

"Four hundred..."

"Eight hundred, my lord, and the letter is yers."

"Three hundred..."

"Yer a hard, hard man. A rich aristocrat such as yerself should be prepared to shell out proper for to protect such a sweet angel as his lady wife."

"Be off with you!"

"I'll take the five hundred," said Mrs. Raffle quickly, opening her bag, and pulled forth the letter.

Geoffrey snatched it, smoothing the creases, and read it quickly through. Then again slowly, carefully. "Who wrote this?" When she would hesitate, he stepped closer menacingly. "Who wrote this, you bloodsucker, or do I have to choke the information out of you?"

Mrs. Raffle, having spent her life dealing with tough men, stepped back uncertainly before his threat. "I don't know who wrote it. I swear to ye. But I warrant it has something to do with Elmo Sewell. He was there last night. And when I asked what the likes of yer lady was doing at my place, he told me she had gambling fever and a taste for young lads. I was only trying to supply the demands of a wealthy client, when ye came charging in."

Geoffrey turned his back to stride to the window, putting distance between him and the woman. "You may go, Mrs. Raffle."

"But yer lordship, it's an uncommon cold day, and I was hoping to moisten my lips with a little something," wheedled Mrs. Raffle, looking with longing at the array of crystal decanters on the sideboards, all of which gleamed with tempting amber liquid.

Quick as a cat, the marquis spun from the window. "Humphrey!" he shouted, fully aware the butler would be hovering just outside the door. He then turned hard eyes on the woman. "I have never struck a woman, Mrs. Raffle, but if you do not take yourself out of my sight, I shall moisten your lips with your own blood. Humphrey, take this person to the front door and see that she leaves. If one word passes her lips, call the authorities and have her arrested. The charge will be extortion and kidnapping."

"And right he'll be, too!" joined in Milty with a dark look. This rather sizable gentleman standing against her too was her undoing, and she fled.

Geoffrey marched to the hearth and stood silently looking into the fire until the door slammed behind Mrs. Raffle. "I'll kill him," he stated simply.

"And then I shall kill him next," replied Milty in agreement. "Let's go. We'll probably find him at Brook's."

The famous club was thin of company, but as expected, Elmo Sewell was seated at one of the windows with a circle of ribald fellows who, like him, hung about on the fringes of society, always eager to advance themselves at the expense of someone else.

With little warning, Lord Wyse strode up to their table with Lord Philpotts close behind him. All fell silent; some even cringed away from the thunder on his face as the marquis removed his tan York gloves and struck Elmo Sewell sharply across the face with them. "You have plotted and schemed in the most despicable manner against my wife, Elmo Sewell," announced Geoffrey. "I demand satisfaction."

"You're mad," Elmo countered with a tight, fixed smile. "I refuse to talk to you. You have lost your mind. I have witnesses to that fact."

Geoffrey lifted Elmo's glass of spirits and dashed the entire contents full in his face. "What do I have to do to make you accept my challenge, you coward?" he demanded.

Elmo lifted a hand to swipe the stinging spirits from his eyes. Even so, he might have been able to withstand the marquis's challenge, but then one of his companions snickered slightly, bruising his ego severely. "All right, I'll meet you! And God in Heaven, I will kill you!" growled Elmo Sewell, leaping to his feet.

Geoffrey slammed Elmo back into his chair with a firmly placed palm in the middle of his chest, and curled his lip in disgust. "I believe you are in some way related to me, Sewell, which only compounds the insult. You are a disgrace to the Hetherington name."

Elmo shivered with hatred. "How dare you say I am not worthy of the Hetheringtons! Were it not for you I would have my own estates and my own title. Did you honestly think I'd stand by and see you father brats on that common little slut you married? Call me a disgrace, would you? Name your seconds, by God. I'll see you in hell well before me!"

There were plenty who would volunteer to stand up for both men, if for no other reason than to see blood. A time was set for dawn at Chalk Walk in Hyde Park. Leaving Brook's, Geoffrey signaled his groom to trail behind as he elected to walk some of the fury away. Ever faithful Milty trailed his friend through the sooty snow of London, for what seemed like hours to the viscount, who was breaking in new boots in the most brutal manner possible.

Milty was the first to speak. "They say Elmo Sewell is a good man with a sword."

"So am I," remarked Geoffrey, and both fell silent again. Melting snowflakes ran down his face like tears and glinted off his snowy cravat. Fear and worry for his little wife consumed him. He remembered all her shy and hesitant approaches and how he had brutally snubbed her, hiding his hurt feelings behind a mask of formality. How could he have been so blind as to think she could embroil herself in such seediness as Ma Raffle's sort? He contemplated Elmo Sewell. How had it been possible for one man, and not even a man who moved in the same circles as himself and Rose, to carry forth such an intricate plot with such efficiency? Abruptly he stopped dead in his tracks, deep in thought. Milty ambled aimlessly round him in the snow like a pet dog.

"Sharon!" cried Geoffrey. "She had to have been a part of this plot. Think of it, man. It was she who told me of Rose's gambling...and sent me to Ma Raffle's last night!" He swung abruptly about to signal for his mount. Once mounted, he thundered off in the direction of Clarence Square, where his mother had reported Sharon had taken up residence once her welcome had been cut short at Lady Lavitia's Grosvenor Square town house. Milty dutifully followed.

Sharon Bartley-Bacon was seated in the drawing room with Lord Abernathy. When the Marquis of Hetherington strode forcefully into the room followed closely by a frowning, rather formidable Lord Philpotts, she fluttered to her feet, with guilt and terror etched on her face.

"A word with you in private, Miss Bartley-Bacon," said

Geoffrey, pointedly holding open the door and frowning at the elderly lord. "If you will excuse us, Lord Abernathy."

Lord Abernathy wheezed to his feet, and stepped in front of Sharon. "I say, Hetherington, I can't be ordered from the room that way. This is outrageous behavior. This lady is my fiancée, and if you insist on compromising her in such a fashion, I must make it my business to call you out."

"If that is your wish, Lord Abernathy," Geoffrey grated. "As I have plans to meet with another gentleman at Chalk Walk this next dawn, I can accommodate you soon after I have completed my business with him. Lord Philpotts is acting as second. Register your time preference with him. Miss Bartley-Bacon?"

Sharon's eyes flashed to Lord Wyse's stern face and knew the game was up. There might yet be a way to save the day, and her engagement, but only if she got rid of Lord Abernathy. Turning to the florid man, she leaned slightly toward him and placed a hand upon his arm. "Please excuse me, my lord. It is not as you suspect. Why, it's practically family business, you know. You just seat yourself back down here and I shall be no more than one second," she cajoled. With a pat on his hand, and a limpid smile, she passed through the door ahead of the two lords.

Leading Lord Wyse and the diligently faithful Lord Philpotts to the library, she firmly closed the door behind them for privacy. "You must forgive my Lord Abernathy. I fear he will need a firm hand once we are married."

"So, it seems, will you," said Geoffrey, moving toward her. She backed away before the fury on his face. "I have just discovered Elmo Sewell has been plotting against my wife. He sent her a note to lure her to a certain gaming house. Then the thought came to me, that it was you who so touchingly told me I would find Rose there. Do you have a believable explanation for that?"

Sharon thought quickly. Obviously the marquis did not know of her involvement, or he would be here with recriminations, not questions. She gave him a tremulous smile, and stalled for time to think. "How horrible! I never did like that man. Oh, poor little Rose!"

Geoffrey was not to be taken in so easily. "Yes, poor Rose, indeed. I believe you have been seen in the company of Sewell on more than one occasion, Sharon."

"Well, yes..." Sharon attempted to give the impression that his statement had sparked a memory. "Of course, my dear Geoffrey, it was Mr. Sewell who told me all about Rose going to those awful places. Now that I recollect, he did suggest I speak to you about her behavior. He was so convincing that I did not suspect a plot."

Geoffrey glared hard into her face, seeking to tell if she spoke the truth or if she was attempting yet another deceit. "Is that all?"

"Oh, Geoffrey." She leaned toward him. "After all we've been to each other, you must believe me."

Her mouth was trembling and her large eyes shone with tears. Geoffrey could see no deceit on her face. "Very well, Sharon," he said heavily. "It appears you have been as much a dupe as myself." He stepped back from her in dislike. "Come, Milty. The air is foul in here."

Knowing she must return quickly to Lord Abernathy, Sharon sank into a chair on watery legs. Just one second more, she promised herself, to gather my wits. She rubbed her sweat-slicked palms on her skirt and drew in a ragged breath. She had most certainly barely escaped what surely would have been social death.

But her dilemma was not to be resolved so easily. Unannounced, Elmo Sewell burst into the library, followed closely by the outraged butler. "Have you heard from

Hetherington?'' he demanded, coming to stand over her
with his snow-laden coat dripping.

Sharon shooed the butler away, then drew her skirts
away from Sewell in insult. ''Yes, in fact you just missed
him. If you hurry, you can catch him at the corner.''

''Stop your damn nonsense! Does he know of your part
in this?'' Sharon shook her head. ''Good! You will do one
more thing for me. The bastard is to meet me at Chalk
Walk at five in the morning. You must alert the authorities
and have the duel stopped.''

Sharon surveyed him with contempt. ''You are frightened of Geoffrey?''

''Do as I say and spare me your insults,'' he snapped.

''Oh, very well.'' Sharon sighed. But after he had gone,
she stared out the window as he climbed into his carriage.
A slow smile curved her lips. ''No, I shall not do as you
ask. I shall not alert the authorities, Mr. Sewell. And I hope
to God he kills you. Dead. Dead. *Dead!*''

''Miss Bartley-Bacon, I feel it is imperative that I speak
honestly with you,'' came Lord Abernathy's voice behind
her.

Sharon put her polite face on before she turned to attend
her fiancé. ''Yes, my dear Lord Abernathy. Come, seat
yourself before the fire. You do know how cranky you become when you are unnecessarily chilled.''

The elderly lord did not heed her solicitous comment,
but continued to stand in the doorway. He looked at her
with narrowed eyes, and said in a dead tone, ''Miss Bartley-
Bacon, I took your explanation to heart upon your removal
from Lady Wyse's in Grosvenor Square, and believed you
implicitly when you said you had been unjustly tried there.
I offered you my protection in marriage, and the security
of my home under the care of my sister until our wedding
could take place. But, having had close contact with you

these few weeks, and in light of the events of this day alone, I fear you are not of the character to make my twilight years a pleasure.''

"But...but Charles," Sharon stammered, holding her hands out in pleading. "How will it look if you cry off now? You will smear my reputation."

"No, my dear," he answered. "You have smeared your own reputation. You see, I have heard it all. You are beautiful to look upon, and I fear I allowed that to cloud my thinking. But, alas, you are only beautiful on the outside."

Sharon could only hang her head in pretended shame, and damn all men to hell. Now what? Only one answer came to mind for she knew of the old man's weaknesses. Slowly she raised her hands and began to undo the buttons on her bodice to bare her breasts. Tears filled her eyes. So she had come to this. She foresaw a long life stretching out before her, and it did not look to be a pleasurable one.

The first task Lord Wyse accomplished upon his return to 1 Leicester Street was to instruct his steward, Jay Marsh, to alert two hearty footmen to stand ready to ride hard for Hetherington Harrow at first light with a message to Rose that he would arrive there as soon as weather and business permitted. He also granted Marsh the authority to immediately, and publicly, restore all rights and privileges to the marquise with his heartfelt apologies. Then he retired to his library and closed the door, seeking solitude regardless of Milty's unrestrained protests.

Going to his desk, he pulled several pages of parchment toward him with a purpose in mind. He raised his pen but could only stare down at the paper, seeing Rose's sweet face. What if she did not love him? What if he had waited too late? What if she would never forgive him his abominable treatment of her? The hours stretched out as he searched for the correct phrases to explain what was in his heart in case he should not return alive from Chalk Walk. Sheet after sheet was crumpled and flung toward the hearth as he slaved over the delicate task of explaining to his wife that he had fallen head over heels in love with her and, in retrospect, must have been in love with her for a long time.

Finally, as the night watch moved through the house, dousing candles and banking fires, Geoffrey set his seal to the pages with some sort of satisfaction and peace. Placing the weighty packet on the table for Jay Marsh, he climbed the stairs to his bed. A burdensome heaviness suddenly seemed to have been lifted from his soul. There was nothing else to do but retire to bed and pray that he would acquit himself with honor on the morrow.

As the pale dawn crept across the wintry landscape, Geoffrey stirred from his seat before the window. Having not slept at all, he did not feel particularly tired, or apprehensive. Rising, he dressed himself quickly without rousing his valet. His anger of the day before had not abated one whit, and as he urged his horse through the heavy snow in the direction of Chalk Walk, he was followed by the, for once, silent Lord Philpotts, who had been solemnly waiting for him as he descended the stairs that morning.

The night had also been sleepless for the viscount, but his had been tortured by thoughts. He feared for the safety of his dearest friend, and dreaded the task that might follow the duel. As by right, he would be the one to inform little Rose of her husband's demise, should the contest go against the marquis. The thought of having to perform such a task, to be the one to break Rose's heart, brought him several times to the point of suggesting he be the one to fight Elmo Sewell in Geoffrey's place. For, in truth, any affront to Rose, or to Geoffrey, was also an affront to himself. Although, looking at the marquis's tall, athletic figure riding in front of him, he doubted he could wrest the honor of killing Sewell from him.

The white fields of Chalk Walk were spread out in sleepy silence under their blanket of snow. The surgeon arrived in a hack just as the clock in a neighboring steeple began to strike five, but there was no sign of his opponent.

He did not mean to come, thought Milty with a huge sigh of relief. "The coward is not going to show, Geoffrey," he said, edging his horse nearer to Geoffrey's. "I know a cozy little inn where we can have a spanking breakfast, then set off for Hetherington Harrow. Surprise our Rose, you see."

Geoffrey stayed rigidly upon his horse without replying, his hard narrowed eyes constantly raked over the snowy field. Sewell's seconds arrived together, but still no sign of Elmo Sewell. The steeple clock mournfully struck the quarter past and the faintest gray line of light appeared on the horizon.

"The bastard isn't coming," declared Sewell's second, spitting on the ground to show his disgust. "Come on, Lord Wyse, we'll hunt him down in London, shoot him in his tracks like the cowardly dog he is!"

"We wait!" commanded the marquis in such a voice that the man quickly moved away to stamp his feet in the cold, suddenly worried he might be the brunt of the rather large load of anger the marquis seemed to be sporting. Just when he thought to approach Lord Wyse again, a solitary horseman was heard riding slowly toward them.

Elmo Sewell was desperately looking for the officers of the law. He had given them plenty of time to get there. As he rode across the field, he suddenly realized that Sharon Bartley-Bacon had alerted no one, probably in the hope that he would be cleanly disposed of. With a certain amount of resignation, he slowly dismounted. Being a fair shot and a skilled swordsman did not mean he relished this duel. He was much more comfortable plotting against women. Nevertheless, coats were removed, swords were presented, weapons selected and the duelists squared off facing each other...and Lord Philpotts turned his back.

"Hey! You're one of the seconds. Turn around," the surgeon admonished him.

"I can't watch," admitted Milty, tears forming in his eyes. "Best friend I ever had, you see."

"Come on, man. Your duty to see that there's fair play," he urged, only mollified when Milty dried his eyes and dutifully turned around to watch the duel proceed.

It quickly became evident that both men were out for blood. Sewell proved to be a wicked bladesman, and at times, the marquis was hard-pressed. But Sewell's hate and temper began to get the better of him as his tall opponent skillfully parried every move and escaped every trap. He became wild with rage, lashing and lunging and hacking, his feet sliding on the ground as it became trampled and treacherous with mud.

Suddenly, the marquis missed his own footing and went to his knees in the snow. Elmo Sewell leaped down on him with a tremendous thrust and Milty clamped his eyes closed. He did not see Geoffrey twist away from the glittering point and strike upward. There was a loud gasp, then a long silence, and when the viscount opened his eyes, Elmo Sewell was lying on the ground, his blood staining the white snow a deep crimson. Lord Wyse stood with the point of his blade nicking Elmo's throat, then he snorted and turned away.

"Hetherington!" Elmo gasped. The marquis turned to look down at the wounded man with a bland face. Elmo raised himself up on one elbow. "Sharon Bartley-Bacon," he gasped, out of breath from his exertions, weakening from loss of blood. "She was in the plot from the announcement of your engagement at the Townsend ball. Do not let the bitch off easy."

His voice trailed away and the surgeon bustled forward to inspect the wound. "He'll live, gentlemen. The wound is deep, but not lethal."

"Good," gritted Geoffrey. "He is not worth fleeing the country for. Sewell, if you ever come near my wife again, I shall hunt you down like the vermin you are, and see you hang for conspiracy. Do you hear me?"

Elmo only nodded, his hooded eyes filled with anger and hatred. He shoved the surgeon away and accepted the hand of his second, never taking his eyes off the departing marquis. Do not think I am done with you, Hetherington, he thought. Do not feel safe enough to leave your back unguarded!

Milty held out Geoffrey's coat with smiles of exuberant relief. "Splendid work, Geoffrey. Now let's retire to that inn. Best breakfast in town, I tell you."

Geoffrey shrugged into his coat. "First of all, I have a call to pay on Miss Sharon Bartley-Bacon."

Milty rubbed his growling stomach, but nevertheless followed Geoffrey to the horses. "Won't do any good to confront that cat. Can't slap her in the face with a glove, you know. The worse thing you can do to her is refuse to receive her in your home and ignore her in public. Be the worst thing."

Geoffrey thought a moment, then admitted the validity of Milty's suggestion. Besides, a detour to Clarence Square would only delay his reaching Rose. "Right you are, Milty. Let's retire back to 1 Leicester Street for breakfast, then it's off to Hetherington Harrow for me. Come if you will, my friend, but I'll not rest until I am face-to-face with Rose."

Milty pondered a moment, then announced, "Well, I feel I must come. Our Rose would never forgive me if I let you go careering off alone with the roads near impassable."

Geoffrey swung aboard his mount. "Tell me, Milty, old friend, just at what point did Rose become *our* Rose, instead of *my* Rose?"

Milty directed a slightly exasperated look at the marquis. Perhaps it was time for a bit of harsh truth. "Well, I suppose the first time you chose to ignore her, old boy," he stated rather strongly. "Told you before, she's a deuced pretty little thing and bound to come to trouble if left on her own. Figured it was my place to look after her until you saw fit to come to your bloody senses."

"I see," said Geoffrey with a laugh, taken aback slightly by his friend's candor. "Rest assured, Milty. I shall be taking care of *my* Rose from this day forward. But for now, let's pray this whole affair had ended with Elmo's blood the only one spilt."

Milty swung astride his mount. "Right you are. Now let's make good time to the Harrow, shall we? Can't wait to show Rose my new look. She'll be pleased as punch, she will. Never said much, but now I think back on it... Damn! Must have been deuced uncomfortable for her to be seen in public with me, don't you know...."

Geoffrey, fearing this one-sided conversation might prove lengthy, spun his mount and set off for 1 Leicester Street, leaving Lord Philpotts and his conversation to trail behind him. His one thought was to reach Rose's side in the best time possible.

Chapter Nineteen

The impatient men had different thoughts as they fought their way northward through deep snow, impassable roads and bitter cold. Although it made for an unbearably miserable ride, Geoffrey was glad they had taken the trip under saddle, for a carriage would never had made it through the deeply rutted roads and piled drifts as far as the eye could see. The road was indistinguishable and rendered unfamiliar in more than one place, because most persons of sanity had stayed indoors before the home fires. Just before dark, they struggled around a bend in the road in Balderdash's wake, and drew rein beside the wildly barking dog. A light traveling vehicle was upended in a ditch.

Geoffrey's mouth settled into a hard line as he recognized his own crest upon the door. "Something must have happened to Marsh. They couldn't have made it too far on foot. Probably no farther than the Keg and Kettle at the next intersection."

Milty swung stiffly down, calmed the dog and scanned the ground. "There's tracks aplenty here, foot and wheel. Would seem someone's happened on them and carted them away from the looks of it all," he declared.

"Just in case, keep a sharp eye for them," Geoffrey cautioned.

They rode slowly on, scanning the fields and ditches for any sign of the steward and the footmen. Luckily the snow made the dark less formidable or they might have ridden past the injured men in the night. As they rounded the last bend beside the river, they spied the small country inn, which seemed huddled down in the snow. Relieved at reaching this respite from the cold without finding bodies in the snow, they dismounted and strode into the taproom with the marquis calling loudly for the barkeep.

He was met instead by one of his own footmen, who was descending the stairs, and whose face lit up with relief when he saw the marquis. "Oh, my Lord Wyse," he cried. "We were overturned and Mr. Marsh has gone and snapped his leg. He lies upstairs now in high fever, and Jem and me...well, we was feared to leave him, we was."

"You did well," Geoffrey said, slapping the boy on the shoulder encouragingly. He rapidly mounted the stairs and pushed into the room where Marsh lay bundled and white as death.

Jem, the second footman, jumped to his feet. "Your lordship..."

"How is he doing, Jem?" Geoffrey demanded, placing a hand on the old man's flushed brow.

"The fever seems less, and I think he's resting easier now. The barkeep will go for the physician in the morning...when the roads have cleared somewhat."

"Roads cleared? Humph!" Geoffrey grunted. "That could be spring." He turned to the young footman and put his hand on his shoulder. "You did well to get him here. This is a good, clean place. I will leave you here to wait for the surgeon. Jem will come with me. I must ride on to Hetherington, for I am riddled with anxiety to see my wife.

I shall send Jem back with a sturdy carriage as soon as the roads can be navigated. When the physician agrees to his movement, bring Mr. Marsh to Hetherington. He will heal better in his own home.''

"Yes, my lord," the young man said, solemnly nodding his head.

The marquis's face was drawn and worried as he returned to the taproom. Milty was seated in front of the fire, boots extended to the blaze and a rather large toddy in his hand. Balderdash sprawled at his feet. "Come now, Geoffrey. There's no way we can continue tonight. Even with the daylight, the track is easily lost. The horses are done in, and I might add, me as well.''

Geoffrey sank down across from the viscount and accepted an equally large tankard of warmed whiskey. "I know you are right, but damn, I chafe at the delay. I never should have sent Rose to Hetherington Harrow. And certainly not accompanied by such a caustic note. I very much doubt she has been well treated. You know how Gresham can be.''

Milty chuckled deeply. "Yes, it was a bad rub, that move. And one for which you might have to pay a dear forfeit to the little spitfire. Devil of a temper for such a small person, you know. Pity poor Gresham.''

Geoffrey relaxed somewhat and leaned back with a chuckle. "I fear you are right. Well, as there is nothing to do but sit out the night, we might as well eat hearty, and get our rest. Tomorrow will be another such as today. Blasted weather!''

"Right you are on that," Milty agreed. Then as if a thought suddenly came to him, he added, "I say, old man. You don't happen to have a bracelet or such on you? Might smooth the way a bit. The ladies do like that sort of thing, you know. Especially if it's all sparkling with diamonds or some such...."

Geoffrey looked stunned for a moment, then grinned. "No. No bracelet. But I will go one better. If a bribe is called for, I shall offer Balderdash's head on a platter. Rose does set such store by that cat of hers..."

It was Milty's turn to look stricken. Reaching to draw the wolfhound's head toward him in a decidedly protective gesture, he turned a rather stern glare toward the marquis. "You do understand, of course, Geoffrey, it'll have to be my head first," he ardently vowed.

Elmo Sewell grasped the handle of the door and gave it an energetic pull. Pain ripped through his chest, causing him to gasp and sink to his knee in the snow. "Damn that Hetherington. I'll see him dead, I will."

"Right ye are, gov. Here, best be lettin' me do that kinda stuff. Can't have ye faintin' on me now," the tough at his side declared. "Damn near kilt yerself riding all night as it is."

Elmo levered himself to his feet and shrugged off the man's helping hand. "Just keep your mouth shut and shove that damn door."

The door to the ice cellar fortunately opened inward, for its doorway was banked with snow. It swung in smoothly, showing a long, low cavernous passage to the two men.

The tough shivered mightily. "Don't much like this place, gov."

"You won't have to be here long. Just do as I tell you and we'll be out of here before you know it. Have you go the cat?"

"Right here," he said, holding up a sack with a lump in the bottom. As he gave it a shake, the lump emitted a angry meow. "Lady Luck 'twas smiling on us, gov, when the lady let her cat out that side door, huh?"

"Shut up. Just do as I tell you when I tell you. You hear?" Elmo ordered. He leaned against the wall and held his chest. The hard night's riding had caused the wound to reopen, and now it was bleeding through the bandage and seeping through his shirt. It might well not be lethal, as the surgeon had said, but it certainly was painful. He'd see Hetherington suffered well and thoroughly for doing this to him.

"Willy-y-y," a voice called from the side door.

Both men scurried to the entrance to the ice cellar to crouch in the dark doorway.

"Willy-y-y, where are you?"

Light spilled out into the snow from the open side door, but as yet no one ventured forth. Elmo leaned over to whisper in the tough's ear. "You stay here. Hide behind the door, while I ease outside. Every so often, shake the sack so she can hear the cat. When she steps in, you shove her to the rear of the passage and get out quick. Bolt the door closed behind you. I'll be there. Do you understand?"

"Yeah, gov. I understand, but..." The roughneck hesitated, obviously thinking he might just be locked inside the eerie place and left to freeze as well.

"I said, I'd be outside. It would serve me no good to have you in here with her, you idiot. Just do as I say!" Elmo snarled. Pushing off the wall, he eased outside and around the corner of the building, just as Rose stepped out the door.

"Willy, come here!" Rose called, clearly exasperated. From a short distance came a muffled cry of an obviously distressed feline. "Willy?" When the cry came again, she drew her robe tightly about her night rail, stepped gingerly into the snow and started down the path. When she would have passed the ice cellar doorway, the sack was shaken again, and Willy obligingly let out a loud squall.

"Willy, for goodness' sake, what are you doing in there?" Ducking her head, she stepped through the low doorway. Plucking a candle from the wall niche, she struck a lucifer to the wick and moved slowly down the corridor. Suddenly, a sack was tossed at her feet with a great squabble of hissing and squalling, and she was slammed to the ground by a hand in the middle of her back. The candle guttered and went out just as the slamming door threw the passage into total darkness.

Rose swallowed her scream and lay very still, unsure if her assailant was within or without. When the only sound came from the sack at her side, she eased to her knees. Leaning back against the icy wall, she carefully felt around her for the candle. Assuming she had flung it when she fell, she slid up the wall and felt her way back to the doorway, fearing herself snatched and throttled with each step. Her heart pounded in her ears and she held her breath until she became dizzy. Feeling quickly over the shelf, she grabbed another candle and a lucifer, scattering the rest over the floor in her haste.

Ducking down, in case something was aimed at her head, she struck the lucifer and held it aloft. Relieved to find herself alone, she carefully restored light to the candle. She tugged at the door, but it was securely bolted from the outside and would not budge. Quickly realizing the futility of that escape, she lit as many candles as were on the shelf and planted them on the floor before the door. Only then, when she had some knowledge of her situation, did she hurry back to the sack.

"Willy?" she whispered. The struggling stopped and a low, mournful meow came from the cat. The knot was not overly tight, and in seconds Rose had it worked loose with her fingernails, and had Orange Willy in her arms. His eyes were huge, and she was relieved to see he was much more irritated than hurt. Soothing him in the cradle of her arms, she kissed his furry head before setting him down at her feet. "I'm not sure what we've gotten ourselves into now, Willy, but it doesn't bode too well for our health."

Walking down the passage, she attempted to see if there was another way out. The air became more and more frigid, and she began to shiver. The passage ended in a great vault piled high with glistening blocks of ice and straw. "Ice! Willy, we're in the icehouse. I remember tales of such places on country estates. They draw these blocks of ice from the lake in winter and store them here in this vault to supply ice for summer."

Willy wound around her legs, obviously caring more about leaving this place than the purpose of it. Rose held her candle high above her head. "I don't think there's another door in this end. We must be far beneath the house...."

Suddenly the long stalactite forms hanging from the roof developed masses of red eyes blinking in the wavering candlelight and Rose heard the slow rasping sound of leathering wings. Bats! She gave a faint scream and turned about. Dropping her candle, and snatching Willy from the floor, Rose dashed down the passage. The disturbed bats wheeled and squeaked. Midway, Rose dropped to her knees and flung her flowing skirt over her head and Willy's. Holding tightly to the struggling cat, she crouched as low against the icy stone floor as possible, drawing deep breaths, ordering herself not to faint from fright.

It took hours for the bats to become quiet again. Only then, did Rose ease the robe from her head and release Willy. She was shivering uncontrollably with cold and fright. Who would do such a thing to her? Mrs. Sunday had convinced her that Geoffrey would never plot another's demise, but who else hated her this much? Crawling the last part of the passage, she pressed her ear against the outer door, hearing nothing but the faint sound of wind filtering through as if from another world. She dared not call out for fear of arousing the sleeping bats, and besides, the only person who would possibly be waiting would be the person who had imprisoned her here in the first place.

"Think, Rose, think!" she admonished herself. Orange Willy came to crawl into her lap, shivering with cold and fright also. "Willy, let's put our heads together on this, shall we? Whoever shut us in here felt that this was a fairly obscure place and we'd not be found easily. So, if we're going to be here a great while, perhaps a little conservation on candles might be in order." Licking her finger and thumb, she pinched out all but one of the candles. Wrapping the cat into the folds of her robe, she snuggled him close to her breast for warmth. "I let you out just before dawn, which means there won't be anyone to notice my absence until Lettie decides I've been under the covers long enough. That could be close to luncheon, for Mrs. Sunday is expected. Surely a body wouldn't freeze before luncheon, would it?" She shivered mightily and pressed her ear to the crack in the door again. There were no sounds of a search. Rose began to cry hopelessly. There was no one in the whole world to care if she lived or died.

Geoffrey, Milty and Jem arrived at Hetherington Harrow by luncheon. Turning their mounts over to the stable master, they stomped into the entry demanding food and brandy, both in abundance and as close to the library fire as possible.

"Bonner, where is Gresham? Not taken ill, I hope,"

Geoffrey asked, gladly taking the offered brandy snifter from the extended tray.

"No, my lord," Bonner answered solemnly. "He was relieved of his duties by Lady Wyse...er, not long after her arrival. He will most probably be wishing to speak with you later."

Geoffrey tilted an eyebrow toward Milty with significant meaning. "I fear, with my out-and-out stupidity, I have brought a great deal of insurrection about my household."

"So it would seem," Milty agreed, with a chuckle. "So it would seem."

"Bonner, would you please tell her ladyship that I will await her pleasure here in the library?"

"Of course, your lordship. I shall inform her maid, as her ladyship has yet to descend stairs."

Geoffrey merely nodded, but Milty's eyebrow went up in surprise. "It's not like our Rose to be a lay-abed—" he pursed his lips in contemplation, then his brow cleared "—although, there are seldom worse days than this to spend beneath the coverlet, huh? Besides, this is the country after all. Supposed to rusticate a bit in the country."

"Well, it's a fine muddle when my best friend knows more of my wife's habits than I do. I, for one, am quite eager to see her," Geoffrey said, moving to lean against the mantel and stare into the fire. "I only hope I can make her listen to me. Wouldn't blame her if she tossed me into the snow on my ear, after the way I've treated her."

"Nor I. It was truly abominable of you," Milty said, tossing off his brandy and smacking his lips. He looked about for someone to replenish his snifter or failing that, the decanter itself, completely missing the dumbfounded look on the marquis's face.

The door eased open again to admit Bonner, followed closely by Lettie. Geoffrey turned in eager expectation.

Bonner bowed stiffly. "Your lordship, her ladyship's maid is without. She wishes to speak with you, if you would permit."

"Of course," Geoffrey said, motioning Lettie forward. "What's amiss?"

Bonner cleared his throat uneasily and filled in for the weeping Lettie. "It would seem Mrs. Sunday is here for luncheon and...er, her ladyship is missing, my lord."

"Missing!" exclaimed Geoffrey and Milty in one breath. It took no more than two steps for Geoffrey to reach Lettie and grasp her shoulders roughly. He barely refrained from shaking the words from her. "Since when!"

Intimidated beyond belief, Lettie whipped up the tail of her apron and stuffed it, and her fingers, into her round mouth with a squeak. The scowl on the marquis's face was so fierce, she could only cringe and blubber incoherently. Great tears began to overflow her eyes. Not only was her mistress missing, with Mrs. Sunday in the drawing room for luncheon, now she had to face the formidable marquis with her tale of woe, and she was terribly afraid of him, especially after the way he had banished his poor blameless wife from his sight.

"Here, Geoffrey, best let me," Milty said, drawing the weeping maid away from Geoffrey, and into the nearest chair. "Now here...er—" He glanced up at Bonner to supply the maid's name.

"Lettie, my lord."

"Now, Lettie. There's nothing to fear. Just tell me what you know. When did you suspect your mistress wasn't where she was supposed to be?" the large man asked soothingly.

Geoffrey paced back to the mantel and leaned over to stare into the flames to keep himself from rushing the interrogation with his impatience. If something had happened to Rose, he'd hunt Sewell down and end his life in the most painful manner imaginable.

Lettie, using the same apron tail to swipe at her face, cast nervous glances at the marquis, but answered readily enough. "I—I'm so-so-sorry, m-m lord. It was just after ten."

"That's a girl," encouraged Milty, turning to beam upon Geoffrey's turned back as if to say, see what results mere kindness gleans?

Heartened by Milty's approval, Lettie told her tale, such as it was. "I went to wake her at ten, for you see, Mrs. Sunday is coming for luncheon and I knew she'd want to be up and about."

"Yes, yes. That's as it should be."

"But she wasn't th-there," wailed Lettie.

"Now, hush your weeping. Let's see. Just tell me. Where would she have gone? Has the house been searched?"

"I looked and looked but she has just disappeared."

"No one just disappears. We'll get a search up immediately," Geoffrey said, spurred to action by worry. "Bonner, call out everyone. The women will search the house and the men the grounds. Now, Lettie, can you think of anything else? Anything at all?"

"Well, I don't think she was dressed, my lord. Her red robe was lying just over the foot of her bed, but now it's missing too—" she raised bright eyes as another thought came to her "—and Willy! I haven't seen Willy! She always takes that cat out first thing in the mornings!"

"All right, that narrows it somewhat. Look for any place she might have gone looking for her cat. Perhaps she's injured herself, knocked unconscious or somewhat," ordered Geoffrey, striding rapidly into the entry hall and dragging forth his greatcoat again. "Make haste! Everyone physically able, make a thorough search."

Milty joined him, and began to shrug into his wet coat as well. "That's probably it, you know, Geoffrey. Our Rose was probably chasing her cat and hit her head or something. Probably nothing more," he fretted, trying to ease his own sense of worry as well as the marquis's.

Geoffrey turned a set face toward his friend. Visions of Rose lying injured in the freezing cold, or worse, done in by foul play, filled his head. It seemed as if fate was conspiring with happenstance to keep them apart. What next? That thought was one that he chose to disregard, for it could only be worse than what he faced at present. "Pray God that is all it is, Milty. Pray God," he said.

Chapter Twenty

The day wore on at a snail's pace. Rose, having exhausted herself, first by weeping, then calling at the crack in the door until her voice was hoarse, had finally curled up with Willy, napping fitfully until cramped with cold.

Again and again, she forced herself stiffly to her feet to pace back and forth to bring blood coursing into tingling limbs. She carefully stayed toward the front of the passage as she could not bring herself to disturb the bats again. The lucifers gave out first, and then the candles burned out one after another, until finally Rose was forced to steal quietly down the passage to the ice vault to retrieve the one she'd dropped in her fright. Returning to the entrance, she carefully held the wick to the nearly melted one on the stone floor with a shaky hand. Sitting back, she gathered Willy tightly to her.

"This last one will last no longer than three hours, Willy. And when it goes, we will be left in darkness with the bats. I don't like that idea at all," she whispered into the warm fur. "We need light and warmth. What do you think, Willy? If we tried to set the straw on fire, do you think we'd be overcome by smoke before we ever got warm?" She looked around her once more. "There has to be something I'm overlooking. I escaped Henri, didn't I? Well, I can escape this too. Let's think. The door? Bolted from the outside, too heavy to batter down even if I had a battering ram, and not conducive to pounding as I have the splinters to prove it—'' she yawned widely ''—guess we ought to make a bonfire out of it. But that'd just fill the place with smoke too. Nowhere for the smoke to go...'' She shook her head to ward off the sleepiness that seemed to come over her. "I think I'm freezing, Willy. I don't seem so cold anymore and I'm so sleepy." She yawned again to demonstrate.

Hugging the cat, she levered up the wall and gained her feet again. "We must keep moving, even if we do disturb the bats. You know what we ought to do, Willy. We ought to spook them quite good. Then when they fly out, we'll stop up *their* entrance as well, to keep..." She halted abruptly as the words she had uttered took on meaning for her. As if mocking her sudden insight, the candle behind her gave a flickering spurt and went out.

Rose let out a little squeak and clutched Willy so tightly he yowled a protest. "I'm sorry, Willy. It's all right, really it is. Why, you can see in the dark, can't you? Tell me what you see. Do you see where the bats go in and out? They wouldn't be in here unless there was a way out, would they?" She paced carefully back to the door, with the ideas coming faster and faster. "Bats fly at night. What a strange sight it would be if hundreds of bats suddenly erupted from the ice cellar in the daylight. Wouldn't you come to investigate, Willy?" She kept up this monologue as she felt her way along the floor, seeking the sack. Finally finding it, she carefully stuffed a protesting Willy into it. "It's only for a moment, Willy. I'll lay you right here by the door, so you can be first out when they rush to open it to see about the bats. I promise you, Willy, you'll be the first one out. Please stop your complaining."

Pulling her robe from her shivering body, Rose felt her way back down the passage to the ice vault. Taking a deep breath for courage, she began to flap it mightily over her head, screaming as loudly as her tortured throat would allow. The rapid, sinister rustling of the bats began immediately. They took flight in fright. With their high-pitched squeals in her ears, and the wind from their rapidly beating wings brushing feather-soft against her flesh, clad only in a thin nightrail, her screaming became earnest.

Geoffrey and Milty, in a long line of footmen, all bundled to the teeth in the driving snow, marched through the elaborately laid out gardens, calling at the top of their lungs. They had been at it for hours, yet none dared voice their doubts of finding the mistress alive and well in such weather. Not after such a long time without adequate clothing. Suddenly, the sky over their heads was filled with wheeling, squeaking bats.

"Good Lord," cried Milty, tugging his topper more securely upon his head. "Whatever could that mean? Never saw so many...and in daylight at that. Something must have disturbed them for sure."

Spinning to Bonner, Geoffrey grasped his labels and demanded urgently, "Bats, Bonner! Where in the house would there be bats? That's where we must search! Dark, cavernlike rooms. The wine cellar..."

"The ice vault, my lord!" Bonner exclaimed, pointing to the shadowy side of the stone wall. "I bet it was the ice vault!"

Rose, lying against the door with her robe held tightly over her head, felt the door press inward against her. At first, it did not register that someone was attempting to open the door, but when it did, she felt such terror wash over her. Pray God it was rescue, but the possibility of the villain returning to finish her before rescue could come filled her with terror.

"Who is it?" she called in a raspy voice that wavered with tears. She pressed her weight against the door. "Oh, please tell me who it is."

Geoffrey, planting a stern shoulder to the door, heard her cry. "Rose, it's us. Stand back from the door. Do you hear me, Rose? Step away from the door."

Rose pulled herself to her feet again, and backed away, dragging poor Willy in his sack with her. The door opened effortlessly once her weight was removed, and daylight poured into the corridor. Shielding her eyes, Rose blinked and stared at the men crowding the doorway. Lord Philpotts's pink-cheeked face was the first thing she saw. She flung herself wildly into his arms. "Oh, Milty! I've never been so glad to see anyone in my life," she cried, sobbing mightily.

Milty caught her in his arms and squeezed her tight. Glancing over her head, he surveyed the dark passage. "I say, Rose. This is a deuced uncomfortable place to be on such a cold day."

Giggles of relief and released fear bubbled up in Rose's throat, but were quickly overcome by tears of joy, then great sobs of relief. Milty, totally out of his element with weeping femininity, rolled his eyes toward the marquis for help, and Geoffrey gently disengaged Rose's arms from his neck, feeling desolate that she had not come to him immediately. He had indeed let their estrangement progress too far.

"Milty, continue the search of the grounds. Look for any clue as to the meaning of this. I will see to *my* Rose," Geoffrey ordered.

Milty grinned from ear to ear to hear Geoffrey speak in such proprietary terms of little Rose. Snapping a smart finger to the brim of his topper in acknowledgment, he turned to the grouped men and flapped his arms at them. "Off we go, fellows. Someone has locked the marquise in this damp and cold place with the idea of doing her harm. Spread out now. Watch for clues of any sort that might lead us to the bounder."

Geoffrey swung the sobbing, shivering Rose into his arms and headed toward the nearest side door with long, purposeful strides.

"Willy! Don't leave Willy!" Rose cried, frantically twisting in his arms.

"Bonner! Grab the cat!" Geoffrey called over his shoulder. Striding through the house, he took the stairs two at a time to Rose's bedchamber, calling for a warm bath and brandy as he went, leaving servants scurrying in all directions behind him. Lettie met him at the doorway, wringing her hands and weeping almost as loudly as Rose. "Lettie, quickly, a change of clothing. Something warm. Stoke up the fire also. She's chilled through and through. Oh, and see that the cat's attended too, will you?"

Having anticipated the need, Lettie directed him straight into the dressing room where a tub of steaming water waited. A chenille robe of generous proportions and fuzzy, fleece-lined slippers warmed before the hearth rug. The marquis set Rose on her feet, steadying her with a hand until he was certain she was capable of standing. Without waiting for assistance, he hastily drew the wet, soiled crimson robe from her hands, and stripped the clammy nightrail from her violently shivering body, gritting his teeth to see bruises marring its perfection. Lifting her gently, he sat her in the tub, where she hunched forward with her knees drawn to her chin.

Shrugging off his greatcoat, Geoffrey crouched beside the tub. Taking her hands in his large ones, he laved them with gentleness, shaking his head over the scratches, bruises and splinters. An expression of worry marred his fine face. Her shivering was more pronounced now than when she was found, and he strongly suspected a goodly amount of shock was setting in. "Here now, Tiger's Breath, everything is going to be just fine now, I promise," he murmured. "I'm here to protect you now."

Rose drew a long shaky sigh. Drawing her hands from his, she swept her hair from her face. "Oh, Geoffrey, if only I could believe that," she murmured, clinching her teeth in her attempt to stop their chattering.

"I shall do whatever it takes to make you believe it, Rose," he said, tilting her chin to look into her face. Drawing a fingertip over the porcelain cheek, dirt-smudged and tear-streaked, he saddened at the look of mistrust in her eyes.

Bonner rushed into the bedchamber, unceremoniously bearing a brandy bottle and two glasses, devoid of tray in his haste. Finding the room empty, he called into the dressing room, "My lord?"

"I'll be right back, sweetheart," Geoffrey reassured Rose, then rising swiftly, he left her to Lettie's attentions. "I'm here, Bonner," he said. Crossing to the blazing fire, he wearily rubbed a hand over his face. The hard ride, the worry and the cold were taking their toll on him as well.

"My lord, I took the liberty of bringing a second glass for you," the butler murmured at his elbow.

"Oh, good show, Bonner. Break out a bottle for the men searching outside. They'll be in need of it also," Geoffrey said, taking the bottle and glasses from him. "Have they found anything?"

"I shall check at once," Bonner said, then as an afterthought, "Please tell her ladyship that Willy is in the kitchen, sipping brandied milk and complaining mightily of his mistreatment into the sympathetic ear of Cook."

"I shall tell her," Geoffrey said, with a grin that did not reach his eyes.

Bonner sobered and sketched a slight bow. "I'll see to

the brandy for the men now. Unless there's anything else..."

"That's fine, Bonner," Geoffrey said, without turning from the fire. "Tell Lord Philpotts I'll be downstairs shortly."

Geoffrey dashed a goodly amount of brandy down his throat and stared pensively into the fire. It would seem the fray wasn't over yet. He could not in all good conscience believe anyone of his household would wish harm to their mistress, despite the caustic note he had sent with her to the Harrow. No, he would stake his life on Sewell. In some manner, the attempt on Rose's life was only a continuation of Sewell's plot for his own gain. He should have run the man through and been done with it.

Rose, wrapped snugly in the robe, and her hair piled atop her head showing a freshly scrubbed face, came through the door. Geoffrey stepped to her, to draw her toward the fire and the tufted chair placed there. Placing his snifter in her hand, he lifted it to her lips, urging her to drink. "Sip it slowly, child. It'll help warm you, as well as bring some of the color back into your face. Are you still terribly chilled?"

"Not terribly," Rose murmured, sipping the fiery liquor, which closed her throat and brought forth a cough. She made a face at the taste, but could not help luxuriating in the warmth that swirled to the pit of her stomach.

Geoffrey urged the glass to her lips again. "I've been instructed to tell you Willy is in the kitchen with a great deal of fuss being made over him."

This brought a smile to her face, and a sigh of relief as well. "Thank you," she whispered, looking down at the snifter in her hands.

The marquis drew a stool forward and seated himself in front of Rose. They sat in silence for a moment, then he cupped her chin in his hand to gently tilt her face upward.

"Rose, can you tell me what happened to you? Who would do such a thing?"

"I don't know," she admitted. "I was looking for Willy...he was in a sack in the ice cellar...someone pushed me from behind and bolted the door."

Suddenly, unable to help himself, he came down on one knee in front of her. Drawing her into his arms, he murmured into her hair, "Oh, Tiger's Breath, when I thought I might not find you..."

The warmth of his body seeped into hers and Rose ceased shivering. Suddenly she felt very safe. This was the way it should have been all along, and she never wanted to leave his arms. Tears welled up again and traced over the scrubbed cheeks. "It was so dark, and no one answered my calls. Poor Willy was so frightened..." she said, sobbing.

"Poor Willy, indeed. What about poor little Rose?" Geoffrey soothed, with a soft chuckle. Drawing forth his handkerchief, he dabbed the tears from her face. Then he became quite serious. Sitting back on his stool, he leaned forward earnestly to cup her chin, forcing her eyes to meet his. "Rose, please listen to me. I was wrong. Wrong all along about that thing with Ma Raffle...and other things, too. You see, it was Elmo Sewell trying to come between us all along."

"Elmo Sewell! But why..."

"Shenstone, of course. But that's not important. What's important is the horrid way I've treated you. I was so angry and jealous, I suppose when you didn't want to be near me, well, because...well, because I love you so much." Rose became suddenly quite still. Not at all heartened by that stillness, Geoffrey gathered both of her hands in his and rushed on, "Ah, Tiger's Breath. Hear me out. I know I demanded that we should maintain a *mariage de convenance,* and so it shall remain, if you truly do wish it. I give you my solemn oath, I will not force myself on you, but...well, I was very naive not to realize how such a thing would be. I mean, I certainly did not think I would fall in love with you, but here it is.'' He cleared his throat and continued, ''And I find that I mind very much, very much indeed, if you should fall in love with someone else...regardless of what I said in the past.''

They sat motionless. Geoffrey was almost frightened to look at her face. Dropping his head, he looked instead at his hands folded over her small ones. He dropped his head to press his lips to her hands. His heart ached in his chest, for he truly did not know how he would bear it if she told him to go away.

The fire crackled in the stillness of the room, its light shining brightly on the glossy, walnut brown of his curls. Rose leaned forward and gently laid her forehead against his head like a weary child. ''Oh, Geoffrey. How can you not know that I have loved you since that day you offered to pay for that gown that Sharon tore. I began to think you would never love me back. In fact, I began to think you hated me....''

''Oh, my little love!'' Geoffrey moaned. Gathering her into his arms, he drew her to his lap.

Lettie tiptoed through the room to answer the gentle rapping at the door. A footman stood there. Avid with interest, trying to peep through the crack in the doorway, he delivered his message for his lordship. ''The other lord is requesting his lordship attend him in the library. As quick as can be, he said.''

Geoffrey, catching the message, reluctantly drew back from Rose. ''Ah, my love. I had best go. Perhaps they found something I should know of. I shall be no more than a moment. Will you wait right here for me?''

''For all of my life, Geoffrey,'' she murmured. ''For all of my life.''

Resolutely gaining his feet, Geoffrey reached out to gently ruffle her hair, and this time Rose didn't mind at all.

Upon entering the library, Geoffrey was greeted heartily by Milty. Ensconced before the fire with Balderdash adoringly at his feet, he waved a snifter of his lordship's finest brandy toward his host, and exclaimed in high spirits, "The jig is up, Geoffrey. We've nabbed the fellow."

"You caught someone? Who and where is the bastard? I would like a few words with him," Geoffrey demanded, dark murder coming into his eyes.

"Not possible, my friend," Milty declared, with a shake of his head. "He's already done in."

Accepting that the viscount was probably as weary as himself after their harrowing ride, and cognizant that he owed him a large debt, Geoffrey lowered his tired frame into the chair opposite him and said a silent prayer for patience. "Now, Milty, let's have the tale as straightforward as possible, shall we? I have the strongest desire to be with my wife right at this moment."

Milty beamed upon him and motioned the attending Bonner to bring his lordship a glass. "We found him not too far into that narrow stand of trees to the north of here. Do you know the ones I mean?"

"Very well."

"Good! Can't say he was going very far…dead already, you see…."

"Dead!"

"So we put him in the ice vault. Fitting, don't you think?" Milty chortled at the irony of it all.

"Milty!" threatened Geoffrey, patience wearing thin enough to snap. "A name if you please!"

"Sewell! Amazing strength of hatred, wouldn't you say? Sorely wounded, yet he made it here before us?"

"Good Lord," muttered Geoffrey in disbelief. "Sew-ll..."

"From the looks of it, the ride did him no service. Bled ut, right there in the trees. There was another set of tracks. set the boys on them and expect they'll turn up an ac-omplice soon or later. Good lads, they are."

"Who's good lads?" came a voice in the doorway. At-red in her generous pink robe and fuzzy slippers, with her lossy hair simply caught back with a pink ribbon, Rose ooked very much like a naughty little girl escaping from er nanny. Suddenly Willy's inquisitive orange face ap-eared around her skirts. Leaping to his feet, Balderdash ave one mighty bray and dashed through the doorway and own the entry hall after the fast-disappearing Willy.

"Balderdash!" bellowed Geoffrey, leaping to his feet. .s giving chase to the two seemed too much effort, he irned instead to admonish Rose while drawing her gently the fire. "Rose, you shouldn't be down here! Why aren't ou tucked into bed?"

"I am really quite fine," Rose said, brushing his concern side. "Milty, who are good lads?"

"Why, the fellows Geoffrey employs here at the Harrow, at's who," Milty informed her, then beamed delightedly pon her. "Rose, did you take note of my new look? Geof-ey says I cut a dashing figure."

Rose smiled indulgently, then stepped back to ponder the rge frame so appropriate attired for the country. "Yes, ilty, I would say you are devastatingly handsome. Quite e thing to show off the very marvelous masculinity of ur large frame. I applaud your choices, as I am positive ore than one miss will, come the new season."

"Oh, well, that will only be a plus, as the real premium the absolute comfort," he confided. "I don't even stum-e about anymore. Although I shall truly mourn my swans-wn vest."

Geoffrey, eager to be alone with his newly acquiescent wife, placed a hand beneath Lord Philpotts's arm and hefted him from the chair. "Milty, old man, would it be too much to ask of you to rout Balderdash from his chase...and er, maybe check on those good lads? Perhaps they have returned while we spoke and I would have news of their findings."

"Well, doubt the lads could have gotten back so quickly and I quite think once Balderdash has cornered that cat and had his jowls boxed properly he'll return... Oh, I see!" Milty exclaimed, clapping a hand to his forehead. "Want to be alone with our Rose, huh? Of course, only natural. Best thing too, as the two of you..."

Geoffrey firmly shut the library door on his words, and turned sternly to Rose. "Now, young lady, what are you doing out of bed? You have had a rather trying day, and would not be surprised to see some ill effects from it."

Rose tilted her small nose in the air and addressed him quite clearly. "Why, my lord husband, do you repeatedly treat me like a child, when you know very well, you wish to treat me otherwise?"

Geoffrey was slightly taken aback by her frankness, then gave in to an ever widening grin, flashing the dimple she so loved. "You are quite right, Tiger's Breath. I have no defence for treating you as a child...other than acknowledging the possibility that only by doing so, was I able to keep my distance."

"But, Geoffrey," Rose said with amazement clear in her voice. "Never have I had any desire whatsoever for you to keep distance from me."

Sinking to the sofa beside her, he snuggled her close to him. "Ah, Rose. We have made a muddle of it all, haven't we?"

Rose nodded her head, rubbing her cheek against the scratchiness of his new beard, content to remain in his arms forever. But, at last she drew away a little and began to tell him her story in a faltering voice, of her escape from Henri, of the fear she once had that he wanted to divorce her and marry Sharon Bartley-Bacon.

"Sharon!" Geoffrey exploded, pulling her into his arms again. "I thought I was most clear, right from the start, about my feelings for her. Why, that hellcat was working with Sewell all along."

Rose gave a little sigh of happiness. Feeling brave, thanks to his loving arms, she turned her face up to his. His kisses were tender at first. Then, encouraged by her sweet, innocent willingness, they became deeper, until both found that they were beginning to tremble with passion. Rose encouraged his hands to explore beneath the pink robe, to seek the satin of the pearl flesh he had seen all too briefly in the bathtub. Made bold by the sense of time wasted, she nipped the flesh of his neck and explored the whorls of his ear with a wet tongue, delighted when it brought groans from him.

Geoffrey moved back a bit, rubbing his mouth over her tender lips, then kissing the perfection of each pink nipple in turn. "Hmm, Tiger's Breath, what a cursed tangle. Come, let us find some place less public. I have a great desire to make love to my wife in the most complete manner possible."

"Yes, let's," Rose murmured, reluctant to break the kiss, yet eager to begin her marriage in the way all marriages should begin. When he rose and extended his hand to her with the most beautiful, loving, inviting smile, Rose shyly placed her hand in his. Allowing him to pull her to her feet and back into his arms, she tiptoed to capture his lips and their departure was again delayed.

Just outside the library door, a staunch Lord Philpotts was standing guard with arms folded sternly over his massive chest. Gresham stood before him with several of his accomplices behind him, sputtering and arguing. "I demand you allow me to speak with the marquis, and I demand you allow it immediately. I do not care what you have been told, and I refuse to accept termination of employment by a...a guest!"

"I believe it was the Marquise of Hetherington herself who delivered your termination of employment, not I," Milty countered. Nothing could have induced him to move aside and have Geoffrey and Rose disturbed.

"Bah! That one!" Gresham spat. "The marquis was quite explicit in his instructions to me concerning her. He will not listen to whining complaints from a wife he despises."

"You go too far, my good man!" threatened Milty, uncrossing his arms.

The library door swung open, and Geoffrey led a shyly smiling Rose, radiant with happiness, past a beaming Lord Philpotts. Wrapping an arm protectively about her shoulders, the marquis smiled down into her face, and like sleepwalkers, they moved slowly across the hall and mounted the stairs to their private apartments.

When they had disappeared, Milty grinned at the confused majordomo. "I would say, Mr. Gresham, that there's your answer. I'm sure the marquis can expect your removal, and the removal of your cohorts here, away from Hetherington Harrow by nightfall."

With a stiff bow of acceptance of his fate, Gresham left to attend to his packing.

That night, Milty ate his dinner in a solitary state, as neither Geoffrey and Rose showed any signs of joining him. Later, as he passed through the halls on the way to his apartments, he paused outside the mistress's door. The rumble of Geoffrey's voice came through the door, followed by a rippling laugh from Rose. Milty smiled and moved on. He had never heard her sound so happy. It brought a tear to his eyes and a great long sigh of sentimental longing in his bearlike chest for much the same as Geoffrey had discovered.

Orange Willy came down the hall and wound around his legs. "Misplaced, are you, cat? Well, I suppose a comfy spot on the window seat can be found in my room, since Balderdash has been banned to the stables for ungentlemanly behavior. After all, we bachelors must take care of our own."

The cat willingly accepted the charity, and perched upon the window seat while Milty readied himself for bed. "You know what I shall do, of course. Remarkable that I never thought of it before…but, come morning, I shall set myself to enlist Rose's immediate aid toward acquiring a wife. For, after all, she did say I was the perfect picture of masculinity, didn't she?" he demanded. Carefully laying his new togs over the valet stand, he smoothed a hand over the lapel. "The ladies like that, you know…or perhaps you don't know. Being a cat and all…but still…"

Willy resolutely turned his back on the conversation and curled into a tight ball among the cushions, leaving Lord Philpotts to his lengthy monologue.

* * * * *

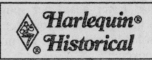

HE SAID

♥

SHE SAID

Explore the mystery of male/female communication in this extraordinary new book from two of your favorite Harlequin authors.

Jasmine Cresswell and Margaret St. George bring you the exciting story of two romantic adversaries—each from their own point of view!

DEV'S STORY. CATHY'S STORY.
As he sees it. As she sees it.
Both sides of the story!

The heat is definitely on, and these two can't stay out of the kitchen!

Don't miss HE SAID, SHE SAID.
Available in July wherever Harlequin books are sold.

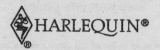

HARLEQUIN®

Coming this summer from
Award-winning author
Theresa Michaels

The Merry Widows
A heartwarming new Western series

"Michaels at her poignantly moving best."
—*Affaire de Coeur*

"Pure magic!" —*The Literary Times*

"A true gem…" —*Rawhide and Lace*

"Will hold you spellbound." —*Rendezvous*

"Emotionally charged…" —*Romantic Times*

**That's what reviewers are saying about
Mary the first book in the Merry Widows trilogy**

Coming in June to a store near you.
Keep your eyes peeled!

Harlequin® Historical

If your tastes run to terrific Medieval Romance, don't miss

The Bride Thief

by Susan Spencer Paul

The exciting conclusion to her Medieval Bride Trilogy

MBT797

KAREN HARPER

She would risk everything for love....

Brett Benton came to America to claim her inheritance:
one half of Sanborn Shipping. The other half belongs to
Alex Sanborn, a man who awakens the dormant passions
within her—a man committed to a cause that is about to test
his courage, his skill...his very life.

Forced to make a devil's bargain, Brett must betray Alex in
order to protect him. Now, only the hope of love can see them
through to...

DAWN'S EARLY LIGHT

Available in June 1997
at your favorite retail outlet.